D0811277

Vendetta in Spain

READERS of *The Golden Spaniard* and other books in which the glamorous Lucretia-José appears with the Duke de Richleau may recall that her parentage was surrounded by mystery. Over the years many people have written, asking for an account of the great romance that led to her birth.

The story takes us back to Spain, in 1906, when the Duke had not yet succeeded his father, and was still the Count de Quesnoy. In these days it is not easy for us to realize that, less than fifty years ago, there was hardly a Monarch or President who could leave his bed in the morning with any certainty that he would live through the day. Anarchism permeated every country in Europe. Not a night passed without groups of fanatics meeting in cellars to plan attempts with knives, pistols or bombs against the representatives of law and order; not a month passed without some royalty or high official falling a victim to their plots.

In Spain, an historic bomb outrage that led to scores of innocent people being killed or injured, gave de Quesnoy ample cause to vow vengeance on the assassins. His attempt to penetrate anarchist circles in Barcelona nearly cost him his life. In San Sebastian, Granada and Cadiz he hunted and was hunted by them in a ruthless vendetta. Only after two years did it end in a final desperate gamble with death.

It is against this background of true history, subtle intrigue, sudden violence, terrorism, blackmail and suspense that there develops the bitter-sweet romance between the gallant young de Quesnoy and the beautiful Condesa Gulia, the wife of a friend he loves and honours. Their frustrated passion leads to a dénouement that rivals in surprise and breath-taking effect the outcome of his vendetta against the anarchists.

BY DENNIS WHEATLEY

NOVELS

The Launching of Roger Brook
The Shadow of Tyburn Tree
The Rising Storm
The Man Who Killed the King
The Dark Secret of Josephine
The Rape of Venice
The Scarlet Impostor
Faked Passports
The Black Baroness
V for Vengeance
Come into My Parlour
Traitors' Gate
The Prisoner in the Mask
The Second Seal
Three Inquisitive People
The Forbidden Territory
The Devil Rides Out
The Golden Spaniard
Strange Conflict

Codeword—Golden Fleece
The Quest of Julian Day
The Sword of Fate
Black August
Contraband
To the Devil—a Daughter
The Eunuch of Stamboul
The Secret War
The Fabulous Valley
Sixty Days to Live
Such Power is Dangerous
Uncharted Seas
The Man Who Missed the War
The Haunting of Toby Jugg
Star of Ill-Omen
They Found Atlantis
The Island Where Time Stands Still
The Ka of Gifford Hillary
Curtain of Fear

WAR PAPERS FOR THE JOINT PLANNING STAFF

Stranger than Fiction

SHORT STORIES

Mediterranean Nights   Gunmen, Gallants and Ghosts

HISTORICAL

A Private Life of Charles II (Illustrated by Frank C. Papé)
Red Eagle (Illustrated) (The Story of the Russian Revolution)
Saturdays with Bricks (Illustrated)

DENNIS WHEATLEY

VENDETTA IN SPAIN

THE BOOK CLUB

121 CHARING CROSS ROAD
LONDON, WC2

© Dennis Wheatley 1961

First published 1961

Printed in Great Britain
by Ebenezer Baylis and Son Ltd
The Trinity Press, Worcester, and London

For

SHELAGH

Still 'the dazzling young Duchess of Westminster'* *who knew and loved Spain at the period of this story.*

*Robert Sencourt in "King Alfonso" (Faber and Faber, 1942)

Contents

1

Death at High Noon

THE principal streets of Madrid presented a riot of colour. From a cloudless sky the sun poured down on the flags of all nations, long strings of pennants and thousands of yards of red and yellow bunting draping the innumerable stands that had been erected on every available space beyond the pavement line. In addition, following the eastern custom brought over by the Moors, carpets, woven rugs and colourful tapestries hung from every window and balcony. On both sides, behind lines of soldiers in bright uniforms, the pavements were a solid mass of people in gala attire. Others filled the stands, every window and even the roof-tops. At intervals along the route there rose tall flagpoles surmounted by gold crowns and bearing shields with the arms of Spain and those of Princess Ena of Battenberg, for King Alfonso XIII had that day, the 31st of May, 1906, married the granddaughter of Queen Victoria.

The side streets, although nearly deserted, were little less gay; for the marriage of the young King, aged twenty, to the beautiful, golden-haired English Princess, aged nineteen, was a most popular one, and even the poorest *Madrileños* had shown their joy by hanging flags and strips of carpet from their windows.

Down one such street behind the Calle Mayor several small groups of smartly-dressed ladies and gentlemen were hurrying. They had just left the church of San Jerónimo in which the wedding mass had been celebrated with great pomp and splendour, and were making their way to a special stand reserved for certain court officials and distinguished guests to witness the procession on its way back to the Palace.

In one of these groups the most striking figure was Armand, Count de Quesnoy, the thirty-one year old son of the ninth Duc de Richleau. He was only a little above medium height but carried himself with the easy grace of a man who had spent most of his life hunting, dancing, fencing and soldiering. His hair was dark and slightly wavy, his forehead broad, his face oval with a rather thin but well moulded mouth, and a pointed chin that showed great determination. His nose was aquiline, his eyes grey, flecked with tiny spots of yellow; at times they could flash with piercing brilliance, and above them a pair of 'devil's eyebrows' tapered up towards his temples. At the moment his slim figure was hidden by the robes of a Knight of the Golden Fleece, and it was his membership of this illustrious Order that had secured for him a place in the church to witness the wedding ceremony.

Beside him, a hand on his arm, was his wife, Angela: a typical English beauty with big pansy-brown eyes and a milk-and-roses complexion. Her forehead was broad, her eyebrows well arched, and her fine jaw-line, square almost to the point of truculence, showed her to have a personality as determined as her husband's. On her high-piled hair she wore an enormous hat decorated with tulle and yellow roses. In spite of the heat she was wearing a dress made of satin. It was also yellow, had leg-of-mutton sleeves, almost touched the ground and was excruciatingly nipped in at the waist above an armour of whalebone corset.

She had been his first great love and he hers; but she had already been married when they met and many vicissitudes had prevented the consummation of their love until at last tragedy had broken the barrier that kept them apart, and fourteen months earlier she had become his Countess.

With them in the group that had slipped away from the church as soon as the *Te Deum* had been sung were Colonel Guy Wyndham and several other officers of the 16th Lancers who had formed Princess Ena's military escort on her journey to Spain. At the end of the side street, on showing their passes, the police made a way for them through the crowd into the Calle Mayor about two-thirds of the way down, where this narrow street in the heart of old Madrid widens out in a small square called the Plaza de la Villa.

There the group separated, the de Quesnoys and several others crossing the square to the stand which had been erected in front of the church of Santa Maria, while Colonel Wyndham and his officers went to a nearby house occupied by a Mr. Young, one of the secretaries at the British Embassy, who had invited them and the British Ambassador, Sir Maurice de Bunsen, to see the procession from its windows.

The stand was already three parts full with Spanish hidalgos and their ladies, and foreign notabilities, whose rank had not been high enough to secure them places in the church, and now the front rows, too, were rapidly filling up with the more exalted representatives of the aristocracy of many nations. De Quesnoy's Order of the Golden Fleece made him a Grandee of Spain; so on that account he ranked among them, but that he and his wife should have been allotted seats in the very front row he knew must be due to the influence of the King's cousin, the young Duc de Vendôme, who was devoted to him.

François de Vendôme had been the instrument chosen by fate to alter the whole course of de Quesnoy's life. The Duc de Richleau was by birth a Frenchman, but he had married a Russian Princess, and since he loathed the French Republican régime he had lived for many years as a voluntary exile on a large property of hers a little to the north of the Carpathians; so de Quesnoy had been born and brought up in Russia.

At the age of eighteen, in order that he might establish his right to French citizenship, he had, against the strong opposition of his father, decided to do his military service in France, and had chosen the Army as his career.

That career had opened with promise, but political differences with his superiors had resulted in his being packed off to insufferably dreary garrison duty in Madagascar. There, for the following two-and-a-half years, he had succeeded in overcoming discomfort and boredom by devoting his abundant spare time to an intensive study of the occult. Then, changes at the War Office had resulted in his being posted to Algeria. At that time France was opening up the interior of North Africa, so while there he was almost constantly on active service against the tribesmen and, as he soon showed himself to be a born cavalry leader, his promotion was rapid. Another three years and he was a Brevet Lt.-Colonel decorated with the Légion d'Honneur.

When at last recalled to France early in 1903 he had hoped to be given employment with a regiment, as the greatest ambition of his life was, in time, to command a Cavalry Division, but fate had decreed otherwise. The Republican government was riddled with corruption, and so fanatically atheist that it was purging the Army of many of its ablest officers solely because they adhered to their religion. A group of patriots had decided that the only remedy was to restore the Monarchy. Among them was an Assistant Chief of Staff named General Laveriac, and he had drawn de Quesnoy into the conspiracy.[1]

The Monarchists' choice for King was the Duc de Vendôme, in whose veins ran the blood of Henry IV, the founder of the Bourbon dynasty. His father had married the Spanish Infanta Maria Alfonsine, so he had been brought up in Spain but, like de Quesnoy, he insisted on going to France to do his military service. Soon after de Quesnoy's return, de Vendôme was due to become an officer-cadet at St. Cyr, and Laveriac had asked the Count to take a post as

[1] See *The Prisoner in the Mask.*

Chief Instructor there so that he might watch over the young Prince and gradually initiate him into the plan to stage a *coup d'état* for the purpose of proclaiming him as François III of France.

De Quesnoy had accepted this most delicate task and in due course de Vendôme—an unambitious but deeply religious young man—had, from a sense of duty, consented to being placed on the Throne. But the conspiracy had been betrayed and de Vendôme arrested. By sacrificing his own liberty de Quesnoy had saved the Prince from acute suffering and probably death. It was for this signal service to a member of the Spanish Royal Family that King Alfonso had made de Quesnoy a Knight of the Golden Fleece. But his career in the French Army was irretrievably ruined. He had been deprived of his commission and could no longer even set foot in France without risking imprisonment for his part in the conspiracy. It was this knowledge, that there was little hope of his ever being able to return to the land of his ancestors, and because he knew how greatly it would please Angela, that had led him at the time of their marriage to become a naturalized British citizen.

The ledge of the stand in the front row of which they sat was only just above the level of the heads of the crowd; but it was no more than three deep there because the stand projected over the pavement in front of the church and there was room for only a thin ribbon of people between the stand and the backs of the soldiers lining that part of the route. In consequence the procession itself would pass within fifteen feet of them. Midday had just chimed so it was now due to start and the street had been cleared, but it would be the best part of an hour before, near its end, the Crown Coach entered the Calle Mayor; for the timing had been arranged to allow for the Royal couple to receive the homage of the great nobles, officials and royalties of Spain before setting out from the church. Suddenly the eager, murmuring crowd began to cheer, a solitary mounted orderly came into view, and a few yards behind him the Captain-General of Madrid.

In his magnificent uniform he made a resplendent figure, but as he passed the stand, followed by a jingling troop of cavalry that headed the procession, it was upon his horse that de Quesnoy's eyes were fixed. It was a pure white Arab, mettlesome, high-stepping and perfectly proportioned. As a fine judge of horseflesh he thought he had never seen a better mount, and he gave an inaudible sigh.

His sigh was not one of envy for the splendid animal, but of regret that he would now never lead another cavalry charge, much less command a Cavalry Division. Had the conspiracy succeeded de Vendôme would, he knew, have rewarded him with one, and after leaving France he had had thoughts of joining the Army of one of the South American Republics in which, for an officer of his experience, there would have been fine prospects; but Angela's having become free to marry him had put an end to such ideas.

As the wife of a French politician she had lived for so long in Paris that the past eighteen months, during which she had been back in England among her own family and old friends, had meant positive bliss for her. He could not possibly ask her to give that up and go with him to an utterly strange life in Latin America; yet there was no other avenue by which he could satisfy his longing to resume his career as a soldier.

Fortunately, however, his father was rich and made him a very handsome allowance. That enabled him and Angela to live in considerable comfort, to enjoy the amenities of London society and to visit friends, or stay at fashionable hotels abroad. For the past fourteen months they had divided their time between such jaunts to the Continent and longish stays with her relatives, mostly at English country houses, in what really had amounted to a prolonged honeymoon. But now he was in negotiation for the lease of a pleasant house just off Berkeley Square, and had resigned himself to settling down to the sort of round that men of his class lived—the London Season, Scotland or a visit to a German spa in August, shooting in the autumn, a month or more somewhere in the Mediterranean after Christmas, hunting in the shires during early spring, then another trip abroad until Ascot, Lord's, Henley and Goodwood came round again.

At first only the thought that he would be sharing it with Angela had made bearable to him the contemplation of such an aimless existence, but early in the year another factor had arisen which now made him regard it much more cheerfully. Angela was expecting a baby in October.

For some reason, perhaps because so great a part of his bachelorhood had been spent in outposts of the French empire, or because he had not met any women other than Angela whom he had wished to marry, he had never thought of himself as a father. But now he was thrilled by the idea. He hoped that she would give him a boy to carry on the ancient title of de Richleau, but the prospect of a girl who might take after her was almost as exciting. Her pregnancy had run a normal course and so far caused her little inconvenience; but from the moment she had told him of it he had shown the greatest concern for her, and he was a little worried at the moment that the walk from the church and the heat might have tired her unduly. To his tender, whispered inquiry she replied with a smile that she felt perfectly well, then she began to fan herself while he opened the big gilt-edged programme they had been given on reaching the stand, and read out to her the names of the regiments and personalities that were now passing within fifteen feet of them.

For over half an hour detachments of cavalry, infantry and artillery went by. Every regiment from the Home Army was represented; black and brown troops had been brought from the Spanish colonies and Berbers in the service of Spain, who loped along on their ungainly camels, from Morocco. Then came the open State landaus and the gilded coaches. In the first carriages were the English Lords and Ladies sent to attend the new Queen. Next came the Great Officers of the Spanish Royal Household, Cardinals in their scarlet and other dignitaries of the Church, then the coaches of the principal Grandees of Spain, the Dukes of Alba, Bailén, Fernan-Núñez, Medina-Sidonia and many more. They were followed by coaches containing members of the Royal Family and many visiting royalties; in the last rode the Prince and Princess of Wales, sent to represent King Edward VII, who was happy to regard himself as the principal sponsor of this royal romance.

Among the dozen or more coaches containing Don Alfonso's relatives there was one that the de Quesnoys gave a special cheer, for in it were the Duc de Vendôme and his family. A few years after his father's death, his mother, the Infanta Maria Alfonsine, had married again, taking as her second husband the Conde Ruiz de Cordoba y Coralles, a member of the great banking family whose head was his elder brother, José. In the coach on its front seat de Vendôme was sitting between the two Condes, his stepfather and stepuncle. Opposite, facing the horses, sat their two wives. Like all the other Spanish ladies in the procession they were wearing the national head-dress, huge combs of tortoiseshell from which were draped mantillas of the finest lace. The Infanta was in her early forties, plump, somewhat heavy-jowled and high-nosed; her sister-in-law, the Condesa Gulia, was much slimmer and it was at her that nine-tenths of the male spectators were now looking.

Although the wife of the older brother, the Condesa was much the younger of the two women, being still only in her early twenties. She was not so dark as the average Spaniard, having Titian hair and a matt-white magnolia complexion; but her eyes were black and held the slumbrous fire which is one of the greatest attractions of the typical Spanish beauty. As the coach passed the stand, those eyes sought de Quesnoy, then remained riveted upon him, but he was quite unconscious of her special interest in himself and his smiles and waves were directed at the family as a whole.

Cannon continued to thunder in the distance, and joy-bells to peal from a score of churches. The crowd had been cheering for close on an hour, yet its *Olés* showed no signs of hoarseness. In fact, as the coach carrying Prince George and Princess Mary of Wales passed the Court stand, a louder than ever burst of cheering thundered along from further up the street, indicating that the Crown coach must have entered the Puerta del Sol—the Piccadilly Circus of Madrid—in which thousands of people were congregated.

A moment later a huge mahogany coach emerged from under the arch of greenery and flowers that spanned the street where it entered the little square. In it were the King's mother, Queen Maria Christina, who had acted as Regent during his long minority, Queen Ena's mother, Princess Beatrice, the Infante Don Carlos and his four-year-old son, Don Alfonso Maria.

Next, in accordance with ancient custom, there came a gold-panelled coach which was empty, and known as 'The Carriage of Respect'. The coaches of the nobility had been drawn by four horses, those of the royalties by six, and now there came into view the eight beautiful Andalusian cream-coloured steeds drawing the Crown coach. It was moving very slowly and as the lead horses came level with the de Quesnoys, owing to some check to the procession in front, it was forced to come to a stop.

The shouts of '*Viva el Rey! Viva la Reina!*' were now deafening. On both sides of the street there was a sea of waving hats and a cascade of blossoms being thrown into the roadway where the coach would pass. The King was leaning out of its left-hand window acknowledging the roar of acclamation that was going up from the stand, and at the same time pointing out to the Queen the old church of Santa Maria that towered up behind it. To see the church better his lovely golden-haired wife, her face radiant with excitement, was leaning right across him. At that moment, from a high window in a house opposite, a big bouquet of flowers was thrown and came swishing down towards the coach.

As the bouquet landed there came a blinding flash, an explosion like a crash of thunder, and a blast that sent nearby troops and people reeling in all directions. A great cloud of black smoke billowed up, so dense that for several moments the coach was hidden in it. Angela was only one of scores of women in the stand who gave a piercing scream, but for once de Quesnoy ignored her.

The cream Andalusians, terrified by the explosion, were rearing, plunging, whinnying. They had already dragged the coach several yards forward and threatened to bolt with it. In an instant de Quesnoy had leapt over the low front of the stand, thrust his way through the panic-stricken people, and was out in the roadway. Flinging himself at the near leader he seized its nose-band, dragged down its head and brought it to a halt.

As the smoke cleared he saw that the English officers in Mr. Young's house nearby had not been less prompt to act than himself. Followed by the British Ambassador they had rushed from the house and Colonel Wyndham was the first to reach the now white-faced Queen who, with the King's arm about her, was standing in the roadway.

He saw, too, that the bomb had exploded under the off-wheel horse, shattering its legs and ripping open its belly. Had the coach not been brought to a halt at the very moment the bomb was thrown it must have been hit and blown to pieces; and, even so, had the Queen not leant right over to look out of its left-hand window she would almost certainly have been struck by several of the splinters.

The royal couple had escaped by a miracle, but the bomb had disintegrated into a hundred deadly fragments, one of them actually cutting in two the gold chain of Carlos III that the King was wearing round his neck, and the others had caused appalling havoc. The coachman had tumbled from his box and lay groaning in the road. Two soldiers lay dead near him and a dozen spectators had been killed or wounded. The Major of the Escort had been thrown from his horse and was smothered with blood, the gilded front of the coach was now dripping red with gore, smears of it showed crimson on the white satin shoes and train of the Queen. There was blood everywhere.

After the first shock she showed great bravery; putting her hand to her heart she even managed to give the horrified crowd a reassuring smile. Don Alfonso, too, displayed the personal courage for which he was already renowned. With perfect calmness he immediately took command of the situation. As his brother-in-law, Don Carlos, came running up he told him to go back to his coach at once and assure the two mothers in it that the Queen and himself were unharmed. Then, as the Crown coach could no longer be used, he kissed his wife and led her forward, shielding her as far as he could from the sight of the dead and wounded, to the empty Coach of Respect, so that they could resume their drive to the Palace in it. At the sight of his calmness the crowd temporarily stunned and murmuring angrily, suddenly broke into renewed cheers, mingled with cries of blessing and thanksgiving.

Having handed the Queen into the coach, the King ordered that it should continue its journey at a slow pace, and got in beside her. De Quesnoy waited until it moved off, then returned to the stand.

As he mounted the steps at its end he saw that a little knot of people were standing bunched together at the place where he and Angela had been sitting. A moment later he joined them. They were facing inward looking down at something and talking in hushed voices. He heard a man among them say, 'And such a beautiful woman, too.' Then, peering between their heads he saw what it was at which they were looking. It was Angela.

She was lying back limply in her own seat against the tier of seats above. Her mouth hung open and the brim of her big hat with the yellow roses now stood up at a grotesque angle owing to the back of it being crushed beneath her head; but someone had reverently crossed her hands upon her breast. A little lower down there was a small jagged hole in her satin dress, a broken strip of corset whalebone protruded from it and its edges were stained with blood.

Transfixed by horror de Quesnoy stared down at her. He had seen death too often not to recognize it on sight. In vain he strove to persuade himself that he was the victim of some ghastly nightmare out of which he would soon struggle with a gasp of relief. The death and bloodshed in the street from which he had just come made the truth only too plain. Barely a second before he jumped from the stand a fragment of the accursed bomb had hit Angela. The thing he stared down on with the gaping mouth in which the tongue lolled back was not his beautiful Angela. She was gone, and with her had gone the child that was to bring them so much joy.

A voice near him said in English, 'Count, I cannot find words to express . . . I, er . . . was seated just behind her. At least she can have felt little pain. As you leapt into the street she gave one cry and fell back. It was all over almost instantly.'

Turning his head slowly de Quesnoy recognized Sir Derek Keppel, who had come over in the suite of the Prince of Wales. Another voice said in Spanish, 'It was so, Señor Conde. I, too, witnessed this tragedy from close by. Look, there are ambulances now arriving in the street. Let us summon one of them to take the poor lady to the hospital.'

'No.' De Quesnoy found his voice suddenly, although it came only as a hoarse croak. 'I'll not have my wife's body exposed in a public morgue.' Stepping forward he picked Angela up in his arms, but then gazed round with haggard eyes, apparently uncertain what to do next.

Another Spaniard spoke. 'Permit me to recall myself to you, Señor Conde. I am the Marqués de la Vera. My carriage is waiting behind the church. Allow me to place it at your disposal.'

Glancing up, de Quesnoy recognized a short, fair-haired man to whom he had been introduced at a reception a few nights earlier. With an effort he blurted out, 'Thank you, Marqués. Please . . . show me the way to it.'

With murmurs of sympathy the little crowd parted. The Marqués led the way, first up the stand then down a staircase behind it, through a narrow alley that ran along one side of the church and so into Madrid's oldest and most picturesque square, the Plaza Mayor. Parallel with the shady colonnades on all its four sides private carriages were lined up waiting for their owners. The Marqués gestured towards one and cast an anxious glance at de Quesnoy, fearing that he must succumb under the weight of his burden. But the Count's slim figure was deceptive; his muscles were iron hard and he was immensely strong. At the moment he was not even conscious of the weight of the body he was carrying but, still half dazed, was saying bitterly to himself over and over again, 'Never again. Never again.'

When they reached the carriage and he had laid Angela on the front seat the Marqués ordered the hood to be put up and said, 'You are staying with the Cordobas, are you not?'

On de Quesnoy's nodding, he ordered his coachman to drive to the Palacio de Cordoba. The Count, Sir Derek and the Marqués settled themselves on the back seat. The little group that had accompanied them, several of whom were openly crying, bowed reverently and crossed themselves; then the carriage pulled out of the line and drove off.

Slowly, for now that the crowds had broken up even the back streets were filled with strolling people, they circumvented the Puerta del Sol and the Calle Alcala, crossed the wide Paseo del Prado and reached a narrow street running parallel to the Calle Serrano. In it was situated the early eighteenth-century Palacio with its long rows of windows from each of which bellied out an ornamental iron grille. Behind the Palace was a spacious garden and beyond that a more modern block facing on the Recoletos, just below the Plaza de Colon, in which the Coralles banking business was conducted.

The Palace was almost deserted, as the two Condes with their wives and de Vendôme had been bidden to the State luncheon at the Royal Palace and the servants had been given leave to go out to see the procession. The elderly janitor, who was still in his box, roused from his siesta as de Quesnoy passed him carrying Angela's body; but as he was not called on he assumed that she had only fainted from the heat, and promptly returned to his basket chair.

De Quesnoy, still with his mind repeating, 'Never again. Never again,' had automatically murmured his thanks to the Marqués and Sir Derek, and now he carried Angela across the hall of the Palace, up one side of the great horseshoe staircase, through the lofty picture gallery and up further flights of stairs to the suite they had been given. In its bedroom he laid her gently on the big four-poster bed, then sank down in a chair beside it, burying his head in his hands.

Meanwhile at the Royal Palace the earlier arrivals knew nothing of the attempted assassination until later ones, who had been within hearing of the bomb's explosion, told them about it.

When the Sovereigns made their appearance everyone crowded round to express sympathy for them in their ordeal, and relief at their escape. The King waved the episode aside as the act of a mad-man and declared that the extraordinary enthusiasm shown by the crowds all along the route was ample proof of the loyalty of the Spanish people, and that they had taken his beautiful Queen to their hearts. He then decreed that the celebrations should continue as if nothing unusual had happened and, soon after one o'clock, he and his guests went in to lunch.

The Cordobas did not get back to their Palacio until well on in the afternoon, then, after a belated siesta, they had to dress and go again to the Royal Palace to attend the State banquet. The Infanta, her husband and de Vendôme went by right of her position as the King's aunt; Conde José and his wife because – apart from the Coralles' millions, which had been brought into the family two generations earlier, making him one of the most powerful men in Spain – he was the head of one of its most ancient families and, as *the* de Cordoba, entitled to address the King as cousin.

Besides the de Quesnoys they had a number of other guests, mostly relatives who lived in the country, staying for the celebrations. These dined in the Palacio then went out to see the fireworks and illuminations. By midnight, tired but cheerful, they returned and congregated in the great drawing-room, from the walls of which tall paintings of past Cordobas by Velasquez, Zurbarán and Goya looked down. They were joined soon afterwards by their host and hostess, the Infanta, Conde Ruiz and François de Vendôme, and settled down with nightcaps to talk over the events of the day.

De Vendôme was helping himself to a brandy and soda from the table of drinks near the door, when his eye was caught by the Major-domo who was standing just outside it. Setting down his glass he stepped over to the man and asked,

'What is it, Eduardo?'

The elderly white-haired servant nervously fingered the silver chain of office that he wore round his neck, and replied, 'Your Highness, I am worried about the Count and Countess de Quesnoy. They did not appear at dinner and none of the staff I have questioned has seen them since they went out this morning. Yet they are upstairs in their suite. Agusto, the footman who is valeting the Count, and the maid who is attending on the Countess, went up to lay out Their Excellencies' evening things. The dressing-room was empty and the bedroom door locked. On their knocking the Count called to them in an angry voice to go away and not come back. Fearing they must be unwell, or perhaps overtired, I went up myself after dinner and offered to bring them something up on a tray, but with the same result. What can possibly have caused them to refuse food and lock themselves in? I am afraid there must be something wrong.'

The Prince's young face showed swift concern, and he said, 'I fear you are right, Eduardo. I'll go up and find out.'

Ten minutes later he re-entered the drawing-room, now white to the lips and with his hands trembling slightly. His mother was the first to catch sight of him, and she exclaimed in a loud voice:

'Whatever is the matter, François? You look as if you had seen a ghost.'

He stared back into her plump face with its fleshy Bourbon nose, then gazed helplessly round at the others. The two Condes, resplendent in satin knee-breeches and full court dress, were standing together: Ruiz was slim and elegant with a pale face and dark side whiskers; José was more strongly built and had a ruddier complexion partially hidden by a flowing moustache and black spade-shaped beard. It was the latter who broke the sudden hush that had fallen, by saying with, for him, unaccustomed sharpness:

'Come, boy! Don't stand there gaping. Tell us what has upset you.'

'It's Angela!' de Vendôme gasped. 'She was struck by a fragment of the bomb and . . . and killed. De Quesnoy brought her back here and carried her up to their room. He's been sitting beside her body all these hours. He . . . he's utterly distraught. I fear for his reason.'

'Dios! but this is terrible,' cried the Infanta. 'We must . . .'

The rest of her sentence was drowned in a chorus of exclamations of horror. De Vendôme had burst into tears. Every face in the room showed shock and distress, with one exception. The beautiful Condesa Gulia was seated in a low chair a little behind the others; her magnificent eyes had narrowed slightly and she was smiling.

One of her guests – an aunt of her husband – happened to turn and catch sight of her expression. Giving her a puzzled look, the old lady said tartly, 'There is nothing to smile at in this, Gulia. To weep for the poor Count would be more fitting.'

Instantly the smile on Gulia's full red lips disappeared, and with a surprised lift of her fine eyebrows she replied, 'Did I appear to be smiling, Doña Inés? I certainly was not. It must have been the shadow thrown on my face by those flowers between us and the lamp standard that deceived you. No one could be more upset by this tragedy than myself.'

But she was lying. She had neither particularly liked nor disliked Angela as a person, and, as she was not an evil woman, she would not have wished her dead. But she was an intensely passionate one and, quite unconsciously, de Quesnoy had aroused in her an emotion that went to the roots of her being.

She had been thinking, 'It was because of his devotion to his wife that he would not even look at me. And now she is dead . . . dead. It will take him time to get over it, but when he has I'll make him look at me with seeing eyes. He'll become my lover then. What bliss that would be. For that I'll risk anything – even José's learning about us and throwing me out into the street.'

2

The Aftermath

THE state of mute despair in which François de Vendôme had found de Quesnoy had certainly given the young man grounds to fear for his friend's reason, but, in fact, the Count was much too well-balanced for even so terrible a shock to affect him permanently. Nevertheless it was not until several days after Angela's funeral that his manner again became anything approaching normal.

During them he spent most of his time in a small sitting-room that de Cordoba had offered him as a sanctum; and, in order not to depress the other guests, had asked to have his meals served there. De Vendôme had brought Father Tomaso, the Cordobas' chaplain, to see him and urge upon him the consolations of religion, but he had politely declined them on the grounds that, although nominally a Catholic, he had long since ceased to be a practising one. However, Angela had become a convert to the Roman faith before her first marriage, so he willingly accepted the good Father's offer to make arrangements for her burial.

The bomb had killed thirty people and wounded over a hundred. On the afternoon of his wedding the King had visited the injured in hospital and he had then ordered that a State funeral should be given to the dead. The majority were conveyed to the cemetery on nine enormous hearses through weeping crowds, but a few of the bereaved families preferred to arrange private interments, among them that of the Marquesa de Tolosa. She had been seated on the second floor balcony of the house from which the bomb had been thrown and, as her family were friends of the Cordobas, Father Tomaso arranged that a Requiem Mass should be celebrated for the Marquesa and Angela together.

While de Quesnoy remained mainly in seclusion he found his greatest solace in his host, who devoted much time to sitting with him. The backgrounds of the two men could hardly have been less similar. De Quesnoy's had been an open-air life of travel, soldiering, war and sport, whereas the Conde had never been outside Europe, neither hunted, fished nor shot, and spent most of his time immersed in his banking activities, his only outdoor interest being as a naturalist with the finest collection of butterflies in the country. Yet they had certain things in common. Both of them came from ancient families and were passionately convinced Monarchists; both were well read and particularly interested in history and ancient religions; and both had a wide knowledge of international relations. So, after a day or two, by coaxing de Quesnoy to discuss these subjects, the Conde found that for a while he could take his guest's mind off his bereavement.

At the end of the week's wedding celebrations the Cordobas' other guests left for their homes and de Quesnoy raised the matter of his own departure; but, as he had not been able to bring himself to make any plans, the Conde insisted that he should stay on, at least for another week or two, and he gladly accepted.

It was no small part of his affliction that with the loss of Angela he had become completely rootless. When writing to break the news of her death to her parents he had also written to his agents instructing them to break off negotiations for the house near Berkeley Square as, now that he had become a widower, it would have been much too large for him. Moreover, although his relations with her family were pleasant enough and he knew they would willingly continue to accept him as a member of it, he found most of them distinctly dull, and without her to make it tolerable he felt most averse to condemning himself to the pointless social life they led.

Thirteen years had elapsed since he had left his boyhood home in Russia, and during them he had been back there only once. It lay in the heart of Central Europe, on the River Pruth near the little town of Jvanets and the best part of 400 miles from the nearest cities: Kiev, Budapest, Bucharest and Odessa; so the only diversion it could offer was hunting. He knew that his father would be pleased to see him, so he might go there for a visit of a month or two, but to settle down there with only the affairs of the estate to occupy him would soon bore him to distraction.

Vienna was the city that he loved best, and he could be sure of a welcome there from many old friends with whom in the past he had painted the town red. But at this juncture the thought of nights spent with Wine, Women and Song appealed to him even less than the more staid social life of London. There remained the possibility of reviving his plan for offering his services as a soldier to one of the South American Republics; but as yet he still felt quite incapable of making any definite decision about his future.

Apart from an intolerable ache caused by the finality of his loss of Angela, only one emotion stirred him repeatedly; it was a fierce craving to see justice done on those responsible for her death. Daily he spoke of this to the Conde, who kept him informed about the progress the police were making in their investigations.

The name of the assassin was Mateo Morral and he was on the police files as an agitator, but had done nothing before throwing the bomb which might have justified his arrest. He had come from Barcelona and was a Catalan of superior type; his bearded face had a mild expression, his hands were well cared-for and he had a general air of middle-class respectability.

The old house from which the bomb had been thrown had been divided up into apartments, and it was Morral's unsuspicious appearance which had enabled him to rent a room on its third floor without anyone suspecting that he might be an anarchist. But when the room had been broken into, it had been found that, in addition to chemicals left over from compounding the explosives for the bomb, there were others that indicated he had been treating himself for syphilis.

Immediately he had thrown the bomb he had rushed downstairs, mingled with the crowd in the street, and succeeded in reaching the office of a Don José Nakens, who was the editor-proprietor of a Republican weekly journal called *The Mutiny*. Nakens had provided him with a change of clothes and found him shelter for the night. He had then managed to escape unrecognized from the city and gone into temporary hiding with another associate at a village on the road to the Escorial. Next day he attempted to board a train at Torréjon de Ardoz, but by then his description had been circulated throughout the length and breadth of Spain, and at the station he was identified. A rural guard who was present had tried to arrest him but Morral had shot him dead with a Browning pistol, and had then used the pistol to kill himself.

Further investigations disclosed that had the anarchists' original plot matured it would have had infinitely more hideous results. A gallery in the church in which the wedding Mass was to be celebrated had been allotted to the Press. With forged credentials Morral had succeeded in obtaining a pass to it and had intended to throw his bomb down into the body of the church at the moment when the King and Queen received the Sacrament. Had he done so the two hundred fragments into which it splintered must have killed not only them but half-a-hundred other royalties, priests and officials grouped about the high altar.

By a dispensation attributable only to God this ghastly slaughter had been prevented by an eleventh-hour alteration of arrangements. It had been suggested that little four-year-old Don Alfonso Maria – who as the son of the King's deceased sister was Heir Apparent to the Throne – was too young to be expected to sit quietly through the long ceremony in the body of the church; so it was decided that he and his attendants should sit in the gallery with his cousin, the fourteen-year-old Princess Pilar, next to him to keep him from becoming restless. The Press then having been relegated to a position that would have made the aiming of the bomb more chancy, Morral had elected to hurl it from his room in the Calle Mayor.

It was on learning this that de Quesnoy burst out:

'What infamy! The imagination reels at the thought of such a massacre. It seems incredible that any human being, let alone an educated man like this Morral, could become so obsessed with vindictiveness against the ruling caste as to plan the murder of men, women and even innocent children indiscriminately. Yet one cannot doubt that he would have turned the church into a shambles had he had the chance. Hell is too good for such Devil's spawn.'

'The disease from which he was suffering had probably affected his brain,' suggested the Conde.

'Perhaps; but what of the others who aided and abetted him – the editor who got him out of Madrid, and the man who hid him in the country? Besides, these anarchists are becoming an ever-increasing menace to established order. In Russia during the past twenty years nihilists have murdered scores of Provincial Governors and other high officials. In France, Italy or Belgium every few months they commit some appalling outrage. Look, too, at the toll they are taking of Europe's rulers. In '94 one of them assassinated President Carnot in Lyons, in '98 another stabbed to death the Empress

Elizabeth of Austria, and in 1900 yet another killed King Humbert of Italy. A dozen other rulers have been wounded or had narrow escapes. Not one of them today can wake up in the morning without the thought that he may be murdered before evening.'

The Conde nodded. 'It is not the first attempt on Don Alfonso, either. Just a year ago a bomb was thrown during his State visit to Paris, while he was driving through the streets with President Loubet. He gave fine proof of his courage on that occasion by leaning out of the carriage window and crying, "*Vive la France!*" Then he turned with a smile to the President and asked, "Was that intended for you or for me?" The President rose to the occasion and replied, "This is the land of equality, Sir." But you are right. These anarchists are a hideous menace. Among their victims that you omitted to name was President McKinley of the United States. His assassination a few years ago shows that their organization must be world-wide.'

'Exactly; and they cannot all be mad, at least not in the accepted sense which would make them medically certifiable.'

'No, they are fanatics; mostly, I think, embittered men who have brooded upon imagined wrongs so long that they have lost all moral sense and are prepared to go to any lengths to avenge themselves upon society.'

'They are responsible for their actions!' de Quesnoy exclaimed harshly. 'And nothing – nothing – can excuse this deliberate treacherous warfare they are waging on unsuspecting people. They should be stamped out like poisonous reptiles. I only wish to God that I knew a way to set about it.'

'I understand how you must feel, and you are right,' the Conde agreed. 'But you may be sure that the police are doing everything possible to that end. Regarding yourself, though, Count; permit me to remark that now eight days have elapsed since your personal tragedy I do feel that you should make an effort to cease brooding upon it. Will you not try to put these villainous anarchists out of your mind and engage it with new interests?'

De Quesnoy sighed. 'I suppose that I ought to, and since you wish it I will make the endeavour; but I fear it will prove a hard task. You see at the moment there is nothing in which I feel I could interest myself.'

'You are interested in art and history.'

'I am, but I have visited the Prado many times and have already seen most of the sights of Madrid.'

'Of course; but I gather you have never been in Southern Spain. Andalusia is the loveliest part of my country and in its cities are some of the most beautiful buildings in the world. The Moors left us finer examples of their great civilization than any that are to be found in North Africa.'

'Were I in a normal state I am sure I should find them fascinating, but at the moment I really could not face a sightseeing tour on my own.'

The Conde smiled. 'My dear friend, we should not dream of allowing you to do so. I have already discussed this proposal with François and he was delighted at the idea of acting as your companion and guide.'

'How good of you both;' de Quesnoy raised a faint smile in reply. 'In that case it would be churlish of me to refuse.'

That evening de Vendôme came up to discuss the trip with him and the places he proposed they should visit. His plan was to go south to Cordoba, across to Seville, then through Jerez de la Frontera to Cadiz; from there down to Algeciras, inland to Ronda, across to the Mediterranean coast at Malaga, inland again to Granada, return to the sea at Alicante, up the coast to Valencia, and so back to Madrid, stopping a few nights or longer, if they felt so inclined, in each of these places.

'But such a tour could take up to two months,' de Quesnoy protested.

'What matter,' the young Prince shrugged. 'Neither of us has any duties to claim him; and among these places there are several that I have never been to myself. Like you, after becoming an exile from France I decided to change my nationality, and I am now a Spaniard. So the more I can see of what is now always to be my country, the better.'

De Quesnoy shook his head. 'That is a plausible excuse, dear boy, and it is charming of you to make it; but you will have many opportunities to visit these places in more cheerful company than mine. I really cannot allow you to saddle yourself with me for more than a couple of weeks. However hard I try not to show my grief it is certain that I shall be moody and preoccupied for a good part of the time.'

'I don't mean to give you the chance to be. We are going by road in my new automobile and whenever you show signs of depression I intend to make you drive it.'

'What!' exclaimed the Count, sitting up with a jerk. 'But I've never driven an automobile in my life. I hate the damn' smelly unreliable things.'

The Prince laughed. 'Being, like yourself, a lover of horses, until quite recently I shared your prejudice. But soon everyone will be driving one; so you'll have to learn sooner or later, and this is an excellent opportunity. The new models don't break down like the early types, either; at least not every few miles, and having to keep your mind on the machine will keep it off everything else.'

Next day, the 9th of June, they set out. De Vendôme's car was a six-cylinder Hispano Suiza and capable of doing sixty miles an hour on the flat; but horses were still apt to shy at cars, so their progress was slow through the city and suburbs of Madrid, and it was not until tea-time that they reached the little town of Aranjuez, which is in miniature to Madrid what Versailles is to Paris. The Prince's mother had a villa there so it was one of his homes, in which he had his own suite. They garaged the car there and he ordered beds to be made up, but only caretaker servants were in residence so they dined at a restaurant on the south bank of the Tagus. The river there ran through woods that formed a charming setting, and for dessert they had a great bowl of freshly-picked strawberries.

On the 10th the road, curving south-eastward across the plain of New Castile, proved a dreary stretch and was almost deserted, but it could hardly have been bettered as a place for the Prince to give de Quesnoy his first lessons in driving. By nightfall they reached Manzanares, and on the 11th covered another long, flat stretch until late afternoon when they entered more picturesque hilly country. So far the surface of the roads had been far from good, but now to the ruts and potholes were added sudden twists and unexpected gullies that could be negotiated well enough by muleteers and ox carts, but presented most unpleasant traps for motorists. The high-sprung chassis with its narrow tyres bucked alarmingly from side to side and it took all de Vendômes's newly acquired skill to get them that night to Linares. Their last lap to Cordoba ran through the Sierra Morena and for most of the way followed the course of the Guadalquivir. The mountain scenery was magnificent, but it proved a gruelling drive and they were both heartily glad to reach the white city from which at one time a Caliph had ruled all Spain.

In its oldest part lay the ancestral home of the Condes de Cordoba, a rambling two-storey house with airy, sparsely-furnished rooms built round three carefully tended gardens. Jasmin, bougainvillaea and climbing geraniums covered their walls, the fronds of tall palms rustled high above, orange, lemon and loquat trees were enclosed by low-clipped hedges, there were roses in great profusion with many other flowers and fountains that tinkled faintly into lily pools. It was typical of several such *Casas* that de Quesnoy was to see in the next ten days.

They spent three days there while de Vendôme took his guest to see the Cathedral, once a magnificent Mosque – with its nineteen aisles of Moorish arches and amazing labyrinth of nearly a thousand columns made from different coloured marbles – several fine *Casas* and Renaissance churches, the statue of the Grand Captain, Gonzalo González – upon the bronze charger and body of which a white marble head sits so incongruously – and the thousand-year-old Synagogue in the narrow maze-like streets of the old Jewish quarter.

On the 16th they did the eighty-seven miles to Seville, the most fascinating of all the Spanish cities, and there they remained five days. De Quesnoy was impressed with the Cathedral, which he thought even finer than that at Toledo, and intrigued by the amazing collection of bejewelled chalices and reliquaries in its treasury. The Alcázar Palace, with its perfectly proportioned halls and courts of Moorish stonework carved to appear as delicate as lace, walls of tiles patterned by time to the most roseate hues and lovely gardens in which grew a profusion of jacarandas, oleanders and rare flowering shrubs, all delighted him so much that he paid it three visits. But by the end of five days he was surfeited with the sight of Baroque altars, charming patios glimpsed through iron grilles, Spanish old masters, Moorish fountains and the endless fine tapestries that graced the walls of the big private *Casas*.

Sensing his boredom de Vendôme suggested that they should push on to Jerez, so on the 22nd they took the road south through a smiling countryside of rolling downs across which well-husbanded plantations of olive trees alternated with fields of corn. While in Seville they had occupied a private suite in the palatial Alfonso XII Hotel, and de Vendôme had tactfully declined invitations from the Albas and other of his acquaintances who lived in the city, because he knew that de Quesnoy was still averse to going into society. But he had never before been to Jerez, and if they were to see anything of the wine industry, of which that charming little town is the centre, there was no escape from accepting the hospitality of the Sherry Barons.

For two days Williams, Domeques and Gonzalez in turn initiated them into the mysteries: took them to see vineyards and presses and over vast Bodegas in which were stacked tens of thousands of casks of sherry. As a lover of fine wine de Quesnoy enjoyed sampling the rare Manzanillas, Amontillados, and very old rich Olorosos, and he seemed at last a little more like his normal self. But when de Vendôme suggested going on to Cadiz he shook his head.

'No, François. You must forgive me. I enjoyed Cordoba and

Seville, but for the present I could not face another church or picture gallery. I really think that we should return to Madrid and that I should take a definite decision on how to employ myself in the future.'

The younger man's face fell, then after a moment he said, 'All right; let's cut out Cadiz and go straight down to Algeciras. We can bathe there and could hire a boat to do some sailing, if you like. That would make a change for you, and you could think out what you mean to do more pleasantly while lounging on a beach than in the stifling heat that by now must be making Madrid almost unbearable.'

It was a sensible suggestion, so de Quesnoy agreed. Next morning they drove southward, meeting again on the road many little groups consisting of heavily-laden donkeys and, jogging along on mules, bronze-faced men in flat-crowned hats and sloe-eyed women wearing colourful skirts and scarves typical of Andalusia.

At Algeciras they stayed at the Reina Cristina, which stands on high ground surrounded by a pleasant garden, and looks out across the blue bay to the Rock of Gibraltar. De Quesnoy had never cared much for sailing so they did not hire a boat, but each morning they took a picnic lunch and drove some five miles to a deserted bay where they spent most of the day, either in the water or baking themselves brown on the golden sands.

Nearly all the other guests at the hotel were English, and after dinner the string band played all the hits from the more recent Gaiety shows but, after a few evenings of sitting in the Palm Court, de Quesnoy again dropped into long periods of moody silence. On their fourth night there, in a new effort to distract him from his thoughts, de Vendôme suggested a visit to the Casino, and they went out to have what they intended to be a mild gamble.

In de Quesnoy's case it proved far from that. He was generous by nature and rich enough to lose a considerable sum without worry, but he was careful about money, so would not normally have risked more than about twenty pounds. But his mind was not on the game, so he made his bets with indifference and several times 'Banco'd' indiscriminately. To everyone's surprise he won again and again, and after an hour's play he suddenly realized that he had a big pile of high denomination chips in front of him. Seeing that his luck was in he began to plunge, and his luck did not desert him. When they left at three o'clock in the morning he had won nearly seven hundred pounds.

Next morning when they met in their private sitting-room for breakfast de Vendôme congratulated him again on his big win. With a twisted smile he said,

'Lucky at cards, unlucky in love. I'd give every penny of it for one half-hour with Angela. But you and your uncle were right. I've got to forget her and make a new life for myself. I shall always remember your kindness to me, François, in taking me on this trip. It has helped a lot, but more sightseeing in Malaga, Granada and the other places won't get me anywhere. From today I mean to put the past behind me and concentrate on re-making my career. If you have no objection we will pack this morning and start back for Madrid. Then, as soon as possible, I mean to sail for South America.'

The young Prince nodded. 'I understand; just as you wish. You are right, of course, to take up soldiering again. It's in your blood, and with the wars and revolutions that are always going on out there you will have no difficulty in obtaining a senior rank in the army of one of the Republics.'

But Fate had other plans for de Quesnoy. When the post arrived there was a letter for him from de Cordoba. A passage in it ran:

François wrote to me from Seville that although you were well, and as cheerful as could be expected in the circumstances, he felt sure that our plan to distract your mind by a tour of Southern Spain was doomed to failure, and that you would not fully recover until you had something definite to occupy it.

Yesterday I spoke of the matter to Don Alfonso. He is greatly concerned for you and he has in mind a mission which he believes may appeal to you. In consequence, S. M. el Rey has commanded me to request you to wait upon him with as little delay as possible at his Palace at Aranjuez, where he is now residing.

3

A Dangerous Mission

DE QUESNOY had refused to interest himself in the oily mysteries of the Hispano Suiza's engine, but had soon mastered the art of driving the machine. His long-acquired feel for the mouths of horses stood him in good stead when taking the wheel, and every day for the past three weeks he had spent an hour or more at it; so, now that he could take turns with de Vendôme in driving, they hoped to do the journey back to Aranjuez in four days.

In that, luck was against them. Between Linares and Valdepeñas they had their first breakdown. Fortunately it occurred within a few miles of the latter place and they were able to hire a team of mules that towed the car into it in something under two hours. But as yet this old market town had no garage and it was only after a prolonged struggle with a telephone system still in its teething stage that the Prince succeeded in getting through to Madrid and arranging for a spare part to be sent off by passenger train that evening. In consequence it was not until July the 3rd that they arrived in Aranjuez.

For the best part of two hundred years the Spanish Royal Family had made a practice of spending some of the hottest months there instead of remaining to swelter in Madrid, and the Infanta Maria Alfonsine had been given a life tenancy of the villa in the Royal Domain, in which they had slept on their outward journey. She and her husband, the Conde Ruiz, were now installed there, and at this time of the year it was also home to de Vendôme; so they drove straight to it.

The villa was, in fact, a miniature palace, playing the rôle that Le Petit Trianon played to Versailles. In the past, Spanish Kings had often kept their mistresses there, but under the Regency of Queen Maria Cristina it had been given a new respectability. It faced on to a pretty little courtyard, was surrounded by woods and contained much beautiful furniture, including a remarkable collection of clocks.

Soon after their arrival a message was sent to the Palace asking when it would be convenient for de Quesnoy to wait upon the King. A reply in Don Alfonso's own hand was delivered that evening. In it he said he thought it preferable that the Count should not come to the Palace; so he would ride over to the villa the following morning.

At eleven o'clock, a fine boyish figure unattended except for a groom, he clattered into the courtyard. Having kissed his aunt and given vigorous handshakes to Conde Ruiz, the Prince and the Count, who had assembled to receive him, with a light, quick step he led the way up to the drawing-room. Refreshments had been set out there and while they drank a glass of champagne he asked de Vendôme and de Quesnoy about their journey; then, after ten minutes, he said to the Infanta:

'Aunt, I have a private matter to discuss with M. le Comte de Quesnoy. You will, I am sure, allow us to make use of your drawing-room.'

De Quesnoy had already met the King a score of times – in England with the Londonderrys and at Eaton Hall, where he had stayed as a guest of the Duke and Duchess of Westminster while courting Queen Ena; in Madrid, when installed as a Knight of the Golden Fleece, at numerous functions there and he had played polo with him – but when the King stood up to acknowledge his aunt's curtsey, as the others smilingly withdrew, the Count could not help being again impressed that one so young should already have acquired such a regal presence.

He was only twenty and looked still younger, but he held himself splendidly upright and this, coupled with his very slender figure, made him appear taller than his medium height. His hair and eyes were dark, his thin face, still cleanshaven, was bronzed, his every movement had springiness and verve, and his mobile mouth broke into frequent smiles. He was wearing a white stock, a long waist-coat, a loose coat and beautifully-cut riding breeches, and his long legs were encased in top-boots polished to the brightness of a mirror.

With amusement and respect the Count recalled hearing about the shock he had given to his ministers when, at the age of sixteen, he had assumed power as a Sovereign. To the surprise and dismay of those elderly gentlemen, after the long and tiring ceremony of taking the oath to observe the Constitution he had declared that he would immediately hold his first Cabinet meeting. At it he had vigorously opposed certain changes that it was planned to make in the army, then laid it down in no uncertain terms that now he was of age the Cabinet's power to bestow rewards was revoked, and that henceforth he alone would decide who was to receive honours and decorations.

When the others had left the room he said at once to de Quesnoy, 'Count, after the tragedy that occurred on the day of my wedding I wrote to you expressing my sympathy in your great loss. I wish to assure you now that my letter was no mere formal condolence. Both the Queen and I felt most deeply for you.'

'Your Majesty is very gracious to concern yourself . . .' murmured the Count.

'But,' the King brushed aside the acknowledgement and hurried on, 'it would be another tragedy if a man of your abilities allowed his grief to turn him into a misanthrope; and that, I was distressed to learn from de Cordoba, there seems some danger of your doing.'

De Quesnoy nodded. 'It is true, Sir. During the past five weeks I've been no fit companion for anyone. But when your summons reached me in Algeciras I had just decided to go to South America and take up soldiering again. A break with the past and new activities will, I hope, in time restore my zest for life.'

'It would be some months at least before you could get there and take up responsibilities weighty enough to distract your mind, whereas I could offer you immediate employment; although I must add that it would be of a very unorthodox nature for a gentleman.'

'Even so, I'd be interested to hear your idea, Sir.'

'De Cordoba also told me that on several occasions you had lamented the fact that there was no way in which you could help to stamp out these accursed anarchists.'

'Nothing, Sir, would give me greater satisfaction.'

'Well, I can give you the chance. But it would entail your assuming a new identity and living for a while in considerable discomfort.'

'From that, I assume your Majesty is suggesting that I should undertake to spy upon these people in collaboration with your police?'

'Spy upon them, yes; but without official assistance of any kind – other than that which I can give you. The very essence of my proposal lies in your having no connection with the police.'

The Count raised his 'devil's eyebrows'. 'I must confess, Sir, I fail to understand. I have no experience in such matters and . . .'

'Oh yes you have. François told me how, after your secret return to Paris, you passed yourself off as a Russian revolutionary, ferreted out the secrets of the Masons, and provided the material that brought about the fall of the Government of that atheist Emile Combes.'

'True;' de Quesnoy gave a faint smile. 'I meant only that I know nothing whatever about Spanish anarchists, and unless your secret police collaborate with me . . .'

'Have I not made myself clear?' the King cut in, a shade impatiently. 'If you agree to undertake this venture I wish you to work entirely independently. I will, of course, furnish you with a certain amount of data with which to begin your investigation, but I intend that the police should be kept in ignorance of your activities.'

'I accept what you say, Sir, but permit me to remark that I fail to see what you can possibly hope to gain by keeping me in a water-tight compartment. It stands to reason that my chances of success would be far greater if I were to have the help of the department of your police that specializes in following up the activities of anarchists.'

'Ha!' exclaimed the King. 'That is just where you are wrong. But since you are a foreigner it is not surprising that you should be puzzled by my attitude. The great majority of my people would be, too, for very few of them have sufficient knowledge of what goes on behind the scenes to realize the difficulties of my situation.'

2

After a moment's pause, he continued, 'To accept this mission will be to court considerable danger, Count; so it is only right that I should disclose to you in confidence my reasons for distrusting my own police. That means going back a long way. I assume that, as an educated man, you know the main outlines of Spanish history; but even at the risk of boring you I must recall some of the events of the past in order to make clear to you the effect they have had on the present.'

Standing up, the King began to pace up and down while reeling off facts and dates that had been familiar to him from his earliest boyhood. 'In the past hundred years the only period in which the Spanish people have enjoyed peace and contentment under a King was the ten years' reign of my father, Don Alfonso XII of blessed memory. I said "under a King", mark you; that is important.

'Let us go back to the era of Napoleon. Charles IV was then King of Spain. He was a weak and foolish man. It is common knowledge that from the time of the French Revolution Queen Maria Louisa's lover, the upstart Godoy, was the real ruler of the country. So weak was the King that his elder son, Ferdinand, conspired to force his abdication, and more or less succeeded. That was in 1808 and Napoleon took advantage of their quarrel to intervene. Like the wily blackguard he was, he pretended to give both his support, tricked them both into coming to France to confer with him, then compelled both to abdicate and put his brother, Joseph Bonaparte, on the throne.

'Joseph proved a much better King than might have been expected. He did his best for the Spanish people and eventually quarrelled with his brother through placing their interests before those of France. But his reign was a terrible period for Spain, because the country became for years the battleground between the French and the Duke of Wellington aided by the Spanish patriots who had risen against their conquerors. You know the end. One after the other Napoleon's Marshals were defeated and by 1814 the French had been driven from the country.

'By then King Charles was dead; so it was Ferdinand who returned from exile to mount the throne. But meanwhile in 1812 the Cortes had met in Cadiz and given Spain a new Constitution. Abroad there seems to be a myth that Spanish sovereigns are absolute; but that is far from being the case. From mediaeval times there have always been Parliaments here that have to some extent restricted the powers of the monarchy. But the Constitution of 1812 went much further than any preceding one, because it was made by men who had been influenced by the democratic principles that emerged from the

French Revolution. That Constitution, with only slight modifications, is still in force and binding upon Spanish sovereigns today. Under it no decree that I may issue is valid unless it is countersigned by one of my Ministers.

'However, Ferdinand VII accepted and swore to observe it. He did nothing of the kind, and proved the worst type of autocrat. You must have seen his portrait by Goya many times. It would be hard to find a more cunning, shifty face, and that was the nature of the man. He had no sooner assumed power than he arrested all the leading Liberals, threw them into prison and confiscated their property. That was the root from which our worst trouble springs. It divided the Spanish people into two camps: those who supported the monarchy – they were in the majority, because, even under bad rulers, Spain has always been monarchist at heart – and a hard core of democrats made bitter by the persecution and determined sooner or later to get control of the Government.

'In 1823, driven to desperation by Ferdinand's arbitrary measures and oppressive taxation, the people revolted and made him a prisoner. But Louis XVIII of France sent an army that crushed the revolution and set him at liberty. One way and another, through trickery, treachery and the support of the Church and foreign troops, he succeeded in ruling as a despot for a quarter of a century. Then, on his very deathbed, this evil genius of my country left Spain another terrible legacy.'

Pausing in his stride for a moment, the King took a drink from his glass, then went on, 'You will, of course, know that in France the Salic law operated, by which no female could ascend the throne; and that with the ending of the Hapsburg dynasty in 1700 Louis XIV's grandson, the Duc d'Anjou, became the first Bourbon King of Spain as Philip V. It was this French Prince who introduced the Salic law, which previously had not applied here. Ninety years later King Charles IV approved a resolution of the Cortes to revoke this law and revert to the old order of succession but, most unfortunately, the decree was never promulgated. Thus, the question whether a female could legally ascend the throne remained debatable.

'Ferdinand VII had no son; so two persons were Heirs Apparent: under the Salic law, his brother, Don Carlos, and under the old law, his daughter by his fourth wife, Queen Maria Cristina. In spite of the most vigorous protests from Don Carlos and many of the highest nobility, on his deathbed he designated as his successor his daughter, the Infanta Isabella, who was then only a child of two.

'Ferdinand had often said with cynical humour that Spain was a bottle of beer of which he was the cork, and that on his death it would blow up. By his malicious decision he ensured that it should. Don Carlos was in many ways a good man, and that he should become King was obviously preferable to saddling the country with the uncertainties of a long minority. Don Carlos decided to fight for what he considered to be his rights, and Spain was plunged into a hideous civil war. Behind him he had the Church, most of the aristocracy and all those best elements in Spain who treasured the old traditions of the country handed down from the time when Spain was a mighty Empire. Yet the forces of the Queen Regent emerged victorious. How, you may well ask? To keep her infant daughter on the throne she took the only course open to her and threw herself into the hands of the Liberals.

'At the date of Ferdinand's death she was still only twenty-six, and an exceptionally lovely woman. She had not long been a widow when she secretly married a Captain in her Guards named Munoz. Incredible as it may sound, still in secret she had nine children by him. The strain of keeping up appearances while leading this double life hardly bears thinking about, and naturally the affairs of the country suffered in consequence; she became a puppet in the hands of factions and military adventurers.

'In 1846 the young Queen, Isabella II, although only thirteen, was declared of age and married to her cousin, the Duke of Cadiz. He was a spineless creature, so the power emanating from the throne continued to be the plaything of unscrupulous intriguers. To worsen matters it soon became evident that she had inherited even more than the normal share of the Bourbon appetites.'

The King paused to smile, took another drink from his glass, which de Quesnoy had refilled, then added, 'Perhaps I should say "appetite" for in this case I have not so much in mind the gastronomic feats of Louis XIV or of Louis XVI, who frequently ate a whole chicken as a single course in a meal, but the amorous endurance which caused Henry of Navarre to be nicknamed *Le Vert Galant*, and led to Louis XV keeping a harem busy in his "*Parc au Cerfs*". Every handsome guardsman Queen Isabella set eyes on became grist to her mill, and her immoralities were so flagrant that after years of misrule by her favourites the people rebelled and threw her out.

'With her to exile in France she took her young son, my father, and in 1870 she abdicated in his favour, but he became King Alfonso XII only in name. Meanwhile, under the Provisional Government of Serrano and General Prim, there ensued two years of semi-anarchy here while the Spanish people demanded a King, and half the Royal Houses in Europe wrangled over who should supply one. Feeling was so intense that it started the Franco-Prussian war, but Prim eventually decided upon Amadeo of Savoy, the second son of King Victor Emanuel II.

'Poor fellow, he was no match for such an imbroglio. Generals, Carlists, Liberals and Cardinals all combined to make his life hell. In a little under three years he threw in his hand and returned to Italy.

'The distracted Cortes then proclaimed a Republic, but the great bulk of the people was bitterly opposed to it and the Government lost all control of them. On any excuse armed mobs surged through the cities looting and murdering, bands of peasants turned themselves into bandits robbing travellers and holding them to ransom. To save Spain, Don Carlos, son of the first Don Carlos, raised his standard in the north and launched the second Carlist war. That only made matters worse, as thousands more Spaniards set about cutting one another's throats.

'In desperation a General named Martinez Campos made a *pronunciamiento* calling on my father to return and ascend the throne. He had just completed his first term as an officer-cadet at Sandhurst. Immediately, he set out for Spain. He was received with tremendous acclamation, but the first task thrust upon him was to defeat the Carlist army. He did so, but at a price. History repeated itself. Once again the Church and the traditionalists – those elements which in any country are the natural supporters of monarchy – had rallied round Don Carlos. To bring peace and keep his throne my father was compelled to become dependent on the Liberals.

'He was a good man and would have made a fine King; but he was unlucky. When he was about my present age he married for love the beautiful Mercedes, daughter of the Duke de Montpensier. They adored one another, but after being Queen for only six months she died. With her death the spirit went out of him. He succeeded in keeping the peace, but only by persuading the Conservatives to make great concessions, and an era of two-party government set in. The Conservative leader, Cánovas, made a dubious pact with the Liberal leader, Sagasta. They rigged the elections and played box and cox, so that when the people became dissatisfied with one party the other went in. That system, which makes a mockery of the people's rights, has now continued here for many years.

'Shortly after Queen Mercedes' death, from a sense of duty my father married again – my beloved mother, who was born the Arch-duchess Maria Cristina of Hapsburg. She bore him two daughters. He died still grieving for Mercedes, at the early age of twenty-eight, and I, as you know, was born a King posthumously.

'My mother is the most wise and saintly woman I have ever

known; but once again Spain faced the uncertainties of a long Regency under a Queen. During my minority no course was open to her but to allow her Ministers to make use of the monarchy as a front to cover their own policies and ambitions. It was owing largely to her tact that the throne survived our war with the United States in '98. It is true that for long Cuba had been shockingly misgoverned and the Americans had some justification in taking it from us to protect their commercial interests there, but there was no justification whatever for those rapacious dollar grubbers to rob us afterwards of the Philippines, and the surrender of this last really valuable fragment of the old Spanish Empire caused our people intense indignation. That, and the loss of our entire fleet, was enough to overturn any throne, but my mother succeeded in riding out the storm, and seeing me crowned.

'Yet in the four years since I attained my majority there have been no less than fourteen political crises and I have had eight Prime Ministers. Such is my inheritance – an ever-increasing pressure from the people to give them a real say in the government of the country, but a Constitution which compels me to accept the policies recommended by politicians who have made a compromise solely to keep themselves in power, and whose views hardly differ whether they label themselves Conservative or Liberal.'

Having swallowed the rest of his wine, the King resumed briskly. 'Now, let us sum up, and assess the results of this hundred years of civil war and dissension through which Spain has passed. Again and again, to preserve the monarchy in its legitimate line Queen Regents and youthful Sovereigns have been compelled to turn for support to the Liberals. And in more recent times so-called Conservative ministers have risen to power only by making big concessions to the Left. In consequence, as nepotism is still rife here, more than half the high posts in my Civil Service are held by Liberals.

'Mark you, I do not suggest for one moment that these men are lacking in patriotism, and I am confident that ninety-nine per cent of the Spanish people are entirely loyal to my person. But the great majority of Liberals of all nationalities have their heads among the clouds. Many of them are fine people with high ideals, their only desire being to better the lot of the masses. Unfortunately they fail to realize that in many countries, of which Spain is one, the bulk of the people is not sufficiently advanced to govern themselves. The result of their measures, as has been proved only too often, is to open the way for revolution. Evil men with extremist views make use of them, then climb to power over their dead bodies. That is the danger here.

'I believe my police to be reasonably efficient. I have no doubt at all that they would not hesitate to arrest anyone whom they had proof was an anarchist, or involved in treasonable activities. But many of the senior officers in the police are Liberals. Those who are hold that every man has a right to express his opinions. They deliberately delude themselves about the degree of danger arising from orators who, under the guise of agitating for reforms, stimulate revolution, and this is particularly so in Barcelona where the police, being Catalans, naturally have a certain sympathy with revolutionaries who cloak their aims under a demand for Catalonian independence. It is these people who spread the doctrines of Karl Marx and Bakúnin, and they are the real root of the trouble. It is they who inspire fanatics and men with a grievance to become active anarchists; yet their activities are condoned by the police on the grounds of permitting free speech. If you could secure evidence that the most prominent of these mob orators, and writers of inflammatory articles, were secretly connected with the bomb plots we would be able to send them to prison, and so make some headway in stamping out the breeding-ground of anarchy. You see now what I have in mind. Do you agree?'

'I do, Sir,' de Quesnoy replied at once.

The King came to a sudden halt in front of the Count, looked at him fixedly, and said, 'Good! And after this long dissertation of mine, may I take it that you understand my reasons for not trusting my police to co-operate fully with you?'

'Indeed yes. Your Majesty could not have explained matters more lucidly.'

'Tell me, then; are you game to carry out an independent investigation?'

'I am. It is just something of this kind that I need at the moment. But you spoke, Sir, of giving me some aid yourself. Since your police are ruled out, what form will it take?'

'I have to go into Madrid this afternoon. I will order the police dossier on Morral and his associates to be sent to the Palace. One of my gentlemen whom I can trust will deliver it to de Cordoba, and François can go into Madrid to collect it from him tomorrow. No official will then know that you have seen it or that it has been out of my possession.'

'That would be excellent. For how long may I keep it?'

'A few days should be sufficient for you to make such notes as you require from it. Should the police ask to have it back I can always put them off by saying that I have not yet had time to study it fully.'

For some ten minutes more they discussed the matter; then Don Alfonso rang the bell, the others came back into the room, and shortly afterwards they all escorted him down to the courtyard.

The arrangement about the dossier worked without a hitch and de Vendôme brought it to the Count on the following afternoon; but it proved far larger than he had expected, and consisted of so many papers that they filled two large suitcases. Delighted to have so much material to examine, de Quesnoy set to work on it that evening.

It was a quiet household. De Vendôme was a deeply religious young man and, with Father Tomaso's help, was endeavouring to catch up in his work as President of numerous Church charities; he was also an exceptionally fine horseman and he had won prizes for jumping at International Horse Shows; so he spent much of his time out riding or playing polo with the King. The Infanta, aided by her lady-in-waiting Doña Isabella, also busied herself with many charities and at other times pottered in her garden. Conde Ruiz was much in Madrid on business and spent most nights there at the family Palacio, as the two brothers were devoted to one another, and, although the Palacio was owned by the elder, it was so spacious that the younger also had a private suite there and he, his wife and his stepson made it their home when living in the capital.

In consequence, de Quesnoy had few interruptions and he spent many hours up in a room at the top of the house, of which he had been given the key, reading and making extracts from the great pile of police reports on Mateo Morral and subversive pamphlets, etc., that had been seized during raids on Nakens' publishing office and the premises of other anarchists suspected of being associated therewith.

Morral, it transpired, was the son of a wealthy cotton spinner who had given him an excellent education, which included sending him for some years to study in Germany. But he was of a morose and brooding disposition and had soon adopted revolutionary views. For a long time past Barcelona had been the centre of an increasingly strong demand for Home Rule for Catalonia, and on Morral's return to his native province he had fervently embraced this movement to break away from the central government. The movement contained many anarchists and Morral became one of them.

At that time the most prominent anarchist in Barcelona was a man named Francisco Ferrer. He had been born at Alélla, a little place some twelve miles outside the city, and was now in his middle forties. As a young man Ferrer had attached himself to Ruiz Zorrilla, the Republican leader of the days of Isabella II and the

Revolutionary period that followed her downfall. After Zorrilla had been sent into exile he settled at Geneva and Ferrer joined him there, later acting as his intermediary with revolutionaries in Spain who had gone into hiding.

In 1885 Ferrer's treasonable activities were discovered, but he had been warned in time and escaped to Paris, where his wife and children joined him. There for a number of years he earned a precarious living as a teacher of languages. Being a very highly-sexed man and an enthusiastic advocate of the anarchist doctrine of Free Love, his home life was not a happy one, and on one occasion his wife had tried to shoot him. However, there was evidently something about him that made a special appeal to women, as he never lacked for mistresses, and a lady named Mlle Meunier, who possessed considerable wealth, had become a disciple of his.

Mlle Meunier was particularly enthusiastic about a scheme he had evolved to bring about revolution by educating promising young students to become atheists and anarchists, and to enable him to proceed with it she left him a valuable block of house property in Paris. A Liberal government in Spain having quashed prosecutions pending against Ferrer and a number of other agitators in exile he had, in 1901, returned to Barcelona and, with Mlle Meunier's money, opened an establishment which he named the *Escuela Moderna*.

Ferrer staffed his school with fellow anarchists, both male and female, then added to it a considerable library and an 'educational' publishing business. The library consisted of Rationalist, Positivist, Revolutionary and Communist books and pamphlets of all kinds, and most of the many accounts of anarchist activities which, for the past twenty years, had met with a ready sale in most European countries. The publishing side produced translations of works by French, German and British sociologists of advanced or revolutionary views, and distributed them to booksellers throughout Spain.

The Church, and numerous other respectable bodies in Barcelona, had protested in the strongest possible terms at young people in their midst being openly led to deny God and become enemies of the State. But such was the strength of the Liberal insistence on maintaining freedom of speech that their protests had been rejected by the authorities, and for the past five years Ferrer had continued without interference to canalize youthful enthusiasm into revolutionary channels and to disseminate literature calculated to inflame the discontented.

Morral had naturally become an intimate of Ferrer and after a time Ferrer had made him the librarian at the *Escuela Moderna*

2*

where one of the women teachers was a Señorita Soledad Villafranca, who was said to be very attractive. She had become one of Ferrer's mistresses and at the same time the mistress of Morral. One theory was that the two men had quarrelled over her and that this had led Morral to plan his attack on the King and Queen to show his mistress what a fine fellow he was. Another theory was that Ferrer had used the Señorita Villafranca to influence Morral into making his attempt, although there was no evidence of this.

In addition to these particulars about Morral and Ferrer the dossier contained brief biographies of Ferrer's teaching staff which showed that, although no criminal act could be imputed to any of them, they all openly proclaimed their allegiance to anarchist principles, and that, at one time or another, most of them had been mixed up with Communists, Collectivists, and other types of advanced Socialists whose object was to bring about a dictatorship of the proletariat.

From the seized pamphlets de Quesnoy gathered that the object of the anarchists was not only to overthrow the existing governments in every country, but also to abolish rule by law. That explained to him a point about their activities which had at times puzzled him. Although since the early 'eighties there had been many attempts to assassinate Monarchs and Presidents, there had been many more against Public Prosecutors and Judges; and it now emerged that whenever an anarchist was caught after an outrage and condemned to death or a long prison sentence, his confederates invariably did their utmost to avenge themselves upon the lawyers who had helped to convict or sentence him.

Ever since de Quesnoy had been a boy, there had also been an increasing number of outrages in connection with labour disturbances, particularly in the mining districts of France and Belgium. Pits had been flooded and hoisting gear and the houses of pit-owners blown up; on many occasions troops had had to be called in and ordered to fire on the mobs before such riots could be quelled. The anarchists took the credit for these dynamitings, but the strikes were clearly Communist-inspired; so the Count naturally assumed, as did most other people of his class, that Marxists, Anarchists, Communists, Syndicalists and Nihilists were more or less interchangeable terms for the same type of people, and that although they might differ slightly in their doctrines their common object was to bring about a Socialist world.

Of one thing there seemed no doubt whatever. As far as Spain was concerned Francisco Ferrer was the root of the trouble. He might never have thrown a bomb himself, or even have assisted in planning any act of violence; but it was inescapable that by corrupting the minds of others he was morally responsible for the deaths of scores of innocent people and, most probably, among them Angela's.

De Quesnoy therefore decided that his only real hope of succeeding in his mission lay in putting Ferrer out of the way; and he made up his mind that he would leave nothing untried which might get him the evidence to send the anarchist to the hangman's rope.

By the end of the week he had finished with the dossier and arranged with de Vendôme to return it to the King.

On the Saturday, de Cordoba and the Condesa Gulia arrived to spend the week-end, and both were delighted to find him much more like his old self. That evening there was a dinner-party – the first he had attended since his wife's death – at which he talked with an animation and cheerfulness which showed that he was at last free from his gloomy preoccupation with her loss. On the Sunday, after attending Mass, they all went for a ride through the woods and in the afternoon had a jolly picnic beside the river. It was soon after their return, and before going up to change for dinner, that, while strolling in the garden, he came upon Gulia sitting on a stone seat alone.

In the warm light of the summer evening she made a lovely picture. Her burnished Titian hair, worn Madonna fashion, caught the light in its side curls, her darker, arched eyebrows and slumbrous black eyes made a striking contrast to her magnolia petal skin. Her full, rich red lips parted, showing small, even, flashing white teeth as she smiled a welcome to him. Yet after one swift glance at his eyes her feminine instinct told her that he was regarding her only with the detached interest that he would have bestowed on a fine marble statue.

When he sat down beside her they talked for a while of his trip with de Vendôme, then she said, 'Now that high summer is here the Court will be moving as usual to San Sebastian, and everyone who matters goes with it; the Embassies and even many big financiers like José, who conducts most of his business from a branch of the bank there. We have a charming villa with a little private bay not far from the city. Both he and I would be so delighted if, when we go north next week, you would accompany us and stay with us for a while.'

Smiling, he shook his head. 'It is most kind of you to ask me, Condesa, but I fear I must refuse. On Monday I am off to Barcelona.'

'Barcelona!' she repeated, opening wide her splendid eyes. 'Whatever for? At this time of year you will find the heat there intolerable.'

Her husband knew of the mission he had been given by the

King, as also did de Vendôme, who had spoken of it in front of his mother and Conde Ruiz; so he saw no reason for concealing it from her. After drawing for a moment on the Hoyo de Monterry cigar he was smoking, he replied, 'Please regard it as a secret except from your family, who already know about it, but I am going to Barcelona to hunt anarchists.'

She gave him a long, steady look then said without a suggestion of a smile, 'In that case you need not go so far as Barcelona. You had better begin by hunting me. I am an anarchist.'

4

Anarchists and Anarchists

DE QUESNOY's 'devil's eyebrows' shot up as he exclaimed, 'You can't be serious!'

'I am,' she assured him, and her full, cupid's-bow mouth broke into a smile. That smile, although he did not realize it, was one of secret triumph. She had played her cards well. Her shock tactics had succeeded. He was staring at her, and for the first time consciously, in an attempt to assess her personality as a woman.

He gave a quick shake of his head. 'I refuse to believe it. What you say does not make sense.'

'It would if you knew more about me. I am a niece of Miguel de Unamuno.'

The Count's broad forehead wrinkled again, and he said, 'Unamuno? I seem to have heard the name as that of an educationalist; is he not a Professor?'

'He is that and much more. He is also a philosopher and now acknowledged as one of the greatest brains that Spain has produced in the past century. His book, *The Tragic Sense of Life in Men and Peoples*, is already a classic. You should read it.'

'I fear that my Spanish has not yet reached a standard high enough for me to appreciate the nuances of a philosophical treatise. And even if it had, since you imply that your uncle favours violence as a means of bringing about a change in the social order, it is quite certain that I should find myself strongly opposed to his views.'

'He does not advocate violence; he is simply a clear-thinking man with the highest ideals. His wish is to see Spain legally transformed into a true democracy in which all men are equal.'

De Quesnoy took another pull on his cigar, and said, 'I see. On the face of it, then, your uncle is a Socialist. That does not tally with your implication that you imbibed anarchist doctrines from him.'

'No; since I have been old enough to think for myself I have moved much further to the Left. I find a great deal of sound sense in the philosophy of the anarchists.'

Again the Count regarded his lovely companion with a puzzled frown. 'Do you really mean that? Had you been given Morral's opportunity on Don Alfonso's wedding day would you have thrown the bomb?'

Gulia tossed back her head and laughed. 'Of course not. How could you even suggest that I might?'

'To be an anarchist is synonymous with holding a belief in the justification of using violence to achieve one's ends.'

'No, my dear Count; in that you are entirely wrong. In Spain today there are at least a million anarchists, but I doubt if a thousand of them would kill to further the general acceptance of their principles.'

'Oh come, Doña Gulia; when you speak of a million surely you are confusing anarchism with socialism, and lumping the two together.'

'Indeed I am not. There are many more Socialists than that. By far the greater part of the workers in Madrid, Valencia, Bilboa, Seville and Cadiz is Socialist, whereas the anarchists are concentrated in other areas of the country. The million I spoke of consists of a great part of the workers of Catalonia and the peasantry of Andalusia.'

'The peasantry of Andalusia! You amaze me. I had thought that in Spain, like most other countries, the agricultural population was the main support of the Conservatives.'

'It is not so here. The great part of the land consists of huge estates owned by absentee landlords who draw their wealth from their properties but never go near them. For generations the wretched tillers of the soil have been forced to work for a miserable pittance under slave-driving bailiffs, or starve. Can you wonder that they would like to throw off the yoke and keep for themselves the results of their labours?'

'No, that is natural enough. And had I given the matter serious thought I might have guessed that such feelings existed from the appalling poverty I saw in many of the villages during my trip to the south. However, I still feel that we are using terms that have different meanings for us. By anarchists I mean the sort of revolutionaries known as dynamiters, who created a reign of terror in

Paris in '94, when I was a young Cadet at St. Cyr, and fanatics like
Morral. It is true that ever since the 'eighties hardly a month has
passed without one of them exploding a bomb or knifing some
unfortunate person in one country or another. But, even so, their
number must be comparatively limited. On the other hand, these
hundreds of thousands of Catalonian workers and Andalusian
peasants of whom you speak can be striving to gain their ends only
by constitutional methods. Obviously those ends are the abolition
of privilege, the confiscation of wealth through the penal taxation
of the rich and equality for everyone in a Workers' State. What is
that but Socialism?'

She shook her head. 'You have defined Socialism but not
anarchism. They have certain aims in common, of course, but differ
fundamentally in the type of society they wish to bring about.'

After a moment's thought de Quesnoy said, 'What you say
interests me tremendously. During the past week I have had the
opportunity to acquire a considerable amount of information about
the militant anarchists; but I had no idea that their doctrines,
exclusive of violence, were accepted by great numbers of law-
abiding citizens. In common with most people of our class, I think,
I had, too, taken it for granted that, as it is the anarchists who
claim kudos for most of the acts of violence committed during
strikes, they were Socialists with extreme views. Please tell me now
about this fundamental difference between the two creeds.'

'Give me a cigarette, and I will,' Gulia replied.

'So you smoke,' he smiled, producing his case.

She laughed. 'Yes, sometimes in private; although the Infanta
still considers even that somewhat reprehensible in a woman.'

'Indeed?' de Quesnoy raised his eyebrows. 'Having all her life
had to conform to the stiff etiquette of the Spanish Court has
naturally given her a rather forbidding manner, yet I had formed
the impression that beneath it she is a very human person. But no
matter; please go on.'

He lit the cigarette for her and Gulia continued. 'When you said
a while back that the Socialists aim for a Workers' State you were
right. Their aim is to better the lot of the masses by nationalizing
all the social services and canalizing the whole wealth of the country
into the Treasury, so that it should be redistributed by free education, pensions for people who are too old to work, a fund to
support those who are temporarily unemployed through no fault
of their own, demolishing slums and building great blocks of modern
workers' flats in their place, increasing the number of hospitals and
giving free medical treatment to everyone, and so on.

'To do that would entail the creation of a vast non-productive bureaucracy which would eat up most of the money coming in before any surplus got back through these projects to the people who had earned it. Still worse, the central government would control everything and everybody: where people lived, the hours they worked, what they did with their leisure, and how they brought up their children. Carried to its logical conclusion Socialism becomes Communism, the only difference between the two being that, while the Socialists are prepared to wait until they can gain their ends by legal means, Karl Marx advocated attempts to achieve them more rapidly by insurrection. If either triumphed, in the long run the State would own everything; no one would be permitted to own land or any form of property, or to accumulate money to leave to his relatives. It would be the utter negation of freedom; we would all be slaves of the State.'

De Quesnoy nodded. 'I agree. The whole basis of Socialism is that the government should control the entire wealth of a country and the labouring capacity of its people. To do that would be impossible unless it had absolute power, and used compulsion to force on people the way they should lead their lives. Now, what about anarchism?'

'That is utterly different. The anarchist claims to be a law unto himself. That is no new thing. Zeno, the Greek philosopher who founded the Stoic school, was of that opinion; so were the powerful sect of Gnostics in early Christian times. The doctrine of Atheism was preached by many profound thinkers during the Middle Ages: Joachim, Abbot of Fiore, in Calabria, Amaury of Chartres, and Father John Ball, who played a big part in Wat Tyler's rebellion. It was because the men who took part in that rebellion believed that law enforced by the State was an evil and crippling thing that, on reaching London, their first act was to burn down the great law offices in the Temple.'

'Of course, there have always been individualists all through history. But militant anarchism as we know it began only in the 1870s. What gave rise to this modern creed that has become such a menace to the social order at the present day?'

'Michael Bakúnin did more than anyone to formulate its principles. He argued that the State was a product of religion and an historically necessary evil representing a lower form of civilization out of which mankind is now sufficiently advanced to pass; and he demanded its complete abolition. He wished to do away with all legislation and claimed full autonomy for each nation, region and commune. He also held that all individuals should be given full independence, because one becomes really free only when all others are free. Working upwards from the individual, free federations of communes would become free nations. In such nations everything necessary for production would be owned in common by each Labour group or Commune, and each group would administer its own affairs independently of the others.'

Stubbing out her cigarette, Gulia concluded, 'So you see anarchism is the complete antithesis of Socialism. Not a single *peseta* would be wasted on a non-productive bureaucracy. The millions that even now are squandered in that way would be sufficient for every family to live in comfort. The profits of labour would go to those who earned them, and everyone would have the opportunity to develop their own individualities as they wished. That would be real freedom, and it is that which anarchism offers.'

'In theory the case sounds a good one,' de Quesnoy admitted, 'but in practice I cannot believe that it could be made to work. All the same, I'd like to know more about it.'

'Then to start with you should read Paul Eltzbacher's book called *Anarchism*, in which he gives a very full account of the men he terms the Seven Sages and of the principles they laid down. They were Bakúnin, Proudhon, Max Stirner, Prince Kropotkin, William Godwin, Count Tolstoi, and, I think, yes, the American, Benjamin Tucker. Unfortunately he does not include chapters on Count Carlo Cafiero or Fanelli, the two greatest of Bakúnin's disciples who carried his doctrines to Italy and Spain; but you can learn about them elsewhere.'

'I thought Max Stirner was a close associate of Marx, and so a Communist,' the Count remarked.

'He was at one time. To begin with all these champions of the oppressed masses united to form a common front. It was Bakúnin who organized it by founding the International Working Men's Association. They held a number of Congresses, but it soon became apparent that the views of the principal speakers at them were hopelessly irreconcilable. Marx had the greatest number of followers so he took over the International, while Bakúnin and his followers seceded from it and formed a new Association called the Fédération Jurassienne. It was that body that initiated Propaganda by Deed.'

'What exactly is meant by that?'

'It is the anarchist term for acts of violence. The militant anarchists argue that if one accepts the proposition that all laws and authority are wrong, it becomes right to endeavour to destroy the whole social fabric that law and authority have built up. Since they are in such a small minority they know that they have no hope of attaining their ends by open revolt: but, they reason to themselves like this—"It is for us to set an example and by so doing draw attention to ourselves and our principles. When the masses see that by our deeds we are striking terror into the oppressors they will take heart, acclaim us, rise and overthrow the whole social structure." '

De Quesnoy gave a grim little smile. 'They certainly must have caused plenty of people in high places a lot of sleepless nights. But I think the chances of their ever succeeding in bringing about a revolution are extremely small. And even if they did they would gain nothing by it. They would only have smoothed the path for the Socialists, and ultimately the Communists.'

'You cannot be certain about that,' she objected quickly. 'It would not be so if in the meantime far greater numbers of people had been educated to understand the benefits that anarchism would bring them: that with the abolition of all law they would at last enjoy true freedom.'

'But no society can possibly exist without law.'

'It could, once everybody realized that their own interests are those of mankind in general. It would then be possible to replace the present legal systems, with their frequent injustices and penal codes, by common brotherly customs which would be universally accepted and willingly observed by all.'

He shook his head. 'You paint a Utopia; and I am still amazed to hear that hundreds of thousands of people believe that such a state of things might actually be brought about. Human nature being what it is, this idea that everybody would be content with an equal share of this world's goods and, out of brotherly love, not seek to increase it at the expense of others would never work. It surprises me, too, that a woman so exceptionally intelligent as yourself, Doña Gulia, can possibly suppose that it could. What of all those who are born lazy, the unscrupulous with a lust for power, and thieves and criminals with no laws or police to keep their depradations in check?'

Before she could answer de Vendôme came hurrying through the gardens towards the house. Throwing them a quick smile, he called out, 'Aren't you two coming in to change? If you don't, you'll be late for dinner.'

As they stood up, she said, 'There would be difficulties, of course. Every revolution has to go through its birth pangs; but we'll talk of that another time.' Giving him a quick glance, she added, 'José is aware that I hold Liberal views, but not that they are so far to the Left. To know that I believe in anarchism might distress him.

I have spoken to you so frankly only because you have now become deeply interested in these problems; but I rely on you to regard all I have said as in confidence.'

He bowed. 'I am greatly honoured that you should have given me your confidence, and you may count on me to respect it. But much as I shall look forward to discussing such matters with you again, as I am leaving for Madrid first thing tomorrow morning, I fear it will not be until my return from Barcelona.'

'Get your business there over quickly, then.' She gave him the full benefit of her ravishing smile. 'And please don't think that because I am an anarchist I would ever dream of shielding an assassin, whatever his politics. If you are after one of those people who aided Morral I hope you get him. Have you any idea how long you are likely to be away?'

'None at all, I'm afraid.'

'Well, we shall be at San Sebastian until the end of September. Do please come to stay with us if you can. José would be delighted. You know he is very fond of you, and so am I.'

They had reached the house, and as he held the door open for her he quickly concealed his surprise. Such a declaration by a young woman to a friend of her husband's with whom she had never before held a private conversation was so unconventional as to be startling. But after a moment he decided that he must have misunderstood her. He had a flair for languages and his Spanish was now fluent, but by no means perfect; so he could easily have interpreted wrongly the sense of her remark. She could not have meant that she, too, was very fond of him, but that she, too, would be delighted to see him at San Sebastian.

Nevertheless, as he watched her graceful figure mounting the curved staircase, he found himself thinking that José was a lucky man to have such a lovely and interesting woman for his wife.

Early the following morning, de Vendôme drove the Count into Madrid. Having left the bags he had taken on his trip with his heavier luggage, which was still at the Palacio Cordoba, he went out to make a number of arrangements. He had decided that the best means of penetrating anarchist circles in Barcelona would be to adopt similar measures to those he had used two years before in Paris, when ferreting out the secrets of the Masons, and pose as a Russian refugee; so his first visit was to the Russian Embassy.

The Ambassador, Count Soltikoff, was an old friend of his father's, and had known him from his youth; so he had no hesitation in making certain requests to him and, when asked, giving the true reason for making them.

Having listened to de Quesnoy's plans, the Ambassador thought-fully stroked his grey mutton-chop side whiskers for a moment, then said, 'I can well understand how eagerly His Majesty must have seized on the chance to engage a really trustworthy man of your adventurous disposition in such an undertaking, but I am by no means sure that you would not be wise to tell him that, having thought matters over, you wish to be released from it.'

'Why should I do that?' de Quesnoy asked in surprise. 'This mission is the very thing I needed to take my mind off the great loss I have suffered.'

'Perhaps; but there are better ways of employing yourself which would do so equally well, and possibly more swiftly.'

'I can think of no better way of using my mind and abilities than in an attempt to bring some of these devilish assassins to justice.'

The Ambassador nodded. 'No one would deny the menace that militant anarchism has become to society, and that the men who plan these callous outrages are deserving of death. But to wage war upon and destroy them is a matter for the State, not a private individual.'

'Surely, Your Excellency, it is the duty of every citizen to help protect his fellows by shooting a mad dog, should he be given the opportunity?'

'Of course, but it is not part of our duty to go in search of mad dogs. Or, if you feel that it is, why did you not long since return to Russia, where the nihilists perpetrate more of these bloody outrages than in any other country, and devote your energies to bringing a number of them to the scaffold?'

De Quesnoy shrugged. 'There is the difference that the Ocrana are to be trusted, whereas the Spanish Secret Police are not; so it is only here that my help might prove of value. Besides, I am person-ally concerned in this. These inhuman monsters murdered my poor Angela.'

The shrewd eyes of the older man narrowed a little. 'That is precisely the point that I wished you to admit. You are, in fact, proposing to set out on a vendetta, and deliberately ignoring the divine prohibition expressed by the words "Vengeance is Mine, saith The Lord".'

'I had not thought of it in that light, but I must confess that there is much in what Your Excellency says. I would certainly not have accepted this mission had it not been for the personal motive.'

'Then I beg you, Armand, to reconsider the matter. In my long experience I have never known good come to a man from allowing his bitterness, however well justified, to drive him into taking the law into his own hands. In this case it is true that you will have the law behind you but, even so, should your activities lead to the death of some of these people, it is you who will ultimately be called to account for that by the highest of all tribunals.'

For some twenty minutes, they argued the pros and cons of the matter, but de Quesnoy could not be persuaded to forgo the opportunity he had been given to avenge Angela's death and, at length, the Ambassador reluctantly agreed to aid him by supplying him with certain items which, if at any time his belongings were searched, would substantiate his story that he was a Russian.

Next, after trying several shops that sold second-hand luggage, he succeeded in finding a rather battered trunk that had on it a number of old labels including those of hotels in Constantinople and Athens. Taking it away with him in a hired carriage, he then had himself driven to a number of second-hand clothes shops in which he bought two suits, an overcoat, shoes, and a variety of other items that were in good repair but of the inexpensive kind that might have been worn by a minor official. Lastly he obtained from a bookshop in the Puerta del Sol five, mostly well-thumbed, books in Russian, two of which were histories, two novels by Dostoievsky, and one a collection of Communist tracts by Engels.

After lunch he paid another call at the Embassy and collected three partly-used pencils made in Russia, a block of seven Russian stamps in current use, a small wooden frame with wires across it strung with beads – called an abacus, on which all Russians do their calculating – and a bottle of the Eau de Cologne with which many Russians are in the habit of scenting themselves. In addition, the Ambassador had had some of his Spanish pesetas changed into Russian roubles for him, and handed over a list that he had obtained at the Count's request of all the ships that had called at Valencia during the past fortnight. Among them there was not one that had come from Constantinople, but a Greek ship had arrived on the 6th from the Piraeus; she might have brought him from Athens, which suited him just as well, and having memorized her name he destroyed the list.

Returning to the Palacio Cordoba, de Quesnoy made a thorough examination of his purchases and removed from the clothes all marks which might give away their Spanish origin. He then soaked off from the trunk all the labels except those showing that it had been in Constantinople and Athens, and another which showed that it had been in Salonika. Having dressed in one set of his new garments he packed the rest and the other items into the trunk, had it corded and taken downstairs, then said good-bye to his host and hostess, who had returned from Aranjuez at midday. A hired carriage took him to the Atocha station where he bought a second-class ticket and at a few minutes before seven boarded the night train for Valencia.

Corridor coaches and restaurant cars had so far been introduced only on luxury trains, and there were no second-class sleepers; but the gauge of the Spanish railways being broader than those in other parts of Europe, except Russia, the coaches were somewhat more comfortable. Nevertheless, until night cooled the air a little it was stiflingly hot and, lolling in his corner, with only a bottle of tepid wine to wash down the sandwiches with which he had supplied himself, he found the long journey exceedingly trying.

Arriving in Valencia on the morning of the 13th, he asked a cab driver to take him to a modest hotel in the neighbourhood of the University, and was set down at one in the Calle Don Juan de Austria. There he checked in as Señor Nicolai Chirikov and said that he wanted a room for only a few nights while he carried out some research in the University Library. After a meal in a nearby restaurant he went up to his room and to bed, to make up during the hot hours of the day for some of the sleep he had lost during his night journey.

In the late afternoon he went to the University and, on stating that he was a Russian schoolmaster engaged in writing a book on social conditions in Spain, secured a reader's ticket. He had no intention of writing anything, but put the ticket carefully away as a useful piece of evidence of his new identity. He then drove out to the port and made inquiries about ships sailing for Barcelona. Having learned that a two-thousand-five-hundred-ton cargo vessel, the *Vélez-Rubio*, that plied between the Mediterranean ports and took a few passengers was leaving in three days' time, he ran her Captain to earth in one of the better waterside cafés and, to his satisfaction, arranged for a passage in her.

On the 14th, having nothing to do, he instinctively went to see the Cathedral; but, as was usual in the Spanish churches, the many fine paintings in it by old masters were ill-lit and, having never been cleaned, had become so darkened by time that they were hardly worth looking at. In the Treasury, among the assorted collection of crystal caskets, ornamented with lack-lustre jewels, that contained the bones of Saints, the *piéce de résistance* was a vessel said to be the Holy Grail and sent to Spain for safe-keeping during the persecution of the Christians by the Roman Emperor Valerian; but he found it difficult to believe that a poor carpenter had been given a green agate chalice from which to drink.

His walk round the Botanical Gardens that evening was much more rewarding, as between its groups of tall palms it had a wonderful variety of sub-tropical trees, shrubs and plants. Having found it so pleasant he spent most of the following day there re-reading one of the Dostoievsky novels.

Next morning he left Valencia in the *Vélez-Rubio*. There were only two other passengers on board; a doctor named Luque and his wife. They were a middle-aged couple who had chosen this means of returning from a holiday with relatives in Cartagena. De Quesnoy's reason for travelling by sea was that he wanted to arrive in Barcelona with a few people who knew him as Señor Chirikov, and had he gone by train the opportunity for making acquaintances would have been briefer and much less good. In pursuance of his design, while the ship chugged her way at a modest six knots through the blue waters of the Mediterranean, he sat with the Luques on the after-deck under an awning and soon became on friendly terms with them.

During the course of the afternoon they told him of the life they led and the ramifications of their family, while he told them the story he had invented about himself as Nicolai Chirikov. He said that he was a bachelor, had been a teacher in a private school in Odessa, and that it had been part of his duties to take the senior classes in history. He had taught his pupils what, as a Liberal, he regarded as the truth about the exploitation of the masses both in peace and war by autocrats for their own selfish ends. Some of his pupils had retailed his views to their wealthy parents, and he had been tipped off that the Tsarist police were going into the matter. To avoid arrest, and probable exile to Siberia, he had realized his few assets as swiftly as possible and fled abroad. A Turkish steamer had taken him down to Constantinople. Then, as he had always longed to see Greece, he had gone on via Salonika to Athens. But there was no possibility of earning a living there; so he had accepted an offer by a sea-captain he had met to take him on for a nominal fee to Spain. After a week in Valencia he had decided that he was more likely to find suitable employment in the much larger city of Barcelona; so was going on there.

The Luques proved most understanding and sympathetic, but it was among the ship's officers that de Quesnoy had hoped to find a likely type to sponsor him on his arrival in the Catalonian capital, and, later in the day, he found just such a man in Modesto Pelayo, the *Vélez-Rubio*'s Second Officer. Pelayo, a bearded, bronzed, broad-shouldered man, had started as a seaman before the mast and was now in his early forties; but his lack of general education made it unlikely that he would ever become master of a vessel, and, as he considered himself a thoroughly competent officer, he naturally felt very bitterly about this limitation to his career. That evening, over a bottle of *Anis del Mono* paid for by the Count, Modesto and 'Nicolai' discussed at length the iniquities of the present social system and parted firm friends, the one to go on watch and the other to go to his cabin.

The following evening the *Vélez-Rubio* docked at Barcelona. After promising the Luques to let them know how he got on, de Quesnoy accompanied Pelayo ashore and was taken by him to a clean but inexpensive *pensión* in the Calle de Cabañas, which was not far from the harbour. They then had supper together and afterwards visited a number of bars in each of which they spent an hour or so drinking. In the early hours it was the Count who found a cab and took the befuddled sailor back to his ship in it.

But Pelayo had not been so drunk that he did not remember his promise to call for his new friend next morning and show him Barcelona. By that the Count had not supposed that the convivial rough-diamond intended to take him round yet one more Cathedral or to look at another gallery of Old Masters; but he had thought it probable that the tour would include those symbols of tyranny, the palaces in the old city, and, almost certainly, as Modesto was a seafaring man, the one-time Arsenal of the Kings of Aragon which de Cordoba had told him on no account to miss, as it was now a Nautical Museum and contained many interesting relics of the great Conquistadores. He was therefore considerably surprised when, a quarter of an hour after they had boarded a tram, he saw that it had left the main streets behind and was grinding its way uphill towards the northern outskirts of the city.

On his asking where they were going, Pelayo replied, 'Why, I promised to show you the city, didn't I, and you'll get no better view of it than from Mount Tibidabo.' And he proved unquestionably right. After changing trams in the suburbs, they took a Funicular Railway, but even that did not take them to the top, and for the final lap they had to trudge, with a little crowd of other people who had been in the Funicular, up steep paths through a wood of pines. When at last, breathless and perspiring, they did reach the summit the panorama from it was one never to be forgotten. From a height of sixteen hundred feet they gazed down on the broad coastal plain with the sprawling city spread out with its centre far below them. The air was so clear that they could pick out all the principal buildings and, looking south over many miles of the shimmering Mediterranean, even discern some faint smudges on the horizon that Pelayo said were the Balearic Isles.

The mountain had a broad, flat top on which a number of cafés and restaurants had been built and, as it was a Sunday, they were crowded with people; but Pelayo managed to secure a table at which they sat drinking iced beer while admiring the view. Up there, too, was a permanent fun fair and, after lunching off spider crabs, they patronized some of its sideshows.

Late in the afternoon they returned to the city and, much to de Quesnoy's secret satisfaction, the evening, if less relaxing, proved unexpectedly profitable from the point of view of his mission; for Modesto took him to a club to which he belonged that was a branch of the Somaten.

Among the subversive pamphlets which had formed part of the papers that Don Alfonso had secured for him there had been some issued by the Somaten, and also a short account of its history; so he was already aware of its activities. It was a disciplined organization that had been formed by private citizens of Barcelona in the Middle Ages with the object of maintaining order, and its motto was 'Peace, peace and again peace'. But in more recent times it had become the spearhead of the movement for Catalan nationalism.

De Quesnoy had both read the arguments for that in the pamphlets and discussed it with de Vendôme; so he knew both sides of the question. The Catalans' case was that their stock inhabited the Mediterranean coast on both sides of the Pyrenees, occupying both the whole of Catalonia and a considerable area of southern France including Marseilles, and that at one time they had been one nation. They therefore claimed that as an individual race, neither French nor Spanish, they were entitled to independence. That their language was still a live one was true, although much more so in the Spanish area than the French, and in Barcelona several papers printed in Catalan were among those with the largest circulation. They had also clung most tenaciously to their racial customs and to certain regional rights extracted through the centuries from their Spanish rulers, and on these they based their case for being given self-government.

The opposite view was that since very ancient times the Catalans never had been independent. Those to the north of the Pyrenees had in Roman times been absorbed into the provinces of Nar-bonensis and Provence and later became subjects of the Kings of France; while those to the south had been absorbed into the province of Hither Baetia and later become subjects of the Kings of Aragon. Therefore, from the time of the marriage of Ferdinand of Aragon to Isabella of Castile in 1469, Catalonia had become an integral part of Spain, and should so remain.

The same arguments applied to the Basques, who were also agitating for independence. On the Atlantic coast their stock had from time immemorial occupied large areas both to the north and south of the Pyrenees, and they even had a language of their own which resembled no other in Europe; but they too had never been a nation and, for many centuries, while those to the north had owed allegiance to the Kings of Navarre, those to the south had owed allegiance to the Kings of Castile.

One might almost as well endeavour, reasoned the anti-separatists, to make a case for the peoples of Brittany and Cornwall becoming one nation with self-government, for they too come of the same stock and had a root language in common, and Brittany at least was – for a long period – a Sovereign State; yet the English Channel has separated them hardly less effectively than the Pyrenees has both the Catalans and the Basques.

For the Spanish Catalans and Basques, union with the French elements of their race could obviously be only a long-term aim, but the agitation by both for Home Rule had in recent years greatly increased. This was especially so among the Catalans as they were the most vigorous and industrious of the Spanish peoples, and much fuel was added to the fire of their unrest by the knowledge that the hard work they put into their commercial ventures led to their having to contribute far more per head in taxation to the central government than did the lazier populations in other parts of Spain.

Since the aim of the Somaten was to throw off the yoke of the monarchy and that of the anarchists to abolish government of any kind – and Doña Gulia had told the Count that Barcelona was the stronghold of Spanish anarchy – he had good grounds for assuming that, both being subversive organizations, many members of the Somaten were also anarchists. In consequence he spared no pains to make himself pleasant to those members of the Club to whom Pelayo introduced him.

In their grave Spanish way they responded readily, and when they learned that he was a refugee from Tsarist persecution they eagerly crowded round pressing him to tell them about conditions in Russia. He willingly obliged, purposely exaggerating the situation by implying that the whole nation, except for a handful of aristocrats, went about in constant terror of having something pinned upon them by the Secret Police, and that every political exile was condemned to the horror of the Siberian salt mines.

Naturally, when the question arose, he declared himself heartily in favour of Catalonian independence, and 'Nicolai Chirikov' was obviously so much a man with the right ideas that by midnight he had been proposed and accepted as a member of the Puerto branch of the Somaten.

His original plan had been to join one of the Barcelona Lodges of Freemasons; since once a Mason always a Mason, and having been initiated in Paris two years earlier he would have had only to find, through the secret hand-grip, a Brother Mason to introduce him. Unlike British Masonry, Continental Masonry had for long been the principal breeding-ground of atheism and revolt. It had originated in Germany and in the mid-eighteenth century been brought by the mystic Illuminatii to France. There it had spread rapidly, so that there were soon Lodges of the Grand Orient in every town of any size; and its inner council had undoubtedly organized the French Revolution. Its ramifications spread all over Europe and it had later been responsible for all those bloody up-heavals that overturned half a dozen governments in the years 1848 and '49. Fifty years later it was still a great secret power capable of bringing about revolts in most countries at any time.

In 1904, in collaboration with the atheist War Minister of France, it had launched a great campaign to undermine the strength of the French Army, and de Quesnoy had become a Freemason with the object of exposing this evil combination. Under the name of Vasili Petrovitch, and posing as a Russian political refugee, he had succeeded in doing so; and now, feeling certain that the Spanish Masonic Lodges would be the natural meeting places for anarchists, he had been contemplating on his way to Barcelona an attempt to repeat the process. Unfortunately, however, having exposed the War Minister he had, at the eleventh hour, been exposed himself; and the Freemasons had learned that their betrayer, Vasili Petrovitch, was in fact Colonel the Count de Quesnoy.

Thus, though remote, there was a slight element of risk in his plan; for although he was using a different Russian name and background, if in a Barcelona Lodge it chanced that he came face to face with a visiting French Mason who had known him in Paris, he would be identified, with results that he did not care to contemplate. In consequence, having had the luck to be made a member of the Somaten, which he felt would serve his purpose equally well, he decided there and then to abandon his idea of again becoming a member of a Masonic Lodge.

To stimulate and direct the political activities of its members was only a part of the Club's function. It was also a social meeting-ground for the officers of merchant ships, Customs officers and other minor officials of the great port. Drinks could be had there at a bar and cold snacks at a buffet. Cards and dice could be played. It also had a library and a small gymnasium; so, quite apart from his special reason for cultivating the company who frequented it, de Quesnoy found it a useful place in which to kill time. And after Modesto Pelayo's return to duty in his ship on the Monday the Count found time hang heavily on his hands.

He dared not appear too curious and could only leave it to time to develop his acquaintance with several regular frequenters of the Club, whom he suspected might be anarchists, until one of them either took him into his confidence or, inadvertently, made some incriminating admission. As the Club did not open until after the siesta hour, he was reduced in the mornings to taking long solitary walks or strolling aimlessly along the Ramblas among the colourful crowd that always thronged this principal shopping street of the old town.

The old town appealed to him, but it formed only a small part of the great modern city. Of Barcelona the Spaniards, even in other cities, were intensely proud, as it had made almost their only con- tribution to twentieth-century architecture and town-planning. There were many fine blocks of offices and apartments in it, with electric light, lifts, telephones and other up-to-date innovations, and it was laid out like an American city, in blocks intersected by scores of parallel streets. But de Quesnoy found their sameness both confusing and dreary, and he would have much preferred it had his quest taken him back to the picturesque alleyways of Cordoba or the tranquil, irregular side-streets of Seville.

For him to have spent a pleasant hour or two in any of the better hotels or restaurants would have been to risk being seen going in or out by some members of the Somaten and so, probably, ruining his build-up of himself as a Russian schoolmaster of very limited means. In consequence, as the only alternative to walks in the woods and gardens on the slopes of Montjuich, which lay at the end of the street in which his *pensión* was situated, he again took to sightseeing, but he was always relieved when the hour came for him to resume his rôle as an unsuspected inquiry agent at the Club.

Yet, strange as he afterwards thought it to be, it was not there that he picked up his first real lead to the militant anarchists of Barcelona, but through Doctor Luque.

5

The Infernal Machine

DE QUESNOY had taken the Luques' having asked him to let them know how he was getting on as no more than a casual politeness, but being by habit good-mannered himself, instead of ignoring it he had, on Tuesday, sent the Doctor a line saying that he had found quite comfortable quarters suitable to his modest means, and hoped they had found all well on their arrival home; but he did not really expect that they had taken sufficient interest in a poor refugee to wish to pursue his acquaintance.

However, on the Thursday he received a reply asking him to dine with them on the Saturday. It came from the Señora Luque, whom he had judged to be a good-natured motherly woman and, as he rightly guessed, had been inspired by a kind thought for a lonely foreigner in a strange city.

Their apartment was in one of the new blocks of flats some way to the north of the Plaza de Las Glorias, and on arriving there he found that they had staying with them a Lieutenant Aguilera of the Spanish Navy, who was a nephew of the Doctor.

The Lieutenant had returned a few days before from a long tour of duty in the Canaries, and only that morning the light cruiser in which he had served had been paid off. After the introductions had been made and the Doctor had provided them with aperitifs, the question of the Lieutenant's prospects came up, and it transpired that these were very far from rosy.

The Spanish Navy had never fully recovered from the crushing defeat inflicted on it by Nelson at Trafalgar, and from that time, too, the once mighty Spanish Empire had begun to fall to pieces. Chunk after chunk of South America had revolted, thrown off the Spanish yoke and declared itself a Republic, so that by the 'nineties the only considerable colonies left to Spain, apart from the Canaries, were Cuba, Puerto Rico and the Philippines. This reduction of her Empire militated against any necessity for Spain to attempt again to build up a first class fleet, but with the introduction of ironclads she had continued to build and maintain a navy of the second rank. By 1898 many of its ships were in poor condition and their guns obsolete, although the navy was still a calling in which many thousands of sailors found a career. But then its death blow fell.

Cuba, owing to the exactions and tyranny of a succession of Spanish Governor-Generals, had, for the previous twenty years, been in a state of semi-revolt, and during a good part of that time the great island had been rent by a series of bloody civil wars. In an attempt to suppress the rebels one General, known as 'Butcher' Weyler, had even gone to the length of destroying the insurgents' crops and houses and herding their non-combatant relatives into concentration camps. The United States, becoming alarmed for the big investments her citizens had made in Cuba, sent the battleship *Maine* to protect their interests. From a cause that still remains a mystery, soon after arriving in Havana harbour she blew up.

War followed, and the American Pacific Squadron promptly destroyed the Spanish warships based on the Philippines. Although Spain's main fleet was ill-equipped and ill-munitioned, she at once dispatched it to the Caribbean. It reached Santiago safely but was there blockaded by a much more powerful American fleet. Meanwhile, the Americans had landed troops and were about to attack the city from its landward side. The Spanish Admiral, Cervera, decided that his honour demanded he should leave harbour and fight, although he knew his choice to be suicidal. His fleet was totally destroyed.

This annihilation of the Spanish Navy had occurred only eight years ago. Since then no new ships of any size had been built; so Lieutenant Aguilera had been extremely lucky to get his last posting in one of the few remaining cruisers. And as there were still hundreds of naval officers of experience intriguing to be given further sea service he had good grounds for fearing that he might never get another.

Over a hearty meal of *escudella* soup, chicken cooked *a la cilindrón* and a chocolate cake layered with thick cream, which they washed down with the local Alella wine, the Lieutenant continued futilely to resurrect and inveigh against the brutal greed of past Generals, the criminal stupidity of the statesmen and the unbending pride of the Admiral, which had combined to threaten him at the age of twenty-eight with an abrupt termination to his career.

De Quesnoy, having had his own career as a soldier cut short, although for very different reasons, sympathized with him; but he became distinctly bored by the conversation as, despite several attempts by Señora Luque and himself, they seemed unable to get away from the subject.

In Spanish homes it is customary for guests not to linger for long after dinner; so having partaken of a small glass of Anis in the sitting-room, the Count made a move to leave. But the Senora waved him back to his chair and said:

'Don't go for a little while. You have not yet told us how you like Barcelona.'

'It is a beautiful city,' he replied politely, 'and I find the people most courteous and friendly. The old town appeals to me particularly, owing to my interest in history.'

'Have you visited the Cathedral?' asked the Lieutenant.

As de Quesnoy shook his head, the young man went on, 'You should, then. Not for its religious associations, as I gather from a remark you made at dinner you are not that way inclined. But in it is the huge crucifix that Don John of Austria had nailed to the mainmast of his flagship when he defeated the Turkish fleet at the battle of Lepanto.'

'Indeed!' the Count raised his eyebrows. 'Yes, I must certainly see that, for Lepanto was one of the decisive battles of the world.'

'I imagine,' the Doctor put in with a smile, 'that our friend has been too busy looking for a job to do much sightseeing.'

'Yes, indeed,' de Quesnoy agreed, 'but so far I have had no luck. As you may recall, I am hoping to find a post as a schoolmaster and that is not easy without the right kind of introductions.'

The Señora glanced at her husband and remarked, 'I wonder if Francisco Ferrer could help?'

De Quesnoy's face remained impassive, but his heart gave a jump. Ferrer's name stood at the very top of the mental list he had made of people whose activities he intended to investigate whilst in Barcelona. But he was too experienced a hunter to rush his fences. To have invented some excuse for introducing himself to Ferrer might easily have aroused the anarchist's suspicions, and he had not intended even to fish for an opening until he had been long enough in the city to have made many other acquaintances who would vouch for him as an enemy of established authority. Only then, perhaps towards the end of the following week, had he meant to go to the library that Ferrer ran and, by becoming a subscriber, open the way to a possible meeting. But it had been because Ferrer was a schoolmaster that he had elected to pose as a schoolmaster himself, hoping that their apparent community of interests might help him to establish relations with his quarry. Now it looked as if his idea was about to bear fruit. Praying that the Doctor's reply might be favourable, he held his breath while awaiting it. After a moment the mild-mannered little man said:

'Yes, my love. Ferrer might know of a post that would suit Señor Chirikov. We must arrange for them to meet.'

While refraining from showing any special enthusiasm, the Count bowed a courteous acknowledgement. 'For such an introduction I should be most grateful.'

'Most evenings Señor Ferrer takes an aperitif at the Café Ronda,' the Doctor went on. 'It lies in the Calle de Ronda about half-way between the Plaza de la Universidad and the Plaza de Cataluña. Would it be agreeable to you to meet me there at about six o'clock on . . . let us say Tuesday?'

'My time is still my own, so entirely yours.'

'Then I will get in touch with Ferrer and unless I let you know to the contrary we'll meet on Tuesday evening.'

With that understanding the Count thanked his hosts and took his departure. On his way home he marvelled that so lucky a break should have come from such an unexpected quarter; but, great as his hopes were of it producing concrete results, during the days that followed he did not neglect the cultivation of his acquaintances at the Somaten club.

On the Tuesday he arrived at the Café Ronda promptly on time and sat down at one of the tables on the pavement. Some twenty minutes later Doctor Luque arrived and they had hardly exchanged greetings when they were joined by a small dark man in his middle forties, who was wearing a panama hat and gold pince-nez. As he lifted his hat on being introduced to de Quesnoy the Count saw that he had an exceptionally high, narrow forehead. He spoke with the abrupt aggressiveness of a man suffering from an inferiority complex, and his glance from behind the thick-lensed eyeglasses struck de Quesnoy as slightly shifty. But he greeted the Doctor as an old friend, and on being told that the Count was a Russian political refugee shook hands with him warmly.

When drinks had been ordered 'Nicolai Chirikov' was called on to give an account of himself. As he had known Odessa well in his youth it was easy for him to talk of the city and the imaginary school there in which, according to his story, he had become a master. He had, too, meticulously worked out the details of his fictitious journey into exile, and from Valencia onwards Luque could vouch for it. His appearance, accent and the attitude of mind he displayed all contributed to the impression that he was a Russian, and from the outset it was clear that Ferrer never for a moment suspected him to be anything but what he made himself out to be.

After they had been talking for some while Ferrer asked de Quesnoy in what subjects he specialized, to which he replied 'History and literature and, of course, I could teach Russian.'

Ferrer pursed his thin-lipped mouth. 'I take it you mean Russian history.'

'Yes; although I am fairly well up in the history of other countries, particularly in so far as it has affected my own.'

'I thought as much.' The suggestion of a sneer appeared on Ferrer's face. 'It is the same story everywhere. Each country teaches its young little except about its own triumphs, and consistently perverts the truth as the means of justifying the wars started by Kings for their own aggrandizement. My system is very different. In my school we devote a first course to ancient civilizations and the rise of the priestly caste which by spreading superstition became an aristocracy that battened on the people. In the second course we deal with the principal religions of modern times, showing how each has hindered rather than helped the development of mankind, and caused untold misery through its adherents launching wars in an endeavour to force their faith on others. Then the final course deals with the rise of democracy, and the strivings now in progress by the masses in every country to throw off the yoke of tyranny and achieve the individual freedom which is their right.'

'Then it is a fine work you are doing,' commented de Quesnoy with feigned enthusiasm.

'It is,' agreed Ferrer, 'but I think it hardly likely that you have sufficient knowledge of international movements to aid me in it; even if I had a vacancy for a history master, which I have not.'

'How about a master to teach Russian, though?' Luque suggested.

Ferrer shook his high, narrow head. 'I have French and German masters, of course, but Russian is of little use outside Russia; and I could afford neither to employ a Russian teacher nor the time in my schedule for my students to attend lessons in Russian. However, I might be able to send Señor Chirikov a few pupils for private tuition.'

'That would be a great kindness,' smiled the Count, 'because I was able to bring only a limited sum out of Russia with me and, although it is sufficient for my present needs, unless I can find some means of supplementing it I shall soon be in difficulties. As a matter of fact I already have cards in two newspaper shops advertising myself as a teacher of Russian, but so far I have had no applicants for lessons.'

In the latter statement de Quesnoy was telling the truth, since he had decided that to take such a step was necessary to support his cover: although he was hoping that nobody would take advantage of his offer, since to have to waste his time teaching Russian was the last thing he wanted.

For another half hour they sat over a second round of drinks comparing the progress of workers' movements in Spain and Russia;

then the party broke up. But before they parted Ferrer asked de Quesnoy if he would like to see over his school and, on the Count's accepting, he said:

'Unlike ordinary schools we have sessions all the year round; so although next week we shall be in August I shall still be as busy as ever. We have evening classes, too, for those who have to earn their living in the daytime; but none on Sundays because the law still kept in force through the influence of the Church does not permit it. So the best time for you to come would be on Sunday morning. Shall we say at about eleven?'

'That would suit me admirably,' the Count replied; and as he strolled back down the colourful ever-crowded Ramblas to his dreary little *pensión* he felt well satisfied with the course events were taking.

On the Sunday he found the *Escuela Moderna* to be housed in an old mansion in a street just off the Ronda de Antonio, which was not far from the University; and he guessed that Ferrer had chosen its location so that it should be handy for University students with Leftish leanings who elected to take some of his courses in addition to their official curriculum.

He was admitted by an elderly janitor who took him up to the top floor of the house which, when it had been converted, Ferrer had turned into his own living quarters. Ferrer took him to his study, a room lined with bookshelves on which, as de Quesnoy saw at a glance, in addition to books in several languages, there were many hundreds of pamphlets. They had only just sat down when the door opened again and a buxom young woman carrying a tray with glasses and sherry came in. She had fine eyes and a full, moist mouth, but overwide nostrils in a *retroussé* nose and a very fleshy jowl robbed her of any claim to be a real beauty.

Ferrer introduced her as his wife, and as de Quesnoy bowed he studied her with interest. He knew that she had no legal claim to that status and wondered if she was Soledad Villafranca, who had also been Morral's mistress, or if she was a new acquisition in Ferrer's long line of conquests. That such an unprepossessing man should possess the power to attract a succession of women appeared strange; but the Count knew that a man's features played only a minor part in stimulating female inclinations, and that whatever the major quality was to have for his bedfellow this passionate-looking young creature, who must be at least twenty years younger than himself, Ferrer must have it.

He treated her, too, more like a servant than a wife; for as soon as she had filled their sherry glasses, although she showed an

3

inclination to linger and join in their conversation, he as good as ordered her out of the room.

Having offered his guest a cheroot he sat back in his chair and launched out into an enthusiastic description of his school. Latin and Greek he declared to be a waste of time, and acquiring an extensive knowledge of literature and art a luxury which could be afforded only if one intended to take them up as a means of livelihood or make them one's chosen recreation. Grammar and syntax he also declared to be unnecessary, except for a would-be writer, as all that the average man needed was the ability to make himself understood with reasonable clarity. Naturally, everyone should have a basic knowledge of most subjects taken in a normal education, but the really important thing was that both men and women should concentrate from their 'teens onward on some course of study which would enable them to become useful members of society.

He had as pupils boys, girls and also grown-up men and women. When they came to him they had to select one, or at most two, fields suited to their abilities in which to specialize. All had to go through the three courses in history that he had outlined to de Quesnoy at their earlier meeting, in order that they might fully understand the development of mankind, their obligations to their fellow-men, and become workers in the international movement to free the masses from their centuries-old slavery. But apart from this sociological instruction all their other time was given to developing their natural talents. There was a section in which pupils could graduate through carpentry, plumbing and practical building to architecture, another in which they could graduate through typing and shorthand to secretarial duties or journalism, and sections teaching cooking and household management, engineering and technology, chemistry and science, and agriculture. In addition, extra courses could be taken in French and German and in literature and art.

Now that the matter was put to him de Quesnoy was inclined to agree that in normal schools much time was wasted drilling into pupils matter that could be of little value to them later in life, and that for men and women who would have to earn their own living this new system of education, in which they devoted their energies to acquiring practical knowledge in specialized fields while still young, had much to commend it. But one thing stood out a mile. The heart and soul of Señor Francisco Ferrer's *Escuela Moderna* lay in the course which all pupils were compelled to take, whereby he disseminated his doctrines for the abolition of the Church and State and the emergence of a classless society.

In the Count's mind there lay no shadow of doubt that Ferrer's school was the root from which the Spanish anarchist movement was fostered and supplied every year with scores of young enthusiastic recruits. It now remained to discover whether he was content only to spread his mental poison, or if he actually encouraged the more fanatical of his disciples to undertake Propaganda by Deed.

Far from disclosing even a suggestion of his thoughts, de Quesnoy expressed the greatest interest in Ferrer's work and gave it the highest praise. When they had finished their drinks the schoolmaster stood up and proposed to show his guest over the premises. Following him downstairs de Quesnoy duly inspected the rows of typewriters in one room, the long carpenter's bench in another, the drawing-boards of the technicians in a third, and so on, until they came to a laboratory. In it two youngish men stood side by side bending over one of the slabs, their backs turned to the door. At the noise of the door opening they both swung round and, after a moment's hesitation, Ferrer introduced them:

'My two sons, Benigno and Sanchez; Señor Chirikov, who has recently arrived from Russia.'

If appearances went for anything the brothers had had different mothers. Benigno was small, sandy-haired, intelligent-looking and had both his father's high forehead and sharp nose. He gave the impression of being about twenty-six. Sanchez was a big man, dark to the point of swarthiness, with the coarse features of a peasant and narrow eyes that suggested he had inherited a peasant's cunning. De Quesnoy put him down as about twenty-one.

As the Count walked forward to shake hands with them his glance took in the slab at which they had been working. On it there was a metal canister, the works from the inside of a small clock, some slabs of stuff that looked like toffee, and several strands of thin wire. Having been a soldier he immediately recognized the slabs as dynamite and realized that the brothers had been constructing an infernal machine.

Ferrer, too, had immediately grasped the situation. His face suddenly dark with anger, he snapped at his sons, 'I have told you before. I will not allow you to construct such things here. The . . . the workshop at the mine in which they are used is the place for that.'

De Quesnoy could not tell if Ferrer's anger was real. If it was it lent support to the police reports about him, which stated that, although he openly preached the doctrines of anarchy, he was opposed to violence and had no connection with the militant anarchists. On the other hand it might be simulated and the implication that the explosives were to be put to a legitimate use in a mine a clumsy attempt to cover up the use his sons were making of the laboratory.

For a few tense moments the Count seethed with real rage, but of the fierce and internal variety. Whether Ferrer's outburst was genuine or not, clockwork infernal machines were never used in mines. The two young men were making a bomb, and there could be little doubt how they meant to use it. There could be little doubt either that it was here, in this laboratory, that Morral had learnt how to make the sort of bomb that had killed Angela. And it was more than likely that it was the Ferrers who had taught him how to do so. At the thought de Quesnoy clenched his hands until the nails dug into his palms and his knuckles went white. He felt a terrible temptation to whip out the little revolver he always carried and shoot them where they stood.

With a great effort he mastered it. To execute two men who he felt convinced had played a part in bringing about Angela's death would give him a grim satisfaction; but if he held his hand for the moment he now had a lead which might enable him to destroy the whole brood of assassins root and branch, and that would be a far more fitting memorial to her.

His brain clicked over. He had the lead, but if he did not take it at once it might be lost. Still outwardly calm, and ignoring what Ferrer had said about a mine, he stepped over to the slab, picked up the works of the little clock and remarked:

'I wonder that you still use these things. Their ticking often gives them away so that they are discovered before they are timed to go off. It is far better to use a small phial of acid which, in a given time, eats through its container, and then a thin wire, the snapping of which detonates the bomb.'

For a moment there was a stunned silence, while the brothers stared at him uncertainly, then he added with a smile, 'My cousin is a nihilist and at his home in Odessa I sometimes used to help him make his bombs; so I know quite a lot about such things.'

Both brothers gave a sudden sigh of relief, then the face of the elder lit up and he exclaimed, 'Then you are one of us! Welcome to Barcelona, Señor Chirikov; it is a pleasure to meet you.'

Ferrer had remained scowling in the background. Now he burst out: 'You young fools. I've warned you time and again to stop associating with the militants. You'll end by getting yourselves shot. I warn you, too, Señor Chirikov. Have nothing to do with these young hotheads. I make no secret of my views, but we'll not achieve our ends by violence.'

The sandy-haired Benigno turned to de Quesnoy. 'Sanchez and I are sorry to disagree with our father, but he is old-fashioned and out-of-date. We'll get nowhere by just talking. We've done little else for far too long. Our only hope lies in Propaganda by Deed and in terrorizing all those who attempt to suppress us.'

'Right or wrong,' Ferrer declared harshly, 'I'll not allow you to use this house to make engines of destruction. Take your things, or better still, render them safe, and throw them in the dustbin, then get out. Now, Señor Chirikov, come with me and I will show you the rest of our premises.'

'One moment, Father,' the black-browed Sanchez intervened. 'I'd like to hear something about the Russian nihilists at first hand, and I'm sure Benigno would too. What about having a drink with us this evening, Señor Chirikov?'

'I should be happy to,' de Quesnoy replied, with difficulty concealing his elation at this chance to win the confidence of two active anarchists. 'Where shall we meet?'

'It would be better still if the Señor would dine with us,' suggested Benigno. 'We'd have longer to talk then, and could go out to the Font de Lleo at Montjuich.'

On de Quesnoy's accepting, as the restaurant was some way outside the town, it was arranged that the brothers should pick him up at seven o'clock near the Columna de Colón, which was not far from his *pensión*. Then, having said good-bye to them for the present, he accompanied the now sullen Ferrer on a tour of the library, the foundry, the kitchens and the publishing part of the establishment.

When, nearly an hour later, he left the *Escuela Moderna* he had plenty to think about, and the problem uppermost in his mind was the question whether Ferrer was genuinely opposed to violence or had been playing a part. He had certainly appeared to be in earnest, and Benigno's attitude to his father supported a belief that he had been. On the other hand, if Ferrer's sons had been using the laboratory against his express wishes it seemed strange that they had not at least taken the precaution of locking themselves in before getting to work. If, too, Ferrer's was, in fact, the brain that plotted and directed the anarchist outrages it would be a matter of the first importance that he should be protected from the least breath of suspicion; so it might well be that Benigno had played up to him on a well-established procedure of always making him appear before strangers as only a propagator of anarchist theory. Whichever might prove to be the case, the Count felt that his luck had been very much in that morning and that he could look forward to a promising evening.

By five to seven he was standing outside the Museo Marítimo

opposite the towering column erected to the memory of the dis-
coverer of America; but few Spaniards have much regard for
punctuality, and it was nearly half past before the brothers, without
apology for their lateness, but with cheerful greetings, picked him
up in a one-horse *coche*.

Montjuich is a great hill rising to six hundred feet in height on
the western outskirts of Barcelona. Towards the sea its side is
almost sheer, so the approach to its summit has to be made from
the landward side, and even there the slope upward round a succession of hairpin bends is so steep that de Quesnoy felt pity for the
poor lean horse drawing them and, half-way up, insisted on getting
out. The Ferrers thought his conduct strange, but attributed it to
Russian eccentricity, and good-naturedly joined him.

At the top of the hill they got into the carriage again and drove
through pines, palms and tamarisks towards its southern slope, on
which stood the restaurant. From its terrace there was a fine view
of the great rambling castle that for centuries had dominated
Barcelona, and one could see for many miles out to sea.

Even before they sat down at one of the tables in the garden,
the clothes of people at others and the waiters hurrying about in
spotless white aprons told de Quesnoy that it was a much more
expensive place than he had expected the Ferrers to take him to, and
he wondered that they could afford it.

For a moment he put it down to Spanish pride in showing a
foreigner round, coupled with a generous desire to do him well;
but, in spite of the rather shoddy suits all three of them were wearing,
the head waiter hurried up to take their order, and it then emerged
that the brothers often came there on Sundays in the summer. That
caused the Count to think again, and he recalled the fact that in
Russia it was common knowledge that the nihilists not only committed assassinations, but also robbed banks and blackmailed
wealthy people. They justified such crimes by saying that they were
committed as their only means of raising funds to continue their
political campaign and support their comrades who were in hiding.
But de Quesnoy thought it probable that in some cases a part of
the proceeds was kept back; and he had no reason to suppose that
the activities and morals of the Spanish anarchists differed much
from those of the Russian nihilists.

As the evening advanced he formed the opinion that Sanchez,
anyhow, was in the movement mainly for what he could get out of
it. The burly, coarse-featured young man gulped down the rich
dishes he had ordered with a zest that implied that he could not
have enough of them, and each time he filled his mouth with wine

his eye roved round the prettier of the women at the nearby tables. In Spain no respectable woman then ever took a meal in public; so the majority of them were the better class of kept girls out for the evening with their mostly middle-aged lovers, and two of them, no doubt attracted by Sanchez's fine physique, covertly returned his glances. Although he did not actually say so his attitude clearly conveyed that this was the sort of life he visualized himself living when equality for all had been achieved, and that he would be entitled then to the best of food and wine all the time, with no nonsense about any monied class having first call on the prettiest women.

Benigno was very different and, de Quesnoy soon decided, a true fanatic. He seemed little interested in what he ate and drank, and not the least in any of the good-looking girls at nearby tables; but he was intensely interested in all the Count had to say on the condition of the Russian workers. Sanchez was interested only in the accounts that their guest gave them of high officials being blown to pieces, shot, knifed or poisoned, whereas Benigno wanted to know what wages the workers received, the cost of rent and food, the percentage of them that contributed the little they could afford towards the freedom movements, and the answers to a score of similar questions.

De Quesnoy succeeded in satisfying both of them, although in the case of Benigno he was compelled to use guesswork in answering most of his inquiries. The evening therefore proved a great success, and as they drove back through the cool night air to the city the brothers pressed their new friend to keep in touch with them and to come out with them again. To maintain the rôle he was playing he had to say that, to his regret, his very limited resources did not permit him to return their hospitality on the scale they had entertained him; but, as he had felt sure they would, they brushed that objection aside, declaring that among friends the bill should be paid by whoever happened to have most money.

Thinking over the evening as he undressed in his bed-sitting-room, with its cheap furniture and faded wallpaper, two things were uppermost in the Count's mind: one was the pleasure he had derived, after making do for a fortnight on indifferent food, from a meal of lobsters, duck and wood strawberries with cream; the other was how strange it was that Benigno, who was far the more intelligent of the two, apparently failed to see his younger brother as he was – a gross, brutal egoist who camouflaged his selfish appetites under a veneer of back-slapping good fellowship – and quite clearly worshipped the ground he walked on.

On the Monday, and again on Tuesday, to de Quesnoy's consider-able annoyance Ferrer sent him students who wished to take a course in Russian; so there was nothing for it but to agree to the times that suited them and during those hours assume the rôle of a peda-gogue. Fortunately neither of them could afford more than two hours a week, so they did not greatly interfere with his pursuit of the lines through which he hoped to succeed with his mission.

He had no place in which to give these lessons other than in his bedroom, and it was on returning to it late on the Tuesday night, when he had again been out with the Ferrer brothers, that he found that his things had been searched. Nothing had been taken, and he had little doubt that on Ferrer's instructions one of the students had returned to his room during his absence to vet its contents; so he had good reason to be glad about the precautions he had taken.

Most evenings he continued to put in at his branch of the Somaten; but in addition to Tuesday evening he also spent that of Friday with the Ferrer brothers, taking them to the club for a snack meal. He was, however, a little surprised to find that they did not know any of its members.

When Sunday morning came round again he decided to pay Ferrer another visit. To thank him for having sent the two students was excuse enough, and Ferrer received him without any trace of the moody anger he had displayed when they had last parted. After they had talked for a few minutes in the hallway of Ferrer's apart-ment, in order to prolong the conversation de Quesnoy asked if he might borrow a few books. Ferrer then took him down to the library, which on Sundays was closed to the public.

Having found the shelves containing books in French, de Quesnoy looked through them and chose three. One was a work in support of the expulsion of the religious Orders from France by the govern-ment of the atheist Emile Combes, another was on the brutal exploitation of the negroes in the Congo by their Belgian overlords, and the third was a translation from the German of Paul Eltz-bacher's book, *Anarchism*, which Doña Gulia had recommended to him.

After glancing at their titles Ferrer remarked, 'An interesting choice; but as you intend to settle here I should have thought that it would have paid you better to improve your knowledge of Spanish, rather than to struggle through serious works in French.'

De Quesnoy smiled. 'French is my second language. I both read and speak it fluently.' By way of explanation he transposed the nationalities of his parents, and added, 'My mother was a French-woman.'

Ferrer raised his thinly-marked eyebrows. 'Indeed!' Then after
a short pause he went on, 'That being the case I think I could offer
you employment—although it would be only of a temporary nature.
My French master, Emile Degas, has been ill for some time. Poor
fellow, he is suffering from a cancer and in great pain. I have
arranged for a new man to take his place, but he will not be arriving
from France until towards the end of the month. In the meantime
I would have liked to relieve Degas of his duties, but the classes must
go on. Do you think you would be competent to take them, so that
I could release him at once to receive full-time treatment?'

'Certainly,' replied the Count. 'I have taken French classes before,
and my Spanish is quite good enough for me to do so here. I would,
too, be grateful for the chance to earn a little more money.'

Accordingly it was settled that on the following day he should
take over from Monsieur Degas; and when he arrived at the school
he found the unfortunate Frenchman only too willing to give up his
duties. Ferrer explained that, as less than forty of the pupils took
French, Degas held only two classes, a junior and a senior, each for
an hour a day, and that the rest of his time had been spent giving
instruction in cooking, as he had once been a professional chef.
About the cooking lessons Ferrer said he had already made other
arrangements and had relieved Degas of them nearly a month ago.
He added that although Señor Chirikov would be only a part-time
teacher, he wished him to enjoy the same amenities as the other
masters. Then he left him with the Frenchman.

Degas showed de Quesnoy the work his two classes were doing,
and later took one of them in his presence, after which he took him
to the masters' common-room at the back of the house. Soon after
midday the other masters began to troop in, among them Sanchez
and Benigno. The former, as the Count had already learned, ran the
foundry for the students who were learning metal-work, and the
latter acted as Editor for the publishing business.

There were eleven masters in all and three women teachers; and
as de Quesnoy shook hands with them in turn, he decided that he
had rarely met a group of such strong individualists. Their clothes
and manners showed them all to be eccentrics, but he soon found
that, apart from Sanchez, their level of intelligence was unusually
high, and he had little doubt that they were all fanatical atheists
hand-picked by Ferrer to aid him in his work. Next door to the
common-room there was a small dining-room, and having crowded
into it they ate for lunch the dishes produced by the cooking class
held that morning.

During the days that followed de Quesnoy spent most of the

hours, when he was neither taking his French classes nor coaching his two private students in Russian, browsing in the *Escuela Moderna* library.

One thing that amazed him was the enormous number of weekly and monthly journals either openly published by anarchist groups or carrying articles in defence of anarchists who had been caught after committing outrages and brought to trial. They ran into hundreds and were produced not only in every European country but also the United States and South America. The greatest number were published in France, and that he had never before seen any of them he attributed to their probably being put on sale only in the poorer quarters of Paris, Lyons, Marseilles and other cities. Many of them had been suppressed after publishing only a few issues, but a similarity of set-up and contributors showed that in the majority of such cases the periodical had, after a short interval, been revived under another name. That this spate of agitator literature continued unabated could be taken as fair proof that Doña Gulia's contention, that hundreds of thousands of Spaniards were convinced anarchists, was correct. From that, he judged by the number of anarchist publications throughout the world, if there were a million Spanish anarchists their total number must run to anything between five and ten millions.

In the course of his reading he was interested to find that, as the legislative bodies of States were produced by elections, and anarchists were pledged to abolish all legal procedure, the majority of them considered it to be inconsistent with their principles to use the vote. There were, however, exceptions and one of their most prominent leaders, Count Carlo Cafiero, had laid it down in an article published by 'Le Droit Social' in Lyons that: 'Our action must be permanent rebellion by speech, by writing, by the dagger, by the gun, by dynamite, and even by the voting paper; for everything unlawful is of service to us.'

He was, too, greatly intrigued to learn the real reason that lay behind Kaiser Wilhelm II having, soon after he ascended the throne, 'dropped the pilot', as had been termed his dismissal from office of his Chancellor, the mighty Bismarck, who had been the most outstanding figure in European politics for a quarter of a century.

After the two abortive attempts in 1878 by the anarchists Emil Hoedel and Karl Nobiling to assassinate Kaiser Wilhelm I, the Chancellor had initiated a ruthless drive against all revolutionary organizations in Germany. In Berlin alone no less than 563 persons were brought to trial for expressing in either writing or speech approval of those attempts; only 42 were acquitted and the remainder received sentences between them amounting to 812 years' imprisonment.

It was not without reason that Bismarck was known as the Iron Chancellor, and in the years that followed he used an iron hand in putting down all manifestations of Socialism in Germany; so that ten years later when Kaiser Wilhelm II succeeded to the throne he had virtually beaten it down into impotence. The new ruler, however, was an exceptionally vain man and, working to make himself popular with the masses, in 1890 he refused to renew the anti-Socialist laws.

This was the root of the quarrel between the Monarch and the great statesman. Bismarck ceased to be Chancellor and was reported to have said: 'One must either fight Socialism or yield to it. I prefer the former course, the Emperor prefers the latter. That is why I have retired.'

De Quesnoy also learned much about the various types of anarchist. A few, such a Prince Kropotkin, Count Cafiero and Count Tolstoi, who came from the upper classes, were men with excellent brains but a kink that had led them to strive for the realization of their ideals entirely regardless of consequences, although Tolstoi had propagated his ideas solely by word and been opposed to any form of violence. A much larger number came from the middle classes and were again idealists, but mostly men like Morral, whose morbid natures had led them, after long brooding upon the sufferings of the poor, to commit their crimes as a protest against a system which gave only a limited number of people power and wealth.

But the vast majority were drawn from the dregs of society and these could be divided into two categories: men who had been dogged by persistent ill-luck, and habitual criminals.

Typical of the first category had been Auguste Vaillant, who had thrown a bomb in the French Chamber of Deputies in 1893. After only a rudimentary education he had been thrown penniless on the world at the age of fourteen. That he was not without spirit had been shown by his having emigrated in turn to both Algeria and the Argentine in endeavours to make a career for himself, but fortune had refused to smile on him in either; and on his return to Paris, he had been unable to secure a better post than that of a junior clerk at the miserable salary of eighty francs a month – then worth about 16s. a week. Having become infected with anarchist doctrines while in the Argentine he had decided to give his life as a means of demonstrating social injustice. By saving a few sous a week the poor wretch had gradually built up a store of chemicals to make his bomb, and loaded it with little scraps of iron that he had picked up. It had proved such a poor affair that the old nails in it had fallen on the heads of the Deputies without injuring any of them. Nevertheless, he had been condemned to death and, in spite of a nation-wide agitation for his reprieve, sent to the guillotine.

Later there appeared little doubt that it was President Carnot's refusal to commute Vaillant's sentence that led to his assassination in Lyons the following year. The young Italian, Santo-Geronimo Caserio, who avenged Vaillant by stabbing the President to death, had also been almost totally uneducated; he had been put to slave in a bakery at the age of thirteen, and had never known anything but the direst poverty.

It was, however, clear that the anarchist doctrine of the rejection of all authority had a great appeal to the criminal mind, and during the past twenty years hundreds of criminals, when brought to trial, had defiantly proclaimed themselves from the dock to be anarchists.

Of this type a man of half-French, half-German, blood, named François Ravachol, had been an outstanding example. His first exploit had been to break into the house of an old gentleman who was said to keep there a considerable sum of money. Finding the old man in bed, he split his head open with a chopper, then chased the elderly housekeeper out into the road and murdered her also. A few years later, hearing that the Countess de Rochetaillé had been buried wearing her valuable jewels, he went by night to the cemetery. Being possessed of enormous strength he succeeded in raising two slabs of stone that covered the grave, weighing respectively 260 and 330 lb., broke open the coffin and, from rage at finding nothing of value, desecrated the corpse. Another of his crimes was the brutal murder of an old hermit who had accumulated a hoard of gold. He then became interested in the anarchist movement, owing to the wide publicity given to it by serious disturbances in Paris on May Day, 1891. The police had broken up a procession and two of the principal anarchist agitators who led it, Descamp and Dardare, had been arrested and sentenced to five and three years' hard labour by a judge named Benoit. They had become known in Socialist circles as 'the Clichy martyrs' and Ravachol decided to revenge them. For that purpose he and his associates had stolen one hundred and twenty dynamite cartridges. With these they had twice blown up M. Benoit's apartment and committed many other outrages, which had initiated the '92–'94 anarchist reign of terror in Paris.

Although de Quesnoy continued occasionally to look in at the branch of the Somaten to which he belonged, he now spent most of his evenings in the masters' common-room. As the majority of its members lived in cheerless bed-sitting-rooms, they used it at night for games of chess, or whiling away the time denouncing to one another the iniquities of the régime. Such discussions were followed by him closely, but he could never find more than a hint in them that the speakers might be involved in active measures towards bringing about an anarchist Utopia.

Nevertheless, these hints were sufficient to convince him that some, if not all, of them were in touch with the militants, and his belief was strengthened by his having soon learned that all of them were Freemasons. After a while he formed the conclusion that they would have spoken more openly in front of him had he not been there only as a temporary, and it was on that account they were deliberately exercising a certain degree of caution.

However, one of the women teachers was both more virulent and inclined to be somewhat less discreet than the others; so he decided to play up to her and give her the impression that he wanted to start an *affaire* with her, on the chance that she would talk more freely if he could get her on her own. Her name was Dolores Mendoza and she was obviously of Jewish extraction but, as he learned later, her mother was an Argonese, and from her she had inherited a pair of pale blue eyes which, in her sallow face, made her rather striking.

In his second week there he asked her out to dinner and she readily accepted. On the Tuesday evening they had a modest meal at a fish restaurant down by the harbour, but he plied her liberally with wine and under its stimulus she talked animatedly on a variety of subjects. She was very intense and, like her fellow-teachers, had no sense of humour; so in spite of her intelligence he found her rather a bore. Now and then he turned the conversation to politics, but she shied off the subject and he refrained from pressing it, as he felt that on the first occasion they were out together it would be bad tactics.

At the end of dinner he got two surprises. In keeping with her anarchist principles, when the bill was brought she insisted on paying half. The second was more in the nature of a nasty shock. As the waiter went off to get their change, she said, 'Well, shall we go back to your place or would you like to come to mine?'

He had no doubts about what she meant, and silently cursed himself for not having taken into account that the anarchists believed in free love, and that it was considered a point of honour by the most orthodox of their women to give themselves to anyone who wanted them; and he had certainly led her to suppose that he found her very attractive.

After racking his wits for a moment for a way to escape without offending her from the tricky situation in which he had landed himself, he said, 'I've rather peculiar views about that sort of thing. I think that to get the best out of it, the first time should be something one can look back on with special pleasure. I mean not just a roll on a bed and a good-night kiss, but a real long session. Afterwards, of course, one takes any opportunity that offers; but what I would really like is for us to go down to some little place on the Costa Brava for a week-end together. I'm prepared to wait for that, if you are.'

Her pale blue eyes regarded him with faint surprise, then she smiled and said, 'Perhaps you're right. Anyhow it shows that you must like me a lot, and I'm rather flattered. Let's do that, then. But I can't next week-end. I'm already engaged to spend Saturday night with another friend of mine.'

Inwardly he sighed with relief. He had anyhow gained an eleven-day respite; time enough to pump her if that was possible, and later he could think up some excuse to drop her.

Two nights later Sanchez took him out to dinner, and by chance he learned how it was that Ferrer's swarthy younger son always had a pocketful of money. He was wearing a gaudy new jacket and a handsome red satin cummerbund, and late in the evening, after they had been drinking fairly heavily, de Quesnoy congratulated him on his finery, remarking that he was lucky to be able to afford it.

Sanchez closed one of his sloe-like eyes in a leery wink, and replied, 'I paid for them with some of the money from my little Marquesa, and there's plenty more where it came from.'

'You are lucky in having a rich mistress, then,' the Count commented with a smile.

'She's not my mistress, though I don't doubt I could make her let me have her if I wanted to. But she's too skinny for my liking.' Suddenly he lowered his voice and became confidential. 'Her husband is an old dotard and she's having an *affaire* with her groom. He's a friend of mine and he told me about it. I put up a little scheme to him and we fixed things up between us. They have their fun in the woods when they are out riding together. He took me out and showed me their favourite love-nest among the bushes. I borrowed a camera and after a bit of practice with it went out and lay in wait for them. I got two lovely snaps while he was keeping her good and busy. They were some pictures, I can tell you. Her face was turned sideways and her eyes were closed, but there was no mistaking what they were up to. I sent her a couple of copies and told her where to leave the cash. She's paid up handsomely for the past three months and I split with my friend; although, of course, she doesn't know that and is still potty about him.'

De Quesnoy laughed and, as he was expected to, praised Sanchez's cunning but mentally he promised himself that, when in due course he had collected enough evidence to get the Ferrer brothers arrested, he would see to it that Sanchez received a special beating-up for this despicable blackmail.

On the Saturday Ferrer told 'Señor Chirikov' that he had received a letter from Monsieur Gérault, the new French master, who was also to teach physics, that he would be arriving on Monday; but as his train did not get in until the evening the French classes were to be taken as usual on that day.

By then, owing mainly to the numerous evenings he had spent in the masters' common-room, the Count had acquired a considerably wider knowledge of anarchist affairs and of the divergence of the views expounded by the principal exponents of its philosophy.

He learned that while the pacific Jean Jacques Rousseau and the two most blood-lusting fiends of the French Revolution, René Hébert and Anacharsis Clootz, were all looked on as 'Saints' in the movement, Robespierre, who had sent ten times as many people to their death as the last two put together, was anathema to them because he had made himself virtually a dictator.

He had heard discussed the attempt of the Utopian Robert Owen to found a Socialist community at New Harmony, Indiana, and of that made later at Cincinnati by his disciple, Josiah Warren, to run a 'time store' on the principle of exchanging services instead of paying for them in money.

He also became aware of the subtle difference between anarchism and nihilism. The former wished to destroy the existing order, but had plans for building a new one consisting of free Labour groups and free Communes; whereas, with true Russian pessimism, the latter's aim was simply to annihilate every form of authority, then sit back and let matters take whatever course they would.

From his reading and these conversations he formed one definite conclusion. It was that the belief generally held, that all active anarchists were members of a world-wide organization and received their orders from some secret headquarters – probably in London – where their outrages were planned, was a complete myth.

Their first principle – the rejection of all authority – made that belief, even theoretically, untenable; and a careful analysis of their crimes showed beyond all doubt that they did not even have regional headquarters in individual countries or cities.

This explained why such a high proportion of their attempts, particularly against well-guarded Heads of State, had proved failures. Had they been carefully planned and properly financed many more of them must have met with success. But examination showed that nearly all these attempts had been made by individuals who had imbibed anarchist doctrines and were either solitaries or at most had only a very small group of associates.

The travesty of a bomb that Vaillant had thrown in the Chamber of Deputies had been made by himself out of the poorest possible materials. Caserio, on hearing that President Carnot was to open the Colonial Exhibition at Lyons, had set out to assassinate him from the Mediterranean port of Cette, but he had not enough money to buy even a third-class railway ticket for the whole journey; so he had had to walk the last eighteen miles on the afternoon preceding his attack. Luccheni, who stabbed to death the Empress Elizabeth of Austria, purchased a knife for the purpose for twelve francs; but fearing that his money might not last out until he could find an opportunity to strike the Empress down, he induced the shopkeeper to take it back. Instead, he bought for less than one franc a long file set in a wooden handle and, after sharpening it to a needle point, used it as a stiletto to do the deed.

It was obvious that had any of these assassins been directed by some central committee, they would have been furnished with proper weapons and ample money to aid them in carrying out their murderous intent.

However, it did seem to de Quesnoy that there were grounds for believing that the Barcelona anarchists differed from others in this respect. This he believed to be because they were strongly influenced by the Syndicalists who, while accepting anarchist principles, held somewhat more practical views about the establishment of a new social order after the present one had been destroyed. There was also the fact that the bombs used by the Spanish anarchists were no home-made toys, as witness the terrible devastation caused by the one that Morral had hurled at the Royal coach, and this implied that either they were supplied by some central headquarters or that there was such a centre where potential assassins received instruction in making them.

That no international world-headquarters of anarchism existed was a sad blow to the Count, since he had hoped that through the Barcelona anarchists he might eventually learn its whereabouts, in due course penetrate it and, sooner or later, find means to blow sky-high the brains directing the movement. But it had proved to be a nebulous creature that could not be brought to grief by any single act. He could only console himself with the thought that he might still deal a crippling blow against the Spanish anarchists if he could secure evidence that it was Ferrer to whom they looked for support and direction.

On the Sunday he wrote a long letter to de Cordoba, giving an account of his doings since his arrival in Barcelona, reporting on the situation as he saw it, and stating his hopes of securing evidence which would show that Ferrer and some of his associates had known in advance of Morral's intentions; all of which he asked should be passed on to Don Alfonso.

When Monday came de Quesnoy decided that as it would be his last chance to share the common-room with the other masters, he would spend the evening there. After he had had dinner he went in to find Dolores Mendoza playing chess with Jovellenos, who took the higher maths class, and three other men sitting talking politics as usual. They were Zapatro, who taught architecture, Herr Schmidt, the German master, and Benigno. De Quesnoy settled down with those three and the interminable discussion went on according to custom. Spaniards by habit sit up late so these sessions often went on until past midnight, and it was about eleven o'clock when Benigno remarked:

'Sanchez should be here soon now. My father gave him the job of meeting this new man, Gérault, at the station and bringing him here. His train was due in at a little after ten.'

He had hardly finished speaking when the door opened and Sanchez came in with a small, weedy little middle-aged man. Dolores and Jovellenos glanced up but did not break off their game; the other four came to their feet to greet the newcomer. Sanchez introduced them in turn and coming last to the Count said:

'This is Señor Chirikov. He is a Russian but speaks French like a native, and owing to the retirement through illness of your predecessor he has been deputizing for you as French master until your arrival.'

De Quesnoy murmured a conventional greeting and put out his hand, but the other did not take it. He was staring at the Count with murder in his eyes. Suddenly he cried:

'He is no Russian! He is a Frenchman! I know this man. He can have come among you only as a spy. Two years ago in Paris he penetrated the secrets of the Freemasons and brought about the fall of the Combes government. He is that notorious monarchist, Colonel the Count de Quesnoy.'

Unmasked

FOR a moment utter silence descended on the small room. Every one of the eight people in it remained perfectly still, as though temporarily paralysed by the waving of a magician's wand. Even their breathing was not perceptible, and the smoke from their cigarettes and pipes hung unmoving in faint blue strata. Although they made no movement the pulses of all of them had quickened. Their thoughts were racing and the atmosphere was tense with the invisible radiations those thoughts made upon it.

De Quesnoy needed no telling that, for him, the silence was pregnant with menace. The men about him were declared enemies of society. He had every reason to believe them either actively concerned in carrying out assassinations or, at least, helping to plan them. Since they felt no scruples during attempts to murder their chosen victims, about innocent people often being killed or maimed, it was certain that, should they be convinced he was a spy, they would show no mercy to him.

Taken completely off his guard, during those seconds of explosive quiet, he stared at the weedy little Frenchman who had denounced him. Then, rallying his wits in an attempt to save himself, his face suddenly took on an expression of angry amazement. His 'devil's eyebrows' shot up into his forehead and in a voice sharp with indignation, he cried:

'Monsieur! How dare you make such an accusation. You are entirely mistaken.'

'Nothing of the kind!' Gérault snapped back. 'You were the leader of the conspiracy to put the Duc de Vendôme on the throne, and later you passed yourself off under the name of Vasili Petrovitch. It was you who bribed that absinthe-besotted traitor, Bidegain, to steal the *fiches* from the files of the Grand Lodge, and letters from the War Minister to our Secretary-General, Vadecard. I would know you again anywhere.'

'I haven't an idea what you are talking about,' stormed the Count. 'I've never seen you before in my life.'

As he made the latter statement he would have been prepared to swear to it. The lined face, beady brown eyes and thin drooping moustache of the Frenchman were entirely strange to him; but during the months he had lived in a Montparnasse boarding-house as Petrovitch he had been introduced to scores of Freemasons and attended a dozen or more Lodge meetings, so he could not have remembered the faces of a tenth of those he had met or rubbed shoulders with.

On the other hand, as the wrecker of their attempt to sabotage the French Army, they had ample cause to remember him; and not just vaguely as a man they had seen a few times, for his description had been circulated by the police and photographs of him had appeared in all the papers. Ten months earlier his participation in the abortive conspiracy to place de Vendôme on the throne had brought him nation-wide publicity, so the Press had seized on his reappearance in Paris as front-page news, and his features had temporarily become as well known as those of the atheist War Minister whom he had succeeded in hounding out of office.

It was that which made his return to France, even temporarily and under another name, still almost certain to lead to his arrest; but as he was in Spain and it was getting on for two years since such notoriety had been thrust upon him, he had considered negligible the chances of his being recognized by one of the class of people with whom he intended to mix in Barcelona. He had even regarded the risk as so remote that he had contemplated joining a Masonic Lodge there; so he felt that fate had played him a really scurvy trick in confronting him with an enemy who could swear to his identity.

Hiding his apprehension that he might fail in his attempt to bluff matters out, he gave a swift glance round at the other occupants of the room. Dolores and Jovellenos had come to their feet. The tall, stoop-shouldered mathematics master was peering through his spectacles at Gérault; but Dolores's pale-blue eyes now seemed to be protruding slightly and were fixed on him with evident suspicion. Zapatro and Herr Schmidt he could not see, as both of them were standing a little behind him; but Sanchez's low brow was furrowed and his mouth grim, while Benigno was regarding him with a puzzled frown.

Meanwhile Gérault had returned to the attack. Wrinkling up his nose he retorted with a vicious sneer, 'So you have never seen me in your life, eh? No doubt the noble Count considered me too insignificant a person to register in his aristocratic memory. But I have seen him, with Lazare, with Forain and with others whom he deceived with his glib tongue so that he might lie his way into our Brotherhood. I tell you, comrades, he is a traitor; a spy. If we had caught him in Paris we'd have had him garrotted by *apaches* and paid them handsomely for their trouble.'

De Quesnoy was well aware that there were plenty of dock-rats in Barcelona who, with no questions asked, would prove ready enough to play a similar part for a few hundred pesetas. Whether these people of Ferrer's were militant anarchists or only abettors, unless he could convince them that Gérault was mistaken, he thought it more than probable that they would decide to arrange matters so that next morning his corpse would be found floating in the harbour. His heart was beating quickly now but he realized that his best hope lay in maintaining a calm appearance. He said more quietly:

'Really, this is fantastic. All of you here have known me for quite a while. Have you ever heard me say anything which might lead you to suppose that I am this French Count of whom Monsieur Gérault speaks?'

'If you are, you would not be such a fool as to do so,' said Benigno in a non-committal voice.

'But I am not a Frenchman, and I have never been to France,' lied the Count.

'Yet I am told you speak French like a native, although you say you are a Russian,' Gérault put in. 'Colonel de Quesnoy also spoke French fluently, while pretending to be a Russian refugee.'

'Perhaps, but what of it? There are thousands of Russians who have fled from Tzarist persecution and are now scattered over western Europe. French is the second language of all educated Russians, and unless they spoke it fairly well few people outside Russia would understand them.'

'Yes, yes; but that is only a minor point. I recognize you. Those eyes of yours are unmistakable. Your face and figure too all tally with those of the man who called himself Petrovitch. If we were in Paris I could easily turn up a photograph . . .'

'This is absurd,' the Count broke in. 'A mere resemblance. How can you possibly be certain when it is close on two years since you saw this man Petrovitch?'

The words were no sooner out of de Quesnoy's mouth than he knew that he had blundered. Drawing back his lips in a snarl Gérault spat at him, 'So you are aware how long ago it is since Petrovitch – or to give him his real name, the Comte de Quesnoy – escaped from France? Yet when I spoke of him a minute ago you asserted that you had no idea what I was talking about.'

'That's true!' exclaimed Sanchez, his dark eyes narrowing still further.

'He is a spy all right,' Dolores cried with sudden venom. 'I suspected that he might not be quite what he seemed when he took me out to dinner and tried to pump me. This makes it certain.'

Zapatro spoke from behind de Quesnoy's left shoulder. 'If he is, although we have been cautious at times when he has been with us, he could have picked up quite a lot from our conversation; so we must look on him as dangerous.'

In an effort to restore the situation the Count rounded on him and said sharply, 'All this is no more than speculation, and most unjust to me. The very first day I came to this house, on entering the laboratory I found Sanchez and Benigno busy putting together an infernal machine. If I had come here as a spy that would have been evidence enough for me to have had the place raided and them arrested. But I did nothing of the kind. Instead I suggested a method by which they could make the bomb more efficient.'

'That is certainly the truth,' Benigno agreed. 'But I think I may be able to provide an indisputable answer to this riddle. For years past Father has taken the best illustrated papers of France, England and Germany; and he keeps the back numbers up in his study. I feel sure I remember reading an article about the Vendôme conspiracy and it is bound to have had photographs of the principal participants.' Turning to Gérault, he added, 'Tell me the dates to look for; then I'll go upstairs and see if I can find the article.'

'He was last hunted by the police in Paris in November, 1904,' replied the Frenchman quickly. 'But the conspiracy was unmasked in December, 1903. Round about either time you should find articles about him.'

As Benigno hurried from the room, slamming the door behind him, de Quesnoy found himself faced with a dilemma that might spell life or death for him. As Petrovitch, he had worn a beard and shaved off the upper points of his 'devil's' eyebrows. But no photographs had ever been taken of him like that. All those used by the Press had been of him as a Chief Instructor at St. Cyr and, except that he had then had a cavalry moustache, they differed very little from his appearance as it was at present. Therefore if Benigno found an illustrated article it would prove conclusive evidence against him.

But Benigno might fail to find any proof of his identity. If so, de Quesnoy wondered, what then? It would be his word against Gérault's. In that case they could hardly do otherwise than let him go. But either way this meant an end to 'Nicolai Chirikov's' activities in Barcelona. It was certain that having come under such grave suspicion Ferrer and Co. would not trust him an inch further. They would, too, send out a warning about him to all their associates. To clinch matters Gérault would, no doubt, go hurrying off to the City Library and there turn up illustrated articles about the

Vendôme conspiracy to prove himself right. After, or even before, that happened, the Count now realized, the sooner he was out of Barcelona the better for his health.

With a jerk his mind came back to the present, and the disturbing knowledge that he had first to get out of that room alive.

As had been his custom since arriving in Barcelona he had on him a small pearl-handled revolver. He carried it thrust into his trouser top just above his left hip. It was scarcely more than a toy affair, for had he carried a larger weapon the bulge under his coat would have been noticeable; but its bullets were big enough to kill a man if fired at close range.

All the same, he felt distinctly dubious about the prospects of his suddenly whipping out such a miniature firearm and with it terrifying the group about him into allowing him to walk un-molested out of the house. Even with Benigno absent he would still be up against five men and Dolores; and, unless he made use of the weapon immediately, three of the men were near enough to snatch it from him.

Swiftly he decided that he had only one chance of getting clear away. That was to shoot Gérault, who was standing right in front of him. And not merely to wound him in the arm or leg, but shoot him in the face so that he at once collapsed, then spring over his body to the door while the others were still too paralysed by shock to intervene.

Yet such a move could have most disastrous consequences. At the best of times it was difficult to take accurate aim with a very small revolver, and in this case there would be no time to take proper aim at all. The bullet might pierce one of Gérault's eyes and enter his brain, or pass through his mouth and sever his spinal cord.

The Count had killed too many North African tribesmen, fighting gallantly for what they believed to be their rights, to feel any qualms about taking life; and since Gérault had evidently been chosen by Ferrer as a master at the *Escuela Moderna* because he was an anarchist, de Quesnoy would have felt no compunction at all about shooting him down as the price of his own liberty. But if he did, how long would he keep that liberty?

Even if it could be proved that Gérault had taken part in militant anarchist activities, which was doubtful, to have killed him in such circumstances would, under the criminal law of Spain, be murder just the same. The Ferrer brothers would start a hue and cry and at once inform the police. Once that happened, de Quesnoy knew the odds were that he would be arrested before morning. Had he had an official status he might have got away with it on a plea of self-defence; but he had not, and honour demanded that he should not disclose that Don Alfonso had sent him on this mission while deliberately concealing it from his own police.

Gérault's death would be regarded as the result of a private quarrel between two of Ferrer's associates, and the Government authorities in Barcelona would welcome the opportunity of ridding themselves of another of his group; so it was certain that they would demand the death penalty for Nicolai Chirikov. Don Alfonso would, of course, hear of the affair and it would cause him the gravest possible embarrassment. To save the Count's life he might privately disclose to his Minister of Justice that de Quesnoy had been acting for him, but it was too much to expect that he would court the resentment of his whole police force by admitting publicly that he had gone behind their backs. So de Quesnoy would still have to stand his trial for murder, and the best he could hope for was a backstairs instruction to the judge that he should be let off with a term of imprisonment.

These thoughts rushed pell-mell through the Count's brain, and decided him that the long-term risks of shooting his way out considerably outweighed his present danger. There was still a chance that Benigno might fail to find an article with his photograph, and that with the case against him unproven he might be allowed to go.

Even supposing he was definitely identified, that might not mean the worst. That they would set upon and kill him themselves seemed unlikely, or that they would send for some thug to play the part of executioner there and then. It was more probable that he would escape for the moment with a beating-up and then being thrown out.

Later that night, no doubt, they would offer the leader of some criminal gang a handsome sum to make away with him. Gérault would certainly urge them to do that. But given even an hour's grace he should be able to save himself. He had nothing at his lodgings that he valued, so he need not risk returning to it. Providing that he was not seriously injured in the beating they might give him before they let him go, he could go to earth for the night in one of the suburbs of the city, or be in a train well away from it long before any gang could get on his track.

Slightly easier in his mind owing to these latest speculations, but still highly apprehensive, he waited anxiously for Benigno's return. He had been gone no more than five minutes, yet it seemed far longer; and the others, as keyed up as the Count, were openly showing their impatience. None of them spoke, yet the silence was not complete. Even as they listened with tense expectancy to catch Benigno's footfalls as he clattered down the back stairs, one or other of them made some restless movement, easing their position or giving a little nervous cough.

At last the sound of the expected footfalls reached them. Next moment Benigno threw open the door. Two swift paces brought him into the room. In his hand he held a glossy magazine. Waving it he exclaimed excitedly:

'It's him! It's him without a doubt!'

Dolores ran forward crying 'Let me see' and almost snatched the magazine from him. Jovellenos followed her. Sanchez closed in on Benigno from the other side. Zapatro, also anxious to get a look, brushed past the Count, and even Gérault turned his head in Benigno's direction.

It was de Quesnoy's opportunity. They were all crowded round Benigno with, for the moment, one thought only in their minds – to see what this notorious conspirator, monarchist and spy looked like in the photograph. The group were between the Count and the door, but that could not be helped. Between it and the wall there were a few feet of space and by swerving round them in a violent dash he might get through the door before they realized that he was making a dash for it. Whether he would be able to reach the front door, get it open and leap out into the street before they were upon him lay in the lap of the gods. Such a chance to get clean away was most unlikely to occur again. He took it.

In one bound he reached Jovellenos, between whose back and the wall he meant to pass. But as he landed he felt a violent tug upon his armpits and shoulders. It jerked him upright and almost pulled him over backwards. At the same moment there came a tearing sound. He had forgotten that Herr Schmidt was still standing behind him. The German had seen him tense his muscles for his spring and, as he made it, grabbed the skirt of his jacket with both hands.

Instantly the group about Benigno fell apart and turned upon the escaping imposter. Schmidt was left holding a long strip of the Count's cheap cotton jacket that had torn away, but the pull on it had halted him in his tracks. As Jovellenos swung round and tried to grab him he struck the tall maths master under the chin and sent him reeling back against Dolores. But Zapatro, a middle-aged but bull-like little man, threw himself forward. De Quesnoy side-stepped the anarchist's rush to find himself facing Gérault. With savage pleasure he smashed his fist into the Frenchman's face. The blow broke his nose, it spurted blood, and with a wail of agony he flopped to his knees.

His collapse brought down Benigno too, as in the act of springing into the fray Gérault's falling body knocked him off balance. For a

moment their forms, writhing on the floor, left a clear space in front
of the Count. He used it to pull out his little revolver. As Zapatro
charged him again he fired. The bullet hit the architect in the left
shoulder. Halting, he gave a cry and clapped his right hand to the
wounded place.

De Quesnoy swivelled round and aimed again, this time at
Sanchez, who at the moment the fight started had jumped sideways
to block the doorway. Feet spread wide apart, hands on hips, head
thrust forward, he stood there now a bulky human barrier, seemingly impassable. Yet a shot could move him.

It was never fired. Flinging herself forward Dolores grasped
de Quesnoy's arm with both her hands. Throwing her whole weight
upon it, she bore it down. In vain he strove to shake her off. Next
moment Schmidt had collared him round the neck and dragged him
backwards. Stooping his head he bit into the German's wrist. With
a yelp and an oath Schmidt let go.

Dolores had transferred her hold to the Count's hand and was
clawing at it in an attempt to get the revolver from him. Suddenly
it went off. She screamed; the bullet had lodged in the calf of her
right leg. Momentarily free once more, de Quesnoy again jerked
up the little weapon and turned towards the door. Sanchez still
stood framed in it, and now he had a long thin knife in his hand.
As the Count swung round to face him he threw it.

De Quesnoy had never been nearer death. Thrown with practised
skill the glittering blade should have pierced his throat just below
his Adam's apple. But at the very instant it was thrown Schmidt
struck him a violent blow on the back of the head with a thick,
round, eighteen-inch-long ebony ruler. His head was knocked forward and slightly sideways. The knife streaked over his shoulder,
nicked the German's left ear and sped on to bury its point in a
wooden cupboard.

With stars and circles flashing in blackness before his eyes
de Quesnoy reeled forward. Dropping his revolver, he crashed into
Zapatro. They fell to the floor together. Although the small bullet
had penetrated the architect's shoulder it had done him no serious
injury. Next moment he had both his hands round the Count's
throat. De Quesnoy was half stunned but instinctively brought up
his right knee. Zapatro gave a gasp as it caught him in the stomach.
He released his grasp; but now the Count was down, Schmidt,
Jovellenos and Benigno all flung themselves upon him. In vain he
kicked and twisted, they grabbed his arms, forced him over on his
face and pulled them behind him. Jovellenos quickly took off a
stringy black tie he was wearing and with it they tied his wrists.

Schmidt then hauled him to his feet and Zapatro struck him in the face. He staggered back, tottered, and collapsed with a crash into one of the hardwood elbow-chairs.

Breathless, exhausted, aching from a dozen bruises and still bemused from the blow on the head, for the next few minutes he was only vaguely conscious of what was going on around him. Gérault crouched moaning on the sofa, his smashed face buried in his hands, blood trickling through his fingers. Dolores had pulled down her stocking and with a stream of muttered swear-words was examining the tiny wound in the calf of her leg. The others stood in a semicircle glowering down at the Count while they strove to get their breath back. As their panting eased it was Jovellenos who asked:

'What shall we do with him?'

'Put an end to him, of course,' Zapatro replied hoarsely. 'He has invited it. Not only is he dangerous to our organization; the swine tried to kill me.'

'You're right,' Sanchez supported him. 'He would have killed me too had not Dolores seized his arm.'

For a moment she stopped her cursing to put in, 'The bullets are only pellets. With that little pea-shooter he could not have killed anyone, except by a freak shot. But that's not the point. He is a monarchist spy and may have ferreted out all sorts of things about us. We have no alternative but to eliminate him.'

Sanchez had pulled his long knife from the cupboard. Giving it a flourish he cried, '*Dios!* That is obvious. Why do we wait? Bring him along the passage, some of you, and hold his head over the basin. I'll do the rest.'

De Quesnoy's wits were gradually coming back. Dully it impinged on his mind that Sanchez meant to have him dragged to the lavatory and there cut his throat. A tremor of horror ran through him as he had a vivid mental picture of himself with his head in the cracked, dirty basin and his blood gurgling down the waste. With an effort he struggled into a more upright position, but Zapatro gave him a kick on the shin and snarled at him to stay still.

So far Benigno had taken no part in these swift exchanges; now he spoke in his precise voice. 'All that Dolores said is true, but we cannot deal with him out of hand like this.'

'Why not?' asked Sanchez truculently.

'Because all decisions in matters concerning a death sentence are always taken by our father.'

'Since he is not here we must act for him.'

'Benigno is right,' said Jovellenos. 'We ought to wait until Señor Ferrer returns.'

'But he will not be back until tomorrow,' Zapatro objected. 'The committee that is planning the attempt on Quiroga will be sitting till the small hours, and he told me that he meant to spend the rest of the night with Pedro Conesa.'

Dolores tittered. 'You mean with Conesa's daughter, Teresa? She's a hot little piece if ever there was one, and our *vert galant* never misses the chance of a tumble with her whenever he has to go out to the mill.'

'Anyway, he will not be back before first school is due to start; so we must deal with this man ourselves,' Zapatro gestured towards the Count. 'We dare not let him go, even temporarily; and there is nowhere here where we could hold him prisoner without risk that he would either escape or be found by one of the students.'

'I am averse to taking any irrevocable step until it has received Señor Ferrer's approval,' Jovellenos declared. 'Why should we not take our prisoner up to the private apartment? We could get the Señora Ferrer to turn out a cupboard and lock him into it. She could keep an eye on him and no one would discover him there.'

'No one except the police!' Dolores rounded on her recent chess opponent with a sudden sneer. 'You are talking like a fool, Enriquez. You forget that he is a spy. The odds are that after every evening he spends here he reports to the police all that we have said. He must know that he has been walking on a razor's edge, and probably has some arrangement with them that, should he fail to make his report by a given hour, they are to assume that we have caught him out, and raid the place in the hope of rescuing him.'

'She's talking sense,' cried Sanchez. 'It's not often that we disperse before midnight, so we've no need to fear a raid for some hours yet; but the sooner we get this job done the better.'

Benigno laid a hand on his arm. 'Calm yourself, brother, I beg. Remember the rule our father has laid down. It is that in this house no act of violence should be permitted. I agree that this man must die. He actually saw us manufacturing a bomb. Little more would be needed for us to find ourselves facing a firing squad. But he must not be executed yet, and not here.'

'What reason can you possibly advance for postponing the death of this louse?'

'Only that such matters have always been left to our father's judgment. It is just possible that he may be making use of this man.'

'Nonsense! Is it likely that he would be doing so without having warned us about him? No. He is a spy; and in such cases our father has only one verdict. In the past few years we have had several through our hands. You know as well as I do that in every case he has ordered their execution.'

'True. I know it,' admitted Benigno. 'But not here. Not in this house. After what Dolores has just said how can you fail to realize the danger? Should the police raid us in the early hours as she suggests, think what they might find – blood all over the place, and perhaps even his body if we had not had time to get it out of the house. It is just that sort of ill chance that our father has always so wisely guarded against.'

Sanchez laughed and slapped his thigh. 'You need have no fears on that score, brother. I've just thought of a better plan than to cut his throat. We can dispose of him without leaving a trace by burning him up a limb at a time in the furnace in my foundry.'

7

To be Disposed of Without Trace

FOR the past few minutes de Quesnoy had been conscious of a warm wetness at the back of his neck. It was the blood that had trickled down from the nasty cut on his head made by the heavy ruler with which Schmidt had struck him down. He had no idea of the size or shape of the wound, for the whole back of his head felt as though it had been bashed in. The pain was agonizing and the pulses in his skull throbbed as though it was about to burst. Yet he was just capable of taking in what was said by the group clustered about him.

At Sanchez's proposal to kill him in a way that would also dispose of his body, the saliva ran hot in his mouth and his flesh crept. Courageous as he was, the idea of being burnt alive filled him with fear and horror. When Ferrer had taken him over the *Escuela Moderna* he had been shown the foundry in which Sanchez gave classes in metal-work. The furnace in it was a fair-sized one but certainly not large enough to take a body, and Sanchez had spoken of burning him in it a limb at a time. To kill and cut him up first would mean spilling quarts of his blood – the very thing they wanted to avoid – so the intention must be to thrust him in head or feet first, then reverse the process, until the white-hot interior of the furnace had baked his limbs dry of blood, and only then cut up the charred remains for final cremation.

It was possible that they might first strangle or knock him on the head, but he had a ghastly conviction that they would not show him even that much mercy. It was based on his knowledge of the extraordinary contradiction that was a salient feature of the Spanish character. Normally they were sensitive and generous and would go out of their way to avoid hurting another person's feelings. They adored their children, lavishing on them pretty clothes and toys that they could often ill-afford, and in Spain there were fewer cases of cruelty to children than in any other country in Europe. Yet they worked and beat their animals to death, and the favourite national pastime was the bullring.

The Count had been to a number of bullfights, and while he was filled with admiration for the bravery and skill of the Matadors, as they pirouetted within inches of the bull and even allowed it to tear with its horns the gold lace from the breast of their costumes, he had been baffled and sickened by the part that horses were forced to play in this cruel sport.

It had been explained to him that the whole object of the elaborate playing of the bull was to wear down its strength, so that the great muscles in its neck tired until, when facing the Matador, it could no longer hold up its head, thus enabling him to plunge his sword between its horns and through its shoulder straight down into its heart; and that for the mounted men to rear their horses right on to the bull, so that it had to take the whole weight of horse and man on its horns, was simply a part of the wearing-down process. Even so, it shocked and amazed him that thousands of women as well as men could burst into excited applause at the sight of a screaming horse falling with its guts torn out by the horns of a bull.

Their cruelty, too, was not confined to animals. In the Carlist wars few prisoners had been taken, and both sides had committed unmentionable barbarities on hundreds of the enemy they had captured. Worse still, if possible, had been their treatment of nuns and priests during the frequent revolts and revolutions of the past century. It had been common practice to rape the younger nuns to death, and burning priests had become a favourite sport.

But de Quesnoy was not now thinking of either bullfights or the devilish cruelties of the civil wars – only that hatred could turn Spaniards from delightful companions into merciless fiends in less time than it took to eat a meal; and if there was any conceivable way in which he could save himself from the ghastly death proposed for him.

During the years he had been exiled to dreary garrison duty

in Madagascar he had occupied his mind almost exclusively by an intensive study of the occult. It was an English missionary who had first interested him in it, by telling him that as the people of the huge island were a mixture of negro stock and Polynesians, who had arrived there on fleets of rafts during a great migration, the present witch-doctors had inherited a knowledge of both African and Pacific magic, so were probably more skilled in practising it than any others in the world. His prolonged study of the secret art had taught him many things; among them how to hypnotize, and how, by methods similar to Yoga, to render his body almost impervious to normal cold or heat.

Any attempt to hypnotize the hostile group now staring at him, in a few moments and in his present condition, he knew to be hopeless; and that to prevent oneself from being burnt when thrust into a white-hot furnace was beyond the powers of even the greatest Mage. But there remained the possibility that he might succeed in throwing himself into a self-induced trance.

If he could succeed in that he would, for all practical purposes, be temporarily dead, and so not feel the searing of the flames. Yet he had no sooner thought of the idea than he abandoned it. To achieve complete immunity such a trance would have to be of extreme depth, and to bring about such a state required time, solitude and complete quiet; all of which, in his present circumstances, would be denied him. By a great effort, he might force his spirit out of his body, but only on to the lowest astral plane; and the intense pain as his nerves began to scorch would bring it back to his body almost instantly.

These thoughts flashed through his mind within a few seconds of Sanchez having spoken. Then another swiftly took their place. The question of disposing of his body quickly and without trace had arisen only because Dolores had put into the heads of the others that he was in league with the police and that, if he failed to make his nightly report to them, some time before morning they would raid the house to find out what had happened to him. He must tell them that he was acting on his own, had no connection whatever with the police then they might adopt Jovellenos's suggestion of locking him up in a cupboard upstairs until Ferrer returned in the morning. Anything was better than being roasted in the furnace. But would they believe him? No; not even if he swore by everything he held holy that they had nothing to fear from the police. Why should they?

Yet it was their fear of a police raid that decided matters. For a few moments they had all stood silent, considering Sanchez's proposal. Then Schmidt spoke, in awkward Spanish with a heavy accent.

'To burn him is no good. The fat of human corpses makes a smell most horrible. It would the house stink out. Also in a short time to destroy all traces is not possible. Pieces of calcined bones would be found, buttons from his clothes, other things. If we had twenty-four hours, yes, perhaps. But if the house raided before morning is, enough evidence they will find to prove him murdered by us.'

De Quesnoy's heart gave a bound of relief, for he knew that the German's argument was unchallengeable; but he also knew that, even if he had escaped burning, his life was not worth an hour's purchase, and Zapatro confirmed him in that belief by saying angrily:

'But we cannot let him go. That is out of the question.'

The tall Jovellenos eyed the architect dubiously. 'I suppose you are right, but I have a feeling that he may prove more dangerous to us dead than alive. After all, there is no certainty that the police will raid the house just because he has failed to report to them on a single occasion. Anyway, I am still in favour of locking him up until Señor Ferrer returns and gives us a ruling on what is to be done with him.'

For some minutes Gérault had ceased moaning. Now, he took his hands from his battered face and, his throat still half-choked by blood from his broken nose, gulped out, 'He must die . . . In the name of the Grand Lodge of the Orient, I demand it . . . You do not know this man as I do . . . He is resolute, resourceful and cunning as a serpent . . . Unless you kill him while you have the chance he will find some means to escape . . . Then he will get us all arrested . . . He is the arch-enemy of us all . . . Kill him, I say . . . Kill him or you will have cause to regret it.'

Dolores nodded. 'You are right, Monsieur. But we come back to the question of how to set about it without leaving any traces.'

'In the poison cupboard of the laboratory prussic acid I have seen,' volunteered Schmidt. 'A dose we could give him and all is over very quickly.'

'Escobedo always locks the cupboard up before he goes home, and takes the key with him,' said Jovellenos. 'We would have to break it open, and it is a stout one. We would also have to provide Escobedo with some explanation to give his class in the morning; otherwise it is certain that on finding the lock of the cupboard broken they would start asking awkward questions.'

'Why waste time and go to so much trouble?' Gérault's thick, half-choked voice came again. With a gesture towards Sanchez, he went on. 'Look at those great hands of yours . . . Are they not strong enough to strangle him?'

Once more Benigno intervened. 'You are all talking like fools. However we killed him we would still be left with his body, and in disposing of it have to run a considerable risk. We dare not bury it in the cellar or the yard. If the police do come they would find . . .'

'We are not such fools as to do that,' Zapatro interrupted him.

'I did not suppose you were,' Benigno retorted icily. 'But the only alternative is to carry it out of the house. A body is not an easy thing to disguise. We might run into the police on the door-step.'

'If we don't waste endless time arguing there is little chance of that,' Dolores shrugged. 'It is most unlikely that they will come to find out what has happened to him for hours yet.'

'I agree. But, as I was about to add, other people are certain to see us. Say we put the body into a big trunk and loaded it on to our covered cart, you can be sure that when the police started to make inquiries they would learn about it, and want to know what was in the trunk and where we took it. Another thing: where do you suggest that we should dump his body?'

'On some rubbish heap on the outskirts of the city,' Sanchez suggested. 'Or in a dark alley down by the docks.'

'In either place it would be found within twenty-four hours and identified by the police as that of the spy they know to have got in among us. People who had seen us load a trunk on to our cart at this hour would testify, and in no time we would find ourselves in the dock.'

'Then what the devil are we to do?' exclaimed Sanchez impatiently.

'He must appear to have died as the result of an accident, or disappear altogether,' Benigno replied in a firm voice. 'It is in arranging such matters in similar cases that our father has shown such ingenuity. Our only safe course is to take our prisoner out to the mill and leave it to father to decide what is to be done with him.'

'I disagree . . . I disagree . . .' spluttered Gérault. 'You should kill him now . . . If I felt stronger I would do it myself . . . We'll get rid of the body somehow . . . We could bury it in the woods and it would not be found for months.'

The others, now impressed by Benigno's arguments and not wanting to run any unnecessary risk, ignored the Frenchman. But Zapatro raised the objection, 'We would still have to get him out of the house and, as you said yourself just now, there is always the possibility that the police might come upon us while we are at it, or of some nosy parker of a patrolman wanting to know what we were up to.'

Benigno shrugged. 'The cases are entirely different. In the first we should be caught with a corpse on our hands, in the second only a live man that we had trussed up; so we could not be charged with murder.'

'Our friend Benigno is right,' said Jovellenos. 'From the beginning I have been all in favour of leaving this dangerous business to Señor Ferrer's judgment.'

Sanchez gave a grudging assent. 'I'd have liked to slit his throat. But you are the cleverest among us, brother; so let it be as you say.'

The others nodded agreement, except for Gérault, who continued to clamour nasally for the prisoner's death. Instead of listening to him they began to discuss ways and means of getting the Count out to the mill.

With his nerves as taut as piano wires de Quesnoy had listened to every word of the heated argument on how, with the least risk, to terminate his earthly existence. Now, he could at least breathe again. Even this respite of an hour or two might provide him with some chance to escape from the clutches of his enemies. Yet he was not even remotely sanguine. It seemed certain that he could not expect Ferrer to aid him in any way, and the others, with the possible exception of Jovellenos, were set upon his death. Their only concern was to avoid committing any act which might later be cited to show that they had taken a hand in murdering him. Benigno's caution had resulted in a very temporary postponement of sentence, but it could not be counted as more than that.

It was Dolores who suggested rolling the Count up in a carpet, and Benigno who improved upon this ruse for camouflaging his being got out of the house by the idea of also loading on to the cart some chairs and packing cases; so that passers-by should get the impression that they were engaged in moving some odds and ends of furniture.

Sanchez went off to get the horse and cart from a mews a little way down the street. Schmidt produced a somewhat grubby handkerchief and gagged de Quesnoy with it, while the others pushed back the furniture. When the Count was hauled to his feet he made no attempt to struggle. He knew that to do so would be futile, and he was still weak and in great pain. He could only hope that the ride in the cart would be a long one; so that by

4

the time they reached the mill he would have got enough strength
back to stand some chance in a bid to regain his freedom.

Zapatro gave him a push from behind and hooked one of his
legs from under him, so that he fell on his face. Gérault then
gave him a vicious kick on the side of the head that again rendered
him nearly unconscious, and he was only vaguely aware through
a mist of pain that he was being rolled up in the threadbare carpet
that had long done duty in the masters' common-room.

Presently he felt himself lifted and carried some distance, then
down the front steps. A minute later he was heaved up and thrown
down with a bump on the floor of the covered cart. The sickening
jolt to his injured head sent such a spasm of agony through it that
he fainted.

When he came to, his heart was pounding heavily from its
effort to draw enough air down into his lungs. His head was some
way from the nearest open end of the carpet and, in addition,
a corner of the handkerchief gagging his mouth had flapped up
in front of his nostrils, so for a moment he feared that he was
about to suffocate. But by exerting his will he managed to change
his breathing from desperate gasps to slow regular intakes, so
that the corner of the handkerchief was no longer drawn with
each breath tight up against his nose.

Inside the tube that encased him it was black as pitch. His
hands were still bound behind him and he could make no movement, except slight ones with his feet. The *Escuela Moderna* was
not distinguished by its cleanliness, so the old carpet was gritty
with dust and stank of the tobacco ash and wine that had been
spilt upon it. For how long he had been unconscious he did not
know, but now he hoped desperately that the journey would soon
be over and so bring him relief from his agonizing imprisonment.

Actually he had been out only for a few minutes. The cart was
moving up-hill and at a walking pace. As it jogged on he was
given ample opportunity to think over the events of the evening
and the terrible plight in which Gérault's arrival had landed him.
Even while waging his fight for sufficient air and striving to ease
his cramped muscles, he was bitterly aware of the irony of the
situation. He had set out to secure evidence that Ferrer was the
brain behind the militant anarchists of Spain, and he had got it.

Zapatro had said that Ferrer was attending a meeting that was
planning the attempt on Quiroga, and the Quiroga referred to
could hardly be anyone other than the Captain-General of Barcelona. The others, too, evidently feeling it no longer necessary to
exercise caution about what they said in front of a man they

had already condemned to death, had made several mentions of Ferrer's care to divert suspicion from himself and his ingenuity in eliminating without trace spies and traitors. In de Quesnoy's mind there was no longer a shadow of doubt that the whole staff of the *Escuela Moderna* were militant anarchists and that Ferrer was the king-pin of the movement. But now there seemed little hope of his being able to use the information, let alone warn General Quiroga that a plot was on foot to assassinate him.

At last the nightmare journey came to an end. The covered cart rumbled to a halt, but de Quesnoy was not taken out of it. For a further ten minutes he lay half stifled and sweating profusely in his smelly cocoon while, as he rightly supposed, those who had come with the cart were making a full report about him to Ferrer. Then he heard the back-board of the cart smack down, was drawn out of it, carried some way and dropped with a bump that again sent spasms of agony shooting through his wounds. Next moment he was rolled over and over till free of the carpet, then pulled to his feet.

Temporarily dazzled by the light, he at first registered only that he was in a low-ceilinged room with a number of people staring at him. After a few blinks his sight cleared and he saw that he was in the sort of parlour to be found by the thousand in the suburbs of any big city. At a small table in its centre Ferrer was sitting; on his right there was a giant of a man with a bushy upturned moustache, on his left was a bald man of about fifty, and beside him a youth with the wide-spaced eyes of a fanatic. Behind Ferrer, Benigno was standing. Schmidt and Sanchez, as the Count saw by a swift glance to left and right, were the two men who had dragged him up on to his feet.

Benigno had laid the illustrated magazine, opened at the page carrying the damning photograph, on the table in front of his father. As they looked first at it and then at him, the bald man said, 'It's him right enough. But I am amazed, Francesco, that you did not vet him before taking him into your employ, even temporarily.'

Ferrer gave an angry shrug. 'I did, Manuel, as far as was possible, soon after I first met him. I sent Rubén Pineda, a young student, to take Russian lessons from him, and later Pineda returned to search his room after he had gone out. There were all sorts of things in it that only a Russian would normally have possessed, and the branch of the Somaten he joined confirmed that he had come from Constantinople via Greece and Valencia.'

'Gérault told us that he is a past-master at such tricks,' Benigno put in. 'Apparently he really is half-Russian and succeeded in passing himself off in Paris for several months as a refugee from Tsarist persecution.'

The giant on Ferrer's right poured himself another glass of wine from a carafe that stood on the table, and said, 'To rake up the past is only waste of time. All we have to do is to make certain that after tonight he never again has a chance to play stool-pigeon to the police.'

'Of course,' Ferrer agreed, 'but remember, Pedro, that he has been employed at the school and I don't want the police descending on it and carting us all off to be grilled, as they certainly would if there is the least suspicion that his life had been taken because he had found out too much about us.'

'Why not put him on a railway line near a level crossing,' suggested the young man with the widely-spaced eyes. 'It would be assumed that, finding the gates shut, he became impatient, thought he could cross in time, but just failed to do so.'

Ferrer shook his head. 'No, Alvaro. Since the police must be aware that he has got in amongst us his death, even apparently by accident, would arouse their suspicions and lead to an exhaustive investigation. He must disappear, so that there is no body for them to examine and no point at which to start their inquiry.'

'Gérault suggested that we should bury him in the woods,' remarked Sanchez.

'I don't like that idea,' announced the bald-headed Manuel. 'It is a dark night. We'd need lanterns to select a suitable spot for a grave, to dig it and then clear up afterwards so that it wouldn't be obvious that the ground had been recently disturbed. We might easily be caught red-handed while at the job, or seen and spied on by a couple of lovers, then followed back here and afterwards denounced to the police.'

'There is also the danger of dogs or wild-pigs rooting up a newly buried body,' put in Benigno. 'It would not be the first time that has happened.'

'It is a pity that we no longer have access to Garcia's lime kiln,' Ferrer murmured. 'We could have got rid of him there as we did that traitor Zorrilla.'

'We might get rid of him in the mill,' said the giant Pedro thoughtfully.

De Quesnoy did his best to suppress a shudder. The thought of being crushed and slowly ground to death between two great millstones was very nearly as bad as that of being burnt alive. But that was not what Pedro had in mind and, after a short pause he went on:

'If we threw him down the shaft into the flour he couldn't possibly get out, and the odds are that within ten minutes he'll be dead from suffocation. Anyhow, when we start to grind that would finish him.'

With his recent experience of stifling in the roll of carpet still vivid in his thoughts, this proposal struck the Count as even grimmer than being crushed to death. The night was hot and he was sweating already, but he broke out into a new sweat as his captors gave Pedro's suggestion serious consideration and discussed its possibilities in detail.

It transpired that some years before a workman, unseen by his companions, had fallen from a gallery that ran high up round the interior of the mill-shaft. It had been supposed that he had disappeared for some reason of his own, and the truth had come to light only some months later, as the flour chamber was completely emptied and cleaned out only two or three times a year. Between cleanings, two big doors in the base of the shaft were opened every few days and whatever quantity of flour required to fill orders was shovelled out into sacks. But Conesa, as resident foreman of the mill, could enter the chamber at any time. He would see to it that the Count's body lay buried well away from the doors and undiscovered until the next cleaning, which would not take place until a little before Christmas. When the body came to light its features would be unrecognizable and the face would have grown hair, so it could be suggested to the local authorities that the corpse was that of a tramp, and probably a drunken one, who had broken in to steal, but by a door that led only up to the top of the building, and there had the ill-luck to fall from the gallery. In any case, the chances of the body being identified as that of the monarchist spy who had disappeared in the late summer would be so remote as to be negligible.

While de Quesnoy listened, his blood chilled again. As he had no connection with the police no search would be made for him anyway. In due course de Vendôme, the Cordobas and, perhaps, Don Alfonso, would become puzzled at not hearing from him and set inquiries on foot about him; but long before that was likely to happen he would be a desiccated corpse buried under several feet of flour, or in a pauper's grave as an unidentified tramp.

Having decided that Pedro's suggestion met their requirements, Ferrer said to him, 'Very well. You go with Sanchez and Schmidt. Take him away and make certain that he does not survive. I can settle the final details for the attempt on Quiroga with the others.'

De Quesnoy was still suffering from blinding pains in the head, and his breathing continued to be painful from the dust he had drawn down into his lungs during the three-quarters of an hour that he had lain rolled up in the carpet. As the grip of Sanchez and Schmidt tightened on his arms to drag him from the room he kicked out, began to struggle violently and to gurgle pleas and protests through the gag that was still tied over his mouth. Yet he knew that neither the little strength that was left in him, nor prayers if he could have made them coherently, would avail to save him.

When they had pushed and pulled him out of the house he glimpsed the covered cart in which they had brought him there, and realized that it was a dark night with no moon; but a myriad stars were shining overhead and gave enough light for him to get some idea of his surroundings. The small house stood in a corner of a big walled yard, next to it was a building that might be used as offices in the daytime, and beyond that a lofty warehouse. Opposite them the mill towered up into the darkness with, to one side of it, the long upward-sloping tunnel through which the buckets of grain were hoisted on an endless chain up to the grinders. The mill itself formed a square stack about forty feet in height, and before he had had time to take in more his captors had hustled him over to it.

Pedro produced a key and unlocked a door in its base which gave on to a dark stairway. The Count's struggles had become feeble now, and the three of them half-dragged, half-carried him up several flights of stairs to its top. There they came out on a small landing, and while they paused there to get their breath back Pedro shone a torch round.

Its beam, first levelled straight ahead, lit up the grinders, then, as he flashed it about, showed a catwalk which ran round all four sides of the building and was obviously used by workmen to reach the machinery when it needed oiling or repairs. The grinders formed a circular mass, which at that level filled the whole chamber except for the width of the catwalk and in each corner a triangular space. De Quesnoy was pushed along the narrow gallery till he was standing opposite the corner space to the left of the door by which they had entered. Pedro directed his torch downward and its beam was reflected on the white sea of milled flour that lay twenty feet below them.

Sanchez untied the Count's wrists. Pedro held his arms while Schmidt removed the gag from his mouth. Futile as he knew it to be, he began to shout for help with all his remaining strength;

but Pedro gave him a sharp jab under the chin. It made his teeth rattle, sent another blinding pain through his head, and temporarily silenced him.

Next moment the giant foreman picked him up bodily, lifted him over the rail of the catwalk and let him drop. With arms and legs splayed out in all directions, he hurtled head downwards into the deep suffocating bed of flour.

8

The Ordeal in the Mill

HAD de Quesnoy fallen from that height on to a harder substance his neck must have been broken, but the powder-fine flour was not even packed tightly, as would have been the case had it been shovelled from one place to another; it was just as it had floated down from the grinders so almost as aerated as if it had been a vast cushion of feathers.

Head first, he plunged into it and seconds later was immersed up to the hips, with even his outstretched arms buried a foot or more deep; yet the impact had been sufficient to drive the breath out of his body.

Instinctively, he gasped for air. As his mouth opened the flour fell into it and more flour trickled down, filling his nostrils. He knew then that he was on the very brink of death. Unless he could free his head in the next few minutes he would suffocate. Already, with little air left in his lungs, there was a terrible constriction in his chest. It felt as though iron bands had been passed round it and were swiftly being screwed tighter.

Summoning up his will-power he forced himself to remain still for a moment, then with his remaining breath he blew down his nostrils. As it cleared them he made a desperate effort with his hands and forearms to force himself upward. It was only partially successful, but it brought him temporary relief. The pressure he had exerted had forced the flour beneath him into a solid mass and so created what amounted to an air bubble about his head and shoulders. He was able to draw in a breath of air before more flour fell in from above and filled the gap.

Now, although still half buried, to his unutterable relief it flashed upon him that there was a way in which he could save himself.

The whole bed of flour was so highly aerated that he only had to keep pressing it down in front of his face to get more air. Yet he was still not out of the wood. The mouthful of flour that he had gulped in now threatened to choke him. In vain he tried to spit it out. It had formed into a paste cloying all round his teeth and such of it as he had tried to swallow had stuck in his gullet.

In great pain and with failing strength, but no lessening of endeavour, he continued his fight for life. Several more seemingly endless minutes passed while he writhed and struggled in the darkness. At last, his resolution was rewarded. Somehow he had freed his head and shoulders and pulled himself out of the morass of flour. Now, lying spreadeagled on his back, he gradually recovered from his exertions.

A good twenty minutes passed before he made any attempt to explore his surroundings, then he sat up and looked about him. Already it had dawned on him that although when Pedro had shone his torch downward the flour chamber had appeared to be a pit of utter blackness, it was not so in fact. It was very faintly lit by starlight percolating through two dirt-encrusted windows set high up in opposite walls.

The chamber itself was about twenty feet square and, judging by the glimpse that de Quesnoy had caught of it from outside, he believed it to be about forty feet high. As the grinding machinery must occupy the upper ten feet, and he was lying some twenty feet below it, it could be assumed that the bed of flour was about ten feet deep. If that were so, the doors that Pedro had mentioned, by which the flour was shovelled out as required into sacks, must be well below the surface; so even if he could find them, it would be impossible to force them open.

Assuming that the flour was ten feet deep, the windows were a good bit more than half-way up the walls so could not be reached, and the walls, being sheer, and without protrusions of any kind, were completely unscaleable. However, it occurred to him that if he could make a solid mound of flour under one of the windows, he might be able to jump up to it.

Getting to his feet he ploughed his way over towards the nearest. With each step he took his foot sank knee-deep into the flour, as though it was the lightest form of snow, and at every movement he made, a big puff of it rose up filling the air with a little cloud of particles. Standing beneath the window he found that its sill was a good seven feet above the level of the flour and, as his feet were sunk nearly a foot deep in the flour, when he stretched his hands up as far as they would go his finger-tips were still some eighteen inches short of the sill.

Desperately tired and still racked by a blinding headache as he was, he began a laborious attempt to erect a solid platform below the window. Had he had a spade he might have accomplished the job by an hour's steady work, but he had no instrument of any kind, so was reduced to using his hands and feet. Going down on his knees he swept armfuls of flour forward, stood up to trample them flat, then repeated the process.

It proved a labour of Hercules. All the time he was moving the flour it billowed up in clouds about him, powdering his hair and eyebrows white, and stifling and blinding him so that every few minutes he was compelled to cease until the clouds had settled and he could get back his breath. For over two hours he stuck to this terrible task. By the end of that time he had succeeded in raising a short ramp a little over a foot, but it needed another six or eight inches for him to get a firm grasp on the window sill.

By then he was utterly exhausted and knew that even though his life depended on it he could do no more. His only hope now was that in the morning a workman to whom he could shout for help would come up on to the catwalk to do something to the machinery, or that by throwing something through the window he might attract attention to himself. Slumping down on the soft flour he fell into a deep sleep.

When he awoke he knew from the brighter light that filled the chamber that it was morning. The horrors of the past night flooded back into his mind, and it was only then he realized that someone was shouting at him. Staring up from where he lay he saw the figure of a man leaning over the rail of the catwalk. The mass of machinery filling most of the space in the top of the chamber made it semi-dark up there. Yet, even as a surge of hope that he was about to be rescued ran through him, that hope was killed. He could now make out the form of the man more clearly, and it was the giant Pedro.

'So you're still alive,' Pedro shouted down to him. 'Well, you won't be for long.'

Staggering to his feet, de Quesnoy shouted back. 'Get me out! I'll pay you anything you ask. I'm rich. The others needn't know. For God's sake get me out. What does it matter to you if I live or die? Don't throw away this chance never to have to work again. Save me and I'll hand over to you a fortune.'

But Pedro only gave a bellow of laughter, then walked back along

4*

the catwalk. Like the knell of doom for de Quesnoy, the door slammed behind him.

At the threat that he would not now remain alive for long, the Count recalled what had been said the night before about his being dead from suffocation within ten minutes, but that, should he not be, when they started to grind that would finish him. With renewed fears he stared upward. A moment later there came the sound of turning wheels and clanking machinery. The grinders had been set in motion.

From them a white mist floated down. It was composed of millions of tiny particles finer than any snow. Hastily de Quesnoy ploughed his way to the nearest corner where, not being directly under the grinder, the mist was slightly less dense. Pulling out his handkerchief, he tied it over his mouth and nose then, tearing off his jacket, he put that over his head and drew its skirts close about his shoulders. But even with such protection he knew that a soft-footed death was about to steal relentlessly upon him.

Unlike a sand-storm there was no rushing wind and sharp whipping of grains against everything they encountered. The flour descended in an even, semi-transparent cascade and in utter silence. But like sand raised by a desert whirlwind the particles penetrated every nook and cranny. Within a quarter of an hour at the most the handkerchief across the lower part of his face would become so thickly coated that it would no longer serve as a filter. Then, every breath he was forced to draw would be laden with those death-dealing particles. Another quarter of an hour of mounting agony and his lungs would cease to function. At last complete despair seized him.

But not for long. Suddenly a thought recurred to him that had crossed his mind the previous evening, when Sanchez had proposed to burn him alive in the furnace. If he could throw himself into a deep trance he might survive. Once he had succeeded in suspending his animation he would no longer need to breathe; so his lungs would remain static and uncloyed by the flour. Here, he had two of the requirements for such an operation – solitude and complete quiet in which to concentrate. The trance, too, need not be so deep as would have been required to render the body impervious to the pain of burning. Time was the third requirement; but if he concentrated to the utmost of his power, allowing no other thought to distract him even for a second, he should be able to get out of his body within ten minutes.

Lying down, with his coat still wrapped about his head, he

tensed all his muscles three times, then relaxed completely. Breathing with the rhythm he had been taught, and not even flickering an eyelid, he remained absolutely still. Gradually his breathing grew fainter and at length it ceased. His spirit was now upon the astral plane and his body only an inanimate figure to which it could still give life by returning, but was for the time being attached only by a form of spiritual telephone wire known to occultists as the Silver Cord.

To the step he had taken there was a minor benefit attached in addition to the saving of his life. The body is like a battery that can be recharged with the electricity that gives it vitality only when the spirit is absent from it during a trance or sleep. Denied all sleep indefinitely it runs down and peters out. The deeper the sleep the more beneficial, and a trance being deeper than any sleep it was certain that his physical condition would be greatly improved on his return.

For several hours he remained scarcely conscious of his body; then he began to feel a growing urge to go back into it. Soon after he had done so he became aware that all his limbs were being pressed down by a quite considerable weight; then he realized that he must have been buried by the falling flour. His handkerchief was still over the lower part of his face and his jacket covering his head. Without removing them, he kicked out with hands and feet until he was sitting up with his head and shoulders well above the new flour level. A moment of listening assured him that the mill machinery was no longer working. Pulling off the jacket and handkerchief he looked around him.

Judging by the light that came from the windows he thought it to be late afternoon or early evening. He judged, too, that the day's grinding of flour had raised the level by well over a foot. His heart gave a bound of hope. It looked now as if he should be able to reach the window. Getting to his feet, he began to plough his way towards it.

As he did so it was borne in on him that, although he felt better in himself and much stronger, he was far from recovered from his injuries. He had been hit on the head by Schmidt, kicked on it by Gérault, kicked on the shin by Zapatro and struck under the jaw by Pedro; in addition to which he had been so roughly handled, particularly by Sanchez, that he had a score of minor cuts and bruises. Although his hours of trance had restored his energy they had done little to ease his afflictions and very soon his head was again throbbing painfully.

Nevertheless he set to at once to heighten the mound he had

made with further layers of firmly pressed-down flour. Again its particles half-stifled him and covered him from head to foot with a coat of white, but after half an hour he had raised the mound sufficiently to get his hands well above the window sill.

The next thing was to break the window so that he could climb out. It had four panes, each about one foot six wide by two foot six high. Wrapping his fist in his handkerchief he smashed the two lower ones and several large pieces of glass fell outward from each. He then had to prise out the smaller jagged pieces that had been left round their lower edges; those at the top he could not reach.

Crouching down, he made a spring and caught at the central bar with the object of drawing himself up by it. The wood was old and partly rotten. It could not take his weight, and snapped. He went over backwards to fall half buried in the soft flour behind him. Picking himself up he saw that at least the bar had brought away with it two of the larger remaining triangles of glass, and there was now an opening big enough for him to get through easily.

On his second jump he grasped the sill, got his elbows on it, thrust his head and shoulders through the opening, then wriggled forward until he had the sill under his middle and was half hanging out. But one glance downwards confirmed what he had feared. The sill of the window was over twenty feet above the cobbles of the yard outside.

He had hoped that he might get away without help; so that while Pedro, Ferrer and the rest believed him to be safely dead and buried beneath the flour, he could lodge with the police a charge of attempted murder against them. But that was obviously impossible. A drop of twenty feet on to cobbles was easily enough to kill a man. He might break his neck, or anyhow a leg, and perhaps as a result of such an impact sustain some serious internal injury.

To call for help might bring Pedro on the scene; but as it was still daylight there must be other people about, so it seemed unlikely that the giant foreman would dare to risk another attempt on his life. Anyhow, he could not hang indefinitely half out of the window with its sill pressing up painfully into his stomach; so the chance must be taken that it would be Pedro who answered his shouts. In any case he would be bound to hear that his intended victim had been rescued, so would warn the others and they would all go into hiding. But that, de Quesnoy decided grimly, was of no great moment as he would spare no pains to have them hunted down.

At the very moment he had made up his mind to shout, two work-men emerged from the warehouse on the opposite side of the yard. He called to them loudly; they looked up, saw him, and with exclamations of surprise came running towards the window.

'Help me down,' he cried. 'Quickly, I beg you. Help me down.'

They both stared up at him in amazement, then the elder, who was a bearded man, said to his companion, 'Quick, Antoine. Run and fetch Señor Conesa.'

As the other turned and started off across the yard, the bearded man called up to de Quesnoy, 'How the devil did you get there?'

'Never mind that,' the Count called back. 'Get a ladder. Help me down.'

After glancing uncertainly about him, the man said, 'We'll need a tall one; bigger than I could carry on my own. But we'll get one in a minute.'

The younger fellow had reached the little house beside the office block and was hammering on its door. A minute later it opened and the giant form of Pedro stood framed in it. Only then de Quesnoy remembered that the name Conesa had been mentioned in connection with the mill while Benigno was urging on his companions that their captive should be taken to it. Obviously, it was Pedro's surname.

Pedro and the man who had gone to fetch him came hurrying over. The former looked up with a scowl, then turned to the other two and said, 'Go get a ladder: the tall one out of the ware-house.'

When they were out of earshot he said angrily to the Count, 'To have lived through today you must have nine lives, like a cat.'

'I have,' replied de Quesnoy, 'but you have only one; and if you wish to keep it you would be wise to lose not a moment in going into hiding.'

But, as the Count feared would be the case, the implied threat failed to stampede Pedro into running off and leaving the others to rescue him. The burly foreman remained standing there, his great arms akimbo, until the other two returned with the ladder.

Having had them set it up alongside the window, Pedro said to them, 'The fellow must be a tramp who broke in for a night's shelter, then fell off the gallery. He is obviously a down-and-out, and was probably drunk.'

'That's a lie,' cried de Quesnoy. 'I'm no tramp. One of you run and fetch the police. Then you shall know how I came to be here.'

Ignoring him, Pedro went on. 'The poor chap must have near

died of suffocation and it looks as if the terror of it drove him
potty. Anyhow, he is in a pretty bad way and will need attention.
Go and fetch the first aid kit from the office, Luis, and you, Antoine,
run across to my house and tell my girl to put water on to boil.
I'm quite strong enough to get him down on my own.'

'Stop!' called the Count. 'Stop! For God's sake don't leave me
with him.' But the two men took no notice of him and ran off to
do the jobs they had been given.

With a grim smile Pedro began to ascend the ladder.

De Quesnoy broke out into a cold sweat. Pedro could only have
sent the other two away in order to make another attempt on
his life while no one was watching. But what form would it take?
To push him back into the flour chamber would not kill him,
and how could his disappearance be explained when the others
returned – as they were certain to within a matter of minutes?

Pedro had now reached the level of the window. The Count
felt so certain that his intentions were evil that he decided to drop
back into the flour chamber of his own accord. His decision was
taken a second too late. As he moved Pedro shot out a huge hand,
grabbed him by the wrist and snarled:

'Thought you'd got away with it, didn't you? Well, Monsieur
clever Count, you haven't, see? Know what I'm going to do with
you? I mean to break your neck then let you drop down on to
the cobbles. I've already put it in the minds of my chaps that
you've gone barmy. If I tell them you struggled with me and I
lost my hold on you, they'll swallow it all right.'

As he spoke he was dragging de Quesnoy towards him. In vain
the Count endeavoured to cling to the window sill. He had no
purchase for his feet or back from which he could exert his own
strength, and the great brute who was pulling him out of the window
was far stronger.

The tussle lasted no more than a minute. De Quesnoy's knees,
then his feet, came over the sill, and he swung out into space supported only by Pedro's grip on his wrist. But the grip took the
strain of his weight until he crashed sideways into the ladder
and got a foot on to one of its rungs. He was below Pedro, his
face on a level with the backs of the giant's knees. For a moment
they remained almost still while recovering a little from their
efforts. Then Pedro turned sideways on the ladder and gave the
Count's arm a series of jerks so violent that they threatened to
pull it from its socket. The pain was so excruciating that de Quesnoy
was forced to stumble up the ladder rung by rung until his head
was on a level with Pedro's waist.

But now, in order to do de Quesnoy any vital injury, Pedro had to change his grip and with one of his hands he was hanging on to the ladder. In that lay the Count's one advantage, for although Pedro had him by one of his wrists his other hand was free.

When a youth in Russia, he had often participated in the national sport of wrestling, and later he had for a while studied the art of judo. One of its secrets he had learned was that by a certain grip on the shoulder with the thumb inclined downwards towards the collar-bone a muscle can be pressed which causes exquisite pain. In desperation he now stretched up his free hand as far as it would go and exerted this grip on Pedro.

The anarchist gave a scream of agony, his eyes bulged and his body jerked forward. The result was that he lost his grip on the ladder. De Quesnoy snatched at it to save himself, but the weight of Pedro's big body falling outwards against him broke his hold before he could grasp it firmly. Next moment, with arms and legs still entangled, they went hurtling down on to the cobbles. They hit them with such force that, almost instantly, both of them were rendered unconscious.

As semi-consciousness returned to de Quesnoy he gradually became aware that he was in hospital. He was in no great pain but knew himself to be extremely ill. The vaguely-seen coifs of nuns came into his vision from time to time and a doctor coming to give him an injection confirmed his impression that he was being kept under morphia. A little later he was propped up to be sick and wondered to find himself in a common ward, for as yet no memory had returned which would have explained to him how he came to be there. He assumed that he must have been brought in from a street accident, but he did not realize that he was in Barcelona and from Spanish being spoken by the people about him he gained the impression that he was in Madrid.

For what seemed to him a very long time he lay comatose, only rousing a little now and then when they bathed his head or gave him another injection; and all the while he knew that he was hovering between life and death.

At length a time came when, having lapsed into complete unconsciousness, he found himself outside his body and looking down on to it. His head was swathed in bandages, his left shoulder was strapped up, and a mound over his left leg showed that it was in splints.

Now, his mind cleared as suddenly as if a curtain had been

drawn back. He knew that most of his injuries were the result of his fall from the ladder and was again fully aware of all the events which had led up to it.

As he regarded himself, two nuns came to his bedside followed by a priest carrying the Host. The nuns knelt and for a few moments there came the mutter of prayers while the priest administered Extreme Unction. Then the Count noticed that screens had already been drawn round the bed.

'So,' he thought, 'they expect me to die tonight. In fact, in their eyes I am already as good as dead. I must show them that I am not. I must return to my body at once, and next time anyone comes to the bedside make some movement. Otherwise they'll put me in the mortuary, then bury me.'

He willed himself downward towards his nostrils, but his act of will brought him little nearer to them. Its failure revealed to him how weak and attenuated his Silver Cord had become. In sudden panic he realized that it might break at any moment. If it did he would never be able to get back into his body, and would be really dead.

9

A Ghost in the Night

No one can be positive about what happens after death. Like the very beginning of all things and the meaning of eternity, it is one of the great mysteries and not meant for man to know. But throughout the ages a limited number of people have had experiences upon which they are at least justified in basing almost unanswerable arguments for the survival of the spirit and a belief that they have succeeded in lifting a corner of the veil.

In every period and country there have been people who, after profound meditation and long training, have acquired the ability to will the spirit that animates them out of their bodies while those bodies are still living. That they have actually done so has been proved by their remaining in a state of suspended animation for many days without any form of sustenance and, while in a state of trance, appearing in spirit form to convey messages and warnings to persons at a great distance. From this it is logical to conclude that when the body dies its ego does not die with it, but passes on to some new form of activity; and that those who have been able to leave their bodies while alive and return to them have brought back a certain degree of knowledge about the laws that govern life and so-called death.

That knowledge has been judged by wise men to be unfitting for mortals who have not yet achieved a certain state of advancement, and so in every age had become the jealously-guarded secret of a few enlightened individuals who have mostly been members of an inner circle of some priestly caste. Yet such enlightened ones have always been willing to share that knowledge with those whom they recognize as sufficiently advanced not to abuse it. And de Quesnoy had been chosen as one of those fitted to receive instruction in these great mysteries.

He knew one of the fundamental laws to be that while a person can shorten his life by taking it, no one can add one second to the span of life on earth allotted to him on each incarnation. And he recognized that it might be that his time had come to leave his present body for good.

To do so would now be easy, and in many ways it held out a tempting prospect. While away from earth he would again be with numerous long-time friends who were also out of incarnation for the time being, and some of whom he could not have had the joy of seeing for many generations. He would also see others who had died before him in his present life – Angela among them.

But it would not be the same as living with her on earth. He knew too that never again would they be reincarnated in the same period with similar bodies. Sooner or later the bond between them, as with his other long-time friends, would ensure their coming together again on earth in some relationship, but until that happened they would be no more to one another than companions in the Fields of Asphodel, the Land of Sekhet-Aaru, the Gardens beneath which Rivers Flow – as various peoples had termed the enchanted country in which spirits out of incarnation awaited their return to earth. It was this knowledge which, after his first weeks of grief, had enabled him to put thoughts of Angela, all but occasionally, out of his mind. Since arriving in Barcelona he had accepted their love as a closed chapter in one of his many lives.

Each life on earth he knew to be like a term in school, during which one must learn the new lessons set for one and strive to overcome some weakness of character, whereas to be out of incarnation meant a long and joyous holiday with no tests to pass, no ailments or accidents and no cares of any kind; so the thought of that alone was a big inducement to make no further effort and allow his Silver Cord to disintegrate.

Yet there was also the thought that after that glorious holiday there was no escaping the law which would send him back to earth again in a new incarnation. What form would it take?

He knew the widely-spread Indian belief, that an ill-spent life on earth might result in one's being reincarnated as an animal, or even an insect, to be a heresy. No soul that had once achieved human status was ever sent back as a part of one of the group souls that animated the lower species of creation. Those, too, who had advanced as far as he had always returned with some part of the knowledge they had acquired in previous lives lying dormant within them; so, except in cases where they still had to learn some special lesson, such as humility, they were given an opportunity to become in some degree members of some governing class.

But in this incarnation he had been born the heir to a Duke, and given a fine body, a handsome face and plenty of money. He could hardly expect such good fortune and so easy a path next time. He was, too, still only in his early thirties; so he might yet do great things.

It was then it occurred to him that he might no longer have a fine body. Obviously it had received a most savage battering and, as a result of the fall of twenty feet, might have some internal injury that would make him a cripple for the rest of his life. His astral vision having an X-ray quality not granted with ordinary-human sight, he began to examine it thoroughly and assess the full amount of the damage it had sustained.

His scalp was cut at the back of his head and his skull slightly cracked at the side some way above the right ear; more serious, there were broken skin and a huge bruise across the centre of his forehead and it was this which had caused his temporary loss of memory. His left collar-bone was broken, two of his ribs were cracked, and his left leg was broken about six inches above the ankle; but it was a clean break, not a compound fracture, and he could see no sign of internal haemorrhage. His lungs, however, were severely inflamed, which might lead to pneumonia.

Summing matters up he decided that, once over the initial shock to the system caused by such multiple injuries, there was none among them that should prevent him within a few weeks, or at worst months, from riding, fighting and loving again. So it would still be a fine body, and a sad waste to leave it – and all the other good things that went with it – for an unknown future. But he greatly doubted now if he had any choice.

On that another thought came to him. Perhaps the choice had been left to him in order to test his will-power. If so, he must not shirk the test. It was the law that as long as one had the power to keep life in one's body one should do so. Even those who died under torture were expected to stick it out to the limit of their endurance. They were paying off a debt for some evil they had done to another in the past, and were not given more pain than with extreme fortitude they could bear; so to give up the ghost prematurely left part of the debt unpaid, and was a minor form of suicide. It was possible – no, certain – that if he lived on there were numerous debts that it had been decreed that he should pay during his incarnation as Armand de Quesnoy. The thought decided him. He must make an all-out attempt to get back.

He had hardly taken the decision when a doctor appeared with a lay sister behind him. Taking the wrist of the body, the doctor felt for a pulse, dropped the wrist, then turned up one of the eyelids, glanced at the eye, and shut it. Turning to the lay sister he said, 'He's gone. You can start washing the body and preparing it for burial whenever you like.'

Swiftly now de Quesnoy began to concentrate. No relaxation of muscles was first required, but the employment of a thought rhythm, then the creation of a mental image of the body breathing to that rhythm. Had his Silver Cord had its normal strength the lungs would have responded at once, but now they seemed impenetrable. Yet very slowly the outline of the bed and body on which he was looking down began to blur. For two more long minutes of concentration, so intense that his mind became an agony in the void, he could still see them faintly. Then they disappeared. At the same instant his Silver Cord thickened, he felt a pull upon it that carried him downwards as though borne by a wind of hurricane strength. Two great tunnels – his nostrils magnified a hundred times – opened in front of him and within a matter of seconds he became conscious again of the weight of his limbs.

For several minutes, utterly exhausted by his effort, he made no attempt to move. The lay sister emerged from behind one of the screens wheeling a small table with a bowl of water and some bandages on it. She stripped down the bed-clothes but still he made no sign. He knew that his hold on life remained most precarious, and that even an effort to sit up might prove so great a strain that it would drive his spirit out of his body again, and this time once and for all.

It was not until she put her hands flat on his stomach to press it empty that he summoned what little strength he had to show that he was still alive. For one awful moment he feared it was too little even to make his vocal cords work; but as she threw her weight upon him he succeeded in letting out a deep groan.

Exclaiming 'Saints defend us; he's not yet gone after all!' she ran off and next minute returned with the doctor.

While he was making a quick examination, de Quesnoy succeeded in slightly fluttering his eyelashes to confirm that the woman had not raised a false alarm. The doctor sent for his hypodermic and hot-water bottles, other nuns came to busy themselves about the bedside, and a quarter of an hour later the Count, now carefully tucked up again, had responded satisfactorily to their treatment.

During the forty-eight hours that followed, it continued to be touch and go; but by the Friday night he felt himself to be out of danger, and after a good night's sleep he woke on Saturday morning feeling much stronger. The nun who had charge of him, seeing that for the first time since being brought in he appeared sufficiently recovered to answer a few questions, asked him his name and the address of his nearest relative. But he shook his head as though he had lost his memory, because he wanted time to think matters over before giving an account of himself.

That day during his waking periods he considered his situation. Pedro Conesa could not possibly have escaped with only bruises. He must either have been killed or severely injured, and if he was alive the odds were that he was occupying a bed in the same ward. If that was so, de Quesnoy reasoned, and Pedro was in much the same state as himself, he had little cause to worry; but if within the next few days Pedro became capable of leaving his bed, he must not delay long in taking special precautions. The anarchist must know that as soon as his intended victim had sufficiently recovered he would bring a charge of attempted murder against him and, in view of his declared intention when on top of the ladder to break the Count's neck, it was highly probable that in a bid to save himself he would, one night when all was quiet, make a final attempt to murder him.

Next, what about Ferrer? Pedro's daughter would certainly have informed him of all that had occurred at the mill. He, too, his sons and all those who had played a part in Monday evening's events must fear that the Count's recovery would lead to their arrest. Perhaps, however, they believed that as it would be only his word against that of all of them they would be able to bluff the matter out. They might quite well succeed in that as they must have many fellow-anarchists who would certainly not stick at committing perjury to provide them with alibis for the night in question.

At first the Count thought the chances were that they would get away with it, but later in the day he revised his opinion. The bearded Luis and young Antoine could be called as independent witnesses that he had been trapped in the flour chamber. How could he have got there unless his account of what had happened was the truth? In Barcelona midnight was not regarded as a late hour, so quite a number of passing people must have seen the Ferrer brothers and their companions loading the carpet and some pieces of furniture on to the covered cart. If they could be found that would be strong supporting evidence. Lastly, Zapatro had received a bullet in his shoulder and Dolores one in the calf of her leg. Even if the pellets had been abstracted by a trusted friend it would be several weeks before the marks of the wounds disappeared entirely; and the same applied to Gérault's broken nose. No, taken together all this should prove ample to convict them.

That meant then, de Quesnoy reasoned, that Ferrer and Co. must at the moment be exceedingly anxious that he should die. It could be taken for granted that among the medical students who came round the wards of the hospital they would have a spy who was keeping them informed of his condition. Once they learned that it looked as if he would soon be well enough to make a statement to the police the odds were that they would do their utmost to kill him off.

How, he wondered, would they make the attempt? In hospital an overdose of a drug offered the simplest means, and one in which there was a big possibility that no one would suspect that murder had been committed. At the thought, he thanked God that he was in the care of nuns, since their religion made anarchists anathema to them; so there was no likelihood of one of them being got at.

Perhaps, then, the anarchists would use their favourite weapon, the bomb. If there was a student of their persuasion spying for them, they might induce him to bring in a deadly little packet and secret it somewhere in or near the bed during the round of the ward that the students made each morning with the house surgeon. It would not be easy to do so unnoticed while a little crowd was standing round the bed; but he might, perhaps, drop his notebook and while stooping to recover it push the bomb under the bed.

Still under the influence of the secrecy about his real self which had become second nature to him during the past six weeks, the Count had at first intended to say 'Nicolai Chirikov' when the time came that he had to answer the question about his name. But on consideration he decided that it was pointless to do so. The mission on which he had come to Barcelona had been abruptly terminated by Gérault's having identified him as de Quesnoy. Even if he were in a state to do so he could carry it no further under the name of Chirikov, or any other.

Moreover, he realized now that if he wanted to get out of the hospital alive he must secure police protection. If he sent for the police he was still much too weak to give them a full account of himself, and they might not be inclined to pay very much attention to the fears of a Russian refugee; whereas the name de Quesnoy would ring a bell with them. Angela's having been assassinated during the wedding-day attempt on the King and Queen, and his having come to Barcelona with the idea of avenging her death on the anarchists made obvious sense: they provided an adequate reason for his now needing protection from them. He would, of course, maintain that it had been an entirely private venture, so Don Alfonso's interest in it would continue to remain secret.

That evening he spoke coherently for the first time and asked the nun in whose care he was what had happened to the man who had fallen off the ladder with him. Crossing herself, she said, 'He is dead; God rest his soul. He fell on his head, and they say that his great weight caused it to smash like an eggshell; so he could have known little about it.'

This news was a great relief to the Count, as it removed his most immediate danger. When she asked his name he gave it simply as de Quesnoy, then added weakly that in the morning he wished to make a statement to the police.

When morning came the house surgeon arrived early at his bedside, congratulated him on the improvement he had made, and said: 'I understand you wish to make a statement to the police about how the accident occurred, but I don't think it in the least necessary, particularly as the inquest on the man who fell with you is now over. In any case I couldn't possibly allow you to strain yourself by talking for any length of time. It will be some days yet before you are fit to do that.'

For a minute the Count considered this unexpected hitch in his plans. He was not strong enough to enter into a full explanation, or argue; yet if he failed to get police protection fairly soon now he might pay for it with his life. So also, if a bomb was used, might many other unfortunate people in the ward, as the anarchists were completely ruthless about killing the innocent if in a general massacre there was a fair chance of including the person they wished to assassinate.

At length he said, 'Send a telegram . . . please.'

Producing a pencil from the pocket of his jacket, the doctor lifted his note-pad and, expecting that his patient wanted to notify some relative of his whereabouts, smiled amiably.

'His Highness the Duke de Vendôme,' the Count began slowly.

Lowering his note-pad the doctor frowned. 'When you were brought in they said you were a tramp. You cannot be serious in wishing to send a telegram to a member of the Royal Family.'

'I am a Knight of the Golden Fleece,' de Quesnoy said with a faint smile.

The doctor almost dropped his note-pad, then wondered if he was being made a fool of, but decided that his patient was too ill to play practical jokes. Meanwhile the Count went on. 'Banco de Coralles, Madrid . . . Am helpless . . . and in great danger . . . require police protection urgently . . . General Quiroga also in danger . . . Armand de Quesnoy.'

Having taken down the message the doctor looked up quickly and said, 'Are you . . . surely you must be the Conde de Quesnoy whose Condesa was among . . .'

De Quesnoy nodded; then, exhausted by his effort, he closed his eyes. He had no idea of François's present whereabouts and thought it unlikely that he was in Madrid, but the Bank would be certain to know where he was and forward the telegram to him immediately.

Late that evening his action took effect. The Captain-General of the City himself came striding into the ward followed by the Superintendent of the Hospital, the doctor who had been looking after de Quesnoy, and numerous other people.

General Quiroga had met the Count at a pre-wedding reception at the Royal Palace in Madrid. Halting at his bedside he peered for a moment at the bandaged head, then turning to the others he said, 'Yes. It is no hoax. This is the Conde de Quesnoy.'

Turning back to the Count, he went on, 'I am indeed sorry to find you in such a bad way, Señor Conde. But be assured that from this moment you may set your mind at rest with regard to your safety. Can you tell me what danger it is that threatens you and, it seems, also myself?'

'Anarchists,' replied the Count. 'I got in among them . . . but was found out . . . They are plotting to kill you . . . Don't know any details . . . Mustn't talk much yet . . . either.'

The broad-shouldered General gave a grim smile. 'The attempt on me was made on Wednesday, by a young man named Alvaro Barbestro. We caught him, but I escaped, as I have several times before. I expect they'll get me one day, though; so thanks for the intended warning. Are there any particular precautions you would like me to take in your own case?'

'Ferrer,' de Quesnoy murmured. 'Whole staff of *Escuela Moderna* nest of murderers . . . Good thing if you could . . . could hold them on some pretext . . . till I . . . I . . . well enough to bring charge.'

'That's enough,' announced the doctor. 'He really must not talk any more for the present, Your Excellency.'

The General nodded. 'Of course; of course. Anyhow, that is all I want to know for the moment. Please see that he has every possible attention; and have him moved to a private ward – that is, if being moved would not be too great a strain on him.'

'I'd prefer not to move him yet,' the doctor replied, 'but you may rely on us to make him as comfortable as we can.'

To the Count, the General said, 'Señor Conde, my compliments and best wishes for your speedy recovery. Should you desire anything you have only to command me.' Then he touched his gold-braided kepi in salute, gave some swift instructions to a member of his staff, and strode away.

The patients in the beds on either side of de Quesnoy were moved and the beds taken away to be replaced by screens, which had the effect of creating a private ward for him. Two Guardia Civil then sat down on chairs where one of the beds had been. They were armed with pistols and under orders that one or other of them should remain with him night and day. Considerably relieved by these precautions for his safety, he drifted off to sleep and had his first really good night.

Monday passed without incident but on Tuesday morning de Vendôme appeared. He had received the Count's telegram, relayed from Madrid, at San Sebastian, where he was staying with his step-uncle and aunt at their villa. The train service across country was so bad that he had decided that it would be quicker to take the express down to Madrid, then come up from there to Barcelona on the night train. Owing to his devotion to de Quesnoy he had suffered acute anxiety about him for the past thirty-six hours; so he was greatly relieved to find him safe and over the crisis that had threatened his life.

The guards temporarily withdrew and, as the Count could now talk for a while without exhausting himself, he gave his young friend an outline of his misadventure. Having assured himself that the invalid lacked for nothing the Prince went off to see General Quiroga.

Later in the morning he returned to report that the General had had Ferrer and a number of masters at the *Escuela Moderna* arrested, and produced a list of their names. Benigno, Gérault, Zapatro, and Jovellenos were among them, but not those of Sanchez or Schmidt, and there was no mention of Dolores Mendoza. De Quesnoy asked that the last three should be picked up if possible. With the same object he also gave descriptions of the bald-headed Manuel, who had been with Ferrer when he was brought to Pedro's house. The young man with the widely-spaced eyes who had been with them was obviously Alvaro Barbestro, and he had already been caught after making his attempt on General Quiroga.

After telephoning this message to the Captain-General, de Vendôme again returned to the Count and said, 'Since several of the assassins who have reason to fear you are still at large, General Quiroga feels that the sooner you are out of Barcelona the better. The anarchist movement is so strong here that they can call on innumerable people to help them, and by killing you they could still save Ferrer and the rest, because there would then be no one to bring a case against them. In spite of the guard at your bedside, as these people are desperate they may take any risk to get you, or perhaps chuck a bomb through the window on the off-chance that you might be among its victims. There is no doubt that you would be much safer somewhere outside Catalonia.'

'But I can't leave Barcelona before I've given evidence against Ferrer and these other devils that the General has laid by the heels,' the Count protested.

De Vendôme smiled. 'There is no reason why you shouldn't. Owing to there having been so many anarchist outrages here many civil rights have for a long time been suspended. Under his powers as Captain-General of the City Quiroga can hold them on suspicion for as long as he likes. You won't be fit to go into court for several weeks yet and you can convalesce just as well elsewhere—better in fact. In any case it is my intention to move you as soon as you are up to it, and take you back to San Sebastian with me. When you are fully recovered you can return here for the trial.'

'In that case,' murmured de Quesnoy, 'by all means speak to my doctor and make whatever arrangements you like.'

That afternoon two doctors made a thorough examination of

the Count. Their verdict was that they would not normally have allowed his removal for another week; but in view of the danger to himself and, possibly, other patients in the hospital as long as he remained there, providing he did not have a relapse he could be moved after a further forty-eight hours.

On the Thursday morning de Vendôme told him the latest news from General Quiroga. It was that Dolores had been arrested at Port-Bou while attempting to get over the frontier into France; but the other two had evidently decided to take no chances and left the *Escuela Moderna* the day after the attempt on de Quesnoy. A man answering Sanchez's description was said by a booking clerk at the railway station to have taken a ticket for Granada, where he was now being hunted, and the German was known to have left Spain via Puigcerda.

It had been decided that the invalid was less likely to suffer a set-back if moved by slow trains than expresses; so instead of going down to Madrid they were to travel via Lerida, Huesca and Pamplona. In the late afternoon, having thanked all those who had looked after him, de Quesnoy was carried on a stretcher down to an ambulance and, accompanied by de Vendôme and two nurses the Prince had hired, started on the first stage of his journey.

Normally they would have had to change trains three times, but to save his friend from unnecessary jolting and exposure on station platforms de Vendôme had arranged for a special coach in which they could all eat, sleep and remain permanently until reaching San Sebastian. That this meant the coach having to be shunted into sidings and remaining there for several hours was a good rather than a bad thing, as it enabled the Count to get three long periods of complete rest during the journey. Even so, when the trains were moving, the rhythmic thudding of their turning wheels jarred the newly-set breaks in his bones and gave him the worst headache he had had for some days.

By the second day he was running a high temperature and, when in the afternoon they reached San Sebastian, de Vendôme was acutely worried about him. At the station they were met by de Cordoba, a doctor, two more nurses and one of the new motor ambulances. With it moving at little more than fifteen miles an hour, the sick man was taken the last three miles to the Conde's villa outside the town.

There Doña Gulia was waiting to welcome her invalid-guest, but he did not even recognize her, as his relapse had brought on a period of delirium. She had had one of the ground-floor rooms with french windows looking out on the garden turned into a bedroom for him, because de Vendôme had telegraphed particulars of his injuries and she had realized that with a game leg stairs would be awkward for him for some time to come. He was put to bed and everything that the doctor and nurses could do for him was done.

For a few hours he lay in a drug-induced sleep, then late in the evening became conscious for the first time since he had left the train. At the sight of the comfortably furnished room and the face of a strange nurse at his bedside he realized that the nightmare journey was over. She took his temperature, noted with relief that though still high it had gone down a point, gave him a cooling drink, then began to bathe his forehead with eau-de-Cologne. The gentle massage soothed his pain and soon he dropped off to sleep again.

Sometime during the night he had a dream. He was still in the same room and a figure was standing at his bedside. He knew instinctively that it was not that of the nurse, and as he raised his eyes to the face now bent above him he saw that it was Gulia.

The night-light on the table on the far side of his bed lit up her pale face against the frame of her Titian hair, which was parted Madonna fashion in the centre and fell in two thick plaits on either side of her matt-white cheeks. The flame of the night-light was reflected in her great dark eyes and bright enough to show the colour of her full, rich red lips. Behind her all was darkness.

As he gazed up at her he was thinking, 'How dazzling her beauty is. She is like some superb marble statue, yet it is easy to guess that in the arms of a lover she would take fire and melt in soul-shaking passion.' Then he rebuked himself. 'She is José's wife so I must not allow myself to think of her like that, even in a dream.'

The figure moved, turned a little and extended two hands. Gently they took his pillowed head between them. Their palms felt as cool as alabaster against his cheeks. Slowly the lovely head came down and for a full minute the soft, warm lips were pressed on his.

He closed his eyes, drawing in the fragrance that was now all about him. The lips and hands were gently withdrawn. When he opened his eyes the ghostly figure had disappeared. It was only a dream. It could have been only a dream. Yet he distinctly heard a click, and could have sworn that it had been made by the latch on the closing of his bedroom door.

10

The Beautiful Anarchist

IT took another thirty-six hours for de Quesnoy to make up the
ground lost through his set-back; but after that he began to recover
rapidly, and on the 10th of September he was allowed to get up
in his room for an hour in the late afternoon. Sixteen days had
elapsed since his fall, all his bruises had disappeared, the cuts
on his head had healed, his ribs and collar-bone had mended
and, owing to his excellent health, his body had made good the
blood it had lost. At times he still suffered from severe headaches,
but it was now only his broken leg that kept him a prisoner. When
the plaster cast was removed from it the doctor had pronounced
the mend to be satisfactory and it was a great relief to exchange
the rigid casing for a much more comfortable supporting bandage,
but he was not allowed until some days after that to put his foot
to the ground.

As soon as he had been in a condition to do so he had dictated
to de Cordoba a full account of all that had befallen him in Barcelona, for transmission to the King, who was in residence at San
Sebastian. From then onward the Conde and de Vendôme came
in three or four times a day to sit with him for a while, but he
knew that on many of these occasions de Cordoba would normally
have been immersed in his banking affairs and that the Prince,
in addition to certain duties he had to perform, would, while at
this seaside resort, normally be amusing himself playing tennis
or polo or bathing with parties of other young people; so as
de Quesnoy grew stronger he told them that he would soon be
about again and urged them to resume their usual activities.

After some pressing they agreed to look in on him after breakfast each morning and not make any long visits till the evenings.
It was then he learned, too, that normally the Conde's business
necessitated his spending one or two nights a week in Madrid.
But by his thought for his friends the Count penalized himself
considerably, as he was left with no one to talk to all day and
he found that reading soon brought on his headaches. Doña Gulia
often accompanied her husband or de Vendôme on visits to him,
and when she learnt that he could not read for any length of
time she volunteered to read to him. In consequence, by the time
he was well enough to leave his bed it was already an established

custom that Gulia and her duenna, Doña Eulalia, should sit with him for an hour or more in the mornings and again after the siesta.

On his second time up he was allowed to try out his crutches and, although he felt rather shaky, he managed to walk with them round the small flower-bordered patio on to which his room faced. After that he took his meals at an iron table out there and received his visitors at it.

Three days later the doctor agreed to Gulia's suggestion that it would do the patient good to have a dip in the sea, providing someone was close at hand all the time to support him should he lose his balance. A private bay lay on the far side of the house. It was a quarter-mile-wide half-moon of lovely golden sand screened at either end by pine-covered headlands. At one side of it there stood a row of gaily painted wooden huts with a group of chairs, tables and striped sun umbrellas in front of them.

A footman named Ricardo, who had been allotted to the Count as his valet, and another footman, carried him in a chair with two poles lashed to it down to one of the huts. Ricardo helped him to undress and change into a borrowed bathing dress then, acting as a human crutch, escorted him out to the surf line. As they reached it he looked back and saw Gulia emerge from one of the other huts. Her burnished hair was now hidden under a big white macintosh cap, which made her face look unusually small, and she was wearing an elaborate dark blue costume piped with white. It was of thickish material with a yoke from the shoulders and a full, short skirt; so actually much less could be seen of the upper part of her person than when she was in evening dress; but her legs, normally hidden on all occasions by long skirts, were now bare from just below the knee, and he noted that they were slender and shapely.

On the Biscay coast the sea is nearly always rough and some way out great white combers were breaking over a submerged sand-spit, but nearer inshore it was moderately calm. Even so, neither of them went far out, and on this first day the Count contented himself with paddling and sitting down in the shallows to let the waves wash over him.

Next day he found that when waist deep in the water its buoyancy enabled him to keep his balance while putting only a very little weight on his injured leg; so he was able for the first time to exercise it. The following day he went for a short swim and after his fourth bathe he limped back up the beach to the bathing hut without Richard's help.

From then onward Ricardo and Gulia's maid came down to the shore only to help them change into and out of their bathing things; but Doña Eulalia continued to be their constant companion. However, this plump and indolent ageing lady, whose function it was in the Spanish tradition to protect her beautiful young mistress from unwelcome – or welcome – attempts on her virtue, knew her place as well as her duties. From their first meeting, the strong-willed Gulia had made it plain that she did not consider it part of those duties for a duenna to participate in every conversation she might hold with her husband's men friends, and that at such times Doña Eulalia would be expected to make herself as inconspicuous as possible. Anxious to secure the comforts and good food that went with such a post in a rich household, Doña Eulalia had made no bones about agreeing.

In consequence, while she had had perforce to remain in their immediate proximity when in the bedroom or sitting out in the patio, here on the beach when after bathing they sunned themselves in deck-chairs, she sat under one of the striped umbrellas sewing or dozing a good fifty yards away from them.

As the weather continued calm and warm they now spent a good part of each day down in the bay, usually having a picnic lunch brought out to them there. Sometimes de Vendôme joined them, either alone or with a party of young friends, but for long periods they were on their own and, during them, enjoyed listening to one another's views on a great variety of subjects.

While de Quesnoy swam or limped up and down the golden sands Gulia watched him with covert glances from under her long curling eyelashes. She decided that she had never seen a more beautifully made and supple male body, and that the premature greyness that, as the result of the ordeals he had been through, now streaked his slightly wavy dark hair, added the final touch of distinction to his aquiline features. Disguising her passionate personal interest in him under the guise of normal feminine curiosity, she asked him innumerable questions about himself and these often led to political discussions.

Owing to the time de Quesnoy had spent at the *Escuela Moderna* he was now much better equipped to argue with her upon anarchism and the range of means suggested for bringing about its triumph – from the utter ruthlessness of Bakúnin and Stirner, through violent insurrections as envisaged by Kropotkin, to the peaceful propaganda advocated by Proudhon, the passive resistance of Benjamin Tucker and finally the spread of universal love hoped for by Count Tolstoi.

That she was serious in her belief in anarchism he soon had no lingering doubts; but she was not of the category that would have made even a temporary marriage of convenience with Communism. Neither did she approve of violence. It was simply that she believed that complete anarchism could eliminate poverty and that every individual had the right to live as he pleased.

To find out more about his life with Angela she frequently turned the conversation to England. Although she had never been to that country she had a great admiration for the British and on one occasion she spoke glowingly of the way in which, strong in their own freedom, they refused to be bullied by all the other great nations into refusing to give asylum to political refugees.

He said that he personally had the best of reasons to be grateful to the British on that account, but that soon such refugees might find Switzerland the only country left open to them for, although he was convinced it was not so, there had been accusations from many quarters that the attempt to assassinate King Alfonso and his Queen had been planned in London; and the British were becoming tired of being labelled accessories to murder.

'Had the attempt taken place a year ago they might have altered their law, but they won't now,' she asserted quickly. 'Sir Henry Campbell-Bannerman having ousted the Conservatives from office last December makes that a certainty. No Liberal Government would ever introduce a measure aimed at curtailing the march of humanity towards freedom.'

De Quesnoy gave her an amused glance, and said, 'I fear you are not quite so well up in British politics as you are in many other subjects. As I lived until recently for a good while in England allow me to enlighten you. Liberalism does not mean the same thing there as it does in Spain, Russia and most other Continental countries. The British Liberal party is descended from the Whigs – the great nobles of the eighteenth century who banded together to curb the powers of the Crown. Today it is true that in theory the Liberals represent the interests of the working classes, but whether that is so in fact is highly debatable.'

Having paused to light a cigarette, he went on. 'The main plank in the Liberal platform has for long been Free Trade, and with it they have won the votes of the masses in the towns because, on the face of it, their policy means cheap living. But go a little deeper into the matter and you will find that it has another altogether different aspect. The great strength of the Liberal party lies in the industrial north, and the money to finance industry

comes from the rich manufacturers and the old Whig families
who have invested their wealth in commerce. They are very shrewd
people, and they know that if they can bring the cost of living
down they will then be able to force down wages and derive bigger
profits from their factories.'

'Do you suggest, then, that the Liberal policy is nothing but an
infamous plot?' she asked indignantly.

'Not altogether,' he smiled, 'and the Liberals have introduced
many excellent reforms. But if you go deeply into the matter
you will find that Tory governments have proved better protectors
of the interests of the ordinary people. It was they who first introduced free education, it was they who put a stop to women working
in the mines, it was they who passed the first factory acts and
legislated to prevent little children being forced to labour as though
they were slaves. But to revert to the question of Britain continuing to give asylum to political firebrands from all over Europe,
the last thing the Liberals must want is for such people to spread
discontent in the industrial areas; so they are just as likely to
put up a bar to their entering the country as would be the Tories,
who in your sense of the word are more genuinely Liberal-minded.'

On another occasion they were talking about his early years
spent in Russia when she said, 'The condition of the peasants
and the poorer people must be quite appalling. One cannot wonder
that last year Father Gapon led a revolution there. I know it was
put down with ferocious brutality by the Tsar's Cossacks; but
now that the people have shown their teeth it seems unlikely
that will be the end of the matter. What do you think of their
prospects of gaining their freedom?'

'It all depends what you mean by freedom,' he smiled. 'If they
succeed in overthrowing the monarchy they certainly would not
get it. That could only lead to a blood-bath, after which they
would soon find themselves at the mercy of a committee of mob-
leaders. All revolutions develop in much the same way, and you
have only to recall how in the French Revolution the whole nation
was held in subjection by Robespierre and his Committee of Public
Safety.'

'But it worked out in the end,' she objected. 'The Terror did not
last for very long, and after it was over new laws secured to every
Frenchman his rights as an individual.'

He shrugged. 'Perhaps; but at what a price to the nation. A
million people died in the French Revolution, and that million
represented nearly all that was best in integrity, brains and leadership that had been built up through many generations.'

'Some of the nobles may have been clever, but many were stupid, and the great majority of them were parasites battening on the labour of the people.'

'I was not referring to the nobility. Most of them escaped abroad. The people who were murdered were the solid *bourgeoisie*, who had made the cities of France richer than any others, the lawyers, doctors, scientists, philosophers and the best of the junior officers in the old Army and Navy.'

'Nevertheless there was plenty of leadership shown by Frenchmen in the Napoleonic wars.'

'You mean that there were plenty of brave men prepared blindly to give their lives in battle, because when the wars started they believed their country about to be invaded and overrun. Napoleon everyone admits to have been a genius; but he was an evil one and, remember, a product of the revolution. As a dictator he forced a tyranny on the people far worse than they had suffered under their Kings, and he bled France white in wars with no other object than to achieve his own ambition to become the arbiter of Europe. It was he who took such a terrible toll of the male youth of France that he undermined the stamina of the race for generations. But it was during the Revolution that the worst damage was done. Except for self-seekers and the irresponsible the upper middle-class was virtually wiped out, and France has never recovered. She has since had two Emperors, a Directory, a Bourbon restoration, a Commune, a Constitutional Monarchy and three Republics: all within a hundred years. The strength given to a people by continuity and tradition has been lost, and for a long time now she has been at the mercy of governments formed from little groups of unscrupulous intriguers who barter the votes they control for a share of power.'

'You know too much about France for me to challenge you on what you say,' she shrugged. 'But unless the Russian people dethrone the Tsar, how can they ever hope to better their lot?'

'It is being bettered, although that is probably not apparent to people who don't know very much about Russia. In recent years a lot more power has been given to the Zemstovs – that is, the provincial assemblies. They are local parliaments that have authority to pass laws for their own areas; and after the uprising last year they combined to press the Tsar to give Russia a National Assembly as well. His Imperial Majesty consented and the first Duma met in the autumn. Nearly all its members are men of high principles and broad views; so given a little time many sound reforms should emerge from it.'

Gulia nodded. 'Yes, I read about that. But the Zemstovs can legislate only on matters concerning their own Provinces; and this new National Parliament has been given no power at all. It is only a consultative body.'

'That is more or less true,' de Quesnoy admitted. 'At the root of the trouble are, of course, the Tsar and Tsarina. They shut themselves away with a little clique of hangers-on; so they are hopelessly ill-informed and hear only opinions which lead them to believe that they are still beloved by the great majority of their subjects. Unfortunately the Tsar is ill-educated, stupid and as weak as water; while the Tsarina, who dominates him, is a convinced autocrat, both bigoted and superstitious. It is a tragedy that the throne is not occupied by the Grand Duke Nicholas, or some other Prince who is more in touch with realities.'

'About that you must be right. Anyhow, if they can keep the lid on the pot only by continuing to send thousands of people every year to exile in Siberia, sooner or later it is bound to blow off.'

He gave her a smile. 'In that, my dear Doña Gulia, you are arguing from false premises. It is only when governments show weakness that revolutions succeed. That in France might easily have been held in check had it not been that Louis XVI was too great a fool and sentimentalist to accept the advice of his courageous Queen, and would not allow his loyal troops to suppress the first revolts against his authority. What happened in England during the same period is a fair example of the results of the opposite policy.'

She shook her head. 'I fear I am not sufficiently well up in English history to know to what you are referring.'

'To the effect of the French Revolution on England. At first all classes there welcomed the changes that were taking place on the other side of the Channel, because they believed in constitutional government. It was only when the moderates were overthrown and the Royal Family imprisoned that they began to realize the menace to life, property, justice and true freedom that the revolution had become. By then the virus had spread among their own masses. Agitators started riots in all their principal cities, a mob of fifteen thousand people gathered in north London and at a great mass meeting voted for a Republic. King George III was stoned in his coach on the way to open Parliament. Fortunately for England, in the younger Pitt he had a Minister who would not allow his humanity to deter him from his duty. Pitt brought the garrisons from outlying towns into the suburbs of London, suspended Habeas Corpus, forbade gatherings of more than five persons, and made it a transportable offence to talk treason. A number of hot-heads and would-be demagogues suffered, of course; but by his firmness he saved England from a similar Terror to that which took place in France, and the great bulk of her people from years of misery.'

'Am I to understand, then, that you consider the Tsar's Government is justified in sending all those poor people to slave for life in the salt mines of Siberia, simply because they demand better conditions for the masses?'

Gulia's voice held an angry note, and de Quesnoy sought to calm her by saying quietly, 'Let us get this straight. Persons found guilty of political agitation are never sent to the salt mines. They are exiled only to some city on the far side of the Urals, to keep them from making further mischief in St. Petersburg or Moscow. While living in exile few restraints are placed upon them; they can send for their families, choose their own residence, own property, practise their trade or profession, and enjoy all reasonable freedom. It is only real criminals and people convicted of having participated in nihilist plots who are sent to the salt mines. By ridding European Russia, as far as possible, of agitators, the Government is at least keeping control of the situation. The longer it can continue to do that the better chance there is of the leaders of the Zemstovs, and of the Liberal nobility, persuading the Tsar to agree to allow the new Duma a real voice in the Government. Better conditions for the masses can only be secured by reforms brought about by legal means. I am convinced of that. We can only pray that those already advocated by the best men in Russia will be adopted in time. If they are not I fear you will prove right, and the lid will be blown off the pot. But if it is, just as happened in France, it will mean the massacre not only of the rich, but also of the Liberal-minded intellectuals who are striving to better the lot of the poor, and for the Russian masses a long period of civil war, anarchy, and a far worse tyranny than that under which they live at present.'

It was on the morning after this conversation that a telephone message was received to say that the King intended to come out to the villa. The Conde and de Vendôme had already gone into San Sebastian, so it was Gulia and de Quesnoy who received Don Alfonso. At the far end of the villa from the Count's bedroom there was another patio. Beyond both, and also between them, there extended a delightful garden, with a fountain in its centre faced by a long curved stone seat and a semi-circle of fluted columns carrying busts of Roman Emperors. There, after doing the honours with refreshments, Gulia left the two men.

'Well, my dear Count,' said the young King, 'it seems that you are extremely lucky to be alive; and I am delighted to find that the only ill-effect you now show from your terrible ordeal is a game leg. I read with the greatest interest the report that you dictated for me to José de Cordoba.'

De Quesnoy smiled. 'I thank your Majesty; and I am most grateful, too, for the gracious messages you sent me during the bad time I went through. For some days it was touch and go, but in a week or two I should be completely recovered. My only regret is that I was found out before I could secure conclusive evidence against Ferrer and his fellow assassins.'

'Yes, that was bad luck. But as things turned out their attempt to murder you has given us enough to get all those involved a life-sentence and, perhaps, linked to other charges, sufficient to justify the death penalty.' The King lit a cigarette and went on. 'In any case Alvaro Barbestro's goose is cooked because he was actually seen shooting at General Quiroga; and, I think, Ferrer's too, because you can give evidence that the plot against Quiroga was mentioned before you when they had you in the foreman miller's house, and Ferrer was present.'

'True,' murmured the Count. 'And he is the one above all others that we must endeavour to put out of the way for good. I am convinced that he is their ring-leader. He could even continue to be dangerous in prison. May I ask how matters stand at the moment?'

'Ferrer, his mistress, all his family with the exception of his younger son, and the whole staff of the *Escuela Moderna* are under arrest. The school, of course, is closed. When it was raided a considerable quantity of papers were seized, among them some letters from Morral. There is enough material, anyway, to justify holding these people on suspicion that some, if not all of them, were privy to the attempt made by Morral to assassinate me on my wedding day. Even without your evidence, Ferrer and his closest associates will have great difficulty in proving their innocence, and your testimony will make certain of their conviction.'

'When, Sir, is their trial to take place?'

'At your convenience, my friend,' smiled the King. 'After what they did to you I see no reason why they should not remain kicking their heels in prison for as long as you require treatment for your leg. Those who were not concerned in your attempted murder are tarred with the same brush as the others. Even if not guilty of active anarchism by openly expressing treasonable views, they stimulate fanatics to commit their abominable crimes.'

'I have massage for my leg every morning to get the muscles back into condition, but I think that in about another fortnight I should be finished with that.'

'Very well, then. The trial can take place towards the middle of October. It is my wish that when you go to Barcelona to attend it you should stay with General Quiroga. He will provide a special guard for your protection and you must promise me not to go out without it. The sooner, too, you can leave the city, the better.'

De Quesnoy nodded. 'It certainly seems probable that they will make another attempt to kill me. I am most grateful for your Majesty's concern for me.'

For a while they talked on; then Don Alfonso told the Count that he would be in San Sebastian until the end of the month, and added that as soon as he could move about without discomfort he must come to lunch or dine at the Palace. A few minutes later he got into a trial six-cylinder car that the new Hispano Suiza Company had just made for him, and drove away at top speed.

De Quesnoy was then carried down to the beach with Gulia walking beside him and, a little belatedly, they had their morning bathe. After it, when they had settled themselves in their deck-chairs, she remarked:

'I would not care to be in Don Alfonso's shoes.'

'Why?' he asked. 'From fear that you might be assassinated?'

'He might be at any time; but it was not of that I was thinking. That poor young man has inherited every sort of trouble. Ever since he assumed power four years ago he has been compelled to change his Government every few months. The priests are constantly at him to maintain them in sucking the people's blood and forcing bigotry upon them; the Army has been the other dominant power in Spain for so long that the Generals show open resentment at every reform proposed for it; and in opposition to the other two the Liberals never cease to press him to introduce more democratic measures. It needs only a really serious clash between the Right and Left to start another of our civil wars. If that happened he would lose his throne.'

'I think you unduly pessimistic,' de Quesnoy replied. 'He is intelligent, courageous and has already won the love of the great mass of his people. He has also shown a tact in handling his Ministers that is quite astonishing in one so young. I should be much surprised if he does not find the means for keeping the Blacks, Whites and Reds from one another's throats.'

'He may as long as he does not feel himself to be personally involved. But he can be very high-handed and is extraordinarily pigheaded on some matters, such as the prerogatives of the Crown. Yet, unless he is prepared to sacrifice some part of what he considers to be his rights, a time is certain to come when he will find a great part of the nation against him. Another thing: now that he is a fully-grown man women will begin to play a part in his life and an evil or arrogant one could have a disastrous influence upon him.'

'He is certainly handsome enough for any number of pretty baggages to throw themselves at his head,' the Count said with a smile, 'and as time goes on they will, of course. At present he is said to be deeply in love with his Queen, but one can hardly expect that to last for ever. After all, it's more or less a tradition that Kings are entitled to amuse themselves with mistresses as a relaxation from the burdens of State; so no one will count him much to blame if his name becomes coupled with that of one or more lovely ladies. But I see no reason why he should allow them to dominate him.'

'Just think of his ancestry,' Gulia exclaimed.

'His father was far from being a bad King, and his mother is a most admirable woman in every way: both wise and saintly.'

'That his father's first wife, Mercedes, happened to be his Queen does not alter the fact that he allowed himself to become so besotted about her that when she died he lost interest in everything. And look at his grandmother, Isabella II. There was a born whore if ever there was one. She chose the succession of Generals whom she allowed to ruin the country as though they were stallions, and put each through his paces in her bed.'

Unnoticed by Gulia, de Quesnoy gave her a sidelong glance, as she hurried on. 'Then her mother, Maria Cristina. She was so obsessed with her Captain of the Guards that she had nine children by him, and all of them in secret. When the last of them was only a few hours old she had to put on her State robes and read her official speech at an opening of the Cortes. If allowing oneself to be forced into such a position is not enslavement to passion, tell me what is?'

'Poor woman,' the Count commented. 'But you are right, of course, that the Bourbon blood is particularly easily inflamed. We can only hope that Don Alfonso's share of it will not become overheated to the detriment of himself and his country.'

Meanwhile he was thinking how surprising it was that Doña Gulia should have compared Generals to stallions and spoken of the Queen putting them through their paces in her bed. In high society and mixed company only the most oblique references were ever made to such matters, while it was unheard of for a lady even to mention such a subject when conversing alone with one of her husband's men friends. He then remembered that his parents were middle-class intelligentsia, and that such people, while highly respectable, regarded it as hypocrisy to hedge themselves about with unnatural prudery. Not being a hypocrite himself, he decided that it was refreshing to talk to a beautiful and intelligent woman who was not ashamed to speak her thoughts with frankness. And that was precisely the effect that Gulia had intended her words to have upon him.

After a few more days the Count's leg was strong enough for him to walk unaided in the garden or down to the beach, and de Vendôme suggested that it would make a change for him to go in to San Sebastian. Gulia and Doña Eulalia accompanied them and after leaving the two ladies to do some shopping the Prince drove on through the old town, then along the coast road which almost encircles Monte Urgull, the great castle-topped hill that dominates the harbour, the bay of La Concha, and the city. Pulling up at the road's extremity they sat for a while, now facing inland, to watch the yachts tacking in the bay with, beyond them, the long curved beach of golden sand swarming with holiday-makers enjoying the September sunshine, and at its furthest extremity Monte Izueldo, on a lower slope of which, set in its lovely garden, stood the Royal Palace of Miramar.

Next day they lunched there with the King and afterwards watched him play polo. Soon after they entered the reserved enclosure a number of Gulia's friends came up to her in turn. All of them asked where she had been for the past three weeks and reproached her for declining invitations they had sent her. She explained that she had been looking after a guest who had been seriously ill, and introduced de Quesnoy to them. This resulted in a dozen invitations to lunches, dinners and bathing parties; but each trip in de Vendôme's car had brought on one of the Count's headaches, so he begged to be excused from any social engagements until he had had a further week's convalescence.

Afterwards, while watching the game, his headache wore off, and he wondered a little uneasily if his refusal had been less due to that than a preference for spending long hours on the Cordobas' private beach with Gulia rather than to re-enter the social whirl.

That evening an episode occurred which gave him further cause for some uneasiness. For some time past he had been well enough to change and dine with the family, and at dinner that night de Vendôme remarked to Gulia:

'I hear you have put off the Villalobars from coming to stay. Isn't that rather a pity? It was so jolly here in August with the house full of people; but for quite a time now we've had no company at all – not even a dinner party.'

De Cordoba promptly replied for his wife. 'My dear boy, you seem to forget that we have had other things to occupy us. When our friend Armand arrived he was at death's door; so naturally we got rid of the people who were staying here then as soon as we decently could.'

'Naturally,' agreed the Prince. 'I should have been the last to expect you to do otherwise. But he has been well enough to enjoy talking to other people for quite a while now, and I should have thought you might open up the house again.'

'Yes,' de Cordoba nodded, 'I see no reason why we shouldn't.' Then he glanced at his wife and added, 'Why did you put the Villalobars off, Gulia? After all, it was a long-standing engagement.'

She shrugged the superb shoulders that rose from her green chiffon frock and replied, 'Having cancelled our invitations to half a dozen other people during the past three weeks I suppose it has become a habit, and I did it without thinking. But, anyway, the burden of entertaining falls much more heavily on the hostess than you men realize, and I've been very glad of the respite.'

De Quesnoy had been about to express his regret that his presence there should have upset their autumn programme, but in view of Gulia's last remark he felt that it might be a little tactless to do so. As far as the other two were concerned he felt no qualms of conscience. The Conde, when not immersed in big financial deals, was always happy to go off on expeditions to hunt butter-flies for his collection, and the young Prince led a very full life. Being deeply religious he spent several hours a day at his devotions, and in the rôle of an extremely active President on the councils of numerous Church charities; then he was frequently in attendance on the King and for the rest of the time enjoying himself at parties, mostly in Biarritz, since far greater numbers of the Spanish nobility spent this season of the year over the frontier in the smart French watering-place than in San Sebastian.

However, after their bathe next morning he did raise the matter with Gulia by saying, 'In spite of what you said at dinner last night about entertaining meaning a lot of hard work for the hostess, I fear that devoting your time to me, as you have during my convalescence, must have deprived you of a lot of enjoyment. Even if you hadn't had people here to stay, you must have refused many invitations to luncheons and dinners, and could often have driven into Biarritz.'

'No,' she replied. 'I can see most of my friends any time and a great many of the invitations come from acquaintances whom I wouldn't mind if I never saw again. In Spain, as you must know, except over a luncheon or dinner table women of my class are given little opportunity to converse with men. We are expected to be quite happy making small talk with our own sex; and you can have no idea how ill-educated, stupid, narrow-minded and altogether boring most of the women of the best families can be.'

'From having met a number of them I think I can,' he smiled.

'Then you will understand how greatly I have enjoyed escaping from them to be with you.'

'In spite of the fact that if we carried our political beliefs to their logical conclusions we would cut one another's throats?' he twitted her.

She laughed. 'Yes, in spite of that. After all, politics aren't everything in life. There is another side to it, the personal one; and that is much more important.'

'I agree; and we certainly have a great many things in common.'

'We have; but I should never have found that out if you had not been temporarily incapacitated for ordinary activities, which has led to us spending so many hours alone together. You can't think how I shall miss our talks when you have gone.'

'And I shall too.' He spoke with complete honesty. 'There can be few women of your age who have such a good brain – except perhaps for professional blue-stockings – and as far as I am concerned they don't count. To have heard sound argument on a great variety of subjects coming from the lips of a woman of your beauty and distinction has been a wonderful experience, and one that I shall long remember.'

'Thank you for the compliment,' she smiled. Then, with a little sigh, she added: 'I don't get many these days.'

'Then I'm to blame for that. It's because you have given so much of your time to me instead of getting out and about.'

She shook her head impatiently. 'I don't mean the vapid expressions of admiration with which I am bombarded by José's friends. I was thinking of the honest compliments that I used to receive before I married, from young professors and women who were making something of their lives.'

5 *

'None of us can have everything,' de Quesnoy brought out the old platitude philosophically, 'and surely the acknowledgement of your mental attainments while living in your uncle's circle at the University cannot have meant more to you than being the Condesa de Cordoba.'

'I suppose not,' she murmured a shade uncertainly.

'Oh, come!' he rallied her. 'You have palaces, servants, jewels and beautiful clothes. You bear one of the greatest names in Spain, and that of a charming and intelligent man who adores you.'

Suddenly she turned her head and looked straight at him. Her big dark eyes held his as she asked, 'What grounds have you for assuming that he does?'

For a moment de Quesnoy was nonplussed, then he answered a shade uncertainly, 'Well, it is obvious that José has no interests other than his bank, his butterflies and yourself.'

'Ah!' her eyes flashed. 'You would have been nearer the mark, my friend, if you had stopped short at "butterflies". To have a flutter with his favourite specimen is his real reason for going each week to Madrid.'

There was no mistaking her meaning, and the Count felt acutely embarrassed. The very last thing he wished to do was to discuss with her the private relations between her husband and herself, and he thought it in the worst possible taste for her to have let him have even a glimpse of them.

Yet, after a moment he found excuses for her. Although she looked the part of a youthful great lady to perfection, she was not so by birth. She had been brought up in a very different atmosphere: one in which people were guided more by reason than by inherited prejudice, and were courageous enough to say what they thought frankly – even if it meant being sent to prison. She was a clever woman forced to choose her friends from a circle of, mostly, pleasant fools. She was by nature independent, but now shackled even in her home to a duenna. She was an anarchist in theory and a Republican by conviction, who lived surrounded by die-hard Monarchists.

It struck him, too, that she had paid him the rare compliment of confiding to him her views on many matters; views that she could not possibly have aired to her husband, much less her sister-in-law, the Infanta, or any of the people with whom she came in frequent contact. For some reason that he did not attempt to fathom she had singled him out from all the others and treated him as a trusted friend. If, then, she now wished to tell him of her private life, and he refused to listen, it would destroy the delightful bond that had been established between them and hurt her grievously. After all her kindness to him he could not possibly do that.

Having swiftly collected his thoughts, he said, 'You mean that José keeps a mistress?'

She nodded. 'Yes. I found out only by accident. I came upon a letter from her which he had most stupidly left lying among some other papers he gave me to look through. When I charged him with it he did not deny it. I gather that she is an Andalusian dancing girl and quite a star turn with the castanets.'

De Quesnoy was mildly surprised to learn that his staid friend kept a mistress, but it did not even occur to him to doubt Gulia's statement. Although it was no longer considered *comme il faut* for a noble openly to take pride in being the accepted lover of some leading ballerina or song-bird of the opera, it was still an age in which all over Europe great numbers of rich men, more or less secretly, kept pretty young women in small houses or pleasant apartments; and their wives had been brought up to accept such a situation as nothing to make a great fuss about.

Meanwhile Gulia was going on. 'I feel sure that he conducts his *affaire* most discreetly, and would not admit to it even among his best friends. But he did not marry until getting on in life, and I suppose having a girl who is outside his own circle with whom he can entirely relax had become a habit with him.'

'How long ago is it since you found out?' the Count inquired.

'Just on fifteen months, but I imagine that it had been going on for a long time before that; or if not with this particular woman, then with others.'

'And how long have you been married to him?'

'A little over three years.'

That was not very long, de Quesnoy reflected. But he knew well enough that a man who for twenty years or so had lived with a succession of pretty women could still tire of one who was exceptionally beautiful in a comparatively short time. Only a mental bond created by true love could hold a couple together for a long period of years, and evidently no such bond had been created between José and Gulia. It could only be that he had desired her, marriage had been her price, and she had accepted him for the wealth and position she would enjoy as his Condesa. After a moment, de Quesnoy asked:

'Did you not make an effort to persuade José to break off this liaison?'

She shook her Titian gold curls which, after taking off her
bathing cap, fell like an aureole round her pale face. 'No, I fear
I was too proud for that. I told him that I would not share his
embraces with any woman, and drove him from my room. I told
him that I would not allow him to return to it until he could give
me his word that he had decided for good to give up sleeping
with harlots. But he never has.'

While she spoke she was looking away from de Quesnoy, and
his glance ran over her as she lounged in the deck-chair. She had
a face and figure that might even have tempted Saint Ignatius
Loyola to rise from his shrine at not far distant Pamplona. 'What
a waste,' he thought. 'What a waste, for this divine creature to
be leading the life of a nun.'

At that moment Ricardo came over to tell them that their
luncheon, which they were having on a table outside the bathing
huts, was now ready; so the conversation proceeded no further.

It was Ricardo who, a few days later when helping the Count
to dress, told him that an intruder had been seen the previous
night in the garden. The old man who planted and tended it with
the assistance of two youths had left his cottage to walk across it
to his potting shed for the purpose of sowing some seeds in boxes,
because he subscribed to the ancient belief that certain plants
thrived better if their seed was inserted in earth by moonlight.

He had come upon the intruder outside the drawing-room,
peering into it through a chink between the curtains. On hearing
him approach, the man had turned and run off; but the gardener
had seen him well enough to be certain that he was no one employed about the place, and described him as a tall, broad-shouldered
dark man in his early twenties.

Later in the day de Cordoba discussed the occurrence with
de Quesnoy and they speculated on whether the fellow was a local
rogue contemplating burglary, or an anarchist who had learned
the Count's whereabouts and had come from Barcelona with the
object of endeavouring to put him out of the way.

Fearing that the latter might be the case, the Conde was in
favour of asking for police protection for his guest, but de Quesnoy
said that to have police constantly about the place would be unpleasant for everybody, and declared that he was again quite
strong enough to take care of himself. But he willingly accepted the
loan of de Cordoba's revolver to keep handy in his bedside cupboard.

On Monday the 27th the Conde again left for Madrid. That
day de Quesnoy motored into San Sebastian with de Vendôme

to lunch again with the King, but on this occasion Gulia, not having been included in the command, remained at home. This time the Count found the Queen also present. He had known her as Princess Ena, but it was the first time he had seen her since her wedding, just previous to which, on accepting the Catholic faith, she had taken the name of Victoria Eugenie. He thought that in spite of her youth she looked amazingly regal and, with her mass of golden hair piled high above her milk and roses complexion, indisputably beautiful; so it was no wonder that her husband was in love with her.

She received him very graciously, condoned with him on his accident and congratulated him on his recovery. Don Alfonso also remarked that with his sun-tanned face he now looked the picture of health, and that his limp was hardly noticeable. The King then took him aside and told him that the trial of the Barcelona anarchists had been fixed to open on Monday, October the 11th.

After lunch de Vendôme accompanied the King into Biarritz, where they were to play polo that day, but de Quesnoy excused himself from joining their party because had he crossed the frontier into France he would have risked arrest. Instead he spent the afternoon strolling and sitting in the delightful Miramar gardens with other luncheon guests who had not wished to go to Biarritz. Later he went down into the town, did some shopping for himself, bought a huge box of chocolates for Gulia, and returned to the de Cordoba villa in a hired carriage.

Before changing for dinner, when the weather was fine, the family always had drinks out in the garden by the fountain. Gulia and Doña Eulalia were already seated there when he returned. After presenting the chocolates and receiving Gulia's smiling thanks, he helped himself to a glass of Manzanilla, then gave them an account of the luncheon party. A few minutes later Doña Eulalia tactfully remarked that the light was failing and carried her work and the Moscardo she was drinking off to the back porch of the house, in which a lamp had been lit. De Quesnoy continued to tell Gulia about his afternoon, then for a while they talked of various things.

It was just before they were due to go in to change that she inquired casually, 'Do you ever have dreams?'

'Yes,' he replied. 'Not very often, but occasionally.'

With a smile she asked, 'Have you ever dreamed about me?'

'As a matter of fact I have, once,' he admitted. 'It was on the night that I was brought here.'

She arched her eyebrows. 'Really. I hope it was a nice dream?'

'It was . . . very.' He finished his second glass of sherry. 'I was terribly ill, of course. You appeared at my bedside like a ministering angel from Heaven. After you had gone my fever seemed to abate and I felt much better.'

Rising from the stone seat, she picked up the big box of chocolates and said, 'Ah well; perhaps sometime I will make another appearance in your dreams.'

That night he woke out of a sound sleep. The house was very still and the room was faintly lit by moonlight coming through the french windows. He heard a soft rustle and, fearing an attack, turned swiftly on his other side. She was standing by his bed again.

11

Bedroom Scene at Midnight

FOR a moment de Quesnoy remained absolutely still. This, he knew, was no dream, and the full implication of her midnight visit rushed upon him. Yet his words denied it. Sitting up with a jerk, he exclaimed:

'Gulia! What are you doing here?'

She smiled at him. 'Need you ask?'

The moonlight filtering between the pillars of the patio outside and coming through the french window was sufficient for him to see her quite clearly. Her hair, as on the previous occasion, was parted in the centre, Madonna fashion, and fell in long plaits on either side of her pale face. She was wearing a dressing-gown of dark material, the collar and cuffs of which were trimmed with heavy lace. As she spoke she put out her hands to take his.

'Yes,' he murmured, ignoring her gesture. 'Yes, I know why you've come. But . . .'

'But what? You love me, Armand. I know you do. And I love you.'

'I . . . After our long days together, I feared it might be so.'

'You feared it. Why? To love and to be loved. What is there in life more glorious than that? You do love me, don't you?'

He drew a deep breath. 'Yes, Gulia. I confess it. I would not be human if being constantly with you all through the past month had not played the very devil with my emotions.'

She smiled again. 'Oh sweet confession. I knew it; but what joy to hear you say it. I will confess, too. I've loved you since the first moment I set eyes on you. How I have managed to control my impatience until you were really well again, I cannot think. But now, at last, I am here. To have your arms about me will be no longer a restless dream but a divine reality.'

'No, Gulia; no!' He gave a violent shake of his head. 'However much we love one another, we can't, we mustn't. There is José.'

'What of him?' Her dark eyes flashed and a sudden note of anger crept into her voice. 'I have already told you that he is nothing to me. Nothing!'

'My dear, he is your husband, and . . .'

'He is no longer so. He lost that right when I found him out. Since then I have looked on my body as my own, to do as I will with.'

Again he shook his head, but she went on swiftly. 'As things are between him and me what difference does it make that we are still married? If you and I were deeply religious that would be a different matter. For priest-ridden women who live like nuns for the rest of their lives after their husbands have deserted them, I have only contempt. And you, Armand. I cannot believe that you mean to repel me because you fear to be troubled by remorse at having committed adultery.'

'Adultery, no,' he gave a grim little laugh. 'On that score I've already plenty to answer for. Yet in such cases as I have made love to married women, it has proved no burden on my conscience. You speak, though, of my repelling you. How can you use such a word when you must know that I'm aching to embrace you?'

'Oh my darling!' she gave a quick sigh of relief. 'For a moment you really frightened me. I thought that through some foolish scruple you were about to drive me from you.'

Again she put out her arms and now stooped her head towards his.

His pulses were racing and his brain in a turmoil. He was a virile man and had known no woman since Angela's death, now four months ago. And here was this most lovely creature, whose charm and mind and body all combined to make her so utterly desirable, offering herself to him.

With a desperate effort he fought down his desire, brushed her outstretched hands aside, rolled over and slipped out of the far side of the bed.

'Armand!' she cried, her voice sharp with renewed fear that, after all, she was about to lose him.

'No, Gulia! No!' he gasped, now facing her across the bed. 'You did not let me finish just now when I said that José was your husband. I was about to add that he is also my friend.'

'Your friend. Yes, of course,' she replied impatiently. 'But what of it? You have just admitted that you have several times committed adultery with other women. The husbands of some of them must have been your friends.'

He shook his head. 'You are wrong there. Some were acquaintances, but none my friends. I have never taken the wife of a friend, and never will.'

'Then you shall tonight.' She spoke softly now, but with quiet determination. 'You have admitted that you want me.'

'Of course I do. I am half mad for you, but . . .'

'Then I'll not let you rob yourself and me of the bliss we could know together.' As she spoke she undid her dressing-gown and let it fall to the floor. With his heart beating like a sledgehammer he watched her walk round the foot of the bed towards him.

She was wearing a nightgown of pale blue chiffon. It was goffered under the breasts to accentuate their outline, but otherwise absolutely plain and transparent. When she came round the end of the bed he saw the full perfection of her body, and his breath caught in his throat.

As she approached he backed a little towards the window, but she took a quick step forward, placed both her hands on his shoulders, and murmured: 'Armand, I beseech you to be sensible. José will never know. What difference can it make to him?'

'That's not the point,' he muttered thickly. He was trembling now and made no move to push her hands from his shoulders. 'Not the point. It is that . . . that he trusts me. If he did not he would never have allowed us to spend so much time virtually alone together. I . . . I can't betray him.'

'Darling, he left us alone because he does not care. He is happy with his dancing girls, and you know yourself that he is not mean-spirited. Naturally he would be furious if I openly disgraced him by taking a lover, or even getting myself talked about. But what the eye does not see the heart does not grieve over. He wouldn't wish to know that I had been unfaithful to him, but he would not grudge me a little happiness; and less so if it was with a man like yourself whom he respects and admires. It would not surprise me if he half suspects that we have already become lovers. No

man who really minds about his wife would have given another
the opportunities that he has given you to persuade me to become
your mistress.'

It was a point of view that had not occurred to de Quesnoy.
Perhaps, he thought, she is right. José must realize that she is
made of flesh and blood, and now, at twenty-three, subject to
all the urges of a fully-developed woman. Since he neglects her,
how could he expect her to remain chaste. And I suppose most
men, if left with her day after day, would have had few scruples
about doing their best to persuade her to go to bed with them.
Perhaps I am making a mountain out of a molehill, and throwing
away this wonderful thing for a point of honour that, in the circumstances, José himself would find laughable.

The heady scent she was wearing came like incense to his nostrils.
The nearness of her body set his own on fire. Her eyes fixed on
his were moist with desire; her red lips were a little parted showing
her teeth gleaming white. She slid her arms over his shoulders and
held her flower-like face up for his kiss.

Yet from somewhere inside him he almost heard a voice say,
'This is forbidden. She is my friend's wife. He has trusted me with
her. I have no right to assume that he would not mind if I took
her. That he will never know makes no difference. I shall still have
lost my own self-respect.'

He put up his hands to break her hold and push her from him,
determined now that, whatever she might say, he would resist
temptation. As he moved, her eyes shifted from his to a point over
his left shoulder and she gave a sudden cry.

Turning his head he looked towards the window. From behind
the central pillar of the patio a man had emerged. He was standing now within two feet of the right hand panel of the french
window with something that looked like a black box held up to
his face.

Next second there came a blinding flash. Instantly de Quesnoy's
muscles tensed themselves to meet the shock of the explosion.
For a moment the room and the portico were as bright as on
the brightest day. The light was blinding and for seconds after it
went out he could see the outline of the window and the man
outside it silhouetted in dead black against a deep orange background. But no explosion followed; the window remained un-
shattered. No deadly fragments of glass and iron came whizzing
through the air to tear the flesh of Gulia and himself to ribbons.

It was only when the black and orange dissolved into grey,
and he could see again the familiar features of that side of the

room, that he realized what had happened. It had been no bomb
that the man had set off, but a magnesium flare, and the box-
like thing he had been holding up before his face had been a
camera.

Thrusting Gulia from him, de Quesnoy cried, 'Back to your
room! Don't lose an instant! I'm going after him. The flash and
the noise may wake someone. You must not be found here.'

Before he had finished speaking he had the window open. He
had not forgotten the revolver in his bedside cupboard, but feared
that if he paused to collect it he would lose track of the intruder.
Dashing across the little patio, he halted a second to glance right
and left. To his right, now thirty yards away, he glimpsed between
two groups of palms a dark figure running hard. Launching himself forward he raced down the gravel path. His feet were bare
so the stones cut into them but in the emergency of the moment
he hardly noticed that.

As the man ahead crossed the open space by the fountain, the
Count had a better sight of him. He was taller and had a longer
stride so de Quesnoy's hopes of overtaking him dwindled. For a
second he thought of rousing the household by shouts of 'Stop
thief'; but to do so could not have brought help in time and if
Gulia had not at once obeyed him her presence at the end of the
house in which his bedroom lay might lead to most unwelcome
speculations among the servants.

When he reached the fountain luck came to his aid. His quarry
had taken a short cut across some flower-beds to reach a partly
open wrought-iron gate between two pillars in a tall yew hedge.
Failing to see in the semi-darkness that in the centre of one of
the beds there lay a shallow lily pool, the leaves of the plants
in which almost covered its surface so that no gleam of moonlight
showed on the water, he splashed right into it, tripped and fell.

He scrambled to his feet but had lost a precious minute in
which de Quesnoy had thrown all his strength into a spurt. Before
the man could jump clear of the pond the Count was on him and
they fell in a tangled heap together.

The pond was one of a pair at that end of the garden. It contained only miniature aquatic plants, so was no more than six
feet by four and about eight inches deep. The man's legs and
body were half submerged in it but his head and shoulders were
on dry ground. He was on his back with de Quesnoy on top of
him, and the pale moonlight now revealed his features. He was
Sanchez Ferrer.

'I thought it might be you . . .' panted the Count, as he strove to get a grip on Sanchez's throat, '. . . from the description of the man . . .'

He got no further, but gave a sudden grunt. Sanchez had brought up his right leg with a violent jerk and kneed him in the stomach. The breath was driven from his body. Automatically he let go of Sanchez's neck, doubled up and rolled over gasping with agony. The strapping young anarchist kicked his legs free from the Count's body, struggled up into a sitting position, and whipped out a knife from a sheath under his cummerbund.

Staring upward with bulging eyes, de Quesnoy saw his danger. The twisting muscles of his stomach were still paining him fiercely. He was still incapable of fighting back. His heart missed a beat as Sanchez raised the knife to stab downwards with it. By a super-human effort he threw himself sideways. The knife, aimed to bury itself beneath his ribs, passed under his arm as he flung himself over, and buried itself in a wire basket containing a lily root.

With a curse, Sanchez jerked upon it to pull it free. At the second tug it came out, but he had had to exert so much strength on it that he went over backwards. In a second he was sitting upright again, but even that brief respite had enabled de Quesnoy to draw a little air down into his tortured lungs. As Sanchez raised the knife to stab with it again, the Count's hand shot up and grasped his wrist.

There ensued a tense, silent struggle that lasted a full minute. But de Quesnoy's slim fingers were as strong as steel. Gradually he twisted and forced back his would-be murderer's wrist. Sanchez let out a blasphemous oath, and the knife tinkled on the stone surround of the lily pool.

Flexing his knees, Sanchez heaved himself upright. Still clutching his wrist, the Count was dragged up on to his knees after him. But now he made a fatal error. Slung from a long strap over the anarchist's shoulder there dangled the black leather box that held the camera. It was that, with the damning photograph it must contain, that de Quesnoy felt it all-important to secure. Leaving go of Sanchez's wrist, he made a grab at the box, but missed it.

In an instant Sanchez had turned and, with head down, was again racing towards the wrought-iron gate. Floundering to his feet de Quesnoy dragged them from the mud of the pool and went pelting after him. Ignoring all obstacles Sanchez plunged into a bed of flowering shrubs. His having to force his way through them enabled de Quesnoy to catch him up. Again, the Count made a snatch at the camera case. He missed it, but his fingers grasped the loose skirt of Sanchez's light cotton jacket. Halting in his tracks he attempted to pull the anarchist back by it. There came a tearing sound but the piece of material that he had clutched was wrenched from his hand, and Sanchez bounded forward on to the path on the far side of the bed.

De Quesnoy burst his way through the bushes in pursuit; but it was now his turn to be brought up in mid-career by the unexpected. His foot caught on an exposed root. He was flung violently forward and came down flat across the path, his chin striking one of the stones that formed its further edge. Again the breath was driven out of his body, and the blow to his chin temporarily knocked him out.

It was some minutes before he was sufficiently recovered to pick himself up, and by then he knew that any further attempt to pursue Sanchez would be futile.

As he scrambled painfully to his feet his eye fell upon a nearly square white object lying in the middle of the path. On touching it he realized that it was a piece of cardboard. It was almost four inches long by three wide. Turning it over, he saw it to be a portrait, and the moonlight was just sufficient for him to make out that it was of a woman. Evidently when he had seized Sanchez's coat and dragged upon it, the tear had also ripped the inside pocket and the photograph had fallen out of it.

Carefully now, a lump rising on his chin, his knees grazed and the soles of his bare feet on the sharp ground causing him to wince with every step he took, he made his way back towards his bedroom.

As he approached the house he saw Gulia leaning out of an upstairs window. She called softly down to him, 'Armand; what happened? I pray God you're not hurt.'

'No,' he called back. 'I'm all right; but he got away. It was Sanchez Ferrer. I'll tell you all about it in the morning.'

Going inside, he looked at the portrait under the light. It was of a gipsy dancer, and had been taken by a photographer in Granada. Getting out fresh night clothes he changed out of his mud-covered ones into them, then went along to the cloakroom off the hall to wash himself and bathe his hurts. Back in his room he lowered himself into the armchair and considered for a while what was best to be done.

As it was impossible to guess even in which direction Sanchez had made off it was pointless to telephone the police. Moreover, the police were the last people that de Quesnoy now wished to bring into the matter. He knew little about photography, but was inclined to suppose that it was by no means easy to take good pictures by artificial light; so that taken by Sanchez might not come out. On the other hand it was unlikely that he would have taken it if he had not thought there was a good chance that it would. And if it did it could lead to most appalling trouble.

Gulia, in her transparent nightgown, had been as near naked as made no matter, and she had been facing the window. At the angle from which the picture had been taken his body would probably have shielded one side of her, but as she was nearly as tall as he was her face must have appeared in it over his shoulder, and she had had her arms round his neck. It compromised both of them beyond all possible argument, and for it to fall into the hands of the police would be nearly as bad as if it were shown straight away to José. Therefore, by hook or by crook he must get the negative back.

On re-examining the photograph that Sanchez had dropped he saw that on the back there were scrawled a number of letters and numbers, in most cases having dashes between them. But he could think of no clue to these hieroglyphics.

Glancing at the clock on the mantelpiece, he saw that it was now a quarter past two; so if he woke at six he could still get in the best part of four hours' sleep. Getting into bed he put out the light.

Gulia's visit had greatly disturbed him, but he was decidedly relieved that he had not allowed her to persuade him to make love to her; and Sanchez's appearance on the scene had now given him an excuse to escape further situations in which her beauty might lead him to succumb to temptation. He felt no righteous glow in having rejected her advances. On the contrary he was inclined to think that in refusing so lovely a gift of the gods he might, at times, look back with regret on this lost opportunity to take as his mistress a woman so gifted in so many ways; but at least he was able to go to sleep without any twinge of conscience.

As a soldier, he had long since trained himself to wake at any hour, and within a few minutes of six he opened his eyes. A slight ache in his chin recalled to him at once the events that had taken place during the night and for a short while he lay turning them over in his mind. Then he got out of bed, put on his dressing-gown and walked along to the library. There, he wrote two letters. Both were to Gulia. The first ran:

Dear Doña Gulia,
The intruder who was seen in the garden two nights ago was here again last night. He made an attempt to get into my room,

but fortunately the noise he made trying to force the lock of the window woke me. I jumped out of bed, chased him through the garden and caught, but failed to hold him. (I fear that as a result of our encounter one of your lily pools has suffered sadly.) However, the light was good enough for me to identify him as Sanchez Ferrer.

He will naturally expect me to report the occurrence to the police, as a result of which the San Sebastian district would become too hot to hold him; so the odds are that he will go into hiding again further afield. Last time he was in danger of arrest the police had reason to believe that he went to earth in Granada, and during our struggle last night he dropped a photograph taken in Granada, which makes it as good as certain that he did. But he cannot know that the police suspect that he has a hide-out there so I think it highly probable that he will return to it.

Having considered turning the matter over to the police I have decided against that. There would certainly be delays while statements are taken and passed on to Granada, and it is most unlikely that any of the Granada police could identify Sanchez on sight. Therefore, with the aid of the photograph he dropped, if I act promptly I consider that I stand a better chance of laying him by the heels myself.

Please forgive me for not delaying to make my formal adieux to you, but I am loath to disturb you so early in the morning and must leave the house soon after eight if I am to catch the nine-five for Madrid. (There is just a chance, too, that Sanchez may be on it.)

One more thing. As a knife will be found in or near the lily pool it would be foolish of me to conceal from you that Sanchez attempted to kill me. In consequence, if my idea is correct and I run him to earth in Granada, there is always the possibility that in another attempt he might prove more successful, or that I might be laid up there for a while with another wound.

Therefore, just in case anything prevents my returning to San Sebastian, I would like to express how deep is my gratitude to you, to José and to François for the wonderful care you have taken of me since I was brought to you as a shattered wreck. That I am whole and strong again so soon is due entirely to the unceasing thought that you have so generously given to my nursing and well being. It is a debt that I shall never be able to repay. But I have every hope of returning safely from Granada and later expressing the above sentiments to you in person.

My affectionate regards to you, to José and to François.

Your most devoted and grateful friend,

Armand de Quesnoy.

P.S. There seems nothing to be gained by my going secretly to

Granada; so please tell José that if he wishes to get in touch with me I shall be staying at the new Alhambra Palace Hotel under my own name.

His second letter ran:

My very dear Gulia,

It is imperative that the police should not be brought into this. Sanchez got away with his camera and if it is humanly possible I must get hold of it myself before anyone else sets eyes on the film that it contains.

Why he should have taken a photograph instead of trying to shoot me puzzled me a lot; but I think I have found the answer. To shoot anyone through a thick pane of glass is a chancy business, as the odds are very high on the bullet being deflected and failing to hit its intended victim. Moreover, a shot would have aroused the house and he might have been caught. In any case the whole police force of San Sebastian would have been alerted and on the look-out for him before he could get away from the district.

The probability is that he has been snooping about the place for a fortnight or more. If so he must have seen us many times virtually alone together on the beach and in the garden, and come to the conclusion that we were having an affaire. The idea of blackmail would then automatically have come to his mind, because he told me himself, when he believed me to be an anarchist sympathizer, that for some months past he had been successfully blackmailing an unfortunate Marquesa in Barcelona. His next step would then have been to conceal himself for a number of nights in succession outside the patio which gives on to my bedroom hoping that a chance would arise for him to get a compromising photograph of us.

The obvious assumption is that, if he succeeded, he would use it to demand money. But I do not think that in this case that was his intention or, if so, only as a secondary object of his plan. I have good grounds to believe that the Ferrer family are most strongly united. In any case, the two brothers are devoted to one another, and I feel convinced that Sanchez's mind at the present time is dominated by the wish to save his brother and father.

It may be that he thinks that with this photograph he will be able to blackmail me into refusing to give evidence against them at their forthcoming trial. But to make sure of that, even if I promised not to, would be difficult because it is quite certain that I shall be subpoenaed. My guess is, therefore, that he intends to use the photograph as bait – to lure me into a situation where he, probably aided by several of his anarchist associates, can kill me without risk of being caught.

If I am right, in the course of the next day or two a letter will arrive here for me enclosing a copy of the photograph with a demand for money in exchange for the negative, and directions where I am either to meet him or leave the money.

It is of the utmost importance that you should secure this letter on its arrival so as to guard against any possible chance of its being opened by anyone in error. Destroy the photograph and send the letter on to me at the Alhambra Palace. But with a little luck, aided by the clue to finding him that he dropped during our struggle, by then I shall have located him, taken him by surprise and dealt with him.

And now, my very dear Gulia, what can I say to you other than that I was moved to the depths of my being by all you said to me last night, and that I count your honour as dear to me as my own. Be sure that I will stick at nothing to secure this accursed photograph that now menaces it.

> *I kiss your hands,*
> *Armand.*

Having read the two letters through, he felt that they should serve their respective purposes adequately and that the last paragraph of the more personal one would cause her to feel less badly about his having left without saying good-bye to her. That he had a good excuse to do so was a great relief to him; for, their scene during the night having ended without his either definitely refusing or agreeing to become her lover, he felt sure that had they met again that morning, even for a few moments, she would have done her utmost to extract from him a promise about the future.

To make it would, he knew, have been a hideous temptation. Moreover, realizing from his feelings for her what she must feel about him, he doubted if he could have brought himself to be so brutal as to leave her without hope. Yet, now that fate had temporarily intervened, his instinct was to take it as a sign that he should stick to his resolution not to betray his friend; and, once away from San Sebastian he felt sure that it would strengthen. However much he might now long for her, he could protect himself from weakening by finding some excuse not to come back.

Having put the personal letter inside the one he intended her to show her husband, he tucked them both into an envelope, sealed it carefully, and addressed it to her. Then on his way back through the hall he propped it up on the table there against the mail-box.

By this time the servants were about. Having found Ricardo he told him that he had overnight received a message that his presence was required urgently in Madrid, so he meant to catch the nine-five train. He then asked Ricardo to order a carriage to take him into the city, and to bring him his breakfast in half an hour. It arrived soon after he had bathed and dressed. When he had eaten it, refusing Ricardo's offer to pack for him, he selected the things he was most likely to need, including the revolver that de Cordoba had lent him, and packed them into two portmanteaux. At eight o'clock Ricardo came to collect his luggage and he followed him along to the hall.

As he picked up his overcoat and hat, then turned to follow the footman out to the waiting carriage, a low call came to him. 'Monsieur le Comte!'

He knew it instantly to be Gulia's voice and, swinging round, saw her standing half concealed behind the partially open door to the library. Putting down his things he walked over to it and entered the room. He had never seen her on horseback, but she was dressed in riding habit, and he guessed that she had put it on because the servants who saw her in it would think that she meant to go for a before-breakfast ride, thus being provided with a reason for her being downstairs so unusually early.

Stepping back behind the door she said quickly, 'Armand. As that flash went off I saw that the man was holding up a camera. I was staring straight into it. I had to know if you got the camera from him or, if not, what we should decide to do. I dressed like this and came down meaning to send Ricardo to suggest that you should come for a ride with me. Then I found your letter.'

'You've read it?' he asked.

'Yes; and I think your interpretation of the way that Sanchez's mind has worked is most probably right. What ghastly luck for us that this should have occurred; still worse that you should now have to go into danger again.'

He gave her a reassuring smile. 'Be of good heart. This time it is I who will be able to choose my moment to attack. With a little luck I'll catch him napping.'

'Oh, do be careful!' she begged, suddenly putting up her hands and grasping the lapels of his coat. 'I think I'd die if anything happened to you.'

He placed his hands over hers, but did not seek to loosen her hold on him. 'At least I'll promise not to take any unnecessary risks; but by hook or by crook I must destroy that negative.'

'I know. How long do you think this wretched business will take?'

'It is impossible to say. My guess that he will go back to Granada may be wrong. But anyway I think I'll get a lead to him from there. If not I'll have to wait until you send on to me the letter that I feel pretty certain he will send here. Then it will be up to me to counter any trap he may set for me with a better one of my own.'

'And when you do get back . . . what of the future?'

He shook his head. 'We can't possibly discuss that now. We haven't the time. If I don't go soon, I'll miss my train.'

'But you must have formed some idea what you mean to do when the Barcelona trial is over.'

'Oh that!' He tried to prevent his voice from showing his relief that her question appeared to be impersonal. 'I haven't really decided anything, but I expect I'll take up soldiering again. I've always wanted to command a cavalry division, and I might be given one if I went out to one of the South American Republics.'

'Armand.' She hesitated a second. 'About last night. I do understand how you feel about José. It is just like you to consider yourself bound by the code of chivalry. But it was the thought of deceiving him that really distressed you, wasn't it? I mean . . . Well, you would feel differently if we . . . if we took the bull by the horns and were open with him.'

'Yes,' he nodded. 'That would be quite a different matter. But think of the implications.'

'I did, for most of the night. I love you, Armand. I would go anywhere with you; and I'd like to go to South America.'

He shook his head. 'I'd love to take you there. But I couldn't, Gulia. It's out of the question. You are a Roman Catholic; so you can't get a divorce. How could I expose a woman like you to social ostracism when it leaked out that we were not married?'

'I don't see why it should become known out there if we planned things carefully.'

'Such things always do. But, Gulia, we really mustn't attempt to settle anything without giving the whole matter most careful thought. And I must go now, or I'll miss my train.'

'Very well, then. Kiss me before you go.'

As he took her in his arms she put hers round his neck and drew his face towards hers. Their mouths met in a long, rich kiss. For a full minute they held one another in a firm embrace, then she released him and murmured, 'Go now, dear love. May God protect you and bring you safely back to me.'

Half dazed by the heady emotion her kiss had aroused in him, he gave her a lingering smile, then turned and walked quickly from the room.

Looking after him, she put her hand upon her wildly palpitating heart, while saying to herself, 'I've put my seal upon him. He doesn't realize it yet, but he is now mine.'

12

In the Gipsy's Cave

DE QUESNOY had intended to arrive at the station half an hour before the train was due to leave. Gulia's having waylaid him had cut down that margin a little but he still had plenty of leeway. After buying his ticket he sent a porter ahead with his bags and to keep him a first-class corner seat as near the rear of the train as possible; then he took up a position behind a newspaper kiosk from which he could watch, without making himself conspicuous, the passengers going through the barrier to the Madrid express. It was not until the barrier was about to be closed that he darted through it, ran down the platform, threw a tip to his porter and jumped up into the train.

He had satisfied himself that during his twenty minutes' vigil no one remotely resembling Sanchez had passed the barrier; but there was still the possibility that the anarchist had reached the station before him. As it was an express to the capital from Spain's most fashionable summer resort, the train had no third-class carriages and the firsts and seconds were the newly-introduced corridor coaches. Having taken his seat and given the passengers and attendants time to settle down, he made two slow progresses, first up to the front of the train, then to the guard's van, and back. It took him nearly half an hour, as he paused at every compartment to scan its occupants; but when he had finished his inspection he felt certain that Sanchez was not travelling on the express.

That did not surprise him, for he knew that although the younger Ferrer brother had no great brain he was well endowed with peasant cunning; so he had probably walked or driven during the night to some small town ten or fifteen miles from San Sebastian and would begin his journey south by catching an early-morning local train from there.

On arriving in Madrid, de Quesnoy booked a sleeper on the night express to Granada, then had an early dinner at Boca's, choosing for his main course a dish for which the ancient restaurant was famous – a boiled chicken which was served covered with a yellow sauce made from eggs and sherry, and having some resemblance to a *zabaione*. His first-class sleeper was old-fashioned but spacious and comfortable, so he slept well and arrived in Granada early in the morning on Wednesday the 29th.

He had never before been to this famous city from which for centuries a line of Caliphs had dominated south-eastern Spain, and which later, after the Moors had been driven out, had been greatly embellished by the Catholic Sovereigns, Ferdinand and Isabella. It was set in a vast, fertile plain enclosed by great ranges of mountains, and no finer view of it could be obtained than from the new de-luxe hotel to which the Count had wired from Madrid for rooms.

When he had had a bath and changed he went out on to the balcony. The hotel had been built on the very edge of the precipitous south-western slope of a high plateau that divided the modern city and the old Christian quarter from the original Moorish town. His room looked out over the former and from the balcony on which he stood he could have pitched a peseta down into the nearest street which lay two hundred feet below. The city lay sizzling in the sun but the air up there was cool and invigorating, and the atmosphere crystal clear. Beyond the great huddle of spires, domes and roofs the plain stretched away interminably, walled in on either side by unbroken chains of lofty mountains, those to the left having snow on their peaks gleaming white against the cloudless azure sky.

He took out the photograph that Sanchez had dropped and studied it again. It was a three-quarter length of a sultry-looking beauty. She was wearing a black, flat-crowned, wide-brimmed Andalusian hat tilted sideways on her head, and a fringed silk shawl twisted tightly round her body. Her pose was that traditional with Flamenco dancers: one hand on hip, the other crooked above her head holding castanets. The name of the photographer, which was stamped below the portrait, was Elio, and his studio was in the Calle de San Jerónimo.

De Quesnoy hired a carriage and had himself driven down to the studio. Judging him to be a possible customer of means Señor Elio willingly supplied him with such information as he could. He remembered the woman well. She had not been wearing fancy dress but was a professional Flamenco dancer known as La Torcera – which de Quesnoy later learned meant 'The Wriggler'. The photograph had been taken about six months ago, and on referring to his ledger Señor Elio said that he could not give her address because she had called for the prints. He added, however, that she was certainly a gipsy, so the Count should have no difficulty in finding her if he made inquiries at the gipsy settlement on the hillside beyond the old Moorish town that lay on the far side of the city.

Having thanked him, de Quesnoy declined the suggestion that he should have his photograph taken, and decided to spend the rest of the morning sightseeing.

To his surprise he found the Cathedral to be hidden away behind tall buildings in one of the main streets, and the entrance to it through first a small private house then a tiny patio; but once inside, it was a glory of brightness; all its walls and pillars being made of pure white stone. Having admired a magnificently carved interior door – the great masterpiece of the sculptor Siloe – and the famous Virgin Chapel, he went into the adjacent Capilla Real.

Nearly a third of this much smaller edifice he found to be occupied by four enormous tombs with the most beautiful carvings imaginable. They were those of Ferdinand and Isabella and of their successors, the mad Queen Joan and Philip the Fair of Burgundy, by whose union half Europe fell under the sway of their son, the Emperor Charles V.

A beadle, hovering for a tip, pointed out to de Quesnoy that the stone pillow under Queen Isabella's head had a deeper depression in it than that of King Ferdinand, and told him the amusing legend that it had been deliberately sculpted so because she had had more brains than her husband.

Having a wide knowledge of European history, the Count could well believe that she had; for, although it was Ferdinand who had driven the Moors out of Spain, his Queen had acted as his Quartermaster-General, and without the extraordinary feats of organization she performed he could never have achieved his victories. It was Isabella, too, who had had the vision to finance Columbus's voyage to America. The tragedy was that a woman so brilliant and so good in herself should also have been so much under the sway of pitiless priests that she had allowed them to found the Holy Office, and encouraged the terrible work of the Spanish Inquisition.

The beadle then took him down a flight of steps to a level below the huge tombs, where there was a glass panel through which he could see the actual dust-covered coffins of these two sovereigns who, by their marriage, had brought Spain under one crown and made her a great nation.

In the sacristy he saw the crown, sceptre and mass-book used

by Isabella, and King Ferdinand's sword. Then, having had enough
of churches for the day, he went out to wander round the streets
of the old town. The Moorish bazaar delighted him, as it consisted of a series of open arcades criss-crossing one another, and
each lined on both sides with shops only the width of a single
narrow arch, in which craftsmen of all kinds were still plying ancient
trades.

On returning to his hotel he asked the hall-porter to find out
for him if a dancer known as La Torcera was still living in the
gipsy settlement and, if so, how he could locate her habitation.
After lunch he slept through the afternoon, then before dinner
he went for a walk through the woods which covered the greater
part of the Alhambra height, on which the hotel was situated.

He was thinking only of Gulia, and wondered what he had
better do about her. To disclose frankly to de Cordoba that they
had fallen desperately in love and intended to run away together
was certainly not as despicable as entering on an adulterous liaison
behind his back; yet it seemed to de Quesnoy that even the former
course was highly reprehensible since, had his friend not shown
his trust in him by allowing him to spend so much time alone with
Gulia, the present situation would never have arisen.

There was another side to the matter, too. If Gulia was right
in her belief that her husband was indifferent to her entering on
an *affaire*, provided she was discreet, and José found out that
they had become lovers, he might not mind very much; whereas
he might mind very much indeed if his whole life were disrupted
by his wife being taken away from him.

With a wry smile de Quesnoy thought how, in his case, history
was repeating itself, in that for the second time in his life he should
be contemplating running away with a married woman. He recalled
the many times he and Angela had wrestled with the pros and
cons of an elopement. In her case he would not have had the
least scruple about taking her from her villainous husband, but
she had had a greater sense of loyalty than Gulia and had insisted
on remaining with her husband until he could surmount his financial
difficulties. Gulia, on the other hand, was willing not only to
sacrifice a much greater name and position for him, but also to
share with him the uncertainties of a soldier's life in South America –
a thing that Angela would never have agreed to even after they were
legally married.

'Legally married'; he repeated the words in his mind. It was
over the difficulty of their becoming so, as long as Angela's husband had been alive, that had caused them such harassing doubts

about whether they should gamble everything by her cutting loose and their first living together openly in, so-called, sin. And that, now, would apply equally with Gulia. There could be no divorce, and de Cordoba might quite well refuse to countenance an appeal to Rome for an annulment of their marriage. Even if he did not obstruct the appeal the Church might refuse to grant it. At best it would take two or three years to come through. And in the meantime Gulia would be living a furtive existence with him under an assumed name, and – a thought that made him see red – be in constant dread of being subjected to slights and insults from people who knew that she was not 'legally married' to him.

After a two hours' walk he decided that, greatly as he desired her, he was neither prepared to disrupt the life of his friend nor place her in such an invidious position; and that he was certainly not going to go back on his original refusal to betray his friend's trust by taking her in secret as his mistress.

Having made this resolve it followed that in no circumstances should he again become a member of the de Cordoba household, either at San Sebastian or in Madrid; for to do so could result only in placing an appalling strain on both Gulia and himself. His first job was to hunt down Sanchez. After that he would have to appear at the Barcelona trial, but that was now barely a fortnight away; so it would be easy to make some excuse for not returning to San Sebastian in the meanwhile. When the trial was over he would spend six or eight weeks with his father in Southern Russia, then he would go to South America and see whether, in a year or so, he could not after all achieve his life-long ambition to be given command of a Cavalry Division.

That evening the hall-porter reported that La Torcera was still living in the gipsy settlement and working in the best troupe of Flamenco dancers, who gave displays in the biggest cave for the wealthier tourists. He then asked if de Quesnoy would like a guide to take him there at ten o'clock, when the dancing started.

The Count replied that he would not be going there until the following evening, and then he would not require a guide but only a carriage to take him to the settlement and bring him back.

The porter pressed him to take a guide, giving as his reason that unless strangers were properly sponsored the gipsies could prove troublesome, as the men were a lawless lot and had been known to demand money with menaces before they would let solitary visitors leave their settlement. But de Quesnoy had no intention of saddling himself with a companion, and he assured the porter that he was quite capable of looking after himself.

His reason for delaying for twenty-four hours before getting in touch with La Torcera was based on a nicely balanced assessment of possibilities. Assuming that after Sanchez's flight from Barcelona he had been living with this woman and, following his stay in San Sebastian, intended to return to her, since he had not caught the Madrid express he could not have got back to Granada before that evening at the earliest. On the other hand, if he meant to return he should be back for certain by the following night. To have questioned La Torcera about him before he arrived would have meant running a grave risk, even if she were heavily bribed, of her warning him directly he did put in an appearance that his hide-out had been discovered; upon which it was certain that he would disappear and again become very difficult to trace.

If Sanchez was living with the gipsies it seemed most unlikely that he would show himself at any of their performances, as to do so would have been to risk some police agent among the spectators identifying him; so while strangers were about he would most probably lie low in the woman's hut. De Quesnoy's hope was that he would be able either to fool or bribe La Torcera into betraying Sanchez by pointing out her hut to him. He could then go straight to it, take Sanchez by surprise and, at the point of his revolver, compel him to give up the incriminating negative.

Next morning, as he had another day to kill, he decided to spend it up on the Alhambra height visiting the world-famous Moorish Palaces with which it was crowned.

First he went to the Generalife, one of the smaller palaces which had been used as a summer residence by the Caliphs and was said to have the loveliest gardens in Spain. He found its long walks of tall clipped hedges a pleasant sight, but no better than those he had seen in similar formal gardens elsewhere. There were, too, roses in great profusion, though their beds were ragged and ill-kept; and by and large he considered the garden of the Alcazar in Seville to be much more beautiful. However, the Generalife possessed one unique feature that it had been well worth coming to see – a very long narrow canal with a hundred fountains playing into it from either side and so forming a continuous arcade of sparkling water-drops rainbow-hued in the brilliant sunshine.

On the other side of the plateau he found that the great palace of the Alhambra more than rivalled the Alcazar in Seville. The buildings, lakes and gardens within its walls covered several acres and from the main fortress-palace a huge square *casbar* towered up to the sky. From its top one could see many miles in every direction, and the great ranges of mountains in the distance made the panorama superb. On the ground level its principal courts were gems at which to wonder. To construct the Court of the Lions and the Court of the Ambassadors, with their delicate pillars of different coloured marbles and incredibly intricate lace work carved from stone, must have taken an army of skilled craftsmen years of devoted labour.

In his imagination he endeavoured to people them again with the colourful throngs that must have inhabited them six hundred years ago: the Caliph, in his huge turban and gorgeous robes, seated on the divan dispensing justice; behind him his Captain of the Guards in chain mail and a spiked helmet of burnished silver, and a huge negro, naked except for a leopard-skin about his loins, the great curved scimitar with which he carried out his task as Executioner resting against his ebony shoulder; the veiled Sultana, seated just below her lord, wearing a bright embroidered jacket and Turkish trousers, her dark hair ablaze with jewels; the Moorish Knights, no darker-skinned than other Mediterranean peoples, clad in surcoats patterned in silks with peacock hues; the slender dancing girls, nude but for diaphanous muslins caught at wrists and ankles by gold bangles.

De Quesnoy appreciated, too, that such scenes had symbolized far more than a marvellous spectacle and the power which came from armed might. There would also have been present elderly men deeply versed in the law derived from the Koran, poets, doctors, architects, mathematicians, astrologers, geographers, and others more learned, more humane and more advanced in thought than any then living in the Christian world. For it was the so-called Infidels who from Cairo, Baghdad, Damascus and Aleppo had inherited and perpetuated the great civilizations of Greece and Rome.

History as written by the Western world accounted it a great triumph that the Moors had been driven out of Europe. It had been for the Christian faith; but in no other way. These cultured people, with their high standard of living and scrupulous bodily cleanliness, had been replaced by Europeans who were little better than barbarians: their highest caste still inhabiting bitterly cold and uncomfortable castles, ignorant, unwashed, lice-ridden, a prey to witchcraft and superstition, and dominated by priests whose cruelty had not been equalled since in ancient times the priests of Moloch had also appeased their God by consigning human victims to the flames.

Pondering upon this, de Quesnoy wondered whether, had the Moors defeated the Christians and, in due course, having become

6

the masters of Europe, carried their culture north, humanity might not have been spared the endless wars between Catholics and Protestants, which had caused such appalling suffering and, perhaps, enjoyed the benefits of science and hygiene several hundred years earlier than, with the Christian victory, had proved the case.

While going through the upper floors of the palace he came to the apartments of the Harem. One of the largest rooms was made delightfully airy from one of its walls being composed only of a row of arches, which gave on to a wide covered balcony. Going out on to it he remained there for a few minutes enjoying the view. The wall of the palace and the cliff on which it was built fell almost sheer to a gorge two hundred feet below. On the far side of the gorge lay the old Moorish city; a huddle of white, red-roofed buildings still surrounded by ancient crenellated walls.

Beyond it the ground rose in a rugged slope pitted with caves and dotted here and there with small clusters of low, white-painted walls that were evidently living quarters built against the hillside. From a few of them smoke spiralled up. In some places it also rose from what, in the distance, looked like short posts set up on parts of the rock where it was fairly flat, but actually they were chimney pots to carry off smoke from cooking fires in caves hidden below them. It was the gipsy settlement.

That night, after he had dined, de Quesnoy had himself driven out there. He was wearing informal evening clothes under a long black cloak and a flat-crowned sombrero. Behind his right hip, hidden by the cloak, he carried de Cordoba's revolver, fully loaded. Behind his left hip, similarly hidden, he had slung a leather bag containing a considerable sum in Spanish gold coins. In his pocket he had another, smaller, bag of gold and a number of loose pieces for immediate expenses.

The driver set him down at the entrance to one of the clusters of low white buildings on the hillside. He gave the man ten pesetas and told him to wait, adding that in no circumstances was he to allow anyone else to hire him, even temporarily for a trip into the city and back, or to send him away, and that on their return to the hotel he should receive four times that sum.

Delighted at the thought of receiving two whole gold pieces for his night's work, the driver declared that for such a munificent *caballero* he would wait a week. He then drove off to a sheltered gully in which were lined up several carriages that had already brought visitors.

Meanwhile de Quesnoy made his way past a low enclosure that held a herd of goats, and through a narrow passage between two

of the hutments that were built into the cliff face. Beyond it there
was an open space the size of which surprised him. A natural cave
had evidently been enlarged until it formed a rough horseshoe
with the roof at its widest part about ten feet high. In it were a
dozen wooden tables, all of which had been set round its walls
to leave a circle of sanded floor in their centre free for the dancers.
It was lit by half a dozen acetylene flares each of which, in its
immediate vicinity, gave off a terrific heat.

No dancing was going on at the moment and all the tables were
occupied, but only about half of them by visitors; at the others
sat one or more of the women of the troupe. The Count was ful-
somely welcomed by the Maestro of the establishment: an elderly
gipsy whose greasy black locks were streaked with grey, and who
sported both gold ear-rings and a gold front tooth.

With many bows the Maestro led him to a table at which one
of the prettier girls was seated. She was rather plump-faced and
had black kiss-curls plastered flat on the upper parts of both her
cheeks. The rest of her hair was piled high and held in place by a
big tortoiseshell comb from which hung down a black lace mantilla. From her shoulders rose many-layered puffs of gauzy material
below which her well-made arms extended; she had a slight cast in
one eye.

De Quesnoy made her a smiling bow, which she acknowledged
with an inclination of the head, then he sat down beside her and
told her that his name was Jaime Avila. She replied that she was
known as La Conchita and had only recently been made a member
of the troupe. A hunchback appeared in front of their table carrying a goat-skin containing wine. Skilfully he squirted a quarter
of a litre of the wine into each of the earthenware mugs that stood
before them and, with a grin, scooped up the pesetas pushed across
to him in payment. The Count lifted his mug to his companion,
murmured '*Salud, Madonna*,' and tried the wine. It was a little
thin and slightly acid but quite drinkable.

His excitement rising now he felt that he was most probably
sitting within a hundred yards of Sanchez's hide-out, he took stock
of the other occupants of the cave. They numbered altogether
about twenty-five, of which ten men, including himself, he put
down as visitors. At the far end of the cave was the band, consisting of two men with guitars who, at the moment, were talking to
a very fat middle-aged woman. The remaining dozen were made
up by the Maestro, the hunchback waiter and the dancers.

His eyes ran swiftly over the women, endeavouring to identify
La Torcera. Except that the colour of their costumes differed they

were all dressed much alike – high combs and mantillas, puffed
sleeves and voluminous skirts made in many layers over numerous
frilly petticoats. But, after a brief scrutiny, he decided that she
must be the woman seated at a table nearly opposite him with
a heavy-jowled, middle-aged man wearing a grey suit and a red
cummerbund.

The guitarists began to strum, then moved into a swift rhythm.
La Conchita excused herself and, with another girl, got up to
dance partnered by the two men of the troupe. Both the latter
were as slim as matadors and, like them, wore skin-tight trousers
which showed the rippling muscles of their thighs and buttocks.

All four of them stamped their heels and made the traditional
provocative gestures of advance and withdrawal originally inspired
by the courting of birds. When the dance was well under way
de Quesnoy beckoned the Maestro over to him and said:

'The dancer opposite is La Torcera, is she not?' and as the man
nodded he went on, 'I have been told that she is amusing to talk
to. Please tell her that after she has danced I should like her to
come to my table.'

The Maestro shook his head. 'I regret, Señor; but for this evening,
as you see, she is already engaged.'

'For the whole evening?' asked the Count.

'Yes, Señor. The señor with whom she sits is a rich merchant
from Alicante. He arrived early and asked for her; so it is certain
that he intends to spend the whole night in her company.'

This was a most annoying development and one for which
de Quesnoy had not bargained. But, now that he had shown himself
among the gipsies, he was most averse to putting off his plan even
for a night. To the Maestro he said, 'I, too, am rich, and I am
prepared to outbid him for her. Be good enough to arrange the
matter.'

'Excellency, I regret,' the Maestro raised his broad shoulders
and spread out his arms in a helpless gesture. 'The señor who is
with her has already made me a generous present with the request
that tonight I should introduce no other admirers to her. How
can I now make a deliberate attempt to rob him of his pleasure?'

As the Maestro moved away the dance was ending. La Conchita
and the other girl were pirouetted by their partners, their skirts
flairing waist high to tantalize the male onlookers with the sight
of their white-stockinged legs, elaborate garters and, above them,
a glimpse of naked thighs.

When La Conchita rejoined the Count, he summoned the hunchback to pour her more wine. Then, having given her time to get

her breath back, he said softly, 'My dear, you are certainly the prettiest woman in the troupe, and had I come here tonight for the purpose of enjoying myself I would ask nothing better than to remain with you. But I have a matter of business that it is imperative that I should discuss with La Torcera. As you see, she is not free, and the Maestro tells me that he has been well paid to refrain from disturbing the tête-à-tête she is engaged in. I want you to give me your help in getting her away from her companion. Now, put your hand under the table.'

When she did so he pressed two gold pieces into her palm. It was much more than she would ordinarily have earned in a night and, a swift glance down having shown her that the coins were gold, she said with an uneasy smile:

'*Mil gracias, Don Jaime.* You are a true caballero. But I am much afraid that I shall be unable to earn this generous present. Since the Maestro has refused to present you to La Torcera, I dare not. And I see no other way in which I can help you.'

'It is quite simple,' he answered her. 'All I wish you to do is to go over to her and make some excuse to get her to go outside with you for a moment. When you have her alone tell her that I will give her five hundred pesetas if she will get rid of her companion.'

'Five hundred pesetas!' repeated La Conchita, her dark eyes opening to their fullest extent. 'Do you really mean that? If so, you must be a Prince travelling incognito.'

'I am; my real name is Kropotkin. Please tell her that – Prince Peter Kropotkin.' He told the glib lie because he thought it certain that the gipsies, being perpetually at war with the law, would be anarchist sympathizers, and that, while it was most unlikely that any of them had ever seen the Prince, Sanchez would most probably have spoken of the famous anarchist leader to La Torcera; so she would be all the more willing to get rid of the man she was with and, perhaps, even disclose Sanchez's whereabouts without being bribed to do so.

La Conchita nodded and stood up. As she crossed the floor a little group came on to it. The fat middle-aged woman, carrying a rush-bottomed chair, placed it opposite the entrance and plumped herself down; the guitarists and three girls grouped themselves round her and, following her lead, they all began to clap in rhythm. A young man, scarcely more than a boy, then entered the circle and began to dance. As he did so, shouts of '*Olé! Olé!*' came from several of the spectators and most of them joined in the clapping.

It was evident that the youth was a favourite and the Count

soon saw that his popularity was justified. Holding himself as stiff as a ramrod, with one hand above his head and the other on his hip, he moved at a snail's pace back and forth and round and round, but the whole time his feet tapped the floor at an incredible speed, changing their beat only for an occasional stamp at each sudden cessation of the clapping.

Meanwhile, with a little smile of satisfaction, de Quesnoy saw La Torcera and La Conchita leave the cave together. They were absent for about five minutes, then they both returned and the latter rejoined him. Leaning towards him, she said:

'As I feared, the matter is not easy. It is against all custom for one of us to leave a patron with whom the Maestro has provided us. We may do so only if it transpires that he has no money or is so drunk that he becomes troublesome and insulting. She cannot therefore send him away or come over to you. But, of course, here as elsewhere there are times when disputes arise between two men, both of whom desire the company of one woman. If you decide to attempt to get rid of him yourself, she will not take his part but will remain passive; and she is naturally much flattered by your interest in her. It remains now for you to make up your mind whether your wish to get her to yourself is worth risking what may prove an unpleasant scene.'

De Quesnoy had already considered going over to La Torcera's table and boldly asking her to leave it with him, but it was obvious that such a step would result in high words and probably a fracas. If that happened, he feared that the Maestro and other men of the troupe would join in and, as he would clearly be in the wrong, side with the merchant from Alicante. As he was carrying a revolver he had no doubts about his ability to protect himself and get out of the place unharmed, but having to do so would promptly terminate any chance of his achieving the object with which he had come there. Turning to the girl beside him, he said:

'I had thought of doing what you suggest, but there would not be much point to it if it resulted in my being thrown out. From the way you speak, though, that does not always follow. Do you think the Maestro and the others would leave me a free field to get rid of the other fellow?'

She gave a quick nod. 'Yes. What woman does not enjoy having two men fight over her? La Torcera would see to it that you had fair play. All gipsies love watching a fight, too, so our men would not interfere – that is unless either of you drew a knife. They would then from fear of a killing, for we do not like to give the police an excuse to come nosing about up here.'

'Thank you, my dear. In telling me that you really have been helpful.' With a grim little smile, the Count made to stand up. But she quickly laid a hand on his arm, and said:

'Not yet. La Torcera is about to dance. You must wait now until her dance is over.'

La Torcera was partnered by the taller of the two men who had danced before. Now that she was standing up and the Count had a closer view of her, he saw that she was both a taller and bigger woman than he had so far judged her to be. She was handsome, but in a coarse way, and smallpox had left her with a slight pitting on the lower part of her right cheek. Her features and her skin, which was a shade darker than that of the other women, suggested that she had a touch of Moorish blood. As a Flamenco dancer she was clearly in the front rank, clacking her castanets in perfect timing with the beat of the guitars, jerking back her head with admirably simulated violence, and swaying her big shapely hips in sensuous invitation. Twice as she came round to face de Quesnoy she gave him a smile and raised an interrogative eyebrow.

He did not wait until she had finished her dance, but after it had been going on for some while he bid a smiling adieu to La Conchita, then stood up and skirted the floor until he reached the table opposite. It had occurred to him that to get his way without a scene was at least worth trying, and this was the time to attempt it; so, with a bow to the merchant from Alicante, he addressed him with the utmost politeness.

'Señor, allow me to introduce myself. I am Prince Peter Kropotkin. You may perhaps have heard of me. Most of my life has been spent championing the underdog, and I have a particular admiration for the gipsies. They show such a praiseworthy independence of spirit, and are a living example of my contention that life may be enjoyed without resorting to the law or owning personal property. No doubt it is a similar admiration for them that has brought you here tonight.'

The man gave him a puzzled look and replied, 'Well, not exactly, Señor Prince. As a matter of fact I came here because I enjoy their Flamenco music and watching them dance.'

'Ah!' beamed the Count. 'That is quite understandable; and I see that we shall soon be able to arrange matters.' As he spoke he pulled out a chair, added 'Permit me' and, without waiting for the other's consent, sat down.

'Arrange matters,' the merchant frowned. 'I don't understand what you are talking about, and this table . . .'

'Exactly. It is about this table we have to arrange. As you have come here only to listen to the music and watch the dancing you will, I am sure, have no objection to moving to another.'

'I'll do nothing of the kind,' came the angry retort. 'This is La Torcera's table, and I have booked her to spend the evening with me.'

'That is unfortunate, because it so happens that I have matters to discuss with her that are of much more importance than any of the sweet nothings that you may have visualized yourself whispering in her ear. May I suggest that you should whisper them instead to the young woman I have just left. She is called La Conchita and . . .'

At that moment La Torcera was facing the table at which they sat. Taking a flower from behind her ear she threw it between them. No one could say that it had not been intended for her admirer from Alicante; but it was de Quesnoy who caught it and blew her a kiss.

The merchant had gone red in the face and burst out, 'You may be a Prince, but I'll see you damned before I'll give way to you. My money is as good as yours, and . . .'

'Forgive me,' the Count interrupted. 'You have, no doubt, made certain disbursements to the Maestro, and also perhaps to the lady. I should have mentioned that I will willingly refund them to you.'

'That's not the point,' the other thrust out his chin aggressively. 'You've no right to . . .'

'No; there is only one point,' de Quesnoy's voice was silky as he came quickly to his feet and moved round the table. 'It is whether you are prepared quietly to vacate the chair upon which you are sitting, or whether I must forcibly remove you from it.'

The merchant was a strongly-built, broad-shouldered man of about forty. Turning his face up with a sneer, he muttered, 'You dare to lay a hand on me and I'll break every bone in your body.'

'I would regret to have to soil my fingers,' retorted the Count, his grey eyes now hard and brilliant. Next second he had hooked his foot under the nearest back leg of the chair and given a violent jerk upon it. Had it stood the strain and lifted the merchant must have slid off its far side. As it was, the leg being of flimsy wood, it snapped and he was precipitated sideways towards de Quesnoy. The Count took a quick pace back and the unfortunate man hit the ground at his feet with a heavy thud.

Up to that moment no one else in the cave had noticed their quarrel, because attention had been concentrated on the dancers.

But, at that moment, after a final spin by La Torcera with her skirts flaired out about her like a cartwheel, the dance ended. There came a burst of clapping and *Olés!* but they quickly subsided and all eyes were turned on her table, on the far side of which, now screaming curses, the merchant had just staggered to his feet.

De Quesnoy was not quarrelsome by nature, but in North Africa and elsewhere he had been involved in enough similar scenes to know that the art of getting onlookers on one's side was to make one's adversary look ridiculous. His arm shot out from beneath his cloak like a piston. With his forefinger and thumb he seized upon the merchant's fleshy nose and proceeded to wring it.

The wretched man clawed frantically at the Count's hand but could not break the grip. Suffering acute pain, blinded by tears and giving vent to a low wailing, he staggered from side to side with his head held down to the level of de Quesnoy's chest, while the ring of spectators who had formed about them gave way to peals of laughter.

When at length the Count did let go, his victim staggered back, his hands to his bleeding nose and, turning, blundered away towards the entrance to the cave.

As the laughter subsided de Quesnoy bowed the smiling La Torcera to her chair, beckoned up the hunchback to give them wine, and called to him to fill the mugs of the whole company. This evoked a chorus of clapping and loud *Olés!* in appreciation of his generosity then the occupants of the cave who, since his arrival, had increased to about forty, settled down again.

For a while the Count kept his conversation with La Torcera to compliments and urbanities. He said that having heard a great deal about her he had been most eager to meet her, and that as he was staying only one night in Granada he had seen no other course but to take the steps that he had to become acquainted with her. She said how flattered she was by his attentions and congratulated him on the way in which he had so skilfully relieved her of the merchant's company without resorting to an unseemly brawl. He paid her compliments on the finished artistry of her dancing. She replied that for anyone born with the gift it was then only a matter of hard training, and that with anyone as handsome as himself showing special interest in her performance, that had naturally encouraged her to put her heart into it.

He then declared that he was abysmally ignorant about Flamenco and asked her to enlighten him on some of the finer points of its technique. She willingly obliged and was still discoursing on the subject when another party of dancers arranged themselves. Now

6*

the whole troupe, except for herself and the girl who had danced at the same time, took the floor. The haunting music began and the four couples started to stamp their feet and gyrate.

For a few minutes de Quesnoy watched them, then he said, 'I find it terribly hot in here. Let's go outside and get a breath of air.'

'But you will miss the dancing,' she declared. 'And you are wearing a heavy cloak. No wonder you are hot. Take it off.'

He shook his head. 'No; I prefer to keep my cloak on. And it is not that which makes me hot. It is the smoke and the closeness of the atmosphere. As for the dancing, I can watch it again later.' Standing up, he took her gently by the arm and added, 'Come! I pray you, humour me. Let us go outside for a while and look at the stars.'

Assuming that he wanted to get over the first fences of making love to her, she gave him a roguish smile and let him lead her from the cave. Outside it was broad moonlight, and he saw with relief that no one was about. Still holding her arm he guided her over to one side where a great hump of rock threw a deep shadow. Halting there he turned, faced her, and said:

'Señorita, I have greatly enjoyed meeting you; but I must now tell you the real purpose of my visit. I have come here to discuss an urgent matter with Sanchez Ferrer.'

For a moment she did not reply; then she asked, 'Are you then a friend of his?'

De Quesnoy nodded, and lied, 'Yes; a most intimate friend. Please take me to him without delay.'

By way of answer she drew back her head, then like a striking cobra spat straight into his face.

13

A Strange Partnership

LA TORCERA'S spittle had barely landed on de Quesnoy's chin when both his hands shot out. They seized her wrists and brought them together with a smack in front of her. A second later he had put into practice a trick that he had taught his troops in North Africa for use when alone with a prisoner whom they suspected had a knife concealed in his robes. With a swift move of his right hand, before she had a chance to pull her wrists apart, he had grasped them both, then with his left hand he imprisoned both her thumbs.

Too late she made a violent effort to pull away from him. She was now as much his prisoner as if with his left hand he had a firm grip on a chain by which she was handcuffed to him; and his right hand was free. His grey eyes were blazing. Lifting his hand, he snarled:

'You bitch! Had you been a man I would have half-killed you for that.' Then he slapped her hard three times across the face.

At the sting of his slaps the black pupils of her eyes expanded, narrowing the surround of yellowish white, and tears sprang to them. She choked, gasped and gulped in a breath to shout for help. But again he was too quick for her. Pulling his revolver from under his cloak he jabbed it into her stomach, half-winding her. As she gave another gasp and almost doubled up, he drew it back, held it in front of her face, and snapped:

'This is loaded. Give one cry and you will never dance again.'

Panting, and with the tears now streaming down her coffee-coloured cheeks, she straightened herself. For a moment they stared at one another in silence, then he said:

'I came here to speak with Sanchez. Had you not behaved like a fool I would have paid you well for taking me to him. As things are you'll get no reward but will take me to him just the same.'

'I can't,' she muttered thickly.

He gave a cynical little laugh. 'D'you expect me to believe that?'

'Believe it or not, I cannot. He is no longer here.'

'That we shall see. If he is here, no doubt while strangers are about he will be skulking in your sleeping quarters. You will walk ahead of me and lead me to them. But I warn you, I am a crack shot. Should you attempt to run for it, shout a warning to him as we approach, or play me any other trick, I'll put a bullet through your ankle.' With a contemptuous gesture, as he released his hold on her thumbs, he flung her hands away from him.

Without a word she turned and, with her head now held high, set off along the cliff-face. As he followed her, he considered the possibility that she might be telling the truth. If so, he would have had all his trouble for nothing. He had all along been conscious that the evidence for his belief that he would find Sanchez in Granada was very slender. It was based only on the police report that he had taken a ticket to go there when he had fled from Barcelona, and the photograph of La Torcera that he had dropped. She had just admitted that he had been there, but that might have been only to lie low before making his trip to San Sebastian.

On the other hand, if Sanchez had returned he could have got back only that day, and it seemed most unlikely that he would have left again within a few hours. Besides, the Count reasoned that an obviously primitive and passionate woman like La Torcera would lie to protect her lover was to be expected. The thing he could not understand was where he had slipped up and enabled her to guess that he was not a friend of Sanchez's but an enemy. Having weighed the pros and cons, worried as he now was that he might be about to suffer a grievous disappointment, he still thought it a fifty-fifty chance that he would surprise Sanchez in her quarters. But it then occurred to him that she might yet try to cheat him, so he said:

'I have another warning for you. If you take me to the quarters of some other woman, pretending that they are yours, you may fool me for the moment, but you will live to regret it. Tomorrow I can easily bribe someone to check up, and if I find you've tricked me I'll come back here when you least expect it. By the time I've done with you you'll not have the looks ever to attract a man again.'

'I'll not trick you,' she flung back over her shoulder. 'I've no need. I tell you Sanchez has gone from here. There is my lodging, just ahead of us.'

They had rounded a bend in the cliff and were approaching a six-feet high wall of whitewashed brick with a low door in its centre, which was evidently the entrance to a small cave. Catching up with her, he took her right hand and swiftly twisted it up in a half-nelson behind her back, as he said softly:

'Now; no nonsense. I am aware of Sanchez's skill in throwing a knife and I've no mind to have one in my chest. But he won't throw one at you, so you are going to stand in front of me. You will now call him by name so that he comes to the door of the cave. You are to call his name, mind, and not a word more.'

Obediently she called 'Sanchez!' There was no reply. But as no light was filtering through the cracks round the door de Quesnoy thought it possible that Sanchez was sleeping; so he made her call again, louder. Still there came no reply. After waiting a good minute the Count told her to call again, but the cave remained in darkness and there was no sound of movement from within it.

Releasing her arm, de Quesnoy said, 'It seems that you were telling the truth. Go into the cave now, leave the door wide open and light a candle or a lamp. If you have a knife there I warn you not to touch it. Remember, I can still put a bullet through your foot.'

With a shrug she did as he had told her. Through the open door he saw her light an oil lamp then, with his revolver still at the ready, he followed her inside.

The cave was no more than ten feet deep and a little less in width. From six feet in height at its entrance its rough-hewn ceiling sloped down to four at the back where there was a brick hearth with a chimney and a few iron cooking pots. Along one wall there was a truckle bed, against the other a long trestle table on which stood an enamel basin, toilet things, a mirror, and an array of cosmetics; in front of it stood a single chair.

As the Count put his foot over the door sill La Torcera drew back a little in the confined space, dropped him a mocking curtsy and said sarcastically, 'Enter, noble Prince, and be pleased to search my vast apartment; but have a care when crawling under the bed lest the giant who lies concealed there should seize upon and devour you.'

De Quesnoy gave her a half-smile. 'I admit that after all the unnecessary precautions I took against Sanchez being warned of my approach, you have the laugh of me. Incidentally, too, I am not a Prince. I used Kropotkin's name only because I thought you might know it and that it would influence you the more readily to take me to Sanchez.'

'Neither are you a friend of Sanchez,' she took him up quickly. 'That was made very clear from your fear that he would send a knife whizzing at you.'

'No,' he agreed. 'It would be pointless for me to continue to pretend that Sanchez and I are anything but enemies.'

Her black eyes, no longer misted by tears, flashed angrily. Stamping her foot, she burst out, 'Then why in the name of Shaitan did you not tell me so in the first place?'

'Because I believed him to be your lover.'

'What led you to believe that?'

Putting up his revolver, he showed her the photograph of herself and said, 'On about the twenty-fourth of August Sanchez fled from Barcelona and there was some reason to think that he had gone to Granada. Recently he has been in San Sebastian. Four nights ago I had a fight with him, and this photograph fell out of his pocket. As it was taken in Granada, that confirmed my belief that he had been lying low here. From that it was no great jump to the assumption that he was your lover and you had been hiding him.'

With a glance at the photograph she muttered sullenly, 'You were right. He came here first last summer on a holiday. He is a handsome devil and I let him have his way with me. That lasted for about ten days. He turned up again this August and told me that he was on the run. I had no permanent lover at the moment; so we took up with one another where we had left off and I let him share my cave.'

'How long did he remain here this time?'

'About a fortnight. He left on a Wednesday. I think . . . yes . . . it was September the 8th.'

'And he has not been back since. Today, I mean; even to see you for an hour or leave a message for you?'

'He neither has been back, nor will be.'

'You cannot be sure of that. I believe him to be making his way south by slow trains and branch lines. That could easily take him a day longer than I reckoned on. He may quite well turn up to-morrow.'

'I tell you he will not. He will never return here; no, not if you wait for him till Doomsday.'

'How can you be so certain of that?'

La Torcera's face suddenly contorted into a fierce scowl and she cried, 'Because he knows that if he did I'd stick a knife in his guts. He left me for another woman, and not content with that the swine stole my savings to go off with her.'

Convinced that all this time she had been lying to protect her lover, de Quesnoy had remained blind to any other possibility. But her bitter words had the ring of truth. Now it flashed upon him that he had completely misinterpreted her act of spitting in his face. She had done so not because he had somehow given it away that he was after Sanchez's blood, but because she had accepted his statement that he was Sanchez's intimate friend.

He gave a rueful laugh. 'It seems that for the past quarter of an hour we have been at cross purposes. That was my fault, of course; although I had no means of guessing that Sanchez had given you grounds to hate him. Still, now that we understand one another we must work together, and with luck I'll be able to aid you in getting your revenge. Have you any idea where he would be likely to have made for after leaving San Sebastian last Tuesday?'

She shook her head. 'No, none. I wish I had. I'd give a year's work to get even with him.'

'While he was here did he never mention to you any other places in which he had friends who might have hidden him?'

'No. He spoke little of his affairs, except when following in the newspapers what had occurred after he left Barcelona. The school his father ran there was closed by the police, and his father, brother and many of his friends were arrested. He attributed all this ill-fortune to a Conde de Quesnoy who, according to news he received here through the anarchist grape-vine, had had a miraculous escape from death and had denounced them all.'

De Quesnoy smiled. 'Although I am not a Prince I can give you my word that I am a Conde. I am that Conde de Quesnoy of whom he spoke. It is true that I denounced these anarchists and Sanchez's having escaped the net is one reason why I am hunting him. But I suppose you have anarchist sympathies yourself; so had you not personal grounds for wishing to be revenged you would refuse to help me catch him.'

She shrugged. 'I think we gipsies are all anarchists at heart, but we have enough troubles without mixing ourselves up in politics; and all of us thought the attempt to kill the handsome young King and his bride a most wicked thing. That you are an anarchist-hater and hunting Sanchez on that account makes no difference to me. I'd still aid you to catch him if I could, but I see no way to do so.'

After a moment's thought, de Quesnoy asked, 'What of this woman for whom he deserted you? Tell me about her.'

'She was not one of the troupe, but a girl of the town named Inez Giudice; a little red-headed bitch in her early twenties.'

'Was she a native of Granada?'

'No. After they had gone I made inquiries about her and I learned that she had been living in Granada for only about six months. She is the daughter of a Cadiz shipwright, and had been brought up there.'

'That may prove a clue worth having,' murmured the Count. 'Since Sanchez was being hunted by the police he would still have had to keep under cover, and if she had lived in Cadiz all her life she would have friends there who could hide him; particularly as with your savings they would have had ample money to make it worth-while for such friends of hers to aid them. It seems to me that the odds are definitely on their having gone to Cadiz.'

La Torcera nodded. 'You are probably right. But about the money, I have no wish to mislead you. It was not the savings of a lifetime; no more than about eight hundred pesetas. I had put by a considerably greater sum, but I confess that last spring I squandered it on a handsome young matador for whom I developed a sudden foolish passion.'

'Eight hundred pesetas,' repeated the Count. 'No, that would not have kept them very long if they had to use money to keep still tongues in other people's heads. And Sanchez was in no position to earn any money. If he has returned to her they must by now be on their uppers.'

With a shrug and a cynical smile La Torcera replied, 'At all events they'll not starve. She is a whore by profession, and you may be sure that Sanchez would feel no scruples about sending her out on to the streets to earn enough to keep him in food and wine.'

'Did you ever see her?' the Count asked.

'Yes; she was twice brought here to see the troupe perform by a man who enjoyed Flamenco. He was, I suppose, one of her regular patrons. Sometimes Sanchez used to watch the dancing from behind the curtain that screens the entrance to the big cave. That is probably how he first saw her and became enamoured of her. But every few nights he became bored from having nothing to do up here, and in spite of the risk he ran I could not prevent him from going down into the city. It must have been on one such occasion that he saw her again and became acquainted with her. In any case, after he had left me, and I was near distraught with grief and rage, the brother of one of the girls in the troupe told me that he had seen them together on the station platform. That is how I know that it was she who took him from me.'

'Then you would be able to recognize her?'

'Yes, anywhere,' La Torcera's eyes glowed with vindictiveness. 'And should I ever come upon her I'll pull every hair from her red head.'

'I think not,' said de Quesnoy quietly. 'At least not until after she has led us to Sanchez.'

La Torcera glowered at him. 'What do you mean by that?'

'I mean that as there seems a good chance that he went with her to Cadiz and by now has rejoined her there, it is my intention that we too should pay a visit to that ancient port. Since you say you would have no difficulty in recognizing her and the city is of no great size, by haunting the bars and public places where prostitutes ply their trade it should not be long before you spot her and can find out where they are lodging. Once you have done that I will settle accounts with Sanchez for both of us; his woman I shall be happy to leave to you.'

Her eyes grew round and she stammered, 'But the troupe! I . . . I could not leave them. It . . . it is my living.'

Putting a hand under his cloak, he unhitched the small sack

of gold behind his left hip, produced it, and threw it with a clang on the trestle table. 'That contains a thousand pesetas,' he said; 'more than the sum of which Sanchez robbed you. If we succeed in this business I will give you in addition four times that amount. Whatever happens, any woman who has mastered the art of Flamenco dancing as ably as yourself should have little difficulty in securing employment in another troupe, even if this one will not receive you back; so you can regard the greater part of this money as a bonus.'

Still staring at him a shade uncertainly, she stretched out a hand and lifted the bag. On its weight reassuring her that it really contained gold, she nodded slowly. 'Very well, then. When do you wish me to start?'

'Now,' he replied. 'As soon as you have packed your things. The sooner we arrive in Cadiz the better.'

'No!' she shook her head. 'That really is not possible. I am due to dance again in about twenty minutes.'

He had made up his mind to take her with him, in case if he left her there till morning she should mention her intentions to any other member of the gipsy fraternity and, through a grape-vine, they should reach Sanchez.

'That cannot be helped,' he said firmly. 'You must cut your dance and come with me. I intend that we should leave Granada by the first fast train going west tomorrow; and that may mean an early start. Get your things together, now; and be quick about it.'

'I cannot go in these clothes,' she protested.

'True. Then I will go outside while you change.' As he spoke he picked up the bag of gold from the table.

Her eyes suddenly fierce again, she made a snatch at it and exclaimed, 'You said that was for me! I'll not leave here without it.'

'It is for you, but I don't mean to chance your changing your mind during the night about coming with me to Cadiz.' Opening the bag he poured about a third of its contents into his palm, laid the little heap of coins on the table, and added, 'There is an earnest of my good faith. The rest you shall have when we are on the train tomorrow.'

Leaving the cave he walked some way down the hill to the gully in which the carriages that had brought visitors were waiting, found his driver, roused him from sleep and told him to get ready to return to the city. By the time he had climbed the slope again a good ten minutes had elapsed; so, after he had knocked on the door outside the cave and she had told him to come in, he found that she had finished changing.

Her high comb, mantilla and dancer's frock with its scores of flounces had disappeared. Dressed now in a grey coat and skirt, and wearing elastic-sided black boots and a black sombrero, she was just starting to pack her things into a large, finely-woven oblong basket, which had beside it a similar basket to fit over its top.

While walking back up the hill it had occurred to him as strange that since Sanchez had deserted her for another woman early in September, he should still be carrying her portrait at the end of the month; and he asked her if she could account for it.

She replied that she could not; so he took it out again, showed it to her, and asked if the rows of letters and figures on its back conveyed anything to her.

After looking at it for a moment she said, 'They don't mean anything to me; but might not the letters stand for towns and the figures be the times of trains leaving them?'

That possibility had already occurred to de Quesnoy, and he had even thought of attempting to check them against the Spanish timetable; but that would have entailed many hours of work and, even if successful, still left him in ignorance as to which of a score of trains Sanchez might have taken. Now that La Torcera had had the same thought it strengthened his opinion and, if Sanchez had used the back of the photograph to list a number of trains, that would account for his having kept it.

When she had finished packing he helped her put a strap round the big oblong basket. She put out the lamp and locked the door to her dwelling after them; then they walked side by side down the hill to the carriage.

By the time they reached the hotel it was past two o'clock in the morning and there was only a night porter on duty. When the Count asked for a room for La Torcera the man had already taken in the fact that she was a gipsy; but, knowing that it was not for him to question the vagaries of the hotel's wealthy patrons, he quickly checked his glance of disapproval. If the management chose to make a tactful remonstrance in the morning, that was their affair. Producing the key to a single room at the back on the upper floor, he picked up her basket with barely-concealed reluctance and took her up in the lift.

Meanwhile de Quesnoy had gone behind the porter's desk, found a timetable and was looking up trains. The direct route from Granada to Cadiz was via Antequera and Ronda, but that meant going by slow trains and making two changes. The alternative was to go round by Seville, which meant an extra fifty miles, but at 8.30 there was an express to Seville and Cadiz was only another forty-odd miles on from there; so he decided on the latter.

On a note pad he wrote a line for La Torcera, 'I have ordered breakfast to be taken up to you with this at a quarter to seven. Please be packed and ready to leave at eight sharp. You will find me down in the hall. de Q.'

When the porter returned he gave the note to him with instructions about breakfast for himself and his guest, and asked that his bill should be ready without fail at five minutes to eight. Then he tipped the man well and went up to bed.

Next morning at the station he asked La Torcera if she would like a book for the journey or only magazines. She replied that she had had little schooling and could read only large print slowly; so he bought her some picture papers to look at, and also a box of chocolates. These unexpected attentions by him removed the expression of rather sullen suspicion she had worn during their drive down from the hotel, and after he had fulfilled his promise to give her the rest of the gold in the little sack he felt confident that, in spite of the high-handed way in which he had treated her, he had now won her allegiance.

Although they were leaving the mighty range of the Sierra Nevada behind, the greater part of the journey was through desolate but picturesque mountain country. For much of the time the train was winding its way round bends along a narrow track with a precipitous gorge on one side, so, although termed an express its speed often dropped to thirty miles an hour. But to some extent it made up for that on entering the comparatively flat country farther west and they reached Seville a little before half-past one.

After a meal in the station restaurant, they drove to a small hotel that the Count had noticed during his first visit to the city, which appeared pleasant but unpretentious. There he booked a room for La Torcera and, having given her some more money, told her to go out and buy a hat and clothes of a more fashionable kind than those she had on at the moment, then to return and get changed. He too went out on a brief shopping expedition to buy for her a leather portmanteau, an eyeshade, a crooked stick and, at a secondhand shop for a few pesetas, a greasy old black cotton hood and robe such as were worn by the poorest elderly peasant women.

Having completed his purchases he put the robe in the suitcase and returned to the hotel. Finding that it was still only four o'clock and as the evening train for Cadiz did not leave till six, he sent the portmanteau up to La Torcera's room with a message that ran: 'Repack your things, the old robe, and the clothes you were wearing in this, and give your travelling basket to the chambermaid. Please be down in the hall ready to leave at half past five.' Then he went out to pay another visit to the Alcazar.

The last time he had been in the old Moorish Palace had been barely a fortnight after Angela's death, so he was now in a much more suitable frame of mind to appreciate its beauties. This time he found even more to wonder at in the Salon de Embajadores and the patios de las Munecas and de las Doncellas, with their slender pillars and stone tracery mirrored in the brightly-polished marble floors, and he could not now make up his mind if these glorious Courts or those of the Alcazar in Granada were the more beautiful. But afterwards, when he took a short stroll in the garden, he saw at once that he had been right in thinking it far superior to that of the much vaunted Generalife.

Soon after his return to the little hotel, La Torcera came downstairs. She was now wearing a dress that swept the ground, of smooth fawn cloth decorated with appliqué work, had huge puffed out sleeves and a ruched collar. On her head was balanced a large hat crowned by a mountain of violets.

He smiled his approval and had a carriage summoned to take them to the station. On the way she asked him why he had sent her up the filthy old robe, and he replied, 'Because, much as I regret having to ask you to do so, you will shortly have to wear it instead of your pretty new clothes. We cannot afford to risk having Sanchez or his woman recognize you, and perhaps take alarm; so it is part of a disguise that I have bought for you.'

The journey from Seville to Cadiz took only a little over an hour and the last ten miles of it was along a narrow isthmus that ran from south to north with a bulge at its extremity on which stood the city. The western side of the isthmus, washed by the Atlantic, formed part of the coastline running up towards Portugal, while the eastern side faced a mile-wide lake or, rather, gulf. This vast land-locked harbour made Cadiz one of the finest natural ports in Europe, and as de Quesnoy gazed at it from the window of the train he visualized the great fleets of galleons that once must have lain sheltered there, either assembling before setting sail for the Indies, or just returned laden with gold and silver from Mexico and Peru.

He then recalled that it was here that Sir Francis Drake had, as they said, 'Singed the King of Spain's beard.' The English

Admiral had caught assembling there a powerful squadron that was intended to form part of the Armada and, having sailed right in, had burnt or sunk the greater part of it. 'What bold courageous devils those islanders were; and they're still at it today carrying their Union Jack into all the still-unclaimed parts of Africa, Asia and the Pacific,' was the thought that ran through the Count's mind. Then, to the surprise of La Torcera, he burst out laughing, for he had suddenly remembered that he was now of British nationality himself.

Dotted along the peninsula there were villages and one quite considerable town. At all of them on both shores, tents, rows of bathing huts, concert platforms on the sand just above the tide level, roundabouts, swings and booths, showed that these long beaches were favourite holiday resorts. But now most of them were closed and there were only a few groups sitting or strolling in the evening light; for it was the 1st of October and the holiday season was over.

When they alighted at the station they found it to be on the narrow neck of the isthmus, adjacent to the main port, so they had a further mile's drive through the city to its northern extremity where lay the big hotels and the wealthy modern residential quarter. Before leaving Granada that morning the Count had wired to the Hotel Atlántico for a suite, and on reaching the hotel they were shown straight up to it. The bedrooms, on either side of a private sitting-room, looked out across the public gardens to the sea, and La Torcera, whose only experience of a luxury hotel had been sleeping in one for a few hours the previous night, did not seek to hide her amazement at the elegance and comfort.

Although, for Spain, it was still early to dine, de Quesnoy sent for the head waiter, chose dinner and ordered it to be served in the sitting-room in half an hour. By the time they had unpacked and he had freshened himself up with a wash, the floor-waiter, assisted by a white-aproned *commis*, had laid the table and wheeled in a trolley with spirit-lamps burning under a number of dishes.

When they had dined and fortified themselves with a good bottle of Rioja he glanced at his watch and said to his companion, 'We have done very well. It is not yet half past ten; so the night life of the city can only just be starting. As soon as you are ready we will go out and take a look at it.'

'Tonight!' her face fell. 'But you had me out of bed hours earlier than I usually get up, and in Seville I had time for only half an hour's siesta.'

He shrugged. 'You dozed for quite a while in the train this morning. Anyhow, we cannot afford to lose an evening. I am suggesting not that you should spend the night haunting bars, but that we should make a reconnaissance; then tomorrow night you will not have to waste time finding out the most likely places in which to look for Inez Giudice. While you put on your things I will go downstairs and arrange for a guide.'

A quarter of an hour later, freshly made up and now wearing only a mantilla over her black hair, she joined him below in the lounge. The hall-porter had sent for a guide and after a short wait a page-boy came to fetch them. The guide, who introduced himself as Miguel, was a very small man in his middle thirties with side-whiskers and a leery expression. Obsequiously he bowed them into a hooded carriage and took the small seat opposite them. The coachman, evidently knowing the guide and his usual programme, did not wait for any order but flicked his horse lightly with his whip and they rattled away over the cobbles.

Miguel then proceeded to sound his customers about their tastes. Had he had only a man to deal with he would have come straight to the point, but as his patron had a woman in tow he had to be tactful. There was the remote possibility that she might be his wife, in which case they would wish only to drive through the most brightly-lit streets of the city and round its old walls with a stop at the castle on the point to admire the moonlight shimmering on the Atlantic rollers as they broke over the break-waters. If she was his mistress the odds were that after a short drive he would want to take her on a round of the better night-clubs, where they could dance and at one of which they would sup. But it was his experience that, not infrequently, rich men took their mistresses with them to brothels to watch nude cabaret shows and exhibitions of still more dubious kinds.

After pattering off his piece about Cadiz – known from its white-walled houses as 'The Silver Platter' – being the most beautiful town in Spain and that its climate, warm in winter and cooled by sea breezes in summer, made it the best of all holiday resorts, etc., etc., he went on to say that while its night-life could not rival that of Barcelona or Madrid, it had several *Maisons de Dance* of the first elegance and other establishments at which, if one cared for that sort of thing, one could see groups of young señoritas pose most artistically and see magic lantern displays of a curious and unusual nature.

De Quesnoy told him that they were not interested in señoritas, neither did they wish to dance that evening; but they would like to drive round to see the outsides of these places so that they might decide which they would prefer to patronize another night.

At this Miguel's sallow little face fell, as he saw disappear his hope of collecting a handsome commission from introducing his patrons at numerous places of entertainment. But he obediently gave appropriate orders to the coachman, and they drove down the brightly-lit Calle del Duque de la Victoria to the Plaza General Varela, then made a tour of the streets round about it in which considerable numbers of people were strolling.

Miguel pointed out to them four night-clubs that he recommended, but their fronts were ill-lit and no one was going into any of them. De Quesnoy remarked on this, and their guide said in surprise:

'But, Excellency, it is barely half past eleven. They do not open till midnight and do not really warm up until about two o'clock when people go on to them from the theatre.'

On his visits to Spain the Count had had no occasion to visit a night-club, but he had been to several theatres and recalling that, owing to the very late hours at which the Spanish upper class dined, they did not begin until eleven o'clock, he felt he should have realized that the dance places would not put on their cabarets until still later. To Miguel he said,

'As we do not intend to patronize any of them tonight their not yet being open makes no difference to us. We would like now to look at the ships in the port and drive round the harbour district.'

The driver was duly instructed and turned his carriage in a south-easterly direction. Then Miguel, with new hope in his voice, said, 'Down there is the house where you can see the magic lantern slides. It is owned by a friend of mine, a most respectable lady. The show, of course, could be put on specially for you in private so, if you did not wish you need not mix with other people who might be there. It will cost you only . . .'

'Thank you,' de Quesnoy cut him short. 'We are not interested in magic lantern slides, curious or otherwise. What we do wish to see is how the people of Cadiz amuse themselves at night; so take us, please, to the centre of the locality in which lie the less expensive dance-halls and bars.'

Miguel then had them driven to a Plaza approached from the landward side by three broad avenues all leading up to the palace of the Civil Governor, beyond which lay the docks and harbour. Turning right, out of the Plaza, they entered a maze of narrow streets that evidently formed part of the old city. Here there were so many sauntering couples and groups of men arguing on street corners that the carriage had to proceed at a walk; but that suited de Quesnoy, as it gave him time to ask the names of the streets through which they had passed and make a mental note of the places of entertainment that seemed to be doing most business.

In the poorer quarter night-life was already in full swing. Rows and arches of flaring gas-jets, designed to attract custom, enabled passers-by to see into steamy eating-houses and crowded bars. In a few of the larger cafés girls, tightly swathed in colourful long-fringed silk shawls, were dancing between the tables; while in every street some melody, either plaintive or gay, came to the ear as its notes were plucked out from mandolin or guitar.

To Miguel's frustration, the Count had the carriage driven to and fro through the same half-dozen streets for over an hour while steadfastly refusing even to stop and take a glass of wine anywhere; but when they finally returned to the Atlántico, about half past one in the morning, he was dismissed with a bigger tip than he had expected.

The following day they spent a lazy morning and it was not until after lunch that de Quesnoy discussed his plan in greater detail with La Torcera. He told her then that he wished her to play the part of a semi-blind beggar woman. In every Spanish city there were a legion of poor wretches, mostly cripples, who depended for their meagre livelihood on the coppers they could collect from the charitable. In consequence, pests though they were with their whining interruptions of conversations, there were very few cafés and even restaurants that they were not allowed to enter. His idea was that in this guise La Torcera should make the round of the places they had marked down the previous night in the hope of finding the one in which Inez Giudice plied her trade; and that if she succeeded Inez would remain in ignorance that she had been traced, because the hooded robe and eye-shade would prevent her from recognizing her erstwhile rival.

They filled in the afternoon with a drive right round the sea front that almost entirely encircled the city; then, when the shops reopened after the siesta, they bought a gross of matches, several dozen bootlaces, and a small tray that could be hung from the neck by a strap, so that La Torcera could hawk these wares for which it was customary to give beggars five to ten times their proper value.

That evening, after they had dined in their private sitting-room, the Count gave to La Torcera the eye-shade and the stick he had bought for her to tap her way about with, and they had a dress rehearsal. The gipsy dancer proved clever enough with her make-up to give the lower part of her face, which could still be seen beneath the shade, the appearance of that of a somewhat older woman, and when she tapped her way round the room with hunched shoulders and bent back de Quesnoy congratulated her on her performance.

At half past ten, while most of the hotel guests were still dining, he escorted her downstairs, wished her luck and saw her off into the warm darkness. He then had a word with the head hall-porter and told him a little story to ensure that La Torcera should meet with no difficulty about getting in on her return.

He said that the relative with whom he was sharing his suite was deeply religious and most charitable. Sometimes for several nights in succession she felt the urge to go off on her own and distribute money to the poor, but obviously she could not do so without fear of running into trouble if she went out dressed in her normal fashion. She therefore disguised herself as a beggar-woman and gave away boxes of matches to the destitute, in which they later found not matches but money. He then gave the head porter a handsome tip to pass these particulars on to the night porter.

It annoyed him that he could not participate in the search for Inez and Sanchez; but he would not have known the girl even had he come face to face with her, and to do that with Sanchez was the last thing he wanted, as he would then have been deprived of any chance of taking his enemy by surprise. It was to avoid any risk of doing so that he had elected to stay at the most luxurious hotel in Cadiz, as he and La Torcera could live there without any likelihood of its coming to Sanchez's ears that they were in the city.

He whiled away the next two hours by listening to a concert in the lounge, then went upstairs, changed into a dressing-gown, and did his best to concentrate on a novel by Blasco Ibáñez until La Torcera got back.

She returned about half past two, to report that she had had no luck. From eleven till one o'clock she had peddled her matches and bootlaces in the bistros and dance-halls down by the harbour, and had then moved on to the better-class clubs, at four of which, after tipping their doormen to let her in, she had had a good look round. De Quesnoy was naturally disappointed, although he knew that to expect success in such a quest at the first attempt had really been too much to hope for.

He had already found that he and La Torcera had so little in

common that there were few subjects on which they could talk
with mutual interest. Since, too, he was both rich and handsome
she had, not unnaturally, soon had visions of herself living permanently in clover, so indicated very clearly that she was quite ready
to become his mistress; but he had promptly, though courteously,
poured cold water on her ambitions in that direction. Recognizing
that the only bond between them lay in their common desire to run
Sanchez and Inez to earth, he felt no scruples next day at leaving her
with a pile of picture papers, revelling in the –for her – unusual luxury
of her surroundings, while he went out on his own.

Restrained by caution from going into the main streets of the
city, just in case he was seen by Sanchez, he remained in its wealthy
residential quarter, in the morning amusing himself by shooting
clay pigeons, ejected by a machine for him over the sea-wall,
and in the evening taking a long stroll in the Parque Genoves.

That night they followed the same routine as they had on the
previous one, but again La Torcera had no luck.

Next morning de Quesnoy paid another visit to the park and
sat there for quite a time considering the situation. It was now
October the 3rd, so six days since Sanchez had taken that incriminating photograph in San Sebastian. If it had been his intention
to return to Cadiz he could easily have reached the city, even
by slow trains, three days ago. The inference that he had, had
been drawn only from the fact that his latest woman, Inez Giudice,
was a native of Cadiz. On leaving Granada he might quite well
have gone off with her elsewhere. If so, for the time being there
was no possible means of tracing them.

However, the Count reasoned, six days having elapsed, by now
Sanchez should have made an attempt to exert some form of
blackmail through the photograph. Allowing two days for him
to reach the place where he meant to go to earth, a third for a
letter from him to reach San Sebastian, a fourth for Gulia to send
it on to Granada and a fifth for the hall-porter to forward it on
to him in Cadiz, it should have arrived that morning. As that
schedule made no allowance for delays, de Quesnoy felt it might
easily be another couple of days before Sanchez's ultimatum reached
him.

When it did, the advantage would lie with the enemy, as there
could no longer be any hope of taking him by surprise. To stand
any chance of getting hold of that damnable photograph he,
de Quesnoy, would have to walk into whatever trap Sanchez
might set for him. It was a gloomy prospect; but there was still
a chance that Sanchez might be in Cadiz, or that Inez might be

found and bribed or forced to give information as to his where-abouts; so there must be no relaxing the search for them until the letter turned up to provide a definite, if dangerous, new opening.

That night La Torcera again set off on her quest while the Count kept a lonely vigil. She returned much earlier than expected. It was only a little after midnight and he had not long left the lounge to go up to their suite. To his delight he saw at a glance that she had news. Her eyes sparkling with excitement, she exclaimed:

'I've found her! It was sheer luck. I was doing my act as usual in one of the bars when I overheard two men at a table talking. One said to the other, "Have you been to the Silver Galleon lately? There's a red-head there, a girl named Inez, that I used to know as a kid. She left Cadiz some time ago but she came back last month. She won't play for less than ten pesetas, but you can take my word that she's worth every centavo of it." '

'And then?' asked the Count eagerly.

'I felt sure he must have been speaking of the bitch we're after; so in another bar I asked the whereabouts of the Silver Galleon. It is a fair-sized inn some way from the red-light district but still on the water-front. It lies behind the little park in which stands the memorial to the Cortes. I went off there at once and my luck was in. The place has a cosy little bar and is frequented by the better class of seamen. There were eight or ten of them in there drinking and playing dice, and only two girls: Inez and another. I hung about for a bit and again luck favoured me. One of the men had been standing her drinks and they went out together. I shuffled after them and managed to see that they didn't leave the house. They went upstairs together; so evidently she's got a room there and the landlord is in on it, taking a rake-off on her earnings.'

'I suppose you saw no sign of Sanchez?'

She shook her head. 'No, none. But at that hour it would have been surprising to see them together. If she is keeping him, as I have no doubt she is, the last thing she would do is to go about with her in the evenings. Even if he loitered in the same bar it would soon get round that he was her bully and be likely to scare off her possible customers.'

'That's true. Anyhow, your having run her to earth is half the battle. With luck now, she'll lead me to him.'

For a moment de Quesnoy was tempted to go out there and then on the chance that by the time he reached the Silver Galleon Inez would be back down in the bar hoping to pick up another customer, but he put the idea from him. She might be spending the night with the man who had gone upstairs with her, or when he had left her decide not to come down again; and he did not want to show himself in the bar until he could be reasonably certain that she would be there.

Next morning he made out a draft on the Banco de Coralles for four thousand pesetas in favour of La Torcera. With the thousand he had already given her she would be receiving about £200 for her services, but he did not consider that an excessive price for having enabled him again to get on Sanchez's track, seeing that there had been no other possible way of his doing so.

He thought it very unlikely that her troupe at Granada would refuse to take her back after her few days' absence or, if they did, that she would not be able to get a job as a dancer in a café. In any case, with her normally modest way of living, such a sum would keep her for a year, or provide a much fatter nest egg than that of which Sanchez had robbed her. Even so, as he had promised her the money, he was surprised and touched when, on his giving her the draft, she burst into tears, kissed his hands, called down blessings on him and declared him to be a true *hidalgo*.

Before lunch he went out and bought at a ready-made clothes shop a blue cloth suit with a square-breasted jacket, a muffler and a flat cap with a shiny peak, which would give him a some-what nautical appearance. Then, thinking it probable that he might be up all night, he went to bed in the afternoon and had a long sleep.

In the evening he had an early meal sent up to the sitting-room and afterwards changed into the rig-out that he had bought earlier in the day. No letter forwarded on by Gulia had arrived that morning, so La Torcera's having located Inez Giudice remained his only chance of getting on Sanchez's trail. That he might not have returned to her after his trip to San Sebastian, or had returned and since left her for some other woman, were, the Count realized, depressing possibilities. But should either prove the case he might still hope to deal with Inez as he had with La Torcera and secure from her a new lead to his quarry.

At half past nine, still speculating, not altogether pessimistically, on his chances of settling accounts with Sanchez that night, he walked out of the Hotel Atlántico. He had left La Torcera up in the sitting-room immersed in a new batch of picture papers. Now that she had done the job that he had required of her and he had paid her off, it was his intention the following morning to put her safely on a train back to Granada. The one thing he did not expect was that he would never see her again.

14

The Red-headed Harlot

HAVING been indoors most of the day de Quesnoy had intended to walk to the Silver Galleon, but it was something over a mile away and within a few minutes of leaving the Atlántico there was a distant rumble of thunder, then it came on to rain; so he picked up a carriage. It set him down opposite the flamboyant monument commemorating the Cortes held in Cadiz in 1812, that had given Spain her famous Liberal Constitution, then he walked through the park in the direction La Torcero had told him that the Silver Galleon lay.

He found the inn without difficulty. It stood on a corner and was a rambling old seventeenth-century two-storied building with tiled roofs that buckled here and there, gable windows and an archway in its front that faced on to the park and port. After inspecting its two visible sides, the Count walked through the archway to find, as he expected, that it led to a yard that had stabling for three or four vehicles and about a dozen horses. A covered wagon stood in its centre but no one was about.

On either side of the archway, near its street end, there was a door. From under one only a faint light showed; from the other came a much brighter light and the sound of voices. This door obviously led to the bar. The short, sharp shower was over but de Quesnoy still had the collar of his jacket turned up and now, pulling the peak of his cap well down, he went in.

At a glance he saw it to be a comfortable room furnished with old but solid pieces. In one corner four men were playing dice, farther along two others were seated drinking, a seventh was leaning on the bar and, beyond him, two women were sitting in an inglenook with a table in front of them. Behind the bar stood a broad-shouldered, square-faced man of about fifty with greyish grizzled hair, whom de Quesnoy rightly guessed to be the landlord.

Touching his cap with a murmured *Buenas tardes* to the company, he walked over to the bar and ordered himself a brandy and ginger-ale. It was not a mixture that he particularly liked, but he had found that while the best Spanish brandy, although not comparable with fine French cognac, was quite palatable, the worst could be horrible; so in a place like this it was safer not to take it neat.

The landlord had been chatting with the other men at the bar. As he served the Count, he remarked that it was getting late in the year for a thunderstorm, but it didn't look like coming to much. De Quesnoy replied that it had already stopped raining, which was a pity as it was oppressive and a bit more would have freshened things up. Then the landlord just nodded and moved along to resume his conversation with his earlier customer.

The Count took a drink and lit a cigarette. Both the women behind him were wearing mantillas made from small fluffy black bobbles sewn on to net, but under this head-dress the hair of one of them had certainly been lightish, and as nine out of ten women in Spain were brunettes he felt fairly certain she would prove to be Inez Giudice. It looked, too, as though he had timed his entry well, as he had not wanted to have to linger about there and perhaps be drawn into conversation with other people before she turned up, or, on the other hand, leave his arrival so late that she might have already been picked up by some other man.

When he had smoked a third of his cigarette he glanced round and remained looking at the two girls for a moment as though he had noticed them for the first time. Now, he had no doubt that the fair one was Inez. Her head had been in shadow when he had glanced at her before, but now the rays of a lamp on the bar brought out its vivid red lights. As their eyes met she smiled and closed one of hers in a wink.

Returning her smile, he carried his glass over to their table, asked permission to join them, and then if he might buy them a drink. The red-head asked for a Calisay and the darker woman for an Anis. Having collected the two liqueurs from the bar, the Count told them his name was Jaime. His lead confirmed his belief that the red-head was Inez and the dark one said her name was Beatriz.

Now that de Quesnoy had a chance to look at them closely he saw that Beatriz was by a good bit the older of the two. Her face was very ordinary, with a heavy jowl and a rather bovine but not unpleasant expression. Inez, on the other hand, he decided, would prove distinctly attractive to anyone who liked the *gamine* type. She had a small freckled face with a *retroussé* nose, a wide mouth and merry grey eyes. What he could see of her figure was also good and, barely concealed by the fichu of her bodice, two small plump breasts, pushed up by her stays, pouted invitingly. Even so, experience told him that with such small features she might be more amusing but would not be as passionate as her companion, and would certainly prove more hard-boiled.

For a few minutes they talked platitudes about the weather – how oppressive it was and what a pity that the rain had stopped – then Inez said to him, 'You are not Spanish, are you?'

'No,' he replied, 'I am British, and in my own country I am called James.'

'Are you the master of a ship?' Beatriz inquired.

He shook his head. 'No, only the representative of a Shipping Company. I am out here to make some new arrangements with our agents in Cadiz.'

They asked him how long he had been in the city, whether he had been to Spain before, if he liked the country, and so on; to all of which questions he made suitable replies. But in every case he addressed his replies to Inez, hardly giving her companion a glance.

After ten minutes Beatriz took the hint. Finishing her Anis, she said to Inez with good-natured resignation, 'Well, dear, two's company and three's none, as they say; and you're the lucky one again. Maybe I'll see you later if the gentleman doesn't keep you too long. Have a good time, both of you, and thanks for the drink.'

De Quesnoy did not seek to detain her; but as with a rustle of skirts she stood up to leave them, he said, 'At least permit me to buy you another Anis to drink while you are waiting for a happy encounter with some old or new friend who may arrive to entertain you.'

It was a gracious gesture and both girls smiled their appreciation. When she had settled herself in another corner of the room he took the Anis over to her, then he collected from the bar another Calisay for Inez and another brandy and ginger-ale for himself.

As he sat down again she smiled at him, pouted her mouth, and said the one word, 'Well?'

'Well?' he repeated, returning her smile. 'Do you live far from here?'

'No.' She winked one of her bright grey eyes, then nodded in the direction of the big man behind the bar. 'I live in the house, and Señor Anzana makes no objection to my taking gentlemen friends up to my room. Would you like to see it?'

'Indeed I would,' he told her quickly.

'All right then.' Her grey eyes narrowed a trifle. 'But you understand I want a nice present.'

'Of course,' he nodded, 'that's only fair. But how much? I'm not a rich man, and the money I brought from England has got to last me out.'

'Thirty pesetas,' she suggested.

Knowing her price to be much less, he shook his head. 'No, I can't afford more than twenty.'

She considered for a moment, then nodded. 'Very well then. I wouldn't, if it weren't that I like you. You're different, somehow, to most of the men who come here.'

'I like you too,' he returned the compliment. 'You, too, are different from the sort of girls one expects to find in a place like this.' It was on the tip of his tongue to add, 'I don't wonder that licentious young devil, Sanchez, ran off with you!' but he checked himself in time.

Standing up, she said, 'Let's go upstairs, then.' Simultaneously he rose and walked the length of the bar with her. A few of the men looked up then hid a smile, but most of them took no notice.

They crossed under the archway, entered the door on its far side, and Inez led the way up a flight of stairs. At their top she walked down a corridor in which a dim light was burning. Opening the last door but one on the right she turned, smiled at de Quesnoy, and said, 'Here we are.'

He followed her in and she lit an oil lamp. On taking a quick look round he was conscious of sharp disappointment. It was a small slip-room, hardly more than a cubby-hole and furnished only with a narrow single bed. It seemed that after all she did not live at the Silver Galleon as La Torcero had supposed, but had only professional accommodation there; and even if she used it at times to sleep in, it was quite clear that Sanchez did not share it with her.

Turning away from the lamp, she put her arms round his neck, gave him a swift kiss, and asked, 'Would you like me to undress?'

'I certainly would,' he told her, as his object now was to play for time during which he hoped to get some useful information out of her.

'It will cost you five pesetas more,' she warned him.

'All right,' he agreed. 'You're pretty enough to be worth it.'

At that moment there came a loud crash of thunder and heavy drops of rain began to patter on the roof above.

'Wait a minute,' she said. 'I must shut the window of the other room.'

Picking up the lamp, she stepped over to a door that evidently connected the little room with the last one on that side of the corridor. Opening it, she went through and, by the light of the lamp she had taken with her, de Quesnoy had a fair sight of the room beyond. It was considerably larger than the slip-room in which he stood, with a double bed, chairs, a dressing-table and a wardrobe beside which stood a pair of man's boots.

At her first mention of another room the Count's pulses had quickened, and when his glance lit on the boots he felt a thrill of elation. She was living at the Silver Galleon after all, and a man was living with her. He might not be Sanchez but there was a fifty-fifty chance that he was.

The rain was now streaming down. She had closed the window and picked up the lamp. De Quesnoy's best hope of learning more before resorting to a direct question lay in making her talk as much as possible. As she came back towards him, he asked:

'Why shouldn't we use that room? It looks much more comfortable.'

She gave a quick shake of her small red head. 'No. That is where I sleep. I share it with my man. For business I always use this room.'

Frowning, he feigned uneasiness. 'D'you mean that your husband might come up to that room at any time? If he did he would hear and surprise us.'

'You've no need to worry, dear,' she gave an easy laugh. 'He stays out half the night drinking and arguing with others of his kind at a political club to which he belongs. Even if he did return while I had someone here he knows his own interests better than to make a scene about it.'

Giving no sign of his satisfaction at this strong indication that her man was Sanchez, de Quesnoy continued to frown, and went on:

'I think you have been very unlucky, Inez, in marrying a man who makes use of you like this.'

With a quick shrug, she said, 'He's not really my husband; but he's got all those qualities that attract a woman. I may be a fool, but I'm mad about him.'

The Count threw out a mild sneer. 'He can't be much of a man if he lets others have you.'

It worked. She bridled at once and threw back, 'Speak only of what you know. If he were in work of course he would keep me. But he is a political and wanted by the police on account of some trouble he got into in Barcelona; so he dare not take a job. As things are, it is only right that I should support him.'

That, de Quesnoy felt, clinched the matter. Tonight, at last, his luck was really in. There would now be no need for him even to mention Sanchez to Inez, let alone go through another such performance as he had with La Torcera in order to get another

7

lead to Sanchez's whereabouts. All he had to do was render Inez temporarily helpless and silent to ensure himself a free field. He could then search the bedroom for that damning negative and any prints of it there might be. If he failed to find them he would await Sanchez's return, hold him up at the point of the revolver and force him to reveal their hiding-place. Whether he found them first or had to wait until Sanchez came back, once he had secured them he meant to march Sanchez off to the police station for speedy dispatch to Barcelona so that he could be tried in the coming week with his father and brother.

'Well!' Inez chided him, breaking in on his thoughts. 'Don't look so serious. Just put my little present on that shelf over there, and I'll show you that a Spanish girl can give you a better time than an English one.'

'I doubt it,' he replied with a laugh. 'But get your things off and we'll see.'

As he spoke he produced some money, counted out the agreed amount of pesetas and laid them on the shelf. With a nod of acknowledgement she plucked with both hands at the ruching of her long full skirt and pulled it inside out over her head. For a second he contemplated seizing her and using its folds to muffle her cries; but he decided that his original plan for dealing with the sort of situation that had arisen would save a struggle and prove more satisfactory.

Unbuttoning his square jacket, he took it off. She had rid herself of her petticoat and was standing in bloomers and a cotton bodice. With a well-practised gesture she pushed the bloomers down, gave them a swift kick with her right foot lifting a shapely leg high into the air and, as the bloomers left her toe, caught them in her right hand.

As he unknotted his muffler he laughed his appreciation of her little trick, while thinking that many a sailor home from the seas might travel farther and fare worse than with this lively little red-head.

She then sat down on the edge of the bed to undo the suspender clips that attached her stockings to her long whale-boned stays. It was for her to sit down that he had been waiting. Moving round behind her, ostensibly to hang his coat on a peg in the door to the other room, he pulled from his left hand pocket a silk sock tied at the top and having in it a big fistful of sand. As he swung the sock the sand formed a ball in its toe. With a swish, he brought it down hard on the back of her head.

Stunned by the impact, without even a moan, she heeled over

sideways and slipped off the bed. Picking her up, he laid her back
on it at full length. From a pocket in his coat he took some lengths
of tape with which he tied her wrists and ankles, then he picked
up from the floor a handkerchief she had dropped, and stuffed
it into her mouth. As the handkerchief was quite small it did not
make a very efficient gag, but had he used a larger one there would
have been a possibility that she might suffocate while unconscious,
and he felt confident that the little ball of linen between her tongue
and palate would be quite sufficient to prevent her, when she did
come to, from making a noise loud enough to attract attention.
Finally, he used another length of the tape to make a loop round
her neck, then tied its end to the iron bed-rail above her head, so
that, with her ankles and wrists bound, she could not get off the
bed without choking herself.

As he looked down at his handiwork he thought, 'Poor little
devil, I expect that by this time next week she will be working for
some other blackguard; but with luck tonight I'll rid her of a
murderer.' Then, to console her for the blow on the head, he took
some more money from his pocket and made the amount on the
shelf up to a hundred pesetas.

Readjusting his muffler, he put on his jacket and, while doing
so, he saw that the door on which he had hung it had, at about
chest level, an oblong slit like a letter-box in it. He had not noticed
it before, because on the far side of the door it was masked by
a strip of material the same colour as the paintwork. For a moment
he wondered what purpose it served, then decided that it was
probably used as a spy-hole so that anyone in the big bedroom
could lift the flap, peep through and see what was going on in the
smaller. But, having more important things to think about, he
quickly dismissed it from his mind.

Picking up the lamp he carried it into the larger room and set
it down on a small table. At his first swift glance round his eye
lit on a camera hanging by a strap from a hook on the door giving
on to the corridor. From what he had seen of Sanchez's as they
had struggled together in the moonlight it looked the same. A
moment later he had verified that it was because the leather was
stained from its having been partly submerged in the lily pool.
Opening it up he removed the spool, unrolled the film and held
it up to the light to find that it was a new one, no part of which
had been used.

There was no desk or bureau in the room so he decided that
the chest of drawers was the best place to start his hunt for the
negative. Its contents were almost entirely clothes belonging to

Inez. Quickly he turned them over and thrust his hands into the corners of the drawers, one after another, but they yielded nothing of interest. Next he tried the wardrobe. One hanging space held Inez's dresses, the other garments belonging to Sanchez. He went through the latter most carefully but the pockets had in them only a few old bills, lottery tickets and betting vouchers. The shelves and drawers of the central compartment were evidently shared, and contained scarves, mantillas, socks and shirts. Less hopefully he went to the dressing-table; its two shallow drawers had in them only Inez's manicure and make-up things.

Anxiously now, he stared round for likely hiding places then, stooping, looked under the bed. Beneath it there were three corded wooden boxes. Pulling one of them out he got the cord undone and with the aid of a long steel buttonhook prised the case open. Its contents revealed that Inez was a born hoarder. The box held the oddest collection of junk, valueless except to its owner. He prised open the second box and, to save time, upended it so that its contents spilled out over the floor. Among the pile of old hand-bags, bull-fight programmes, small gaudily painted figures of saints, garter rosettes, a pack of fortune-telling cards and some fancy scent bottles, were two albums. One was half-filled with picture postcards, mostly of a low comic variety or of holiday resorts; the other held photographs, but they were only faded snaps of Inez at various ages and, presumably, her family and friends. The third box held another medley of souvenirs from her perhaps more innocent past.

Angrily, de Quesnoy pushed the three boxes and most of the junk they had contained back under the bed, scrambled to his feet and cast around afresh. His searching eyes stopped again at the wardrobe as the thought came to him that there might be something on top of it. Pulling over a chair, he stepped up on to it and peered into the hollow behind the cornice. Hidden there from ground level lay a flat leather satchel. Seizing it, he jumped down and tried to open it but found it to be locked. Praying that he had at last found what he sought, and not a collection of love letters to Inez, he again used the long steel buttonhook to force its lock. Taking the satchel by its ends he tipped its contents out on to the bed. Twenty or thirty negatives and photographs shot out. One glance at them was enough. His eyes lit with triumph.

Quickly he shuffled through them, seeking the one of Gulia and himself, but he could not find it. Then it struck him that nearly all the prints were very similar. They had a blob of light up in the right-hand top corner and vague whitish figures lower down to the left. Picking up two of them he carried them over to the lamp.

As he examined them under the better light he gave a grim smile. They revealed the use to which the letter-box-like slit in the communicating door between the two rooms was put. While Inez entertained her clients Sanchez took photographs through it. The blob of light was the lamp up on a shelf, turned low; the whitish figures now spoke for themselves.

On examining some of the others the Count found that in many of them Inez's face was turned away but in every one that of the man showed. As photographs all of them were very poor, but in the majority the man's features were clear enough to identify him.

It was easy to see the vile game Sanchez was playing. Having taken his photograph he waited until Inez's customer left her, then slipped out and followed him. Judging by the men down in the bar most of them would be mates and bosuns from cargo vessels, or passengers who had come ashore for the evening from small coasters. On such birds of passage Sanchez would have wasted his time. But all the odds were that quite a number of port officials and local tradesmen also patronized the Silver Galleon. Those who had also patronized Inez would have been traced by Sanchez to their homes and, no doubt, several of the married men among them were now being squeezed by him for a quota of pesetas every week.

De Quesnoy recalled how Sanchez had boasted to him in Barcelona about blackmailing the unfortunate little Marquesa. It would have been his success in that which had led to him adopting as a regular occupation this infamous way of making money. In disgust the Count threw the prints he was holding back on the bed.

Among them he had seen no print that could possibly have been of Gulia and himself, but he had not yet examined the negatives. Gathering them together he took them to the lamp and, one by one, held them up to the light. As he looked at the sixth he gave a little gasp of delight. This was it, and as he stared at the negative he could hardly believe his good fortune.

In the left upper corner there showed the sharply outlined profile of a small bronze bust, one of a pair that had stood on the top of a low secretaire in his room at San Sebastian. For him that identified beyond all doubt the place of which the shot had been taken, but there was nothing else that could, and the only other thing visible on the negative was a little less than half of a woman's body from her raised arm to her foot. Gulia's elbow protruded because her arm had been round his neck. The blinding flash of the magnesium flare made her limbs in the negative dead black, and the diaphanous nightdress she had been wearing had not even blurred the lovely outline from bust to waist and along the curve of her hip. But where her face should have been, and the back of his head and body, the negative was completely blank.

In an instant he guessed the reason. When Sanchez had tripped and fallen flat in the lily pool the camera case must have come into violent contact with the stone rim of the pool or the ground. The jolt must have damaged the camera itself, so that before Sanchez had a chance to develop the film a little light had seeped in and ruined it.

With a sigh of thankfulness he put it in his pocket.

No damning print could have been made from it, so there was no longer the least risk that José de Cordoba would ever learn of his wife's desperate infatuation or believe that his friend had betrayed him with her. Even if by some freak of chance he did see the ruined negative and thought he recognized the bronze bust in it, there was nothing whatever to prove that the portion of woman's body was Gulia's. It might have been another similar bust in another house and any well-made tallish woman. That being the case, the Count decided to keep it as a memento of a night upon which he had been tempted almost beyond endurance.

The fact that the negative had been spoilt explained why Sanchez had made no use of it, and why no blackmailing letter had been forwarded on by Gulia. As de Quesnoy realized that, he wondered what Sanchez was up to now. Inez had said that he spent most of his nights drinking and arguing at a political club. Perhaps on some nights he did, and this was one of them. But he certainly did not spend all of them that way, as was shown by the photographs spread out over the bed.

Suddenly an idea came to the Count that made him laugh. How surprised Sanchez would have been if he had remained lurking in the room that night and, on hearing Inez bring a customer up to the room next door, got his camera ready, then on peering through the letter-box slit found that her customer was the deadly enemy that he believed to be still in San Sebastian.

It was at that moment that he was taken by surprise himself. He heard a noise behind him. Swinging round he saw that the door to the corridor had opened, and framed in the doorway stood Sanchez.

15

The Broken Mirror

THE explanation for Sanchez's unexpected arrival flashed instantly upon de Quesnoy. To guard, as far as possible, against Inez having been picked up by some other man before he reached the Silver Galleon he had gone there early. It could not have been much after a quarter past ten when she had taken him up to her room. Most nights she would probably not have succeeded in attracting a customer who would pay her price until about eleven. His search of the bedroom and looking through the photographs must have taken him longer than he thought and had brought him up to the time when, normally, Sanchez would return with the hope of finding that she had a man with her whom he might be able to photograph and blackmail.

As those thoughts coursed through his mind his hand leapt behind him to pull his revolver from his hip pocket. But Sanchez had recognized and was too quick for him. Giving one shout of surprised rage at finding his hideout had been discovered, the brawny young Spaniard flung himself upon his enemy. The impact was like that made by the charge of a young bull upon an unskilful amateur matador. The Count went over backwards on the bed with Sanchez on top of him. Half the breath was knocked out of his body. His arms had been flung out sideways. Bringing his hands together he grasped Sanchez by the throat. Sanchez dug his powerful chin down just in time and prevented the grasp becoming a stranglehold. With his left fist he struck downward at de Quesnoy's face. The Count jerked his head aside but the blow caught him on the cheek and the side of his aquiline nose. Sanchez's right hand had slid down to his cummerbund. It reappeared holding a long, thin blade. The fist that held it swept up above the prostrate Count. By the light of the lamp he caught the glint of murder in Sanchez's dark eyes. Letting go his hold on Sanchez's neck he shot out a hand and grabbed the wrist that held the knife.

For a few moments there was a tense, desperate struggle. Only the sound of gasps came from the two men. Suddenly the Count raised his head and fixed his teeth in Sanchez's chin. Sanchez let out a howl of agony. At the same instant de Quesnoy gave a violent twist and the knife dropped from the anarchist's hand.

Again they wrestled fiercely. The sweat was pouring off them both. The Count's left hand still grasped Sanchez's right wrist. With their free hands they strove to strike or grasp one another. The blood from the Spaniard's chin mingled with that from de Quesnoy's nose. Making a feint, the Count thrust his hand under Sanchez's guard, seized him by the left ear and pulled upon it. The anarchist gave another yelp of pain. To prevent his ear from being torn off he was forced to roll sideways. The Count gave a heave, threw him over and next moment was on top of him.

But only for a moment. With all his strength Sanchez brought up his right knee. It would have been the finish of de Quesnoy had he not jerked his thighs together and taken the brunt of the blow upon them. Even as it was, he in turn gave a sharp cry followed by a groan, and the upward thrust unseated him. Yet their hands and arms were still interlocked. Simultaneously both gave a violent twist in the same direction. They slid off the bed and landed with a crash on the floor.

Sanchez was underneath. The back of his head struck the boards first, with a hard resounding thud. His body went limp. With a surge of relief the Count realized that he had him at his mercy. It was at that moment, in the sudden silence succeeding the noise of their struggle, that he heard a dragging sound in the next room.

Panting and still trembling from his exertions, he staggered to his feet. He had left the communicating door to the other room partly open, but it was dark in there. Grabbing the door handle, he pulled the door wide. Now there was enough light for him to see inside. Somehow Inez had managed to gnaw through the tape he had put round her neck and tied to the head of the bed. He could see about eight inches of its end still tied to the rail. And she was no longer on the bed. Her wrists and ankles were still tied but she was dragging herself along the floor towards the door that gave on to the corridor.

Taking in the situation at a glance, de Quesnoy guessed that she must have been conscious and working to regain her freedom for some time. Knowing that Sanchez would be returning soon after eleven she had probably been lying there, not daring to move till he came on the scene, but ready to act the moment he did. As she had managed to gnaw through the tape it seemed certain that she had first succeeded in working the gag out of her mouth. At any moment she might scream for help.

De Quesnoy moved to dive through the doorway. His arms were outstretched to seize her, but his hands clutched empty air. A strong arm had been thrown round his neck. It dragged him back. Sanchez had either only feigned being stunned, or his thick skull had saved him from being knocked out for more than a few seconds. He had come swiftly and silently to his feet behind his enemy, and suddenly gained the advantage over him.

For a few moments de Quesnoy strove in vain to break Sanchez's grip. Gasping for breath he felt himself being pulled over backwards by his more powerful antagonist. In desperation he lifted his right foot and kicked out behind him with all his might. His heel caught Sanchez on the shin bone. The sickening pain caused him to relax his hold. De Quesnoy swivelled round within it and jabbed him hard in the stomach. Sanchez was still groggy from having struck his head on the floor. Reeling backwards with the wind knocked out of him, he half doubled up.

Finding herself discovered Inez began to shout. She had now reached the door and was endeavouring to struggle up on to her knees. De Quesnoy knew that if he could not deal with them both in the next few minutes he would be caught like a rat in a trap. But he could not deal with both of them simultaneously.

Although bent half double Sanchez was reaching out a hand across the bed. On it lay the knife that he had been forced to drop. The Count dared not let him snatch it up. With his left hand he grabbed a handful of the Spaniard's coarse, black curly hair and hauled him back.

Out of the corner of his eye he caught a glimpse of Inez, still yelling murder. She had got to her feet and was striving to get a grasp on the door knob. Her hands having been bound palm to palm made that by no means easy; but if she succeeded in opening the door, her shouts would echo down the corridor and carry double the distance they did at the moment.

De Quesnoy decided that if he was to save himself there was only one thing to do. When he had first come upon the cunning, coarsely handsome oaf he now held by the hair, he had been making a bomb in the very laboratory in which it was virtually certain that Morral had learned to make the type of bomb that had killed Angela. A few weeks later he had first wanted to cut de Quesnoy's throat, then suggested roasting him alive, and finally lent a willing hand in an attempt to murder him by suffocation. If more was wanted he was the lowest form of criminal cur who lived on the immoral earnings of women and blackmail.

Lifting his right foot the Count drew back his bent leg. Next second he brought his knee up hard against Sanchez's rump. The anarchist's body reacted to the blow by shooting forward. At the same instant de Quesnoy gave a sudden wrench on his hair, jerking his head violently back. There came the sound of a sharp crack. Sanchez's head suddenly dragged like a ton weight on the hand that grasped his black curls. The Count let go and the limp body slumped across the edge of the bed. He had broken Sanchez's neck.

Swivelling round, de Quesnoy dashed into the small room to secure Inez and muffle her shouts. He was too late. At the very instant he had put an end to Sanchez she had got the door open. As she pushed it wide, her ankles still being tied, she had lost her balance and fallen. Her red hair and most of her body were now out in the corridor and she was screaming at the top of her voice. Still worse, her earlier shouts for help must have been heard, for the Count caught the sound of footsteps pounding up the stairs only twenty feet away.

The corridor was a cul-de-sac ending in a window between the big bedroom and another room opposite. Jumping over Inez's prostrate body de Quesnoy ran to it. From the reconnaissance he had made of the inn before going into its bar, he felt certain that the window overlooked the central courtyard and, as the rooms of the old building had low ceilings, he knew that he would not have far to drop.

But he had overlooked the fact that in old inns windows giving on to landings and passages are rarely opened. When he reached it he found it stuck fast. As he turned away he saw several men, one behind the other, charging down the corridor towards him. Turning, he dashed through the door to the bedroom, slammed it behind him and shot its bolt. The window in there would, he knew, open, because Inez had gone to close it on account of the storm.

Having bolted the door to the corridor had not secured his retreat. The men who were after him could still come through the slip-room. The question which now agitated his racing brain was 'Could he get the window open and drop from it before they were upon him?'

He decided that he could not. That precious minute trying to get the window in the corridor open had robbed him of the vital leeway needed to escape. But there was still a chance. He felt sure he had seen a bolt on the communicating door. If he could close and bolt that he would be temporarily safe.

He sprang round the bed, leapt towards the door and slammed it shut. But only in the nick of time. The leading man, a crop-headed fellow who looked like a Scandinavian bosun, had just stumbled past Inez and was within six feet of him. His fumbling fingers found the bolt on the door. With a gasp of thankfulness, he shot it.

THE BROKEN MIRROR 203

Turning again, he jumped over Sanchez's sprawling legs, pulled the dressing-table aside, and reached the window. Grasping its lower sash he pulled it up and gratefully gulped in the cool night air. At that second there came a resounding crash. The connecting door between the two rooms was only a flimsy affair. The muscular square-head had burst it open with one kick of his heavy boot.

Again, there was not much more than six feet between them. De Quesnoy knew that he could not get through the window before the sailor grabbed him. He had only one course left; to hold him and the others back and, if possible, drive them from the room under the threat of his revolver. Wrenching it out he pointed it at the seaman and shouted:

'Halt! Another step forward and I fire.'

The Scandinavian halted in his tracks. Behind him was a dark-visaged Spaniard. Covered by the bulky form of the man in front of him, he drew a knife. For a moment all the figures in the room were still: the Count standing beside the dressing-table with his revolver levelled, the little mob of men who had come to get him crowded into the doorway and the slip-room beyond it. Then, leaning sideways, the Spaniard threw his knife.

De Quesnoy saw his movement just in time and sprang aside. His swift action saved him. The knife flashed past him through the open window. But calamity followed. One of his feet came down in some spilt blood, either from his own nose or Sanchez's chin. He slipped and went over backwards. As he hit the floor his revolver was knocked from his hand.

For a moment he thought it was all up with him, but as the square-head dived at him he kicked out blindly. It was a lucky stroke. The toe of his boot caught the seaman on the point of the chin. His teeth clicked and he crashed to the floor out cold. The Spaniard had also sprung forward but tripped over the square-head's body and fell upon him. The Count rolled over twice, came up on his feet and grabbed the dressing-table mirror. He had always been told that to break a mirror was an unlucky thing to do, but it was the only weapon close at hand. As the Spaniard rose to come at him again de Quesnoy brought it smashing down on his head. It splintered into a hundred fragments. With blood streaming down his face the Spaniard sank back with a groan on to the unconscious body of the Scandinavian.

Four more men were crowded into the doorway, the brawny grizzled landlord among them. But seeing the way in which the Count had dealt with two of their companions, the nearest of the group – a lean, sallow-faced youngster – now showed reluctance to tackle him. With shouts and curses the other three both urged him on and tried to push past him. The indecision of the young fellow gave de Quesnoy the moment's respite he so badly needed. In one stride he reached the table on which stood the oil lamp. Picking it up he hurled it at them.

With a tinkle of glass its chimney broke. The oil in the container spurted out over two of the men, Sanchez's recumbent body and the side of the bed. Instantly rivulets of fire were running in half a dozen different directions and flames leaping up. Cries of terror came from the men and fresh screams from Inez added to the din.

De Quesnoy wasted no time waiting to see the results of his bombshell. Having thrown it, he stepped back to the window, threw one leg over its low sill, then the other, squirmed over on to his stomach, ducked his head and wriggled out. For a moment he hung from the sill by his hands, then he let himself drop.

As his feet hit the cobbles he tried to flex his knees, but one of his ankles turned over and he pitched sideways to measure his length on the ground. Picking himself up, he darted in the direction of the archway, but as he put his right foot to the ground he gave an 'ouch!' of pain. He had twisted his ankle badly. All the same, he knew that unless he ran for it, and ran hard, he might yet be caught.

Ignoring the pain that shot through his ankle with every stride he took, he gained the archway at a loping run and dived into it. As he did so two men entered its far end from the street. They turned towards the door to the bar, then noticed him and stopped. For him there could be no turning back, and it was too late to pretend, by dropping into a walk, that he was not trying to get away from the place quickly. Running on, he made a sudden swerve and attempted to dart past the two men. But the nearer grabbed him by the arm, swung him round to a halt, and demanded:

'Hi, mate! Where are you off to in such a hurry?'

'It's none of your business! Let me go!' he cried angrily, and strove to drag his arm free. The man had a firm grip on his coat sleeve and refused to be shaken off. For half a minute their tug-of-war continued, then de Quesnoy's heart sank. Faint but clear, coming through the archway there were shouts of:

'Stop thief! Murder! Murder! Stop thief!'

Both the men heard them. The first shot out his free hand and grasped the Count's wrist. The other cried, 'Hang on to him, Emile!' and closed in on de Quesnoy's other side. Able now to bear his own weight only on one foot, he was no match for them. Within a minute they had him fast with one of his arms twisted up behind his back.

They had hardly done so when the burly landlord came crashing down the stairs and out of the door opposite the bar. Taking in the situation at a glance, he cried:

'So you've caught the swine! Well done, lads! Bring him in here.'

Another man had followed the landlord out. With him leading, the other three lugged de Quesnoy up the stairs and back along the corridor to the scene of the affray. Someone had fetched another lamp from one of the other rooms, and during the past five minutes several newcomers had arrived on the scene. As there had been a number of people present when the fire started it had soon been beaten out; so the only signs remaining of it were some oily smoke and the stench of burnt clothing.

At the sight of the prisoner Inez, now freed from her bonds, let out a yell of vindictive delight, and the others shouted their congratulations to his captors.

By the time he had been pushed and pulled into the bedroom it was packed to suffocation. Sanchez's body had been lifted on to the bed and a towel laid over its face, but the bed was shared by the Spaniard over whose head the Count had broken the mirror. He lay moaning beside the corpse while another man mopped at the blood that seeped from cuts on his forehead, nose and ears. The square-head had regained consciousness and was sitting on a chair nursing his injured chin. In addition there were at least ten other people, including Beatriz who had appeared from somewhere in a dressing-gown; and the noise of their excited voices now made a positive babble.

The landlord took charge and shouted loudly for silence; then when their voices fell to a mutter, he said to Inez:

'Now tell us, girl. What happened? How did this start?'

'He's a thief!' she cried. 'The dirty low-down blackguard. We'd only been up here a few minutes when he came round behind me and gave me a wallop on the head. It knocked me right out for about ten minutes. When I came round he had tied me hand and foot and to the bed; and he was in here rummaging through our things to see what he could pilfer. A long time later Sanchez came in and took him by surprise. Then they fought, and I wriggled off the bed to try to get help.'

As she ceased speaking her glance fell on Sanchez. It seemed that in the general excitement it was not until that moment that

she realized that he was really dead. With a heartrending wail
she cast herself upon his body. Beatriz pushed through the crowd,
put her arms about her shoulders and sought to comfort her.
Inez's wails continued and it was only after some minutes, during
which everyone burst into speech again, that they were reduced to
a passionate sobbing.

Her outburst of grief had given de Quesnoy time to recover
a little from the rough handling he had received. A glance round
the room was enough to show him that his position was desperate.
He had killed an inmate of the house, injured two other men and
inflicted nasty burns on several more. His best hope lay in the
fact that most of the frequenters of the Silver Galleon, although
a little rough, looked fairly respectable; so there was a fair hope
that they might hand him over to the police. If they did, he felt
that he had nothing worse to fear than a few nights in the cells,
for he could counter a charge of murder by stating that Sanchez
had been a wanted criminal and he had killed him in self-defence
while endeavouring to secure him so that justice might take its
course; and de Cordoba's influence would then get him a quick
release. But, as he glanced round the crowded room he saw that
everyone who was looking in his direction was glaring at him, and
he realized that it needed only a spark to their anger for the whole
lot of them to set about lynching him.

Again the landlord called for silence, then swung round on
de Quesnoy and snarled at him, 'She's given us the truth, hasn't
she? You can't deny it.'

'I do,' retorted the Count hotly. Having had a few minutes to
think up a line of defence, he went on in a firm voice. 'The señorita
is lying to cover up for her dead fancy-man. I was with her in
the little room and I heard movements in here, so I came through.
I found him about to take a photograph of us through a big slit
in the door. I saw at once that blackmail was his game, and went
for him. We fought, he went over backwards, hit his head on the
chest of drawers and broke his neck. You can't blame me for
that. Meanwhile she had followed me in and was about to rouse
the house. Seeing what had happened I knew that if I was caught
here I'd be for the lockup, and perhaps held there for months
while the police went into the question of the fellow's death. Who
would want that, if there was a chance of avoiding it, eh? I stopped
the hussy's cries and tied her up. But my luck was out. She broke
free and her yells brought some of you on the scene before I could
get away. That's the truth.'

It was a good story, but Inez raised her tousled red head from

Beatriz's shoulder and screamed. 'He's lying! He's lying! He's a thief and a murderer. By the Holy Virgin I swear he's lying.'

'It's the truth, you bitch,' cried the Count, using this term as suitable to the occasion, and the indignation he was feigning as his best hope of convincing his audience so that he might get out of the place alive.

At the foot of the bed lay the leather satchel with the negatives and prints he had taken from it in a little pile near by. Pointing at them, he went on indignantly. 'There's the proof of what I've told you. Just look at them. That's the sort of photograph her pimp was about to take of her and me when I caught him at it.'

Taking a quick step forward the landlord swept the pile into the satchel, tucked it under his arm and said gruffly, 'I'll take charge of those. They're just a lot of old snaps and I've seen them before.'

At his action de Quesnoy's hopes sank. It was a clear indication that the landlord knew about the blackmail racket that Sanchez and Inez had been running, and had been taking a cut from the results of their activities. It swept from beneath his feet the ground of his best line of defence.

Meanwhile Inez had begun to shout again. 'He murdered Sanchez! He murdered him after he'd tied me up. He came here as a thief, I tell you. Look at all my things scattered over the floor.'

Her cry distracted the others from the landlord, preventing any of them looking at the photographs; and she had made a point for which the Count could offer no explanation.

As they glanced round at the junk on the floor and two still open drawers, a tall man with a grey moustache said, 'He's a thief all right. You can see that from the way the room's been searched. He killed her fellow, too. No doubt about that. We must get the police.'

'All right,' de Quesnoy volunteered. 'I'm sticking to my story and quite prepared to tell it to them.'

'No you won't,' the landlord cut in quickly. 'I'm not having the police here.' Glancing round, he added truculently, 'You can't be such a lot of fools as to want the police called in. Those of you who are off ships won't be allowed to sail in them. You'll be held as witnesses. We'd all land ourselves in for weeks of trouble.'

'He's right. That's sense.' 'Yes, we must keep the police out of this,' murmured several of the others.

The Scandinavian stopped massaging his jaw, looked up and said in broken Spanish. 'Then what will we do with him? He has killed a man, hasn't he? That he should go free is wrong.'

'Kill him!' shouted Inez. 'Stick a knife in his belly.'

Her shout was ignored, so she went on. 'Go to it, one of you. A life for a life. That's fair, isn't it? We don't need the police to settle his account. We can do it ourselves.'

Still they ignored her; so she cried, 'You lousy lot of cowards! Give me a knife, one of you, and I'll do it myself.'

The Spaniard whose face had been so badly cut about by the mirror sat up on the bed. With feverish eyes he stared at de Quesnoy, then his features broke into a cruel grin, and he rasped, 'You may spare yourself, señorita. The privilege shall be mine.'

'Shut your trap, Filipo,' snapped the landlord. 'There's been one murder here tonight. I'll not have another done before my eyes.'

A chorus of voices supported him. 'No!' 'Not that! Not that!' 'No! The police might trace him.' 'No, no; we'd all be held responsible.'

'But what will we do with him?' the square-head persisted. 'He has killed a man. That he should be let go free is not just.'

A tubby little man wearing a good reefer jacket and a brand new peaked cap, who had been one of the last to arrive on the scene, replied contemptuously, 'What is there so frightful about a killing? We all know that they happen from time to time in fo'c'sle fights; and in port, like this, when there is trouble over a woman.'

The landlord nodded. 'True enough, Captain Robles. But it's not right that we should let him get away with it altogether. What do you suggest?'

With new hope surging in his breast de Quesnoy stared at the Captain. He had lank black hair, tiny little eyes and an enormously developed jaw. After a moment he said, 'My ship is sailing for Rio in two hours' time. He looks like a seafaring type. I'm short of hands and could do with an extra man in the fo'c'sle. If he doesn't behave we'll soon teach him manners. Slug him under the jaw, one of you, and we'll escort him aboard as though he were a drunk.'

De Quesnoy listened appalled. But with the exception of Inez everyone else accepted Captain Robles's idea as an excellent solution to the problem. The Scandinavian lumbered to his feet, delighted at the chance to avenge himself for the kick under the jaw he had received. The two men who were holding the Count's arms tightened their grip on him. The sailor clenched his big fist and struck him a violent blow on the side of the chin. A black curtain descended in front of his eyes, red stars and circles flashed upon it; then he passed out.

When de Quesnoy came to he found himself in irons. He was lying on a thin straw-filled palliasse in a dark noisome hole. A rocking motion and the noise of a churning propeller told him that he was in a ship at sea. His head was aching abominably, but into his still bemused brain there drifted a picture of red-headed Inez, then of himself smashing the mirror. That had brought him ill-luck indeed.

Then another thought came to him. It was of Count Soltikoff saying 'Vengeance is Mine, saith The Lord'. Sanchez was dead, and his father and the others would shortly be on trial for their lives. But that was little consolation now. By taking the law into his own hands this was where he had landed himself. And there was no escape. He was faced with having to work his way to South America under a brutal captain as a seaman before the mast.

16

Fate Stalks by Night

IT was two and a half years before de Quesnoy returned to Europe. He would not have done so then had he not learnt early in March, 1909, that his father had died. In consequence, when he did return it was as the tenth Duc de Richleau.

One of the blessings granted to mankind is that while it is often possible to recall and, years later, enjoy again in retrospect the most delightful hours of one's life, the emotion of terror, the sensation of pain, the gnawings of hunger, anxiety and jealousy rarely leave a permanent impression on the mind; and even the memories of long periods of distress become blunted by the balm of time.

So, when de Richleau entered the first-class deck cabin of the *de luxe* liner that was to carry him from New Orleans to Hamburg, he did not even give a thought to the very different circumstances in which he had arrived in South America one hundred and thirty-one weeks earlier. By then his mind had telescoped his outward voyage into a few scenes:

His first interview with Captain Robles. The morning after the tramp had sailed from Cadiz he had been taken up, still in irons, from the lazaret to the Captain's cabin. He had told Robles his proper name and offered him five hundred pounds to put back and land him in Cadiz or any other European port. The squat,

baboon-jawed Captain had laughed in his face, and flatly refused
to believe that he was a Count or could lay his hand on one-
tenth of that sum. To threaten him, on arrival in South America,
with prosecution for kidnapping was obviously futile and, de
Quesnoy realized, might even have led to his not being allowed
to land when they got to Rio. The only course left to him had
been to put as cheerful a face as possible on matters and agree
to sign on for the voyage as a deck-hand under his assumed name
of Jaime Avila.

Then of a fight in the fo'c'sle. The rough seamen who were
to be his shipmates were used to minding their own business,
so did not inquire into his. An extra hand meant lightening their
work so most of them gave him a surly welcome and, between
them, fitted him up with spare oddments of kit, such as sea-boots,
oilskins and a razor. But they soon began to put upon the land-
lubber who had arrived in their midst, and he saw that unless he
took a stand his life, from being grim, would become intolerable.
On the third night out he had refused to dubbin the boots of a
brawny half-caste named Vecho. As Vecho was the fo'c'sle bully
the other men did not, as de Quesnoy had feared they might,
gang up against him, but stood by while the two of them fought
it out. It had been a tough encounter with no holds barred; but
after five gruelling minutes de Quesnoy had succeeded in getting
a judo hold on Vecho and made him scream for mercy. From
then on there were no further attempts to make the slim but for-
midable new hand do more than his share of the fo'c'sle chores.

Lastly, on the ship's arrival at Rio after three weeks at sea.
During them the Count's lifelong assumption of leadership had
soon made itself felt. Most of his tasks as a deck-hand required
brawn rather than brains; so he swiftly mastered them and within
a few days had, almost unconsciously, assumed the rôle of leading
hand in his watch; then he had been singled out by the bosun
for any special jobs needing a little ingenuity or skill. That had
not been lost on Captain Robles, who had already realized that
he was an educated man; yet de Quesnoy's surprise can be imagined when, on paying him off in Rio, the Captain had offered
to sign him on for his next voyage as fourth mate. It had then
been the Count's turn to laugh. But he was conscious that had
Robles not shanghaied him he might well have been lynched and
suffered some fatal injury before getting away from the Silver
Galleon; so in spite of the hard time, wretched food and filthy
quarters that he had since been forced to endure, he had taken
leave of the tough little tramp skipper without any ill will.

In 1904, when a guest on the yacht of the American banker Channock Van Ryn, de Quesnoy had made a number of acquaint-ances in Rio, so he had had no difficulty in establishing his real identity there. The Rio branch of Van Ryn's bank had made him a substantial loan, which had enabled him to re-equip himself decently and live in a good hotel while arranging for funds to be sent to him from Europe, and he had at once cabled his father and de Vendôme to let them know his whereabouts and that he was safe and well.

He had also written at length to de Cordoba relating all that had happened in Granada and Cadiz, and saying that it was not his intention to return to Spain. As he pointed out, the trial of the anarchists in Barcelona, having been fixed for October 11th, would by then be over. That he had been rendered incapable of appearing in court to substantiate his personal charges against Francisco Ferrer, his remaining son Benigno, and the others, was unfortunate; but Don Alfonso had been of the opinion that, even without those charges, on the evidence of their anarchist activities found in the *Escuela Moderna*, they would be lucky if they escaped the death penalty and, at the least, would receive long sentences of imprisonment; therefore no useful purpose could be served by his returning and having them brought to trial again.

He added that, had there been the least chance of their being set free, he would have taken the first ship back, but it had always been his intention to go to South America after the trial for the purpose of obtaining a commission in the army of one of the Republics; so, Fate having deposited him there – however uncom-fortable the means she had chosen – he now took that as a good omen of better luck in Latin America than he had met with in Europe during the past year, and meant to remain there at all events for some time to come.

In due course he received a reply from the Conde telling him that, owing to his disappearance, the trial of the anarchists had been postponed. The police had traced his movements and learned from La Torcera, who had returned to Granada, that when in Cadiz he had gone out after Sanchez Ferrer. They had found out about Sanchez's death, but failed to discover what had become of de Quesnoy; so assumed that he had been made away with that same night. In consequence they had written him off as a witness for the prosecution in the Ferrer trial, and were now concentrating their efforts on ferreting out further evidence against the owner and staff of the *Escuela Moderna*. But there was no likelihood whatever of the prisoners being released or, in due course, not receiving long sentences; so de Quesnoy might rest content with the big contribution he had already made to breaking up the nest of vipers which, until August, had flourished in Barcelona.

The Conde concluded by conveying to de Quesnoy Don Alfonso's relief and happiness on learning that he was alive and well, with affectionate messages from Gulia, de Vendôme, the Conde Ruiz, the Infanta Maria Alfonsine, and an expression of his own devoted friendship coupled with the hope that it would not be more than a year or two before they would all enjoy the happiness of having him among them again.

Meanwhile, through his acquaintances in the beautiful capital of Brazil, de Quesnoy had been exploring the possibilities of entering the Brazilian Army. As an ex-Chief Instructor of the French Military Academy of St. Cyr, with several years of distinguished active service in North Africa in addition, his qualifications could not be questioned, and after a few meetings with influential army officers the Minister for War offered him the post of Commandant at the Military College.

He would have preferred to command troops; but it appeared a good opening, so he accepted. Yet he had not long taken up the post before he regretted his decision. In those days, in Latin America, discipline among officers was still as nebulous as it had been in the European armies opposing Napoleon. Young sparks belonging to powerful families were accustomed to sleep out at nights and cut lectures and parades when they pleased but, all the same, they expected to receive the most sought-after appointments when the course was over. By cracking down on them de Quesnoy made himself intensely unpopular, and he soon learned that these wealthy idlers had complained to their influential fathers, with the result that an intrigue was developing to oust him from his job. Fighting he considered his business, but not fighting a haughty oligarchy for the right to force its decadent youth to toe the line and learn to become competent officers. In consequence, in the New Year of 1907 he had resigned and transferred to the army of one of the Central American Republics.

There he had been given the rank of Brigadier-General and sent to fight Indians. Although he found the troops allotted to him illiterate, ragged, and largely recruited from the gaols, and supplies reached him only in an inadequate trickle, he had soon become fascinated by jungle warfare. Not only was it utterly different from his campaigns against well-organized bodies of tribesmen, waged for oases in deserts and through the rocky gorges of the Atlas Mountains, it had a much closer resemblance to big game hunting, which had always been a passion with him. But in this case, instead of stalking dangerous animals for amusement, the object was to make waterways and jungle tracks safe for commerce from attack by murderous savages, and the risk entailed by the hunter was the much greater one of being pipped by a poison-tipped arrow, which could result in a death of excruciating agony.

After three months he had gone down with jungle fever and been invalided back to the capital. While he was convalescing a revolution had taken place and the new War Minister had decided that he would be of more value in helping to reorganize the army than returning to the jungle. By Central American standards the War Minister had been an honest man, and de Quesnoy had done his utmost to bring order out of chaos; but at every turn he had found his efforts baulked by the rivalries of unscrupulous Generals, graft, and every kind of political chicanery. By midsummer he had become so disgusted with the whole business that he had thrown in his hand and accepted an offer from a neighbouring State to become Inspector-General of its forces.

There he had fared little better, as its Government and the higher ranks of its rag, tag and bobtail army had proved equally riddled with corruption. But after a time he had managed to change his job for the command of an expedition to survey the upper reaches of an uncharted river and a great area of territory adjacent to it. That he had enjoyed, as it had meant his being his own master and again living dangerously, which was in his blood. It had entailed further encounters with hostile Indians, hunting an immense variety of big game, and the discovery of an ancient Maya city, ruined and half-submerged in giant creepers yet with many of its intricate carvings still undamaged. But, to his annoyance, the expedition was recalled long before it had completed its work owing to lack of funds to send up to it further essential supplies.

During the eighteen months that followed he had served with the rank of Major-General in the armies of three other Republics. In time he had come to accept the trickery, bribery and ignorance of military matters which was almost universal among his sallow-skinned, black-eyed colleagues, recognizing that their standards were as natural to them as a sense of integrity was to the majority of officers in the armies of the great European nations. Even when telling the most flagrant lies their manners were impeccable, they were most hospitable and intensely chivalrous towards women; so he came to regard them rather as selfish, wicked children than near criminals, and became good friends with a number of the more intelligent among them.

His dream of commanding a Cavalry Division remained as far away as ever since, except for a few squadrons of escort troops for Presidential processions, cavalry hardly existed, and he often thought with regret of the splendidly disciplined and equipped regiment of Spahis he had commanded in North Africa. But the half-Indian peons in the Central American armies were tough little men and earned his admiration.

For most of the time he lived in cities in which the privileged few enjoyed every luxury while the masses, mainly of mixed negroid and native Indian stock with only a rare dash of Spanish blood, plagued by disease, poverty and crushing taxation, barely managed to exist in the most appalling squalor. Yet each time resentment at such a state of things, or frustration at the intransigence and incompetence of his colleagues, had boiled up in him to a point at which he began to consider returning to Europe, he was either sent out to clear another jungle area of marauding Indians, or a revolution engineered by some magnate greedy for more wealth and power had to be crushed.

So for the past two and a half years he had at least lived a life that had not lacked for variety, and frequently provided him with situations in which he could indulge his favourite pastime of gambling his safety against his wits.

Now, as the Duc de Richleau, he had to reorientate himself for his return to countries in which soldiers were not liable to be shot for minor acts of insubordination, where judges sent people to prison for offering them bribes instead of suggesting that the amount of the bribe should be doubled, where one did not have to take constant precautions against catching some terrible disease, or be liable to stumble in a street at night over the body of some poor wretch either struck down by one or knifed; and, in short, where a state of law and order was the rule rather than the exception.

Having crossed the Caribbean to New Orleans, as the nearest port from which he could be sure of making his voyage to Europe in a comfortable liner, he had had to wait there for one for eight days, and for a good part of that time he had amused himself by reading in the big City Library papers and periodicals which would bring him up-to-date with events in the Old World.

In England jovial King Edward VII still occupied the throne, with Asquith as his Prime Minister and a firebrand named Lloyd George as Chancellor of the Exchequer. Led by the latter the Radicals were carrying out a furious agitation to deprive the

House of Lords of its age-old right to veto measures passed by the Lower House. The Southern Irish meanwhile were carrying on an equally furious agitation to be given Home Rule. But the British people, as ever the pioneers in all forms of social welfare, had united in applauding a bill which a few months earlier had introduced Old Age Pensions for the needy.

In France Clemenceau was still Premier, but he was now having great trouble in holding together his coalition of Radicals and Socialists, and there were growing indications that the latter might split off and defeat him at the next election. The suppression of the Paris Commune, and all it stood for, in 1871 was now ancient history; but for a quarter of a century the memory of its threat to property, small as well as large, had made the majority of Frenchmen regard all workers' movements with the gravest suspicion. Since the 'nineties, however, they had gained ground by leaps and bounds. Recently the Marxists had fomented a great wave of militant strikes which, by the sabotaging of plant, had cost the country a vast sum, and had been put down only by adopting emergency measures. The anarchists, too, continued to be equally active and, following an attempt to assassinate President Fallières, were jeopardizing the effectiveness of the army by a great campaign encouraging desertion and denouncing military service.

In Germany Kaiser Wilhelm II continued to give his Chancellor, Prince von Bülow, sleepless nights wondering what new tactless and bellicose utterance he might learn in the morning that his Royal master had given out – generally to some foreign correspondent who had played upon his vanity during a private interview. There had been serious trouble in Germany's Polish provinces and also in Alsace-Lorraine, but a combination of efficient administration backed by the Prussian jack-boot had kept both minorities under control. Commercially, Germany was enjoying an era of great prosperity and there could be no doubt at all that the Kaiser's policies of Colonial expansion and building a High Seas Fleet that could challenge the British Navy had the full support of his people.

Italy was still labouring under a vast burden of debt and the backwardness and superstition of her agricultural population. In the south and in Sicily, the government, the priests and the Mafia competed to rob the peasantry of their last centissimi, and the appalling earthquake that had a few months earlier annihilated the great port of Messina had added greatly to the general distress.

From Vienna the aged Franz-Joseph still ruled his vast multiracial Empire. It was said that he worked stolidly for longer hours

per day than the most conscientious of his civil servants, endeavouring to reconcile Hungarians with Czechs, Poles with Ruthenians,
Austrians with Italians and Croats with Serbs; yet none of his
subject races was content and, many people thought, they were
waiting only for his death to proclaim their independence.

Portugal had for a long while been bankrupt, and in a final
attempt to restore his country's finances King Carlos had allowed
his Prime Minister to assume the powers of a dictator. This had
led, fifteen months earlier, to an attack by a band of assassins
on the Royal carriage. The King and Crown Prince had been
shot dead; the Queen had miraculously escaped a hail of bullets
and her younger son Manuel had been only slightly wounded.
Now, aged nineteen, he wore the Crown, but was no more than
a puppet in the hands of a coalition government which was desperately endeavouring to stave off revolution.

In Spain no event of outstanding importance had taken place,
and since de Richleau was not going there he only glanced through
the back numbers of such Spanish periodicals as were available.
Whatever countries he might decide to visit later he was going
first to Russia, to take up his inheritance; so it was to the state
of things in Russia that he gave the lion's share of his interest.

Only a year before he had been shipped off to South America
the Tsar had at last given way to popular pressure and consented
to elections being held for the purpose of creating a National
Assembly. This first Duma – as it was called – was convened
only as a consultative body. But as soon as it assembled it became
apparent that its members were not going to be content to act
merely as advisers to the government. The two largest parties – the
Liberal Democrats and the Socialists – had both demanded that
the Duma should control the executive. The Tsar had refused to
yield and dissolved his first 'parliament'.

Thereupon the leaders of the Opposition had crossed the frontier
into Finland and issued a violent protest known as the 'Viborg
Manifesto'. It called on the Russian people to refuse to pay taxes
or supply recruits to the Army and Navy until the Duma was
restored. The government had then counter-attacked by establishing special courts to punish terrorists and agitators. A great purge
of Socialists had been carried out and thousands of people sent
into exile.

Early in 1907, by which time things seemed to have quietened
down, elections for a second Duma were held; but, in spite of the
purge, a Liberal–Socialist majority was again returned. The
Tsar's Minister, Count Stolypin, had accused the Socialist members

of conspiracy and demanded their expulsion. A Committee had been appointed to examine the evidence, but the public outcry was so great that, without even waiting for the findings of the Committee, the Tsar had again dissolved the Duma.

There had followed a period of what almost amounted to civil war. On the one hand the Government used its Secret Police, and a vast spy system, with the utmost ruthlessness in an attempt to stamp out all opposition – even executing scores of people for political offences committed two or three years earlier – on the other a great part of the normally law-abiding masses now helped to finance, hide and abet the Nihilists, who succeeded in murdering scores of police and officials.

The Government won, at least to the extent that, when a third Duma was summoned in the autumn of 1907, Stolypin had at last secured the tame assembly he desired. This enabled him to introduce such reforms as he could persuade the Tsar to agree to, and to prepare the way for the measures on which his heart was set. These were designed to substitute private for communal ownership, so that the peasants might own the land on which they worked; for it was his very sensible belief that the possession of private property would prove the best bulwark against revolution.

But matters were not moving swiftly enough for the Socialists and Marxists. They continued their underground warfare with unabated vigour. Not a day passed but shots were fired or a bomb thrown at some relative of the Tsar, one of his Ministers, a General, a Police Chief, or some high official and innumerable police agents were knifed or slugged on the head. And it was in a bomb outrage that de Richleau's father had lost his life.

The old Duke had held no official position of any kind, and had never taken Russian nationality; so he was still technically a Frenchman. He had left his estate only to attend a centenary celebration in Kiev, the capital of the Ukraine, as the guest of the Governor, Count Boris Plackoff, a cousin of his dead wife. As so often happened, the bomb had been badly aimed. None of its splinters even grazed the Governor, but they killed or wounded a dozen soldiers and spectators standing a few yards away from him, the Duke among them.

That both de Quesnoy's wife and father should have met their deaths in the same way was not, in fact, a particularly strange coincidence. Anyone in the vicinity of royalty or a Governor making a public appearance at that time was liable to fall a victim to an assassin; so it was no more surprising than if two people, both of whom at times climbed mountains, should both die as a result of mountaineering accidents. Yet the murder of his father re-aroused in the new Duke all the emotions to which he had been subject two and a half years earlier.

The facts that he had never regarded his father with more than respectful affection, that he had seen very little of him during the past fifteen years, and that he had benefited through his death by coming into a considerable fortune, hardly entered his mind. They were submerged under the salient fact that his parent, while an innocent bystander, had been violently and painfully done to death by a small criminal minority which sought to impose its will by acts of terror upon a vast law-abiding majority.

The news of the assassination had brought back to him vivid memories of Angela, and the way in which their happiness had been terminated with such appalling suddenness. For some days, he was afflicted with periods of bitter brooding, as he thought of what his life might have been were she still alive, and what it had become owing to her death. He would have had a permanent home with the woman who had been his earliest and greatest love, a child now two years old to cherish, the enjoyment of a circle of friends with whom to pass their time in civilized surroundings. As it was, he had been forced to become a soldier of fortune, rootless, without family, and only circles of acquaintances which changed every month as he moved from one appointment to another, engaged in jungle warfare or countering the intrigues of unscrupulous Central American politicians.

Thinking back, it gave him some consolation to recall that, by undertaking his secret mission to Barcelona, he had succeeded in ensuring that Ferrer and his vile crew had been brought to book for the backstage part they had played in Angela's murder, and had been put out of the way for good; but that did not alter the fact that the hydra-headed monster, militant anarchism, was still taking its toll almost daily of innocent victims, and that his father's life had been cut short by Russians of the poisonous Ferrer breed.

For a while he had contemplated offering to serve the Tsar in the same way as he had Don Alfonso, and under an alias seeking to penetrate the inner circles of the Russian Nihilists. But on consideration, he had recalled that the circumstances in Spain and Russia were very different. Don Alfonso had been anxious to employ him because the strongly Liberal element in his own police, especially in Catalonia, made them unreliable. To the Tsar's Secret Police, the *Ocrana*, that did not apply. Far too many of them had fallen victims to the bombs, pistols and knives of the Nihilists for them to have the least scruple about retaliating whenever the opportunity offered. They were already waging a relentless war against the terrorists, and had hundreds of spies constantly endeavouring to penetrate the cells of the assassins; so one more, and especially a man like himself who had not lived in Russia since his boyhood, could make no material difference.

By the time he reached New Orleans, he had decided that there was no place for him in the secret war that the *Ocrana* was waging; so his thoughts instinctively reverted to the type of war which was his own province, and the possibilities of future outbreaks of hostilities in various parts of the world. With that in mind, he looked through all the more serious English, French and German magazines, and read many articles in them to get an unbiased view of what diplomats termed 'The Concert of Europe'.

The standard of the music had certainly not improved while the Duke had been in America, and in the past year the players, large and small, had got so out of tune that for a while it had looked as if they meant to break their instruments over one another's heads.

The Entente Cordiale still held, in spite of some discordant notes between the Anglo-French partners, and Russia, largely owing to a visit by King Edward to the Tsar at Revel in the summer of 1908, had since been drawn away from Germany into what was now a triple Entente. Germany and Austria–Hungary, with Italy as an unenthusiastic third, formed the Triple Alliance, which led by the bellicose Kaiser, was opposing the Entente countries on every major issue.

For the past quarter of a century the ancient sprawling Turkish Empire had been falling to pieces, and it was a further stage in its disintegration which had nearly set the Great Powers at one another's throats. Early in the previous year the Young Turks had deposed the Sultan. Recent memories of the massacre of the Armenians and other horrors perpetrated by the *ancien régime* had secured for the Young Turks general approval of their seizure of power. But it had soon had dangerous repercussions.

Crete, Greece, Serbia and Montenegro had already thrown off the Turkish yoke. Now Bulgaria also proclaimed her independence and Austria, without consultation with the other powers, annexed the Turkish provinces of Bosnia and Herzegovina. As the two provinces were mainly populated by Serbs, Serbia had hoped to absorb them and demanded compensation. Russia, as the natural protector of the Slav races in the Balkans, backed her up, while Germany backed her ally Austria. All through the autumn and winter heated notes had volleyed back and forth between the Great Powers; but a month ago the Kaiser had openly declared his intention of supporting Austria by force of arms if the matter of her annexation of the provinces was further questioned, and Russia had climbed down.

Now, the 'Concert' was playing in reasonably fair harmony again, but in view of the violently nationalistic ambitions animating the several newly-created Balkan States, de Richleau found himself wondering for how long it would continue to do so. He was far too conscious of the appalling consequences which would result from a major war to wish to see all Europe go up in flames; but as a soldier of fortune he regarded with speculative interest the possibility of a war in the Balkans, and that another might break out either in North Africa, owing to Italian ambitions in Tripoli, or North-West Africa, where France had recently seized the Casablanca territories in the teeth of German opposition.

At the moment he was definitely looking forward to taking over and administering the great estate that had been left to him; but instinct told him that his new form of occupation would not satisfy him for very long, and that in a year or so he would once more feel a compelling urge again to use his talents as a soldier. If so, perhaps, after all, he might yet achieve his ambition to command a Cavalry Division in Tripoli, Morocco or the Balkans.

On April 2nd he sailed for Europe, to reach Hamburg after a pleasant but uneventful voyage. From Hamburg he went straight to Vienna and there, in his favourite city, he broke his journey for a week to get the feel of Europe again into his bones.

Frau Sacher, who had known him since his boyhood, received him with delight. In the lofty rooms of her exclusive hotel, with their tall double doors of baize that shut out all sound, he put from him the last unpleasant memories of his time in Latin America – the greedy half-breed politicians and generals, the sweltering heat of the jungle, the constant danger from disease and snake or tarantula bite, the stench of unwashed humanity, and the incessant pestering by flies and mosquitoes – while luxuriating in a huge bed or in the vast marble bath, as big as a Roman sarcophagus.

No sooner had he made known his presence in Vienna than he received a dozen callers and a score of invitations. Friends made in his youth, now Majors and Colonels in crack cavalry regiments, delighted to receive him again into the joyous carefree life of 'wine, women and song' that formed the very heart of Vienna's existence. He was thirty-four years old, strikingly handsome, a lean, bronzed soldier with a ready smile and dark, slightly wavy hair flecked with grey, a Duke who had now also inherited the Austrian title of Count Königstein, rich, unmarried, intelligent, travelled and with decorations that testified to his personal valour. It was not to be wondered at that in the days that followed the most noble families in Vienna unostentatiously put their eligible daughters in his way, and that half a dozen lovely married women indicated very clearly that they would be delighted to enter on an *affaire* with him.

At the end of the week he reluctantly tore himself away and, resisting the temptation to break his journey again for a few nights to see old friends in gay Budapest, crossed the frontier into Russia on the 26th. The following day he reached Jvanets, where he learned to his considerable satisfaction that the nihilist who had thrown the bomb that had killed his father had already been caught and executed.

The great rambling mansion had been built in Catherine II's time and lay deep in the woods some distance from the town. To the north of it there sprawled two acres of stables, glass-houses and farm buildings. He was welcomed by his elderly second cousin, the Countess Olga Plackoff, who had run the house for his father ever since his mother's death twenty years ago; by the silver-haired Abbé Nodier, now in his eighties, who still acted as Chaplain to the household, and by Sergi Mikszath, the Bailiff.

From the Countess Olga and the Abbé he received a detailed account of his father's death; then Mikszath presented the house servants, grooms, gardeners, huntsmen and farm workers all of whom in turn, in the traditional manner, embraced their new master and kissed him on the left shoulder. Many of them were old friends and they begged him to come and live permanently among them. About that he would make no promise, but he smilingly assured them all that whether he did so or not he would retain them in his service and see to it that they were well treated.

As it was now two months since his father's death the household was no longer in mourning; so arrangements could be started at once for the celebrations customary upon a great noble coming into his inheritance. Invitations were dispatched to all the leading families of the Province for the last week in May and a period of great activity ensued in kitchen, farm, cellars, and in preparing many rooms in the house that had for long not been used.

The celebrations were to last a week, and as many of the guests would come from considerable distances, over fifty had to be accommodated; so poor Countess Olga was soon at her wits' end where to put them. But de Richleau came to her aid by hiring additional furniture and converting some of the larger rooms into dormitories for the younger people.

On the morning of the day that his guests were to arrive the Duke carried out a final inspection and was satisfied that they would lack for nothing. In addition to his big house-party, his tenants, everyone employed on the estate, scores of people from the town and hundreds of peasants from round about would all participate on the first and last days of the festivities; so half a dozen big marquees had been erected in the garden and huge stocks of food, vodka, wine and beer had been accumulated.

During the week it rained on only two days and neither of these were those on which the great gatherings took place. On them there were sports of all kinds, horse, foot and troika races, wrestling matches, and ploughing, tree-felling and drinking contests. There were prizes, too, for the best pies cooked by the women, the best embroidery they could produce, the prettiest dresses and the prettiest girls. At night there were fireworks and illuminations; sheep, oxen, boar and deer were roasted whole over bonfires, and the great crowd of revellers sang, danced and staggered about happily drunk until the grey light of dawn dimmed the illuminations.

In the midweek the house-party went for rides, picnics and boating expeditions on the river, held musical evenings and, according to their age, either played whist and baccarat or danced, acted charades, and played guessing games and hide and seek.

On the 29th of the month the great party ended. De Richleau had had to reply to a score of toasts and drink bumper for bumper with innumerable well-wishers, so it had proved a considerable strain. As it had enabled him to renew many old friendships and make a number of new ones he had enjoyed it, but it was with a sense of relief that he waved away the last of his guests.

Earlier in the month he had gone through his father's papers and dealt with all matters arising from them. He had also made several tours of the estate with his bailiff and issued instructions for such improvements as occurred to him. Now that he was on his own he again rode out every morning to inspect farms and coverts, but he found little fresh to remark upon.

The Countess Olga was a pleasant and sensible woman, but she had never been outside Russia and had been immured at Jvanets for the past twenty years; so her conversation was extremely limited. The Abbé Nodier, on the other hand, could talk with wisdom and wit on a great variety of subjects; so it was in his small private sitting-room, the walls of which were lined with hundreds of battered old books, that the Duke spent his evenings. The Abbé had been his tutor and, when young, the tutor of his father before him; so he had no secrets from the old man who, although a saint himself, was always tolerant about the human failings of others. But at this season there was neither hunting nor shooting to be had, the little town of Jvanets could offer de Richleau no recreation and his nearest neighbours lived many versts away; so he soon found his life as a country gentleman extremely boring.

He had received a number of invitations from families that had stayed with him for the celebrations, but the only ones that appealed to him were for later in the year when the shooting started; so he was faced with the problem of how best to fill in the summer months.

He was greatly tempted to return to Vienna; but he had met one starry-eyed little Countess there whom he had found most attractive, and to dally further with her might prove decidedly dangerous. His years in the jungle had not caused him to forget how easily even wary young men could find themselves entangled and be asked their intentions by the fathers of eligible young ladies; and he had no wish to get married again yet. As the London season would be in full swing he thought of visiting England; but it was long time since he had been to a European watering-place and he felt that he would enjoy himself more at a resort where he could swim and be certain of good weather, than at Ascot and in the ballrooms of Mayfair. After considering several, he decided to go down to Yalta in the Crimea.

As usual, having taken a decision, de Richleau acted promptly upon it, and after seven weeks on his estate left it in mid-June. He spent two nights in Odessa to look up old friends and on the 18th of the month arrived in Yalta.

In the same way as the French Riviera owes its delightful climate to the shelter given it by the Alpes Maritimes, so the south-east coast of the Crimea enjoys a similar protection from the Yaila-dagh mountains which run parallel to it some six miles inland, and it has been well-named the Russian Riviera. There is a further similarity between the two in that both present an almost continuous belt of semi-tropical vegetation – palms, mimosa, oleanders, magnolias, camellias, orange, lemon, olive and fig trees – among which rise hundreds of white villas framed in tall cypress trees and with gardens gay with flowers.

This lovely stretch of coast has numerous towns scattered along it and if they are not so large as Nice, Cannes and Monte Carlo, they offer compensation for that in historical interest, as in their vicinity lie many beautiful ruins from the wealthy Greek colony that flourished there before the birth of Christ, Byzantine churches, Venetian fortresses and Turkish mosques.

Winter was the most fashionable time for wealthy Russians to escape from the snows to this sunny pleasure resort, and Yalta was the most fashionable of its towns, because it was there that the Tsar and Grand Dukes had their palaces. But even in the height of summer the promenades were always crowded with holiday-makers, and after the climate in Central America de Richleau found it only pleasantly warm.

At this season most of the big villas were shut, but the Duke knew a few families who had brought their children down for a summer holiday at the seaside; so he was made a member of the Nobles' Club and soon acquired a circle of pleasant acquaintances. Among them was a Baron Bezobrazov who owned a charming villa on the slope a mile or so behind the town, and on several occasions de Richleau went out there to lunch or dine.

One night after he had been in Yalta just on a fortnight he was again asked to dine there, and the Baron told him that it would be a men's party, the *pièce de résistance* of which would be to drink some old Tokay that his cousin had sent him as a present from Hungary. Eight of them sat down to table and remained at it for close on four hours. It was a typical Russian dinner of its kind, at which ten courses were served with an interval between each for pleasant conversation during which another wine was brought round by the *sommelier*. Finally they drank the old Tokay with Muscat grapes and nectarines.

Afterwards the Baron suggested a game of faro; so they adjourned to another room and for a further two hours sat round a table gambling gold ten-, twenty- and fifty-rouble-pieces on the turn of the pack against the two lines of cards on which they had placed their stakes. By two o'clock de Richleau, who was rarely lucky as a gambler, became weary of consistently losing. As he was down some twelve hundred roubles, no one could suggest that he was withdrawing to conserve his winnings; so he got up from the table and asked his host's leave to go home.

The Baron made no demur and said that he would ring for a carriage to take the Duke back to his hotel; but as it was a fine, warm night de Richleau begged him not to bother and said that he would much prefer to walk. Having insisted that none of them should leave the table he thanked his host for a most enjoyable evening, nodded good-bye to the others and went out to the hall where a waiting footman gave him his hat and cloak and saw him out of the front door.

As he walked through the garden he sniffed the air appreciatively. There had been a slight shower and the fragrant atmosphere was refreshing after hours spent savouring the aroma of old brandy in a room heavy with cigar smoke. The moonflowers were out and the moon herself lit the scene for most of the time from a sky that was only about one-third broken cloud.

For the first part of his way down the slope along a road fringed with other villas in their gardens he could see the moonlight glinting on the sea, then the roofs of the town hid it from him. It was just as he was entering the built-up area formed of solid blocks of lower-class dwellings interspersed with small, shuttered shops, that he got the impression that he was being followed.

The streets were deserted, only an occasional light showed in an upper window; the silence was not broken even by the distant rumble of the wheels of a *drosky* over cobbles. De Richleau strained his ears. A few more minutes and he became certain that not far behind him footsteps were echoing his own.

He had not the least reason to suppose that anyone was likely to attack him. It might quite well be that whoever was following him was, like himself, simply walking towards one of the big hotels on the promenade. On the other hand it might be some night-hawk robber who had scented money at the sight of his opera cloak and top hat.

To test the situation he turned out of the street through which he was walking into a narrower one that ran parallel with the sea front. The footsteps still followed and soon closed the gap. They were now only about fifty yards behind. He took a quick look over his shoulder, but the curve of the street prevented him from getting a sight of his shadower. Intrigued now by this possibility of a little excitement after three months of quiet life, he deliberately slowed his pace for the next hundred yards, then turned into the dark opening of an unlit arcade.

Holding his breath, he waited for a minute or more while the footsteps grew louder. At the entrance of the arcade they halted. Leaning forward from a doorway in which he had partially concealed himself, he glimpsed a slim figure peering in his direction. His shadower must have caught sight at the same instant of the white blob made by de Richleau's face. Whipping out a knife, with silent ferocity the man leapt at him.

The poor wretch might have fared better had he attacked a man-eating tiger. The Duke lunged with his malacca cane straight at the face of his assailant. It caught him in the mouth, knocking out three of his teeth. Next second de Richleau's left hand had

8

reached out, seized the wrist of the hand that held the knife, and
borne down upon it. At the same moment his right foot came
up to deliver a sharp kick in his attacker's groin. Finally, having
him off balance, by a violent jerk on his wrist he swung him sideways so that his head smashed the window of the shop in the
doorway of which the Duke had taken temporary cover.

De Richleau released his hold and stepped back. The man
collapsed and fell in a writhing, groaning heap at his feet. He
did not want to go to the bother of charging him, and even felt
a twinge of compassion at the terrible punishment he had inflicted.
Taking a twenty-rouble gold piece from his pocket he was about
to thrust it into one of the man's hands and leave him there when,
attracted by the sound of breaking glass, a policeman came running
up.

Had that policeman not happened to be within earshot the
incident would have ended there, many things might have panned
out very differently, and it is certain that de Richleau's life for
the next few years would not have taken the course it did. But
Fate, in the guise of a stolid Russian policeman, having appeared
on the scene, the Duke now had no alternative but to give an account
of what had happened and agree to charge with assault the man
who lay sprawled in the gutter.

Groaning and blubbering the man was got to his feet, but on
the policeman's questioning him he would not answer so much
as a word. Fortunately the Police Station was not far off and,
partly supported by the burly policeman, he was led there, the Duke
bringing up the rear. At the Station de Richleau again told his
story to an Inspector. The man was again questioned but could
not be induced to reply or even give his name.

This struck both the Duke and the Inspector as queer, since
the man had nothing to gain by keeping silent. He was fair-haired,
dressed in a decent summer-weight suit of gabardine and had not
the appearance of a common thug. His face was smeared with blood
from cuts on the head and the gaps of the three teeth that had been
struck from his mouth, and he stood, now hand-cuffed, with his
eyes cast down; but that would not have prevented the police from
recognizing him had he been a known local criminal.

In exasperation the Inspector turned to de Richleau and said,
'Your Excellency, I mean to get to the bottom of this. We'll find
a way to make him talk. Wait here, please, for a few minutes.'
Then he signed to two of his men to take the prisoner into the
next room, went in after them, and closed the door behind him.

The Duke knew very well the sort of thing that was about to

happen behind the closed door; but he had no power to intervene, even if he had wished to do so. It was common practice in
the countries in which he had spent the past few years and, with
only a slightly lesser degree of brutality, in most European countries
as well. Besides, the man had, after all, tried to knife him, yet
was not a known criminal; so he was now curious to know who
he was and why he had made the attempt.

After about five minutes the door opened again. The prisoner,
blubbering once more, his head hanging slack and supported
between the two policemen, was dragged out. The Inspector followed and, giving the Duke a puzzled look, said:

'We haven't got out of him yet why he attacked Your Excellency,
but perhaps you can enlighten us. He is a Spaniard and his name is
Benigno Ferrer.'

17

Vendetta

DE RICHLEAU could hardly believe his ears, but at the sound of
his name being pronounced the prisoner slowly raised his head
and stared sullenly at him. In spite of the blood-smeared face and
swollen lips the Duke recognized him now. The man was undoubtedly Benigno Ferrer.

In Spanish, the Duke asked him, 'How do you come to be in
Yalta?'

Benigno did not reply, but again let his chin fall on his chest.
The two policemen who were holding his arms gave him a violent
shake and one of them kicked him on the ankle. With a word
de Richleau checked them and said to the Inspector:

'You were right. I know this man and I wish to talk to him in
private. But it is past three o'clock; so I want to get back to my
hotel and to bed. What time will he be brought before the magistrate
in the morning?'

'Ten o'clock, Your Excellency.'

'Very well, then.' De Richleau stood up. 'I will be here at half
past nine.' Taking from his pocket the twenty rouble piece that
he had intended to leave in Benigno's hand before he knew his
identity, he gave it to the policeman who had made the arrest,
congratulating him on his alertness; then he said good night to the
Inspector and left the Station.

On the short walk to his hotel he ruminated on the surprising encounter with a Spanish anarchist in Russia; but, realizing that speculation was futile and that he would learn more about it in a few hours' time, he dismissed the matter from his thoughts. However, it had recalled to him many memories of the months he had spent in Spain and, while he was undressing, a series of pictures flickered through his mind: Angela lying dead, Gérault exposing him as a spy in the *Escuela Moderna*, La Torcera spitting in his face, and the back of Sanchez's head falling limp when his neck was broken – but the most vivid of all was the unforgettable beauty of Gulia de Cordoba when, that last night in San Sebastian, she had walked round the foot of his bed and thrown off her dressing-gown.

It was a long time since he had thought of her and he wondered whether she had become resigned to her position as a neglected wife, or if she had taken a lover. He hoped that she had, for other-wise it seemed certain that she would become embittered and old before her time from having been robbed by convention during the best years of her life of that joy to which every human being was entitled. He felt, too, that for her not to have done so would be a sinful waste, since she had so much to offer and could have brought a period of great happiness to at least one man, and perhaps several.

Not for the first time he cursed his luck that she should have been the wife of a close friend, and that on that account he had felt compelled to deny her and himself the consummation of their mutual passion. Had she been only the wife of an acquaintance for whom he had no affection or respect, he would at least have had the glowing memory of a night in her arms before he had set off after Sanchez; or, had he had no scruples about her hus-band, they might even have decided to let Sanchez do his damnedest and, had exposure of their *affaire* resulted, gone off together.

As things had turned out, Sanchez's photograph having been ruined, he could not, after all, have attempted to blackmail them, and it was by going after him that de Richleau had got himself shanghaied to South America. Still thinking of the scurvy trick Fate had played him, and of what he had missed to keep face with himself, he drifted off to sleep.

At nine-thirty punctually he arrived at the Police Station. The Inspector was still on duty and made no difficulty about having Benigno brought from his cell to a bare little office room so that the Duke could interview him privately.

As soon as the guards withdrew, they seated themselves on

either side of a small table and de Richleau said, 'Now, Ferrer, you will be good enough to tell me what you are doing in Yalta?'

Benigno shook his head. 'It is useless to question me. I have been caught, and that is that. But I shall say nothing.'

'In that case,' replied the Duke, 'you will be acting like a fool. And you certainly are not one. I well remember that during our association in Barcelona I came to the conclusion that you had a much better balanced mind than most of your colleagues. Listen carefully now to what I have to say. I am regarded here as a person of considerable importance. That is why I am allowed to see you alone like this. Shortly you will be put into the dock and charged. Upon whether or not you answer my questions your life now hangs. To see you executed would give me considerable pleasure. But it so happens that one of my besetting sins is curiosity. If you are prepared to give me what I feel that I can accept as a reasonably truthful account of yourself I shall simply state in court that I knew you in Spain as a dangerous political, and that you attacked me because you had an old grudge against me. That will result in you being treated as all political criminals are in Russia these days, and exiled to Siberia. On the other hand, if you refuse to talk I shall state that I knew you to be involved in the bomb plot aimed at killing *S.M. el Rey y la Reina* on their wedding day. That may not be strictly true, but no matter. In your present circumstances, my word will be accepted and under the emergency laws against terrorists which are in force here they will take you away and have you shot. Now, which is it to be?'

'You fiend!' Benigno whispered, lifting his red-rimmed eyes to the Duke's. 'You fiend!'

De Richleau gave a grim little laugh. 'On the contrary, you should look on me as an angel. Not many men whose wife you had helped to murder would forgo this chance to see you dead.'

'I had no hand in that. It is you who are a murderer. You murdered my poor brother.'

'Poor brother indeed!' The Duke's 'devil's' eyebrows shot up. 'That filthy blackmailing young swine! He got off too easily with the quick death that my situation compelled me to give him. But that is beside the point. In twenty minutes you will be taken into court. The life line I have thrown you is running out as we sit here. You had better snatch at it unless you wish to die.'

For a long minute Benigno wrung his thin hands in silence, then he burst out, 'You're right! Even Siberia would be better than a firing squad. What do you wish to know?'

'Why did you come to Russia?'

'To kill you.'

Again de Richleau's eyebrows lifted. 'You astound me. Since you felt the urge to kill I should have thought there were plenty of people in Spain whom you count your enemies and wish dead. What in the world induced you to undertake such a long and expensive journey and choose as your intended victim a man that for years you had not even seen?'

Benigno's eyes suddenly blazed with hate. 'It was you who killed Sanchez. According to your standards he may have had no morals; but he lived as he wished to live and that is how an anarchist should live. I didn't approve of all his actions but he had the right to do as he liked, and I loved him. I loved him more than anything in the world.'

'Then I am sorry for you,' said the Duke, and there was no trace of sarcasm in his tone. 'Love goes a long way to excusing most things. But tell me; how did you discover my whereabouts?'

'My father keeps a book in which he writes a brief account of all anarchist triumphs, wherever they may occur. He told me that your father had been killed in the attempt on General Count Plackoff last February. We felt sure that would bring you back to Europe, and we have correspondents in most of the big cities, so we asked for some of those in the ports to keep a look-out for you. Your arrival in Hamburg was reported to us, then that you were in Vienna and said to be on your way to claim your estate on the far side of the Carpathians. I would have gone there at once, but I didn't know a word of Russian; and having been told that in this vile country the police don't even need a warrant to seize on anyone, I didn't dare risk being picked up and questioned by them until I could speak enough Russian to pass myself off as a Spanish commercial traveller. For six weeks I swotted at your filthy language with a towel round my head; then I travelled to Jvanets. But I missed you by two days. I learned that you had gone down to Odessa, and there that you had gone on to Yalta. I followed you and for over a week I have been hoping for a chance to kill you; but until last night you have always been with other people or driving in a carriage.'

'Your persistence in making such a journey deserves a better reward than that you should now have to continue it for another few thousand miles to Siberia,' de Richleau remarked, this time with a cynical smile. 'But why, since you were prepared to go to such lengths to avenge your brother's death on me, did you not follow me to South America, instead of waiting until I returned to Europe?'

'If I could have, I would,' Benigno scowled. 'But at the time Captain Robles shipped you off there I was in prison. It was over a year before I got out. As soon as I had learned the full details of Sanchez's death and what had happened to you, I wrote to correspondents in Rio. They informed me that you had left Brazil months before and were somewhere in Central America, but no one knew for certain where. I wanted to go out to search for you; but I had very little money and my father wouldn't help me. He said it would be better to wait until . . .'

'Your father!' exclaimed the Duke. 'Did he then escape too?'

'Escape!' repeated Benigno, giving him a blank look. 'Why, no; neither of us escaped. After a year in prison all of us who had been arrested at the time the *Escuela Moderna* was raided were released.'

De Richleau stared at him in astonishment. 'D'you mean to tell me that when you were tried not even your father received more than a twelve months' sentence?'

'We were never brought to trial. Evidently the police decided that they had not enough evidence to convict us; and many influential bodies in Spain who hold Liberal views agitated for us to be given our freedom.'

'And where is your father now?'

For the first time Benigno's face showed the flicker of a smile and his reply was tinged with malice. 'That is no secret. Soon after we were released he started his *Escuela Moderna* again. Not in the city because, the tyrants having confiscated our property, we could not afford to set up in another big house. The school now occupies an old building in a village just outside Barcelona. But, for having been unjustly imprisoned for a year, as was proved when the police had to let him go without preferring a charge against him, he is now looked on by all the Liberals in Spain as a martyr. No one would dare to lay a finger on him.'

At this revelation, de Richleau's thoughts began to race with furious intensity. That Francisco Ferrer, the evil genius who inspired the Spanish anarchists, the man who was basically responsible for the death of Angela and the deaths of scores of other innocent people, should again be at large, filled him with amazement. Why Ferrer and his associates had never been brought to trial seemed to him inexplicable; and that, owing to Liberal pressure, they should have been allowed to go free after only a year in prison shocked him profoundly.

He was quick to realize that, had he not been shanghaied to South America, that could not possibly have happened. They

would undoubtedly have been tried and, on his evidence, convicted. Instead, it now emerged that the dreary weeks he had spent
in Barcelona, the sufferings he had endured there, and the near
loss of his life, had all gone for nothing. He had not, after all,
as he had long believed, succeeded in avenging Angela's death.
For well over a year and a half, Ferrer had been a free man, and
not only free but left at liberty to incite again his admiring disciples to murder.

Benigno's last statement – that no one would now dare to lay
a finger on his father – still echoed in the Duke's brain, but it
needed only an instant's thought for him to realize that about
that the young anarchist was wrong. He, de Richleau, had only
to return to Spain and tell what he knew of Francisco Ferrer on
oath before a magistrate for a warrant to be issued and a policeman to place a heavy hand on Ferrer's shoulder.

Had Benigno known better the man to whom he was speaking, he would have had more care for his father's safety than to
issue such a challenge. It needed only another moment's thought
for the Duke to decide that, while he could have been of little
help to the *Ocrana* in Russia, he could still strike a great blow against
the world-wide menace of anarchism by going again to Spain.
Those grey eyes of his, flecked with their yellow lights, glinted and
with sudden harshness he said to Benigno:

'Whatever your dupes – those guileless, woolly-minded, reform-
for-reform's-sake, besotted Liberals – may think of your father,
I know him to be a disciple of the Devil – a man who has not
only planned murders himself, but has injected his poisonous
philosophy of murder into the minds of scores of earnest, misguided young people and, if he could, would bring about unlimited
misery by overturning all forms of law and order. You may take
it from me, Benigno, that I will either have your father executed
or put behind bars for life, if it is the last thing that I ever do.'

At that moment, the Inspector came in and said that he must
take over the prisoner, as in a few minutes the Court would be
sitting. With a reassuring nod to the white-faced Benigno, the
Duke said, 'Don't worry. I am satisfied now that you did not
mean to kill me'; then, having thanked the Inspector for letting
him talk with the prisoner, he walked back into the outer office.

Benigno's case did not come on for the best part of an hour,
while the Magistrates dealt with other prisoners on minor charges.
Then the Duke was ushered into the witness-box. He told his
story with an air of calm indifference. It was that when in Barcelona nearly three years ago, he had known this man Ferrer as

an agitator who openly proclaimed himself an anarchist. Having heard him make threats against the Captain-General of the City, General Quiroga, he, de Richleau, had informed the authorities, upon which Ferrer had been arrested. No doubt Ferrer had realized who was responsible for his arrest and having, by chance, come upon him, de Richleau, again the previous night, he had sought to avenge himself by inflicting a wound.

With an innocent expression, and apparently in ignorance of the fact that he was overstepping the functions of a witness, de Richleau went on to say, 'It is not for me to suggest to the Court how it should deal with this man. But in view of his past, it seems unlikely that he would have come to this country except at the invitation of the nihilists; or, in any event, having arrived here have not got into touch with them. I feel, therefore, that while the assault on myself might normally be regarded as an ordinary criminal offence, meriting only a few months' imprisonment, having regard to his political background it is quite a possibility that, when freed, he might attack and perhaps murder someone of considerable importance. To send him back to Spain would be a troublesome and costly business, and the Spanish authorities would certainly not thank us; so may I suggest that he should be sent to a place where for a long time to come he will be in no position to do harm to anyone.'

The Magistrates listened to the Duke with deference. As he ceased speaking they nodded their approval; then their Chairman pronounced the sentence which, at that time, had become a commonplace in all the cities of European Russia. 'The Court orders that the prisoner be dispatched forthwith to a penal settlement in Siberia, there to remain during His Imperial Majesty's pleasure.'

As de Richleau left the courtroom, he gave a last glance at Benigno. He had secured from him the information he was anxious to obtain, and he had not cheated him. Many hardened criminals survived for years the harsh life in the Siberian penal settlements; some even succeeded in escaping. But to do so needed resource, great courage and, above all, extreme physical fitness. Benigno had none of those, and the Duke would have been prepared to wager heavy odds that he would not last six months in the salt mines. He felt satisfied that this second member of the foul Ferrer brood would make no further contribution to the infliction of agony and grief on innocent people; it now remained to choke the fount from which the poison sprang.

Back in his hotel, he was unhappily aware that he was now

8*

committed to another trip to Spain. He would so much rather have remained at Yalta, enjoying his morning and evening bathes in the warm waters of the Black Sea, sunning himself on the beach, lunching in some mimosa-scented garden with friends and going to the Casino to dance, or for a mild gamble, in the evenings.

He recalled his talk with Count Soltikoff, before he had set out for Barcelona, and the old Ambassador's quoting the dictum, 'Vengeance is Mine, saith The Lord', when warning him against taking the law into his own hands. And, as it had turned out, his first encounter with the Ferrers had ended disastrously for himself. Yet at that time he had been dominated by bitterness at his loss of Angela, so was impelled by a strong personal motive to reject the Ambassador's advice. Now, after an interval of years, he was able to regard the ethical side of the question dispassionately.

He was an entirely free agent and the choice lay with him. He could either take no action, or do his utmost to have Ferrer shot. Yet, apparently, no one else was in a position to bring the anarchist to justice. That such a rôle should have been cast for him would, he admitted to himself, inescapably brand him, if he took it, as participating in a vendetta. Nevertheless, he decided that the public good must be placed before all other considerations, and that it was his duty to accept this personal responsibility in order, once and for all, to prevent Ferrer from doing further evil.

In consequence, that afternoon he spent nearly three hours in a travel agency. After much discussion, looking up of time-tables and making long-distance calls to the offices of steamship lines in Odessa, he decided that, since he was debarred from travelling through France, his quickest way to reach Spain would be to go down to Constantinople and there pick up a ship which, without further change, would take him right through the Mediterranean to Gibraltar.

Next day, the 4th of July, he left Yalta for Odessa and, with nights spent there and in Constantinople, it was the 16th before he completed his sea voyage. The most likely person to be able to give him a true explanation for the Ferrers' release from prison was, he felt, Don Alfonso and, knowing that from the latter part of July it was the King's custom to reside at San Sebastian, he spent the next two days travelling from south to north through the length of the peninsular. On the evening of the 18th he booked in at the Maria Cristina Hotel, and on the following morning went to sign his name in the book at the Miramar Palace.

He then toyed with the idea of driving out to the Cordoba

villa, but decided against it. He would have, had he been certain of finding the Conde or de Vendôme there; but if it chanced that Gulia was alone on the bathing beach, it would hardly be possible to avoid all reference to their relationship when they had parted and, in view of the attraction the memory of her still exercised over him, he was very anxious to avoid a resumption of their secret intimacy.

On the other hand, to fail to let them know that he was again in San Sebastian would be thought extremely strange; so he wrote and posted a brief letter to Gulia reporting his arrival, saying how much he was looking forward to seeing them all again, and suggesting that he should come out to tell them all his news after the siesta the following afternoon. That, he felt sure, if they were at the villa, would result in an invitation to dinner and ensure that, when he did meet her again, there would be no opportunity for any private conversation between them.

His call at the Palace produced results more swiftly than he expected. After lunch a note from one of Don Alfonso's equerries was delivered to him, commanding him to dine that night. When he entered the yellow drawing-room, he found a mixed company of eight or ten people already assembled, including one couple he had met before. While he was talking to them, the gentleman-in-waiting on duty came up to him with a slip of paper in his hand, glanced at it, and said:

'Your Excellency, I am told that you already know the Condesa de Cordoba. It is His Majesty's pleasure that you should take her in to dinner.'

'I shall be delighted,' smiled the Duke; and, indeed, had he been in a position to arrange such a situation himself, no bridge over to the past could have suited him better.

Two more guests arrived, then the Infanta Maria Alfonsine, Conde Ruiz, Doña Gulia and François de Vendôme. Gulia was dressed in white satin and wearing the priceless Cordoba emeralds. She was now twenty-six and de Richleau caught his breath at the sight of her. He had known many beautiful women but at the moment could not think of one who combined such lovely features, striking colouring and grace of figure.

As she caught sight of him her step faltered, then she gave him a slow smile. First he kissed the Infanta's hand and acknowledged her kindly greeting. Gulia then extended hers and as he took it he saw that it did not betray by the faintest tremor any emotion she might be feeling. De Vendôme and Count Ruiz expressed their delight at his return and upbraided him for not having at once come out to the villa. He explained that he had arrived only the previous evening, been engaged with business most of the day, and that there was a letter in the post suggesting that he should go out there the next afternoon.

By then another couple had arrived, making the party up to eighteen. Two minutes later the big double-doors at the end of the room were thrown open, the guests formed two lines, and the King and Queen advanced between them, graciously acknowledging the deep bows of the men and the curtsies of the women.

They went into dinner in strict order of precedence, Don Alfonso taking in his aunt, the Queen escorted by the Duke de Lécera and de Richleau, as a foreign duke and a Knight of the Golden Fleece, coming next with Gulia on his arm. In consequence, he found himself on the Queen's left.

While not neglecting her other neighbour, she talked to him for the greater part of the long meal. Evidently she was unaware of the dramatic way in which he had left Spain and, having learned that he had been soldiering in Central America, did not pursue the subject. Knowing him to be of British nationality, she talked to him mostly about England – a matter always near her heart – and of the friends he had made there while he was married to Angela. In consequence his conversation with Gulia was perforce fragmentary and impersonal; but at the first opportunity he inquired after her husband, and was relieved to learn that José had not been included in the party only because he was abroad. His banking interests had decided him to make a tour of the South American cities, and he was at present in Bahia.

When the Queen and the ladies withdrew, Don Alfonso called to the Duke to come and sit next to him, and at once inquired how he had fared overseas. De Richleau provided him with an account of some of the ramshackle armies in which he had served, and some amusing instances of the barefaced trickery of Latin American politicians; but he formed the impression that the King's mind was not on the conversation and that he was secretly worrying over something.

Soon after they had joined the ladies an Italian *prima donna* sang several arias for them and between her songs a gifted pianist played pieces by Chopin. When they had finished de Richleau talked for a while with Maria Alfonsine. Although the plump, high-nosed Infanta was only in her middle forties her staidness made her appear older, and she was not a very bright conversationalist; but she had never forgotten how much her son, François, owed to the Duke, and she expressed the greatest pleasure at seeing him again.

Later he managed to catch the eye of the King and, going over to him, said:

'Sir, may I crave a private audience whenever it is convenient? I am anxious to discuss again with Your Majesty the subject about which you did me the honour to speak at Aranjuez.'

Don Alfonso nodded and fingered the small moustache that he had recently grown. 'Yes, certainly, Duke. But not for the present. Although I arrived here only two days ago, much to my annoyance I have to return to Madrid tomorrow. What are your plans?'

'I was hoping that I might be of some further service to Your Majesty.'

Suddenly the King frowned. 'If you were thinking of going to Barcelona again, I do not desire it. In fact I forbid it. There is going to be serious trouble there, and if you were recognized your life would not be worth a peseta.'

'For what I have in mind, to go there might not be necessary.'

'Very well, then. We will talk of the matter on my return. But I may be away for some days. I will send for you when I get back.'

Shortly afterwards the King and Queen wished their guests 'good night' and were bowed and curtsied from the room. As the party started to break up, de Richleau joined his friends and asked them if they would come with him to his hotel for a drink before returning to the villa. Count Ruiz replied that his wife had just complained of a migraine so he must take her home. As it was still quite early and de Vendôme could have chaperoned Gulia, de Richleau was somewhat surprised when she also declined and said quite casually:

'I am sure the account of your adventures will lose nothing by being kept until tomorrow after the siesta.'

She had not even asked him to dinner and it was the placid, good-natured Infanta who, exercising her royal prerogative of inviting people to any house in which she was staying, repaired the omission by saying:

'Come changed, Duke, so that you can stay on and dine.'

Having thanked her and seen them to her carriage, de Richleau, accompanied by de Vendôme, walked back to his hotel. There the two old friends talked until the early hours of the morning and, after the Duke had given a resumé of his doings, the Prince told him about the crises which necessitated Don Alfonso's return to Madrid.

There was serious trouble in Morocco. The Riff tribesmen there were in revolt and had cut the railway line between the valuable Spanish iron mines up country and the port of Melilla. It was even feared that the town might be taken and sacked, so reinforcements were being rushed out there as speedily as possible. However, as the Prince – having served as an officer-cadet under de Richleau at St. Cyr – was competent to judge, the Spanish Army could not compare with that of France as far as training, efficiency and readiness for service were concerned. Moreover, for some reason that no one seemed to understand, the Generals said they could not find enough men to send unless they depleted essential garrisons.

In consequence the War Minister, General Linares, had had the not very bright idea of calling up the Catalan reserves. Since the war in Africa was most unpopular anyway and Barcelona, as ever, more strongly anti-Government than any other city, this, as might have been foreseen, had had the worst possible results. Hundreds of young Catalans liable for service were refusing to join the colours, the city was in a ferment and a General Strike was threatened. A further cause for anxiety was that these troubles now threatened to undermine the value of the peseta in the international money market.

The Duke was aware that there was fighting in Morocco, but had thought it no more than one of the outbursts by hot-headed tribesmen that so frequently took place; and as a heavy censorship was being imposed, his glance through the morning papers had given him no hint of the much more serious trouble at home. Now he no longer wondered that Don Alfonso had appeared so distrait after dinner.

Out at the villa, in the cool of the evening next day, the Cordoba house-party, which included a couple named de Tarancón, assembled round the fountain in the garden to drink iced Manzanilla while de Richleau told them how, while trying to trap an anarchist, he had been shipped off to Rio and of the life he had led in Central American cities and in the jungle.

They expressed the greatest interest and asked many questions, with the one exception of Gulia, who showed by a slight smile now and then that she was listening, but made no comment, and appeared to be half-absorbed in some embroidery that she was doing.

When the men sat over their wine after dinner they discussed the crisis again and the shortcomings of the army. The lean, good-looking Conde Ruiz, as elegant as ever with his curled hair, black sidewhiskers and wearing a velvet burgundy-coloured smoking jacket, was playing host. He maintained that the root of the trouble lay with the Church, because its demands on the State's funds were so great that there was never enough left over to provide the army with all the supplies it needed.

De Tarancón backed him up, declaring that the power the Church continued to wield was far too great. He instanced the fact that all efforts by the Government to limit the number of religious houses had been frustrated, and that quite recently the Prime Minister, Señor Maura, had been forced against his will to appoint a most unpopular monk, Father Nozaleda, as Archbishop of Valencia.

The Conde nodded agreement and went on to castigate a new measure, by which a huge loan was to be raised to compensate the Religious Orders for the damage they had sustained during the Revolution of 1868. He roundly declared that for the Government to accept liability for such a claim after a lapse of half a century and, above all, at the present time, was nothing less than a piece of financial madness.

De Vendôme, however, owing to his strong religious feelings and friendship with many of the leading prelates, argued that the majority of priests lived in dire poverty, and that any nation which did not put the work of God before any other consideration did not deserve to prosper. He then went on to attack the Generals for their incompetence, lack of true patriotism and the high-handed manner in which at times they combined to defy even the King.

Later, in the drawing-room, de Richleau learnt from Gulia further particulars about her husband's trip to South America. The Conde had left Spain early in May and gone first to the Argentine. After a fortnight there he had crossed the Andes to Chile and Peru, returned to stay for a few days in Uruguay, then travelled up the coast to the principal cities of Brazil. He had last written that having completed his business in Bahia he intended to go on an expedition up the Amazon for a few weeks to hunt the wonderful tropical butterflies on the banks of which river they abounded. He would then go on to Venezuela and the capitals of the Central American Republics; so he did not expect to get back much before the end of October.

When the Duke was taking his leave Gulia did not offer him any further invitation, and it was de Vendôme who asked him to come out to bathe with them from the private beach next morning. Only then did she endorse the Prince's pressing with a vague apology for not having thought of suggesting it herself. In view of Gulia's attitude he almost felt that he ought to refuse; but since he was staying in an hotel and all of them must know it to be highly unlikely that he would have any other engagement, to do so would have struck them as very queer, so he accepted.

While he was being driven back to his hotel in one of the Cordoba carriages his mind was occupied in succession by two very different sets of thoughts.

First, distress and sympathy for the young King in his Herculean task of trying to keep the peace between the greedy hidebound Church, semi-mutinous Generals, and the large section of his subjects who was now clamouring for the blood of both.

Secondly, pique at Gulia's attitude towards himself. He had meant to take every possible precaution against being left alone with her. But clearly she had not the least desire for a *tête-à-tête* with him. It was evident that no vestige remained of the burning passion she had felt for him three years ago. That, he could not help feeling, was not very flattering to him; but at least it would enable him to see as much of the Cordobas as he liked without fear of a renewal of their entanglement which, in view of her husband's absence abroad, could have proved all the more dangerous.

His reaction to her apparent coldness only went to show how easily a man of even exceptional intelligence and shrewdness can be fooled by a clever woman who desires him. If he could have seen into Gulia's mind an hour or two later, as she tossed and turned restlessly in her big canopied bed, he would have thought very differently.

18

Put on a Chain

THE beach party the next day was a large one for, in addition to those staying in the villa, Gulia had invited several friends, but what should have been a carefree gathering was overshadowed by the morning's news. The papers, although still reticent, had been allowed by the Censor to print enough to show that a really serious state of affairs existed in Catalona.

One of the party, named Señor Dencás, a wealthy Barcelona

industrialist on holiday, who had been invited by Conde Ruiz, told them that he felt certain that a General Strike would lead to armed risings and, perhaps, even civil war. He added that for several years past the movement for Catalan independence had become so generally accepted that if the workers rose in revolt the majority of the upper and middle classes would give them their support.

Challenged by de Vendôme on his statement that responsible people would join with Marxists and anarchists in fighting the Government, Señor Dencás shrugged his broad shoulders and said, 'After the way in which we Catalans have been treated, what can you expect? We are business people and our principal concern is to earn a decent living. We contribute a far greater share of taxes than any other part of Spain; yet the Government is not content with that, but permits the livelihood of many of us to be threatened by iniquitously unfair competition.'

'In what way?' inquired de Richleau.

'By allowing the Church to engage in commerce,' came the prompt reply. 'The Religious Houses have, of course, always had their industries: farming, the cultivation of vineyards, the manufacture of various local products and so on. No harm in that as long as these things were for the support of their own communities. But in recent years the Church has gone into business. I mean real business, with advertising campaigns, export departments and Fathers who are sales-managers. It gets its labour free so can, anyway, undersell us; but that is not the end of the story. We have to pay a tax on everything we make, but everything made by the Religious Houses is tax free.'

Conde Ruiz nodded. 'Yes, it is utterly wrong. Spain's trade in liqueurs is an example. We have our Anis del Mono, Calisay, Cuarenta y Tres, and many others which could rival the best productions of the French and the Dutch; but abroad they are almost unknown, because the firms that make them are too heavily taxed to be able to afford to popularize them. Whereas Chartreuse swamps the market; and the Fathers who make it at Tarragona, since they were expelled from France at the turn of the century, are positively rolling in money.'

'It is the Church, too,' remarked Dencás, 'that is responsible for the repressive laws that prevent progress. We Catalans are a go-ahead people. We resent being forced to have our children only partially educated because there are so many things that the Church prefers that they should not know, and the absurd censorship which is still maintained on great numbers of foreign books solely because they deal with the lives of men and women in a realistic manner.'

'I suppose there are certain matters in which the Church should adopt a more progressive attitude,' de Vendôme agreed reluctantly, 'but if one once opened the gates to doubt it might result in a land-slide towards free-thinking. The Church is the great bulwark pro-tecting family life and the discipline which it inculcates ensures millions of people maintaining a high standard of conduct. In Spain, too, the Church has played a greater part than in any other country.'

'Ah, now you are talking of the distant past, Prince,' Dencás replied. 'It is true that in the days of Ferdinand and Isabella our great Cardinal Cisneros emancipated the Church of Spain from the domination of Rome, and purged it of all the abuses which were rife among the priesthood all over Europe during the Middle Ages. That is why there was no Reformation here. By the time Cisneros had done his great work there was no more need for reform; so he saved the Spanish people from becoming infected both by the Protestant heresies and the religious civil wars that caused so much misery in other countries. But the state of the Church today is very different from that in which he left it. Under his rule even the highest prelates led the lives of the greatest sim-plicity and self-denial. They were a strength and example to the nation, and Spain's greatness in the sixteenth century was largely due to them. Now the State subsidizes the Church to the tune of 300,000,000 pesetas per annum and in return for it has been so shackled as to become one of the most backward countries in Europe.'

De Vendôme flushed and was obviously about to make an indig-nant protest in defence of his friends the Fathers, but de Tarancón, who had played the part of a listener during the conversation, prevented a possible quarrel by saying that it was quite time for them to go in for another swim.

A few days later the storm broke. A General Strike was declared throughout Catalonia and in Barcelona the workers threw up barricades in the streets. There were anti-Government demonstra-tions in many other cities but San Sebastian, being so largely a holiday resort, remained free from any serious trouble. Life there went on much as usual, except for the rush to secure a paper every time a new edition was put on sale.

After the first beach party to which de Richleau had gone, on the 21st, he became swiftly absorbed into the de Cordoba circle. The Dencás and two other couples at it had asked him to lunch or dine, and Gulia had said pleasantly, if without enthusiasm, that she hoped he would use the beach regularly for his morning bathe.

On the 24th, Conde Ruiz left in haste for Madrid to take charge at this time of crisis of the bank's affairs, from its headquarters; but the Infanta, her lady-in-waiting, the de Tarancóns and de Vendôme all remained at the Villa, and several other friends, like de Richleau, had been made free of the private beach, so most mornings there was a party of from eight to a dozen people swimming and paddling there.

For three days there was desperate fighting in Barcelona, buildings were fired, convents sacked, priests and nuns maltreated; but the discipline and superior weapons of the troops gave them the upper hand. Several hundred rioters were killed and several score of soldiers; the organized resistance to authority collapsed.

At the end of the week the King returned to San Sebastian and next day he sent for de Richleau. The Duke found him working in a small, open-fronted marquee in the garden of the Palace. Don Alfonso sent away the secretary who was with him and, having waved de Richleau to a chair, said:

'When last you were here I had this Barcelona business on my mind, but the situation there is now in hand, so I would like to hear what it is that you wanted to say to me.'

De Richleau gave an account of Benigno's attack on him in Yalta, then went on to say, 'I squared accounts with the younger Ferrer brother in Cadiz before I was shipped off to South America. The other is, by this time, in Siberia and it is most unlikely that he will ever return to plague us further. But I was amazed to hear from him that he and his father were never brought to trial, and that after a year's imprisonment they were allowed to go free. Would Your Majesty care to enlighten me about this extraordinary failure on the part of the authorities to administer justice?'

Don Alfonso made a wry face. 'Yes; to you, Duke, whom these people did their best to murder, it must seem extraordinary. But remember, their friends had succeeded in getting you out of the way, so that you could not have appeared had they been brought to trial; and you were the key witness.'

'But you, Sir, assured me that even if I was prevented from giving evidence against them they would still be awarded the death penalty, or at least a life sentence.'

'I know it! I know it!' the King shrugged impatiently. 'But despite all their efforts the police failed to secure really damning evidence against these people. At least, that is what they said.

And at that time I had a Liberal Cabinet. You should have heard
the fuss they kicked up in defence of this man Ferrer and his
associates. They actually argued that with his *Escuela Moderna*
he had been doing a service to the country, because he provided
an opportunity for a part of the youth of Barcelona to acquire
a much broader education than it could have received in any of
our national Church-sponsored establishments.'

'They may have been right about that,' de Richleau replied,
'but they seem to have left out of account that these people also
corrupted youth. Advanced teaching may be desirable in many
ways, but not if it is of the kind that would do away with law
and order. The freedom to express an opinion is all very well,
but not when it is an older person telling admiring youngsters
that if they do not approve of your Government it is an heroic
thing to murder the officials appointed by it, and that it is nothing
to worry about if they kill a score of bystanders into the bargain.'

'I entirely agree with you, and I was most loath to consent to
the release of the prisoners. Before doing so I had de Cordoba
write to you asking if there was any prospect of you returning
to Europe in the fairly near future. Had there been I would have
insisted on their being held until you were here and could give
evidence at their trial. But de Cordoba received no reply to his
letter. After waiting a final month I had no alternative, short of
quarrelling with my Ministers, but to allow Ferrer and his friends
to be set at liberty.'

The Duke shook his head. 'If de Cordoba's letter was written
ten or eleven months after I left Spain, by the time it should have
reached me I was probably many miles from civilization, buried
deep in one of the Central American jungles. No doubt the bag
of mail in which it was fell off a mule into some swamp or river.
Anyhow, it never reached me. Had it done so, Sir, I can assure
you I would have returned to see to it that Ferrer and Co. got
their deserts. It is for that purpose that I have now come back
to Spain.'

'If only you had returned a month or so ago,' Don Alfonso
murmured.

'What difference would that have made, Sir?'

'It would have made a world of difference. Ferrer and his friends
were then living openly just outside Barcelona, once more spreading their pernicious doctrines. The police could easily have picked
them up and we could have had them brought to trial. That might
well have proved the stitch in time that would have prevented the
recent outbreak of armed revolt in the city. There can be no

question about it, the anarchists were behind that, and if only we could have roped in their leaders a few weeks ago it would have saved many lives, much bloodshed and a great deal of bitterness.'

'There is, then, more reason than ever to arrest them and bring them to trial.'

'True; but that is easier said than done. Warrants are out for them on a charge of having incited the workers to rebellion; but yesterday I had a report that they have already gone to earth, and it may now prove extremely difficult to trace them.'

De Richleau leaned forward and said earnestly, 'Your Majesty. As you are aware, after accepting the mission with which you charged me, I spent the best part of two months in Barcelona posing as a Russian refugee. During that time I got to know a considerable number of people with whom the Ferrers had dealings. Not all of them were anarchists. Many of them must still be living normal lives and it is most unlikely that your police would know that they have ever been acquainted with Ferrer. Through one or more of them I feel confident that I could get on his track. I request Your Majesty's permission to proceed to Barcelona and collaborate with your police in hunting Ferrer down.'

'No.' The young King's voice was firm. 'You served me well, Duke, three years ago in enabling me to break up the original *Escuela Moderna*; but you very nearly lost your life in the process and have since been a marked man. Barcelona is now a veritable hornet's nest, and I'll not allow you to stick your head into it. I refuse to have the blood of so good a friend on my head.'

The Duke sighed. 'I appreciate Your Majesty's consideration for me. But I am a soldier and used to taking my life in my hands, I am determined to get the man Ferrer sooner or later; so I beg you to reconsider your decision.'

'Sooner or later,' repeated the King. 'That is another matter. And nothing would please me better. For the year that Ferrer was in prison anarchist activities in Barcelona practically ceased. Soon after he was released they recommenced and for the past year they have steadily mounted in numbers and violence. There was only one lull. Last November a squadron of the Fleet of Austria–Hungary paid a courtesy visit to Barcelona. My Ministers did their utmost to persuade me not to go there to receive it; but I insisted. The celebrations lasted for three days and during them not one bomb was thrown. Three days without a bomb! It was a record against the sort of thing that had been going on for months, and considered quite remarkable. That gives you the picture.'

'It also gives me a picture of Your Majesty's popularity,' de Richleau smiled.

'True. The reason given for the lull was that anyone who had thrown a bomb at me would have been torn to pieces by the crowd; and that the great majority of my subjects should feel that way about me is most gratifying. But it does not console me for the loss of the hundreds of my loyal officials and soldiers who have been murdered by these evil men. And no sooner had I left Barcelona than their outrages recommenced.'

'May I ask, Sir, what the situation is there now?'

'The back of the revolt has been broken, but mopping up operations are not yet completed. My new Home Secretary, Juan de La Cierva, is a good man. He feels that this may be a chance to clear things up in Barcelona once and for all, and he is taking strong measures. Among others, a house-to-house search is being conducted for arms. But hundreds of the malcontents must still have them and that is why I don't wish you to go there yet. There is too great a risk of your being shot in the back or from a window.'

'Things will never be cleared up in Barcelona until Ferrer is brought to book.'

'No; I fear you are right there.'

'Then when does Your Majesty feel that you might be disposed to let me off my chain, so that I can attend to him?'

'Not until the arrests have ceased and the excitement has died down. Even then it would be better to wait for a little because when the city has been back to normal for a while the ringleaders who have escaped the net will begin to take risks by coming out of hiding now and then. That should make it easier for you to catch your man. May I take it that you are enjoying yourself in San Sebastian?'

'Yes; all my friends are being most kind, Sir.'

'Then you had better remain here, and when the time is ripe I will send for you again.'

Seeing that the interview was over, de Richleau stood up, bowed, and said with a smile, 'I only hope, Sir, that you will refrain from putting too great a strain on my impatience to see this matter through.'

Much disappointed by the restraint Don Alfonso had put upon him the Duke lunched at a restaurant in the town with some friends then, after the siesta, as the visit to the Palace had deprived him of his morning bathe, he drove out to the de Cordoba's beach for an early evening swim.

For the past eight days he had seen Gulia every morning and,

on most days, also later at a luncheon or dinner party; so they
had again dropped quite naturally into the friendly relationship
that had existed between them when he had first become con-
valescent. There was only one subtle difference. Then he had been
tied to his bed or a chair so he had been unable to fetch and carry
for her. Now, having after a few days come to the conclusion
that she had no lover – or, at least, not in her social circle then
in San Sebastian – her first coldness towards him had so titillated
his vanity that, almost insensibly, he had asserted himself by
assuming the rôle of her cavalier. She had accepted his attentions
gracefully and watched with amusement the skilful way in which
he jockeyed other men who were always eager to serve her in small
matters out of the chance to do so; but he and she had never
been alone together for more than a few minutes and no word
of their past feelings for one another had passed between them.

On this evening he had only just changed in one of the beach
huts and walked out on to the sand when he saw Gulia and Doña
Eulalia coming down from the house towards him. As they approached Gulia waved to him and cried:

'I wondered what had happened to you this morning, until
François told me at lunch that you had been sent for to the Palace.
But it's a lovely evening for a bathe and when I saw you from
the house just now I felt I too must come in for a swim.'

Doña Eulalia settled herself with her embroidery in her usual
chair and de Richleau made casual conversation with her while
Gulia was changing. The bathing dress she wore this summer
differed considerably from the one in which she had swum with
him three years ago. The fashion had become both more elegant
and practical. Skirts were now only knee-length, there was no
heavy ruching about the shoulders, no sleeves and the material
was much thinner; so the female form was more obviously dis-
cernible and women were not so heavily handicapped when swimming by the weight of water-soaked serge.

That, perhaps, partly accounted for the fact that Gulia had
become a much stronger swimmer; and when, having joined him
on the foreshore, she suggested that they should swim out to the
point he had no doubts about her ability to cover the distance.

After wading out they swam side by side for ten minutes, then
he shot ahead so as to reach the rocks first and help her up on
to them. Near the point there protruded a flattish slab. It had
been warmed by a long day of sunshine and there was no wind.
Sitting on it they could wriggle their toes in the pools below them
as the gentle swell rose and fell. They were still within sight of

Doña Eulalia, sitting something over a quarter of a mile away in front of the row of beach huts, but apart from that they were as much alone between sea and sky as if they had been on a desert island.

For a few minutes they sat in silence, getting back their breath, then Gulia pulled off her swimming cap, shook out her hair so that it fell over her shoulders, and said, 'Now, Armand, I want to hear what really happened to you in Cadiz. All you've told us is that you killed Sanchez in a fight, but his friends caught you and shipped you off to South America. I want to hear every detail from the moment you left me.'

She alone knew that it was not so much Sanchez that he had gone after as the photograph with which he feared Sanchez meant to blackmail them, and he now gave her the full story of his doings in Granada with La Torcera, in Cadiz with red-headed Inez, and the final scene in the Silver Galleon.

When he had done she sighed. 'And to think that negative had already been ruined before Sanchez made his escape from you in the garden. If only we had known. You would never have been shanghaied, and I would have been spared the worst month of my life. I nearly died from an agony of uncertainty about what had happened to you.'

'My dear,' he murmured gently. 'It distresses me greatly that you should have suffered so much on my account.'

She turned and looked at him, her eyes shining. 'How could it have been otherwise? I loved you desperately. I feared that those devils must have killed you and that I would never see you again.'

'The moment I reached Rio I sent a cable to François and wrote fully to José. It was impossible to let you know what had become of me any sooner.'

'I know; but you might also have written a personal letter to me; if only a line to say that you still loved me and that I need not fear that photograph being produced.'

'I did consider doing that,' he replied after a moment, 'but I felt there was too great a risk of such a letter falling into wrong hands. Had José chanced to open it by mistake, or should you have had an accident or been taken ill, or had he recognized my writing and asked you what was in it, the fat would have been in the fire. He could only have assumed from it that you had become my mistress; and as things never reached that point such a denouement would have been doubly unfortunate.'

Her full lips twitched in a little smile as she asked, 'Have you ever regretted that they didn't reach that point?'

'Often,' he admitted frankly. 'The man isn't born who, having had the chance to make love to you and did not take it, would not afterwards ask himself if he had not been stricken with madness.'

'Thank you for the compliment.' Her smile broadened. 'But I don't doubt you found plenty of lovely young women to console you while you were in the Americas!'

He gave a little laugh. 'Plenty implies a lot; and I have always been a *gourmet* rather than a *gourmand* in such matters. But I'd be a poor fish if for three years I had lived the life of a monk; and the gods were kind enough to send me a few very delightful companions to solace me in my widowerhood. Now tell me about your charming self?'

'I was not made to be a saint, either.' She shrugged her fine shoulders. 'Since we parted I have taken four lovers. Mostly out of boredom, it is true; but at least they have saved me from shrivelling up into a mummy physically, and I have had quite a lot of fun pulling the wool over old Doña Eulalia's eyes in order to give my lovers rendezvous without her suspecting anything.'

'Has José any idea of this?'

'Perhaps; but I rather doubt it. Anyhow, as I told you long ago, I don't think he would have any serious objection provided I managed my *affaires* discreetly.'

For a moment she was silent, then she turned her head again, looked full at him and asked, 'Tell me, Armand; do you still feel any love for me?'

In a flash he saw the danger signal blazing red ahead. 'No,' he said firmly. 'Affection, yes; but love, no. Time is a great healer and I got over that.'

Her Gioconda smile came again. 'You are lying, Armand. You are lying, and you know it.'

'*Dios!*' he exclaimed, suddenly turning to look at her. 'You're right, of course. Seeing what passed between us that last night before I left for Granada – that indelible memory of you – how could I possibly be in your company day after day as I have been recently without again succumbing and desiring you most damnably?'

She gave a low, happy laugh. 'I knew you would. But I had to have a little time to bring you to it. That is why I gave you such a cold reception on your arrival. If I hadn't you would have taken alarm and sheered off, wouldn't you?'

'I suppose I would,' he admitted a shade ruefully. 'But Gulia, though you may look an angel you are certainly a fallen one.

Only a daughter of the Devil would have laid such a snare for anyone in such a position as myself.'

'I'm nothing of the kind,' she laughed again. 'I am just a woman – a woman in search of a man. It so happens that I have a healthy, lovely body and a very much better brain than most members of my sex. I don't have to be told that, I know it; so why shouldn't I use my assets to secure a lover who is healthy, handsome and intelligent too – a man like you?'

'I don't blame you. And I only wish it could be me.'

'Well, why not?' She raised a well-marked eyebrow in faint mockery. 'José is thousands of miles away chasing butterflies – real butterflies this time. The de Tarancóns are going home at the end of the week, and François is leaving too.'

'Is he?' exclaimed de Richleau. 'Why?'

'He has volunteered for service in Morocco, and is going out with the regiment of which last year Don Alfonso made him Colonel-in-Chief. He leaves with the Tarancóns the day after to-morrow. Ruiz is in Madrid. He may return for a night or two occasionally but, apart from him, that leaves only Maria Alfonsine, her lady Doña Isabella and old Eulalia, and as far as human relationships are concerned they are all as blind as bats. Now that there will be room in the house, since I shall be so heavily chaperoned, no breath of scandal could arise if I invited you to come and stay, just as you did before.'

The Duke put his head between his hands and groaned, 'Gulia! Gulia! When Thaïs tempted Paphuntius he was subjected to nothing worse than this. You are an experienced woman of the world and must know how greatly I desire you. I am flattered, too, terribly flattered that you should find me more desirable than other men. But you already know why I cannot allow myself to give way to this temptation.'

'If your reason is still the same, an outmoded chivalry towards the husband who has no use for me,' she replied bitterly, 'then I wish you joy of your hair shirt. But why, in God's name, must you play the Puritan with me when you admit to having had *affaires* with other women?'

'Because José is my friend. It is that which makes the barrier between us.'

'Such scruples may have been valid three years ago. But in all that time you have not even exchanged a word with him. To continue in such an attitude is farcical. It is the behaviour of a Don Quixote – the sort of fool who tilts at windmills.'

'You may be right,' de Richleau admitted miserably. 'But the fact that I have not seen José for three years makes no difference. If he were here he would still count me his friend; so how, without feeling eternal shame at myself, can I take you as my mistress behind his back?'

For a while they were silent, then Gulia said quite calmly, 'Very well. I must accept your decision. There are plenty of other handsome, intelligent men who would willingly become my lover. When I next feel in the mood I'll look round and choose one. All the same I should be loath to lose your friendship. Are you willing that we should forget this conversation and continue to see one another as we have done during the past week?'

He looked up quickly. 'Of course I am. Desire for you physically is only a part of the attraction you have for me. You are more beautiful than any work of art and I delight in looking at you; I love the sound of your voice and watching the workings of that quick mind of yours. I know that I am acting like a fool, but I just can't help it: and half a loaf is better than no bread. If you can forgive me for failing you as a lover and let me continue to be your friend I'll honour you all the more.'

'So be it then.' She gave a sigh of resignation but at the same time smiled at him. 'Once more I'll put away my wicked dreams and try to look on you as a brother. I think I can promise, too, that I'll give you no cause for jealousy. With you about all other men will continue to seem poor game to me, so it's very unlikely that I'll take another lover until I return to Madrid in the autumn.'

Coiling her Titian hair up into a bun she pulled her rubber cap over it, and added, 'I'll play the game by refraining from tempting you further. But should you change your mind before we leave San Sebastian – well, let me know.'

Before he had time to reply she had slid off the rock and was swimming for the shore.

During the next few days and nights she was rarely out of de Richleau's thoughts. His conscience told him that he had done the right thing, but that was little consolation for having deprived himself of what he believed would have been two or three months that he would have been able to look back on as one of the highspots of his life.

He tried to excuse himself for having deprived her of the happiness she sought by arguing that it was not love that drove her to pursue him. Three years ago he believed that it had been. He felt sure that although she might have contemplated taking a lover before they met, she had not done so; and that a woman of her kind would have had to be in love before, for the first time, making

up her mind to be unfaithful to her husband. That he, her husband's
devoted friend, should have chanced to be the man on whom she
had set her heart had been hard indeed.

But now matters were different. Her love for him could not
have endured since she admitted to taking four lovers. Now it
could only be the aftermath of the old physical attraction that she
felt. It was no longer love but lust that had caused her to renew
her attempts to seduce him from his loyalty to his friend. The
proof of that was the casual way in which she had spoken of taking
another lover when she returned to Madrid in the autumn and in
her reaction to his refusal to make her his mistress. If she had
loved him she would have pleaded with him and burst into tears.
Instead, she had taken his refusal quite calmly, and cynically told
him that should he change his mind he had only to let her know.

He asked himself then if he loved her, but about that he could
not decide. She delighted him in so many ways, yet simply to be
in her company was not enough; his whole being yearned for her
embrace so that at times he actually felt a physical pain from it
deep down in his body. And what was that if not lust? Yet where
did lust end and love begin? It was an age-old problem and in-
soluble. He had to admit to himself that there could be little to
choose between their feelings for each other and that it was unfair
to her to assume that love played no part in her desire for him.

On the Thursday evening there was a big farewell party at the
villa for de Vendôme, and on Friday morning they all went to
the station to see him off. The de Tarancóns left by the same train,
but even after their departure Gulia continued to play the game as
she had promised, neither going out of her way to be alone with
de Richleau for a few moments, nor seeking to arouse his jealousy
by flirting with other men who came to the bathing parties at the
villa. Yet every now and then during these days he, perforce,
caught her eye and was tortured by the knowledge that he had
only to say the word for her to give him a secret rendezvous that
would open the gates of heaven for them both.

As he was so deeply committed to her social circle there was
no way in which he could avoid meeting her daily as long as he
remained in San Sebastian; so he seriously contemplated leaving
the city, and would have done so but for his promise to remain
there at Don Alfonso's disposal until the King should consider
the time ripe to let him off his chain. It was therefore with relief
that on returning to his hotel on the Friday night after a dinner
party given by the Dencáses that he found a letter commanding
him to lunch at the Palace next day, and for a few hours he was

able to banish Gulia from his mind by searching it for people he had met in Barcelona who knew Ferrer.

The lunch proved to be a men's party of only six, all of whom were soldiers, and before they went in to lunch the King said to de Richleau, 'I thought it would interest you to join us today, Duke, because we are going to discuss the campaign in Morocco. As you served with the French Army in North Africa you must be well acquainted with the sort of problems we are faced with, and may be able to offer us some sound advice.'

De Richleau bowed his acknowledgements and as soon as they were seated at table the conversation became general. There could be no doubt that the war was most unpopular with the Spanish people and the King told his guests that he was being pressed by certain members of his Cabinet to give it up; but he had refused to do so. He then went on to express a view that was entirely new to the Duke, by saying:

'The greatest tragedy that ever befell our country was the discovery of America by Columbus. Already in Ferdinand and Isabella's time we had secured a foothold in North Africa and once the Moors had been driven out of Spain that was our natural road to expansion. King Ferdinand realized it because being also King of Naples and Sicily the possession of Tunis was important to him. So, too, did Charles V, who was regarded as the champion of Christendom owing to the great expedition he led against the lairs of the Barbary corsairs. Again in Philip II's time, after Don John had defeated the Turks at Lepanto, we should have seized on the chance to break the power of the Sultans, Beys and Satraps in North Africa.

'But during that century when Spain was at the height of her power the energies of her greatest captains were dissipated in the Americas. Admittedly we acquired vast territories and the gold and silver of Mexico and Peru. But what good did it do us? The result was an inflation of our currency that nearly ruined the commerce of the nation, and in the long run we had to spend more in costly expeditions to hold our gains than we got out of them in treasure.

'And where are we today? The last of the American colonies has been lost to us and we have nothing left to show for our centuries of effort in bringing Christianity to the New World. If instead we had devoted those efforts to North Africa while we had the strength we would be the masters of the whole of it from the Libyan border to Casablanca.

'Owing to our dynastic troubles and lack of a forward policy during the nineteenth century, France got ahead of us and made both Algeria and a large part of Morocco her own. But the Anglo-French agreement of 1904 at least stipulated that should the Sultan of Morocco at any time fail to control his subjects, Spain should thereupon become the paramount power within her own sphere of influence. And that, gentlemen, I am determined to do. To fail in it would be to reduce our country permanently to the status of a second-class power.'

Don Alfonso's generals heartily agreed with him and the progress of the campaign, so far, was discussed. After the meal they all adjourned to a room nearly the whole of one wall of which was covered with a great map of Morocco. There were many pins stuck in it carrying different coloured flags, indicating the position of the Spanish forces, and, as far as was known, those of the hordes of revolting tribesmen. General Linares gave an outline of the operations that were taking place and the King asked the other Generals in turn for their views. When they had given them he asked de Richleau if he had any comments and the Duke replied:

'Your Majesty must pardon me if I appear to lay undue stress on the importance of my own arm, but in campaigns of this type the value of cavalry cannot be rated too highly. The enemy is not tied to roads and railheads, he does not need great masses of transport, siege trains, field hospitals and so on to be brought up before he can fight a battle. His mobility enables him to strike with maximum force at one point and only a few days later at another a hundred or more miles away from it. Battalions of infantry can rarely move fast enough to get at him; so their use is limited to holding valuable key points such as oases and valleys through the mountains in which advancing troops might otherwise be ambushed. You might, of course, use them with advantage if you built a series of blockhouses, as Lord Kitchener did in South Africa; but short of establishing such a chain of garrisons to split up the tribes so that they can be dealt with piecemeal in each area, only a force of cavalry at least equal in size to the enemy will enable you to take the initiative and engage him at times of your own choosing until he is finally defeated.'

The Generals, knowing that de Richleau had been appointed a Chief Instructor at St. Cyr following his successes in desert warfare, listened to him with respect, and for over two hours the six men continued to discuss the finer points of the war against the hardy warriors of the Riff.

Before the party broke up the Duke managed to get a private word with Don Alfonso, and said, 'I had hoped, Sir, that you had sent for me today to tell me that you were ready to let me off my chain.'

The King smiled, but shook his head. 'No, my friend. It will be some weeks yet before I'll agree to your paying another visit to Barcelona. Please continue to amuse yourself here for a while longer.' And de Richleau felt that he had no alternative but to say that he would.

As it was a Saturday, Conde Ruiz was at the Cordoba villa for the week-end, and Gulia had arranged a dinner party for that evening, to which she had invited de Richleau. When he got back to his hotel after the long session at the Palace, he was, therefore, much surprised to find a note from her which ran:

A matter of deep concern to the family necessitates my cancelling tonight's dinner party, and for most of tomorrow I expect we shall be discussing measures that may have to be taken with regard to it. So please don't come out to the villa until bathing time on Monday morning. I look forward to seeing you then.

The Duke naturally wondered what the cause of this upset could be, and the only thing he could think of was that the Banco de Coralles might be faced with some major financial crisis. That was certainly a possibility as Spain had not yet fully recovered from the drain made on her resources by the Spanish-American war, and the great expense now entailed by the war in Morocco was already forcing down the value of the peseta.

If that was so, de Richleau thought, it was particularly unfortunate that de Cordoba was in South America and, even if recalled at once, could not be expected to arrive on the scene for at least three weeks; for Ruiz, although an intelligent man, was not a very forceful personality. It was José de Cordoba who really ran the great banking concern and whose brain would be needed to cope successfully with any considerable emergency.

The words 'measures to be taken' in Gulia's note seemed to imply that her husband had appointed her as one of a family committee of Trustees to handle his affairs while he was abroad and – if a financial crisis was the trouble – they might be considering selling some part of the vast family estates to bolster up the Bank's credit. The Duke could only hope for all their sakes that his speculations had no foundation, and spent his time on Sunday with other friends.

When on the Monday morning he arrived at the beach he found Gulia, the Infanta, the two duennas and two young couples who were friends of Gulia's already there, and he was relieved to see that the whole party seemed to be in good spirits. Conde Ruiz had taken the express back to Madrid that morning.

It was not until they were in the sea that de Richleau had any chance for a private word with Gulia. Then, as they were swimming side by side, he said, 'I do hope that this family trouble you mentioned in your note to me was nothing very serious, and that you have succeeded in dealing with it.'

Turning on her side she blew out a mouthful of water, then replied, 'I want to tell you about it, but this is no place to do so. Come back after the siesta. There will be no one else here then and we can talk. But I can't ask you to stay on to dinner.'

More mystified than ever he returned to the town for lunch, whiled away the afternoon, then went out to the villa again at five o'clock. Much to his surprise, instead of taking him through to the garden the butler showed him into the small library on the right of the hall. Gulia was sitting there doing nothing with her hands folded in her lap. There was no sign of Doña Eulalia.

As soon as the door had closed behind him, he said, 'My dear, I've been quite worried about you. What is this mystery? Is there anything I can do to help?'

Her face remained expressionless but her big dark eyes held his as she slowly shook her head. 'No, Armand. There is nothing that any of us can do. José is dead.'

19

When the Heart is Young

For a moment de Richleau stared at her, hardly believing that he could have heard her aright, but she nodded and repeated, 'José is dead. Ruiz brought me the news on Friday night. When I got your message that you were commanded to lunch at the Palace on Saturday, so would bathe from the Casino beach instead of here that morning, I was glad that I didn't have to see you then. I needed a little time to get over the shock.'

'But . . . But,' he stammered, 'why has no announcement been made? Why this morning's bathing party when the house should be in mourning? And you! Damn it, Gulia, you are dressed in pale blue!'

'Come and sit down,' she said, 'and I'll tell you about it.'

As he took a chair opposite to her, she went on, 'When José was out one day catching butterflies on the banks of the Amazon he was attacked by a puma and terribly mauled. With him he had only Patricio Lopex, the valet who has looked after him for years, and the Brazilian crew of the river boat he had hired for his expedition. Patricio and the natives did everything for him that they could, but before they could even get him to a township he died from his wounds. For most of the time, though, he remained conscious, and he was terribly worried about the Bank.'

Gulia paused for a moment and asked for a cigarette. The Duke gave her one and lit it. Then she resumed. 'He had devoted his life to it, and from being quite a small private concern he made it into a great one. Everyone knew that he really was the Bank – its heart and brain – and when he realized that he was dying he was worried that the news of his death might cause a run on it.'

'I can understand that,' de Richleau nodded. 'From your note I got the idea that the Bank was faced with some kind of crisis. But not, of course, the sort that José's death might bring about.'

'He dictated a letter to Patricio and signed it. The letter was to Ruiz and in it he said that he wished the news of his death to be suppressed for at least two months. During them Ruiz was to call in all doubtful loans and convert all speculative securities into gold. By these means, when the news of his death was eventually made public the reserves of the Bank would be so large that no run on it could possibly affect its solvency. He then swore Patricio to secrecy and gave him the money to pay off the boat's crew, with three months' wages in advance if they swore on the Cross that they would not leave their native village for that time. Patricio promised to come home in the first fast ship he could find and he arrived in Madrid on Wednesday.'

'I see,' said the Duke after a moment. 'So you are all having to continue to live as though you did not know that José was dead. What an extraordinary situation.'

'It is. But what else can we do? Ruiz says that but for José's thought for us as he lay dying, in view of the Moroccan crisis that is already rocking the financial stability of the country, the Bank might well have had to close its doors – anyhow temporarily. As it is, if the secret of Jose's death can be kept for six or eight weeks he feels no doubt about being able to face any demands when it is announced.'

'How many people are in the secret?'

'Only Patricio, Ruiz and myself; and, of course, when Ruiz

next comes here you must in no circumstances let him know that I have confided our secret to you. We both promised that we would keep it absolutely to ourselves.'

'I fully understand that. But did Ruiz not even tell his wife?'

'No. Maria Alfonsine would have been safe enough in herself, but she confides everything to Doña Isabella; and she is a born gossip. Besides, it was not necessary. Ruiz had to tell me. After all, I am José's widow. If he had not obtained my consent to concealing José's death for the time being, and carrying on, I might have made great trouble for him later.'

For a moment de Richleau was silent, then he said slowly, 'Yes, you are José's widow.'

She did not smile, but came abruptly to her feet. 'Yes. I am no longer José's wife. I am his widow. That makes a difference, doesn't it?'

At the same moment the Duke stood up. His grey eyes were shining as he exclaimed, 'By God it does!' Next second she was weeping in his arms.

Holding her close, he murmured, 'Don't cry, my love, don't cry. Naturally it has been a great shock to you, but . . .'

'It's not that,' she sobbed. 'Not his death, although . . . although I hate the thought that it was . . . such a horrid one. I . . . I'm crying from happiness. Oh Armand, you can have no idea how much I love you.'

'And I you.' Turning up her face to his he kissed her tenderly on the lips. She threw an arm round his neck and pressed her mouth to his, so that the caress became fierce, passionate, long, breathless.

As their lips at last parted, he whispered, 'When, darling? When?'

'Tonight,' she whispered back. 'Out of respect for José I decided not to see you until this evening; but the past three days have seemed like a week.'

'Oh blessed night! How I wish I could hurry the sun in going down! But wait!' His glowing face suddenly became clouded by a frown. 'It is nearly half past five already. To return to my hotel, pack all my things and return here could not be done in less than two hours. For me to arrive out of the blue and move in just before dinner is going to look very strange to Maria Alfonsine. That is, unless you have already told her that you have invited me to stay here, and we think up some plausible excuse for my arriving at such a late hour.'

Gulia shook her head. 'I've had a lot of time to think about us over the week-end, and I decided that it would be wiser if you did not come to stay. We're going to be so happy, darling; so happy. We'd never be able to conceal it if we were together all day as well as at night. Remember, no one else here knows that I am a widow and now free to do as I like. And although Maria Alfonsine is so straight-laced, I'd hate to hurt her by giving her grounds to suspect that I was being unfaithful to José in his absence.'

'How shall we manage then? I could take rooms for us under a false name in some small hotel, and come out here about midnight in a carriage to fetch you.'

'No, that would be much too risky. I'm so well known in San Sebastian that any servant at an hotel might recognize me.'

'Could you creep down, then, when everyone is asleep, and let me in?'

Again she shook her head. 'That's no good either. Going to and fro from my room would mean passing that of Maria Alfonsine and I know she sleeps lightly. The boards in the corridor creak and she would be certain to hear us. We might get away with it for one night but not as a regular thing.'

'But, beloved; you said tonight, and . . .'

'And I mean it,' she gave a low laugh. 'As I told you, I've had lots of time to think everything out. Kiss me again, then I'll show you how we'll manage.'

After a long embrace she tidied her hair in a mirror, then led him out of the house and round to the back of the stables. Backing on to one corner of them was a large shed. As she opened its door he saw that it housed all the garden implements and on hooks along one wall there was a twelve-foot ladder. Pointing to it she said:

'All you have to do is to carry that fifty yards and set it up beneath my window. Do you remember which it is? I leant out of it that night you fought with Sanchez in the lily pool, half-crazy with fear that he had done you some serious injury.'

He smiled. 'Shall I ever forget. It's the big bay window on the left-hand side of the porch. And your plan, dearest, could not be better. At what hour am I permitted to enter Paradise?'

'I was going to the Floridablanca's party, but I've sent an excuse, and we have no one dining; so we shall go up to bed at about half past eleven. It would be best to give them an hour to settle down. To be on the safe side, say between a quarter to one and one. In order to catch you alone when you arrived I told the others that I was going indoors to write a letter. But we must join them now and pretend that we are not the happiest people in the world.'

When they reached the fountain, round which were sitting the three older ladies and two friends of the Infanta's who had been invited in for drinks, they found it far from easy to conceal their elation; and de Richleau was much relieved when he had been there long enough to take his leave without rudeness, so that he might give an undivided mind to joyful anticipation of the night to come.

Those joyful imaginings were, if possible, surpassed by the reality. De Richleau was very far from being an habitual lecher, but in everything that gave him pleasure he took pride in perfecting himself, and as an expert in the art of love he found Gulia sufficiently experienced to bring out the best in him. As a woman she was just entering her best years, as a man he had not yet left his best years behind. They were as physically perfect as two thoroughbred race-horses, and they were at last able to give free rein to their pent-up passion for one another.

At half past five in the morning, after the Duke had climbed down from her window and put away the ladder, he walked the three miles back into San Sebastian as though he were treading on air. Gulia, meanwhile, lay dozing in her big bed, her lips pressed to a handkerchief that she had exchanged with him for one of hers. She drifted off to sleep, the desperate craving she had had so long for him at last blissfully satisfied.

Right through August and well into September their delight in one another continued unabated.

Gulia's bedroom was far enough away from any other that was occupied for there to be no necessity for them to talk in whispers, and they could romp together both there and in her bathroom without any risk of being heard. Of all pastimes, too, making love is best guaranteed to beget good thirsts and hearty appetites; so from their second night together onward De Richleau brought with him bottles of champagne, fruit, caviare or *foie gras* and a variety of other easily portable delicacies, for which Gulia smuggled up to her room glasses and plates that she concealed during the daytime under her winter underclothes in a drawer. Over these midnight feasts they laughed, joked and teased one another with the zest of happy children until some chance word caused them suddenly to fall silent, exchange a smile of mutual understanding, and stretch out their arms to hold one another close again.

After their second night together it occurred to de Richleau that it was a stupid waste of time and effort for him to walk out to the villa each night and back from it to his hotel in the dawn;

so the next day he went off to a livery stable and hired a horse, arranging for it to be saddled and left ready for him to collect from the night watchman round about midnight. Having ridden out on it he hobbled it in the orchard that lay beyond the garden of the villa, then returned it to the livery stable in the morning. He did not doubt that the people at the livery stable had a shrewd idea of the reason for his taking these night-long rides, yet returning his mount still fresh; but they could not know the place to which he went and, as far as he and Gulia could judge, no one living in the villa had the least suspicion of their clandestine meetings.

Yet no *affaire* ever stands still, and while on neither side was there the least sign of their passion cooling, there soon appeared a subtle change in their relationship to those about them. For the first few days, still having in the forefront of their minds the reason why Gulia had decided against having her lover to live in the house, they maintained an exemplary discretion. But before a week was out they found that it was not enough to spend five or six hours together each night then, perhaps, to see one another only for a morning bathe during the daytime and, if either of them went to an evening party without the other, to have to cut down the time they could give to their secret revels during the hours of darkness.

In consequence, almost imperceptibly they became indifferent to opinion. Both began to refuse invitations to parties to which the other was not invited. If they were not lunching out at the same place it became accepted that de Richleau should stay on after the morning swim and lunch at the villa. As well as bathing from its beach every morning he came out to swim with Gulia again every evening. They could not see enough of one another; they became almost inseparable.

From time to time the Duke was troubled by the thought that their being so constantly together must be giving rise to scandal. That the Infanta was showing her disapproval by an increasing coldness towards him he found distressing because he liked de Vendôme's kindly if somewhat domineering mother; yet he did not greatly mind because he knew that in a few weeks' time she would learn of de Cordoba's death, and when told that Gulia had known of it from early in August would realize that she could not be so greatly blamed for permitting such marked attentions from a gallant. But that Gulia should become talked about among her acquaintances he minded very much, and now and then he endeavoured to persuade her that in the daytime they ought not to be seen about together quite so frequently.

He might have saved his breath for she would not listen to him. In vain he argued that no limit of time was set upon their happiness, and that when she returned to Madrid there was no reason why he should not also go to live in the capital. She replied that there it would not be possible to set a ladder up against her bedroom window, and there would be no bathing or tennis parties; so it would be much more difficult for them to be together frequently, therefore they must make the very utmost of the present.

It was during one of these discussions that, for the only time, they touched on the subject of marriage. Angela had, for him, been the perfect wife, and his memories of her made him wonder if Gulia, who had such an utterly different personality, could bring him the same contentment. Yet, on the other hand, he realized that if he did mean to marry again he might never find another woman who combined such a wealth of attractions, and she left nothing undone to show that she adored him. So without actually proposing he had asked her if she liked the idea of retaining her freedom as a rich widow or would prefer to settle down and have children.

She had taken the question as he meant it – as a feeler about themselves – but had shrugged it off with a laugh, declaring that, delighted as she was to think that he might be contemplating making her his Duchess, nothing could be done about it until José's death had been publicly announced, and it would be time enough then for her to decide if she would risk her figure in order to present him with a little Count de Quesnoy.

In the meantime she continued to insist that they should grasp their present happiness with both hands, regardless of what people might be saying about them; and, taking consolation from the thought that the announcement in the autumn of de Cordoba's death would do much to restore her reputation, he gave way to her.

That people were talking about them was made very evident to him one night towards the end of August when they were both bidden again to dine at the Palace. For a few minutes after dinner he was alone with Don Alfonso, who asked him, 'Are you still as eager as ever to go hunting that wretch Ferrer in Barcelona?'

In view of the wonderful time the Duke was having with Gulia, he was now by no means anxious to leave San Sebastian, and he wished that he had never heard of Ferrer. But he felt in duty bound to reply:

'Indeed I am, Sir.'

The King cocked an amused eyebrow. 'You surprise me, Duke. They tell me that you are far more successful in hunting butterflies than is poor de Cordoba on his expedition up the Amazon. Or at least that you have captured such a beautiful one that you are the envy of every naturalist in San Sebastian.'

De Richleau felt his colour rising, but he bowed and said, 'I fear I am but a poor naturalist, Sir. I have a rooted objection to sticking pins into such lovely creatures; so I am doing no more than provide a most delightful specimen with lettuce leaves until de Cordoba returns and can claim it.'

'Dear me. Then you are not the man I thought you,' smiled the King. 'And you shall go to Barcelona. But still not for another week or two. The city has not settled down sufficiently for me to allow you yet to risk your neck in it.'

It was on the 6th of September that de Richleau next talked with Don Alfonso, having been summoned to wait upon him at the Palace at nine-thirty in the morning. After receiving the Duke in his working room, the King sat back at his desk and, without preamble, said in a business-like way:

'The time has come for you to attempt to run Ferrer to earth and, if you can catch him, render me another considerable service. La Cierva tells me that Barcelona is now quiet. In fact, owing to the many arrests that have taken place and the repressive measures that were rendered necessary by the revolt, it is quieter than it has been for a long time. Only one thing still troubles him: that is the police. I suppose you could not manage without police assistance?'

The Duke shook his head. 'No, Sir. This mission will be very different from that which I undertook three years ago. Then, being totally unknown in Spanish anarchist circles I was able to pose as a political refugee from Russia and get in among them. To attempt to do so again is out of the question. This time my intention is to play the part of a police agent and either bribe or threaten all those I can find who knew Ferrer until one of them cracks and gives me a line on his whereabouts. To do that I must be in possession of police papers, and have the authority to call on the police to pull in anyone I wish for questioning.'

'Yes, I thought that would be the case.' Don Alfonso fiddled with a pencil. 'I asked only because we know that the Barcelona police are not one hundred per cent to be relied upon. Nearly all Catalans of whatever class are Separatists and many are imbued with the principles of anarchism. Had that not been so we could have put an end to the epidemic of bomb outrages there long ago. La Cierva is now carrying out a very thorough investigation into the police organization with a view drastically to reforming it;

but to purge it entirely of its doubtful elements is bound to take time. I mention this only because I think it would be unwise for you to rely too much on police co-operation. They will, of course, all do ostensibly as they are ordered, and the majority are loyal to the Government; but here and there you may find a man who will turn a blind eye to your requirements at a critical moment.'

'I understand, Sir, and will watch out for that sort of thing.'

Producing a letter from a drawer in his desk, the King passed it over, and went on. 'This you are to hand to General Quiroga. You are to live with him in the fortress of Montjuich. He will introduce you to the Chief-of-Police, who will give you all the assistance you may require from him. He will also provide you with a detective who will act as your bodyguard and constant companion. In no circumstances are you to leave the fortress without him. Is that understood?'

De Richleau gave a rueful smile. 'I cannot help regarding with regret these restrictions Your Majesty is placing on my liberty; but I have no alternative other than to bow to your wishes.'

The King stood up. 'I have insisted on them only because I refuse to allow a valued friend to jeopardize his life further than is strictly necessary. Besides,' he added with a sudden boyish smile, 'think how angry your beautiful butterfly would be with me if, knowing that you had undertaken a mission in my service, she was permanently deprived of her supply of lettuce.'

The Duke smiled back. 'I will inform her, Sir, of your gracious concern for her welfare.'

An hour and a half later, while swimming with Gulia in the bay, de Richleau broke the news to her of his impending departure. As there were other people nearby, for the time being she gamely concealed her distress, but that night, when he joined her in her bedroom, she gave way to it. Impartially she cursed Ferrer and the King for being the cause of her lover leaving her, and pleaded with him to put off this mission to Barcelona at least until the end of the month, when she would be returning to Madrid.

He agreed that it was hard that they should have to sacrifice a part, and perhaps all, of the precious time that remained to them in San Sebastian, where they were able to spend most of each night together with little risk of discovery; but he told her that in his interview that morning with Don Alfonso he had received what amounted to orders that could not be disregarded. He could only promise that he would work night and day to lay Ferrer speedily by the heels so that he might not lose a moment in getting back to her.

It proved a night in which tears were mingled with passion, and in a final effort to console her he remained with her longer than he had ever done before. He left her only when, from fear of discovery by the waking servants, it became dangerous to stay longer. Even then he had to break the clasp of her arms from about his neck and put her from him still weeping bitterly.

Much shaken by this emotional parting, he found it a relief to steal through the dawn-lit garden to the orchard. He was always a little anxious that he might find that some prowler had stolen his mount in the night, but he found the horse quietly grazing as usual.

Half an hour later he was back at his hotel and, as he had packed the previous evening, soon after eight he was on his way to Barcelona. He realized that by now Ferrer might well have taken refuge over the frontier. But if that vile poisoner of minds was still in Catalonia, de Richleau had determined that he would not rest content until he looked down on his dead body.

20

Death Claims Three More

WHEN de Richleau arrived in Barcelona the following afternoon he was met at the station by one of the Captain-General's A.D.C.s and taken by him straight out to the grim old fortress of Montjuich. As he shook hands with Quiroga in his office he thought that the past three years, in which the General had been in constant danger of his life, seemed to have had remarkably little effect upon him. He was still the same square, red-faced forceful man with a cheerful decisive manner. When the Duke congratulated him on still being alive, he said with a laugh:

'They may get me yet; but they'll have to show more originality than they have in the past. Nearly all their attempts run to a pattern: some miserable youth lurking in the crowd with a pistol or a bomb. But nine times out of ten their nerves betray them. I'm too old a hand to leave my quarters here except when I have to on official occasions, and then I always go surrounded by a bodyguard with loaded carbines at the ready. My fellows are crack shots and specially trained to spot fanatics intending mischief. Before they can aim or have a chance to throw anything they get a bullet through the head. The tragedy is that we can't possibly manage to give that sort of protection to all our people, and those poisonous vermin have murdered scores of good, honest officials here since last we met.'

De Richleau handed over the King's letter. The General read it through, nodded, and said, 'This confirms the instructions I have already received from His Majesty. Naturally I shall be delighted to have you as my personal guest, and this morning I spoke to Comandante Urgoiti about you. He is the head of the Security Bureau, and will supply the man who is to accompany you on your investigations. I will have them both up here tomorrow morning.'

'If you could arrange for me to meet them this evening I would be grateful,' replied the Duke, 'because I would like to start on my job as soon as possible.'

'Just as you wish.' Quiroga glanced at his watch. 'It is not yet six o'clock; so I will have Urgoiti here between seven and seven-thirty. If you will come with me now, I will show you your quarters.'

'Thank you. There is just one other point. For the purposes of this investigation I feel it would be best to drop my title and call myself by some simple name. I thought of Carlos Gomá.'

The General nodded. 'I think that's wise, and Carlos Gomá would do very well.'

As they left the General's office and crossed a big interior courtyard, de Richleau asked, 'What do you think my chances are of running Ferrer to earth?'

The General shrugged. 'You should be a better judge of that than I. His Majesty informed me in his letter that you have lines of inquiry that the police are unlikely yet to have tried. I know no more than that.'

'I have. What I really meant to ask was, do you think it likely that Ferrer is still in Barcelona?'

'I would say the odds are that he is; or if not in the city, not far from it. You see, here he is accounted a hero, not only by his fanatical followers but also by thousands of misguided people; so he can move from one to another of scores of different hiding places without much fear of being betrayed. And that does not apply to any other part of Spain.'

'My fear was that after the suppression of the riots he might have fled over the border into France.'

'No; the chances are a hundred to one against him having succeeded in doing that. On the last day of the revolt he was known to be still in the city. Several of our prisoners who have turned King's Evidence have sworn to that and, if you can catch him, are prepared to swear at his trial that he was one of the principal instigators of the outbreak. And on the first day of the riots I closed the frontier. I did more. Within twenty-four hours I had replaced all Catalan frontier police, Guardia Civil and port police by non-Catalans on whose loyalty I could depend. We issued to them hundreds of photographs and descriptions of Ferrer and half a dozen other ringleaders. Three of them were caught, and I don't believe for a moment that any of the others slipped through. The frontier has remained closed ever since, and only people with special papers are allowed to cross it.'

'That is excellent news,' smiled the Duke. 'It makes my chances of ferreting him out look better than I had hoped.'

By then they had reached the Captain-General's residence, which consisted of a fine old mansion forming one side of the court-yard. Quiroga showed him first a pleasant sitting-room where he could make himself comfortable until Comandante Urgoiti arrived, then took him up to a bedroom that had been prepared for him. A soldier servant was already unpacking his luggage, and the General left him there to have a wash after his journey.

When he came downstairs to the sitting-room he found there a plump but pretty girl of about seventeen, who introduced herself as Mercedes, the General's daughter. She was busily engaged stitching some gold thread on to a canvas-backed piece of blue velvet, and after some small-talk the Duke asked her what she was making.

With a shy smile, she replied, 'They are to be a pair of bed-room slippers with gold monograms on the toes. I'm making them as a New Year's present. Of course it's a long time yet to the New Year, but I don't work very fast so I thought it just as well to begin early.'

'I suppose they are for your father,' smiled the Duke. 'I'm sure he will be delighted with them.'

She blushed and shook her head. Then, after a little gentle twitting by him, she confided, 'They are for Captain Juan Escalante. He . . . well, he's not exactly my fiancé, because my parents say I am too young to marry yet. But we are hoping that they will let us get engaged in the New Year.'

'I wish you luck then,' smiled the Duke. 'What branch of the service is your friend in?'

'He is a cavalryman, and he has much the smartest troop in his regiment, the 5th Hussars.'

'Is he?' said de Richleau with renewed interest. 'Although I am wearing civilian clothes, I am a cavalryman too.'

Having found a topic of mutual interest they talked on for half an hour, then an orderly arrived with the request that the Duke would accompany him to the General's office.

Over there Quiroga introduced him to Comandante Urgoiti, a short, paunchy, bald man and to Señor Veragua a tall young fellow who had a brown moustache and beard. The Duke had a vague feeling that he had seen the latter somewhere before and was about to question him when he said:

'If your name were not Gomá, señor, I could have sworn that you were a Russian refugee that I knew slightly some years ago. I forget his name but he used to frequent the branch of the Somaten to which I belong.'

De Richleau smiled. 'You are right. During the summer of 1906 I lived for some six weeks here in Barcelona, and I often spent an evening at the Somaten Club down by the harbour.' In pursuance of his policy to conceal as far as possible his true identity, de Richleau refrained from mentioning the secret mission he had then been engaged upon, and its having resulted in the closing of the *Escuela Moderna*. Instead, he added, 'I am surprised, though, that you, as a member of the police force, should still belong to the Somaten. I was given to understand that during the recent revolt it supported the rioters.'

Veragua shook his head. 'It is true that certain Communist elements had worked their way into the Somaten, and got themselves elected as officials at some of its branches. In those where they had secured enough authority they used it to push the members into rash actions; but the majority were against them and after a few days they were thrown out. The Somaten has since been thoroughly purged, and for some while has resumed its ancient function.'

The General nodded. 'Yes, indeed. After the fighting had ceased, the Somaten was of the greatest value in supplying squads of vigilantes to help us restore law and order. They are, of course, all Catalan Separatists; but that is a different matter, as there is nothing illegal about holding such views.'

Urgoiti said that if the Duke would call at Police Headquarters the following morning he would furnish him with a police card, which would enable him to arrest anyone on suspicion or call for help on uniformed men, then proceeded to question him about his plan of campaign. But, bearing in mind Don Alfonso's warning, de Richleau did not mean to risk any leaks through junior detectives to whom the Comandante might mention his activities; so he politely replied that to start with he meant only to make a general reconnaissance.

It was arranged that Veragua should report to 'Señor Gomá' at

eight o'clock the following morning, and the two detectives took
their leave. When they had gone Quiroga unlocked a steel cabinet
and took from it one of a number of pistols, with a box of ammuni-
tion, and said:

'You had better carry this. It may come in useful.'

De Richleau had brought his own revolver, but the weapon the
General handed him was one of the new German automatics. It
carried eight instead of six bullets and, being flat, was easier to
conceal about the person than the old-fashioned pistol with its
revolving magazine. Having examined its mechanism with interest,
he thanked Quiroga, and they then crossed the courtyard to the
residential quarters.

When the Duke had changed he came down to the drawing-
room and was presented to the Señora Quiroga. She was considerably younger than her husband and an elegant woman, who
obviously had social ambitions; for she remarked with a laugh
that had an underlying note of bitterness that, great as was the
honour of being one of the three Captains-General who commanded the forces in Spain's three largest cities, for all the pleasure
her husband and his family got out of it they might as well be
castaways on an island inhabited by hostile savages. And she did
not seek to hide her delight at having as her guest a Grandee of
Spain who was on terms of friendship with the King.

They dined *en famille*, the Señorita Mercedes making a silent
fourth. During the meal the Señora pressed de Richleau to tell
her all the latest gossip of San Sebastian, dragging in at every
opportunity the names of noble families with whom she was
acquainted. The Duke politely obliged, but he felt sorry for the
girl, as it was clear to him that her mother would consent to her
marrying nothing less than a Marquis; so she had little chance of
fulfilling her romance with the handsome Captain Juan Escalante.

After the ladies had left the table de Richleau did not see them
again that night. He and Quiroga sat over their wine for upward
of two hours, while the General gave an interesting account of
the revolt and they had a long discussion about anarchists.

In the morning de Richleau dressed himself in a ready-made
suit that he had bought on his last afternoon in San Sebastian,
then walked across to the General's office. The tall, bearded Veragua
reported there promptly at eight o'clock, and the Duke was somewhat surprised to find that he had arrived in an automobile. In
1906, when de Richleau had learned to drive de Vendôme's Hispano
Suiza, motor-cars had still been a wonder for crowds to gape at.
On his return to Spain he had noticed that many rich people in

San Sebastian now owned them, but for them to be used by the police seemed quite an innovation.

Veragua told him that the Security Bureau kept a dozen machines at the disposal of its officers and, as he had learned to drive one, he had felt that they might get from place to place at which 'Señor Gomá' wished to question people quicker than by any other means.

De Richleau was pleased that his tall young assistant should have shown such initiative, and they set off down the hill into the city to Police Headquarters. There, from the bald-headed Comandante, the Duke received his warrant, then they started on a long round of visits.

As a first bet de Richleau went to the apartment in which the Luques had entertained him to dinner, for it was Doctor Luque who had introduced him to Ferrer. But he learned from the porter of the block that some fifteen months earlier the Luques had left for Cartagena, where they had relatives, and that the Doctor had bought a practice there.

They then went to the Café Ronda, at which Dr. Luque had introduced de Richleau to Ferrer; but the proprietor said that he had not seen Ferrer since the revolt and had no idea where he had got to. Throughout the morning and, ignoring the siesta hours, all through the afternoon, they drove to one place after another at which the Duke hoped that he might pick up some trace of his quarry. These were shops that de Richleau knew to have supplied Ferrer with books, others that had supplied the *Escuela Moderna* with food, restaurants at which he and members of his staff had dined, and cafés they had frequented.

In the majority of cases, in order to avoid its being realized that he was connected with the police, de Richleau left Veragua and the car fifty yards away down the street. Sometimes he announced himself as Señor Carlos Gomá, an old friend of Ferrer's, and furtively inquired his whereabouts; at others he resumed his identity of Nicolai Chirikov, once a master at the *Escuela Moderna*, who, after a long absence from Barcelona, wanted to be put in touch again with the Chief whom he had found such an interesting personality. Occasionally, with those whom he suspected knew something but would not talk, he produced his police pass and threatened them with incarceration in the fortress of Montjuich. But his efforts were of no avail.

Throughout the whole day he drew nothing but blanks and returned a little before eight o'clock in the evening, tired out and cursing the fact that he must again over dinner be subjected to the Señora Quiroga's insatiable appetite for gossip about the Court.

Next day he continued his investigation, mainly on scraps of information he had extracted from various sources. He called on Ferrer's tailor, barber, dentist and a number of his ex-pupils, but neither cajolery nor threats produced any result.

It was not until after he had given Veragua lunch at a small fish restaurant that he remembered the foreman miller's daughter. Thinking again of that fateful night on which Sanchez had first wished to slit his throat, then burn him in a furnace, he recalled Dolores Mendoza saying with a sneer that as Ferrer had gone out to the mill for a conference he would certainly not return until morning, as he 'never missed a chance of a tumble with that hot little piece Teresa Conesa'.

De Richleau had never had an opportunity to learn exactly where the mill was situated, so he had Veragua drive him out to the hospital to which he had been taken. At his request a secretary in the office there turned up the entry recording the admission of himself and Pedro Conesa and from that he got the address of the mill at which they had received their injuries.

It was some way inland on the south-west outskirts of the city and they drove to it. Leaving Veragua outside, de Richleau crossed the yard to the foreman's little house. As he did so he cast a glance at the tall, square stack of the mill building that had such terrifying memories for him; then he rang the bell of the door through which he had been carried rolled up in a carpet.

It was opened by a buxom woman. Her husband proved to be the third successor to Conesa, but as he had been employed at the mill for the past ten years they had known Pedro and his daughter well. The woman said that for the best part of two years the girl had been married. She was now a Señora Irujo and lived in a village about two miles further out.

Having obtained a description of her cottage de Richleau walked back to the car and told his eager young assistant that he thought they really might have got on to something at last, as he had succeeded in tracing one of Ferrer's ex-mistresses, who was much more likely to know what had become of him than any shopkeeper or café proprietor. When they reached the village he followed his usual practice of leaving Veragua with the car about fifty yards short of their destination and proceeded to it on foot.

He found Teresa at home. She was a sluttish-looking young woman with a heavy jowl and strong hips, but fine eyes and a good figure. At the moment he arrived at the open doorway of her cottage she was busy in the kitchen cooking a conserve of melons. Fearful that it might boil over if neglected, without even inquiring his business she threw open the door of a frowsty sitting-room and asked him to wait.

Six or seven minutes later she joined him, carrying an infant on her arm; a toddler clutched at her skirt, and a wide-eyed thumb-sucker of about two-and-a-half pattered in after her.

As she had never seen de Richleau she had no idea that it was he who, by a judo grip, had brought about her father's death. In case the name of Chirikov might ring a bell with her, he presented himself as Carlos Gomá, an old friend of her father's who had recently returned from four years in the United States.

He said that the woman who now lived in the foreman's house at the mill had told him of Pedro's death and he had been greatly distressed to hear of it. Then he went on to speak of those exciting days when he had formed one of the group that had planned the bomb-throwings, making casual mention of the bald-headed Manuel, young Alvaro Barbestro, the Ferrer brothers, Mateo Morral, Dolores Mendoza and the German, Schmidt.

At first she regarded him with obvious suspicion, but he talked with such intimate knowledge of her father's friends that after a little she thawed out. She told him that in the summer of 1906 the group had been betrayed by a French spy, which had resulted in the *Escuela Moderna* being raided and closed, and that for a year the activities of the group had been brought almost to a standstill through most of them being in prison. She added that Barbestro had been shot for an attempt on General Quiroga and Sanchez Ferrer killed in a brawl in Cadiz.

He then asked her about the recent revolt. She described some fights that had taken place locally and the brutality with which the soldiers had treated the workers after they had forced the barricades. Several of her friends had been killed or wounded, and her husband had been among the latter, although fortunately the bullet that hit him had only taken off the lobe of his left ear. She added that, what with the fighting and the arrests that had taken place after it, the ranks of the anarchists had been sadly thinned, and those who had escaped were now all in hiding.

Having deplored this sad state of things, he remarked what hard luck it was on him that the revolt should have taken place only a few weeks before his return, and so deprived him of the chance to renew his old friendships; then he said in his most winning tone:

'But perhaps you could put me in touch with some of them, or know people who could. How about Benigno Ferrer? I hope he is all right. He was a particular friend of mine.'

She shook her head. 'I've no idea where Benigno is; but he

wasn't killed or captured in the revolt. I believe that during it he
was somewhere abroad.'

'His father then? I take it Señor Ferrer is still safe. He is so well
known that had ill befallen him it's certain that I should have seen
it in the papers, or anyhow have heard about it from someone.'

'No; Francisco's all right. It was him really who I knew better
than any of them. Of course he was much older than me; but as
a matter of fact we were great friends.'

De Richleau gave her a slightly doubting smile and said, 'I
suppose anything is possible for such a good-looking girl as you.
But do you really mean to tell me that you succeeded in securing
as an admirer such a famous intellectual as Francisco Ferrer?'

She bridled with pleasure and pointed to the thumb-sucker
who was standing in the doorway. 'If you really want to know,
I had little Francisco, there, by him. These other two are Irujo's;
but I only married him really to give my eldest a father.'

'I hope he makes the boy a good one.'

'Might be worse, I suppose.' She made a grimace. 'It's only
when he's had a skinful of wine that he gets jealous and would
ill-treat the kid if I didn't watch out. Otherwise he just ignores
him and is glad enough to pocket the money Ferrer sends me for
the boy's keep.'

'Ferrer does the decent thing by you, then. Does he ever come
to see you and little Francisco?'

'Oh yes. Ferrer's fond of children, and after he got his school
going again he used to look in fairly regularly. He hasn't been
here since the revolt, though.'

'I hope he sends you your money just the same.'

'Yes. That Mendoza woman you were talking about a while
back brings it. He's living with her now.'

'Since you know where they are I'd be awfully grateful if you'd
give me their address, so that I can look them up.'

De Richleau had made his request sound as casual as he could,
and to conceal the intense excitement with which he awaited her
answer he glanced away from her towards the baby she was holding. When her reply came it was disappointing. After hesitating a
moment, she said:

'No; I couldn't do that. You see, I don't really know anything
about you, do I? And there's a big reward for his capture. For all I
know you might be trying to earn it, or even be one of the police.'

He knew that if she would not talk he had only to arrest her
and turn her over to Urgoiti. Quiroga had told him that under
the fortress of Montjuich there were dungeons that had been handed

over to the secret police in which they held and questioned political prisoners. He had a pretty shrewd idea that the methods used were not far short of the tortures inflicted in those same dungeons during the Middle Ages. Without a doubt they would get out of her the information he was so anxious to obtain; but he thought her a very decent woman and was most loath to bring such a fate upon her.

Deciding to try further persuasion, he laughed and said, 'Oh come, now! You're talking nonsense. I . . .'

At that moment a window pane shattered. He was standing sideways on to it with his back to the open doorway. As the glass tinkled down he glimpsed a black object, about the size of a cricket ball, spinning down into the room. Instantly, he flung himself backwards.

Next second there came the crash of an explosion. A bright orange flash lit the dingy little room. Teresa gave a piercing scream. Dense black smoke billowed up from the floor swiftly spreading and obscuring the scene.

De Richleau's backward plunge had sent little Francisco spinning. The boy burst into howls. Ignoring him the Duke picked himself up and, unhurt except for bruising one elbow, plunged back into the smoke-filled room. Teresa had dropped her baby and collapsed groaning across a small stiff-backed settee. Her skirt was on fire. Snatching up a cushion de Richleau beat out the flames with it, then got his arms beneath her and carried her across the passage to the kitchen. As he did so, through the murk he glimpsed other flames and realized that some of the lighter furniture must have also caught fire from the explosion.

By that time several women neighbours and Veragua had rushed into the cottage. Still choking from the fumes, the Duke shouted to them to get the children and to him to take charge and put out the fire. Meanwhile he had laid Teresa on the floor and, with the swift practised fingers of one who has tended many wounded on battle-fields, was assessing her injuries.

The bomb must have exploded on her right almost at her feet. On that side only charred and tattered remnants of her skirt and petticoats remained, exposing her legs to the thigh. The right one was hopelessly shattered, the left one was also scorched and bleeding. Grabbing a kitchen knife he slit the leather belt she was wearing, then tore open her corset. As he had feared, several bomb splinters had lodged in her right hip and that side of her stomach. Springing up he seized a towel to staunch the blood that was seeping from the wounds.

At that moment a wild-eyed woman burst into the kitchen.

In her arms she was carrying the limp form of Teresa's second child. Hysterically she shouted, 'The poor mite's dead! She's dead! And so's the baby. Oh, Holy Saints defend us!' Then at the sight of Teresa half naked and bleeding on the floor she uttered another wail, turned, and ran from the room.

After her first screams Teresa had uttered only a low moaning, then fallen silent. De Richleau thought she had fainted, but at the shouts of her neighbour she opened her eyes. As he again knelt beside her she asked in a hoarse whisper, 'Francisco. Is he . . . Is he . . .?'

A sweat had broken out on her forehead and the Duke knew that she had not long to live. Kneeling beside her he said gently, 'He is safe, Teresa. As with myself the angle of the wall saved him from injury. But you, Teresa. You have not long and you must think of his future.'

He had her head pillowed on his arm and she nodded weakly. 'Yes . . . I don't want to die . . . I'm afraid to die . . . But the pain inside me . . . I . . . I know I'm finished.'

'You cannot leave the boy to Irujo. Not if Irujo would be unkind to him. Let me take him to Ferrer for you. Ferrer loves him and will see to it that he is given a happy home. But you must tell me where to find Ferrer.'

The sweat was running down her face and she was breathing fast. 'San Cugat,' she panted. 'He now . . . calls himself . . . Olozaga.'

The Duke nodded, then he said earnestly, 'Listen, Teresa. Your father was an anarchist. I expect he brought you up as an atheist and it is generally those who have always said that they do not believe in God who fear most to die. But you have nothing to fear. I promise you that. I'm afraid there is not the time to bring a priest to you; but if you simply say, "Please God, for Jesus Christ's sake, forgive me my sins," that will be enough.'

Her eyes brightened a little. She clutched at his free hand and slowly panted out the words after him. A few minutes later a spasm shook her, then her head rolled sideways and she was dead.

Lowering her head to the floor he put the towel over her face and stood up. According to his own beliefs no deathbed repentance could be of the slightest value. It was not logical that a person who had been mean, cruel and unscrupulous could, by muttering a few words, with or without the assistance of a priest, have the bill receipted for all the suffering they had caused in their lives. Teresa, like everyone else, would have to pay off such ill that she might have done to others, and her untimely, painful death would be only something on account. But, as he washed her blood from his hands at the kitchen sink, he knew that he had at least been right in telling her that she had nothing to fear, and he was glad that he had been able to give her in her last moments the conventional comfort without which a woman of her class might have died in terror.

He was far less happy about having used the fact that she was dying to extract from her Ferrer's whereabouts. But on that score he comforted himself with the thought that if there were not men like Ferrer no bomb would have come through the window to destroy her and her two little children.

As he finished washing, Veragua came in to report that the fire in the sitting-room was out. He was followed by a local policeman, notebook in hand, who had just arrived on the scene and was taking down particulars of the tragedy. De Richleau produced his police-card, made a statement, and said that he intended to take the surviving child away with him. He then collected the still weeping little Francisco, left the policeman in charge, and with Veragua walked along the street to their car.

On the way Veragua congratulated him in the heartiest manner on his narrow escape, and remarked that it had been good luck for him too, as he would have got into frightful trouble if de Richleau had been injured, since he would have failed in his duty as a bodyguard. They then speculated on how any anarchist could have been on hand to throw a bomb and so cut short the questioning of Teresa Irujo. As no one could have known of the Duke's intention to meet her, they decided that the only explanation must be that the enemy had learnt about 'Señor Gomá's' investigation and had been stalking him all day, waiting for a suitable opportunity to throw the bomb, and that only chance had led to the attempt to murder him being made while he was in Teresa's cottage.

As they were driving down the hill Veragua asked if the Duke had managed to get anything out of Teresa during his long talk with her. To which he replied:

'One line that may be worth following. But this affair has been pretty shattering to the nerves, so I think we will take it easy for what remains of the afternoon. You can collect me again from the fortress at nine o'clock. That should give me just time to have a quick dinner.'

Since de Richleau was entirely lacking in nerves of that kind, he was prevaricating. But he had decided not to make his attempt to catch Ferrer until night had fallen and, in the meantime, he had no intention of letting even Veragua know the high hopes he now had for that evening.

When they arrived at Montjuich he carried little Francisco into the Captain-General's residence and gave him temporarily into the charge of one of the woman servants. Then he went upstairs and lay down on his bed.

At seven o'clock he came down to the drawing-room to find Mercedes there alone stitching away at her bedroom slippers. It then occurred to him that she would make a much more responsible protectress for his small thumb-sucker than would her socially-obsessed mother. So he told her Teresa's story and about the tragedy that had occurred that afternoon, and asked if she could find a suitable family among the married N.C.O.s of the garrison in which the boy could be boarded and brought up; adding that he would make over to her a capital sum sufficient to provide a small income for the child's keep.

Mercedes listened with wide eyes, then willingly agreed to his request. Little Francisco was produced from the servants' quarters, his cheerfulness now restored from having been regaled with a surfeit of sugar plums, and Mercedes, delighted with her new charge, carried him off to make arrangements for him to be bathed and put to bed.

De Richleau then telephoned Urgoiti and asked how late he would be remaining at his office, adding that he hoped to bring in a very special prisoner round about eleven o'clock. The Comandante replied that he had plenty of work to occupy him, so he would return to his office after dinner and remain there till midnight.

When the General and his wife came in the Duke again gave the story of the attempt that had been made upon his life that afternoon, and praised their daughter for the willingness she had shown to take charge of the little orphan. He then asked to be excused from changing for dinner, as he had to go out again at nine o'clock, and for the loan of a key to the house as he might not get back until very late. Quiroga provided the key and his wife had dinner put forward by half an hour; so when Veragua arrived in the motor to collect de Richleau they were able to set off without delay.

The village of San Cugat de Vallés lay about seven miles to the north of Barcelona behind the great mountain of Tibidabo. As they had to drive right through the city it was nearly half past nine when they reached it. De Richleau had contemplated a much later raid, with the idea of catching Ferrer in bed. But he had still to find out where the 'Señor Olozaga' lived, and to have made inquiries in the village at a late hour of the night might have resulted in Ferrer's being sent a warning that somebody was after him.

Having halted Veragua well before they came to the village square, the Duke left the car and continued on foot. There was only one café there, and it was somewhat dimly lit, with only a few people sitting at its tables. Seating himself at a vacant one, he ordered a Fundador with water. When the waiter brought it the Duke said casually that he had recently made a contact in San Cugat which would bring him out there on business fairly frequently, and he had been told that some old friends of his named Olozaga had moved into the neighbourhood. Perhaps the waiter could tell him whereabouts they lived, then next time he came out he would look them up.

The waiter replied that a couple of that name lived in a small villa out on the road to Sabadell. It was on the left and easy to recognize as it had a little turret; but they kept themselves very much to themselves and came into the village only to do their shopping.

De Richleau tipped the man, but not too lavishly, took plenty of time about finishing his brandy, then rejoined Veragua. They drove out along the Sabadell road until they sighted the villa with a turret, then backed the car up a side turning on to a patch of grass and left it.

Only then did the Duke tell his eager young companion that he had reason to believe that Ferrer was living in the villa. Walking forward, they reconnoitred it. There was no other building within five hundred yards. On either side of its porch it had a bay window. In that on the right a light showed through drawn curtains. The rest of the house was in darkness.

To his companion de Richleau said in a low voice, 'Either at the back, or more probably at one side, there will be a kitchen entrance. I want you to find and cover it. Should anyone come out, hold them up. If they refuse to surrender or attempt to run for it you are to shoot them down without further warning. For that I accept full responsibility. I'll give you ten minutes to take up your station, then I am going in.'

With a happy grin Veragua produced his automatic, snapped its breech back and forth to make sure that it was in perfect working order, then moved off into the semi-darkness.

Ten minutes can be a very long time when waiting to go into action. More than once de Richleau gave an impatient look at his wrist-watch. Now and again, too, he gave an uneasy glance up and down the road. In spite of the precautions he had taken to keep his investigation secret, the many inquiries he had made about Ferrer must inevitably have led to the anarchists learning about his activities, and the attempt on his life that had been made that afternoon led him to believe that they were doing their utmost to keep constant track of his movements.

But the country road was deserted. No movement of shadow suggested a lurking figure in the hedgerows. At last the ten minutes were up. The villa was some way from the road. With an even step he advanced up the fifty-yard-long garden path and pressed the front door bell.

He stood there, his heart pounding in his chest at the thought of the encounter to come. The peal of the bell shrilled through the silent house, but no one came to answer it. Holding his breath, he listened intently. Muffled sounds of movement came faintly from inside the villa. With a grim smile he rang again.

Still no one came, and he could no longer hear sounds from within. He rang a third time, keeping his finger pressed on the bell push for a full half minute. Footsteps sounded on the far side of the door. There came the noise of bolts being shot back then the door opened a few inches and a female face peered out at him.

With a swift thrust of his knee and shoulder he forced the door further open. Then he jabbed the muzzle of his pistol into the woman's stomach and said:

'Open your mouth and I'll fill you full of lead.'

She gave a gasp and stood back. In the dim light from the single lamp in the hall he now saw that she was his old acquaintance, Dolores Mendoza. Recognizing her brought him a new elation. It meant that Teresa's information had been up-to-date, and that it was unlikely now that he had come out there on a wild goose chase only to find that his quarry had moved on to another hiding place.

Forcing Dolores back a few paces he closed the door, felt behind him with his free hand till he found the key, turned it in the lock, pulled it out and pocketed it. Then he asked Dolores, 'Where is the lavatory?'

Giving him a surprised look, she made a gesture towards the end of the passage. So far it seemed that, after the lapse of years, she had not recognized him. Under the threat of the pistol she obediently turned and led the way down the narrow hall. At its end there was a door in front of which she halted.

'Open it and go inside,' he ordered her. She did as she was bid. He saw that it had a window through which she might squeeze herself. But, even if she did, the villa was so far out in the country that there seemed no possibility of her bringing help on the scene before he had accomplished what he had come to do.

Under the brighter light of the oil lamp burning there his features stood out more clearly. Suddenly her pale blue eyes widened, and she exclaimed, 'Chirikov! No; the French spy – de Quesnoy.'

He nodded. Returning her angry stare with a calm scrutiny he saw that her sallow face had grown much older; but that was not to be wondered at as she had spent a year in the dungeons of Montjuich. With an ironical bow, he remarked:

'I recall that we once talked of spending a week-end together on the Costa Brava. As I would cheerfully have murdered you rather than make love to you, you may consider yourself lucky that you have had three more years of life than you deserve. Sit down now and remain quiet. If you start shouting I shall come back and you will die in this place so well suited to the life you have led.'

Taking the key from the inside of the door he transferred it to the outside, shut the door and locked her in. With his pistol at the ready, he opened and threw back the door on the right-hand side of the passage. No sound broke the stillness indicating any reaction to his swift movement. Having listened intently for a moment he stepped inside.

The room was square and evidently used as a study. Opposite the door there was a large desk. As he stood there, facing him on its front was a solid row of thick reference books, and to its right there was a standard lamp that lit it, making a pool of brightness in the otherwise dim room.

De Richleau had little doubt that up to ten minutes ago Ferrer had been working there. At the ring of the doorbell he would have gone into some prepared hiding place. Had it been in England it might have been a priest's hole; but in Spain there had never been any necessity for such secret rooms. In any case, the house was not old enough to have that sort of thing. Therefore, he would be either in the cellars or up in an attic.

Before going in search of him the Duke decided to take a quick look round. Walking forward to the left-hand side of the desk, he glanced at the paper that lay spread out on it. Somewhat to his surprise he saw that it was a Russian newspaper about two weeks old. He then remembered Ferrer's passion for obtaining first-hand news from all parts of Europe. Beside the paper lay a Russian-Spanish dictionary that Ferrer had evidently been using to look up the meaning of words he did not understand.

As de Richleau's eyes fell upon the dictionary his heart suddenly stood still. The sight of it had rung a terrible bell that summoned up past memories. The last time he had seen a Russian-Spanish dictionary had been three years ago in his lodgings down by Barcelona's commercial harbour. He had then been using one to tutor a student that Ferrer had sent him, named Rubén Pineda. The young man had been one of Ferrer's brightest pupils. Later, on the night that de Richleau had so nearly lost his life, it had emerged that it was Pineda who, on Ferrer's instructions, had searched his lodging and been fooled into believing that he really was a Russian refugee.

But now it was he who had been fooled. Pineda had pulled a very clever bluff. Trusting in the beard he had grown, that three years had elapsed since they had met, and that he had since changed his name, he had said that they had become acquainted at the Somaten Club. That had seemed natural enough. But it was not the truth. Pineda had become Veragua.

The Duke stood beside Ferrer's desk, his mind working like a dynamo. He had left Veragua to guard the back entrance. Instead, by now he might have entered the house with the intention of helping his old master to escape. At that moment he heard a faint sound. Swinging round he saw Veragua standing in the open doorway. The young man had a smile on his face and was pointing a pistol at him.

21

The Twice-turned Tables

As de Richleau stared at the tall, smiling anarchist who now threatened his life, the truth about the afternoon's events flashed upon him. It was not, as he had supposed, that some of Ferrer's friends had learned of the investigation he was making and had been trailing him, waiting for some opportunity to murder him in a place where there would be a good chance of their escaping capture.

He had told no one that he was going to endeavour to trace Teresa – no one except Veragua. And he had not even mentioned her to him until after they had left the mill. But he had then confided to the young man that the woman he was going to see had been Ferrer's mistress, so he had good hopes of getting something out of her.

Had he spent only a few minutes with Teresa it seemed probable that, as with the many other inquiries he had made, Veragua would have taken no action, assuming that he had drawn another blank. But he had remained talking to her for the best part of a quarter of an hour.

Evidently that had led Veragua to assume that Teresa was
giving away information that might lead to Ferrer's capture; so
the time had come to put an abrupt end to 'Señor Gomá's' activities.
Out there in that quiet suburb he stood much less risk of being
seen making his attempt and being captured than he would have
in the city. It must have seemed to him now not only urgent to
eliminate the Duke, but too good a chance to miss. He had left
the automobile, walked up the almost deserted street and lobbed
his bomb through the window.

The whole sequence of events was grasped by the Duke's mind
in a matter of seconds. He knew now that he probably had only
a few more moments to live. Veragua had only to squeeze the
trigger of his pistol and he would be dead. To show that he realized
the situation would prove fatal. Instead, he gave a quick frown and
exclaimed:

'Why the hell are you pointing that thing at me?'

As he spoke he took an unhurried pace sideways and sat down
in the chair behind Ferrer's desk.

The smile on the bearded features of the young man deepened,
and he said, 'Can't you guess?'

'As a matter of fact I can,' de Richleau replied calmly. 'You
are thinking of putting a bullet through me. But I wouldn't, if I
were you. Of course, you think you could get away with it by
putting in a report that Ferrer shot me while I was trying to arrest
him. But you won't. If I die General Quiroga will have you shot.'

'Why should he? There would be no reason whatever for him to
suppose that it was I who had killed you.'

'My dear boy. Had you been longer engaged in the sort of game
we have been playing you would be aware that it is less dangerous
to have close to you an enemy you know than to eliminate him,
so that his work is taken over by another that you don't know.
And from the beginning I have known you to be Pineda.'

Veragua's bearded mouth dropped open in surprise. The point
of his gun also dropped a little. His eyes wide with astonishment,
he exclaimed, 'What! You knew all the time and gave me the
chance . . .'

He got no further. Under cover of the desk behind which he
was sitting, de Richleau had eased out his pistol. Suddenly he
jerked it up so that its barrel came just above the line of reference
books. It spat flame. Four staccato reports shattered the silence
of the house. The first three were from the Duke's automatic. Its
bullets ripped into Veragua's stomach. The last was from Veragua's
gun as a spasm closed his finger on its trigger. The bullet chipped

a splinter low down off the left-hand corner of the desk, then ricocheted off to land in the far wall. With a long-drawn howl the young anarchist collapsed upon the floor.

De Richleau jumped up from the desk. Now that the back entrance of the house was unguarded Ferrer might slip out of it; so he had no time to lose. Veragua, clutching his stomach with both hands, lay writhing in agony in the doorway. The Duke paused only to snatch up the gun that had fallen from Veragua's hand. As he did so he snapped:

'You won't kill any more little children with your bombs, my friend. And I gave it you in the stomach so you should know just how much that poor woman Teresa suffered by your act this afternoon.'

A moment later he had crossed the passage and thrown open a door that seemed the most likely one to lead to the kitchen. It did. No one was there. Beyond it was a small scullery. Entering it, he saw on its far side a door that was evidently the back entrance to the house. The door was bolted and the key was in the lock. Having made certain that it had been turned, he took it out and put it in his pocket. It was certain that Ferrer had not had time to get out of the house since the shooting; so unless Veragua had come upon him lurking in the kitchen quarters and urged him to escape by the back entrance, he was now trapped in it.

De Richleau decided that his best plan would be to search the house from the bottom up, otherwise while he was on an upper floor Ferrer might slip out of a downstairs window. The villa was fairly modern; but most Spanish houses that are larger than a cottage have a cellar, so he swiftly cast round for the entrance to one. He expected to find it somewhere in the back of the premises but a swift scrutiny of the floors convinced him that in none of them was a camouflaged trap-door.

Going out into the hall he paused to listen intently for a moment. He feared now that Ferrer might be making the best of the time he was being given to tie sheets together into a rope; so that he could get away by lowering himself from one of the windows. Not for the first time, the Duke cursed the dubious loyalty of the Catalan police. Had it not been for that he would have brought a score of policemen with him and had the house surrounded; but a leak could have ruined this chance, the like of which might not come again, to catch Ferrer; so he had decided against it.

Dolores had evidently wriggled out of the lavatory window, or was sitting quietly there. The only sound that broke the stillness was Veragua's moaning. Reassured, de Richleau moved a few

paces down the hall towards the door opposite that beside which
Veragua lay, expecting it to lead to a sitting-room. As he did so
he brushed past a red velvet curtain that hung on the side of the
hall formed by a straight staircase that ran up from it. Wondering
why there should be a curtain in such a pointless place, he pulled
it back. The reason became plain. It concealed a door under the
stairs. With grim satisfaction he wrenched it open.

The result was a bitter disappointment. Instead of the flight
of steps leading downward that he had expected, it was full of
coats, macintoshes and a variety of junk. Pushing the door to,
he listened again. There was still no sound from upstairs but
queer noises were now coming from the lavatory. Dolores was
not battering upon its door but seemed to be kicking one of its
walls and uttering muffled cries. What she was up to he had no
idea, and he did not care.

He again took a pace towards what he believed to be the sitting-
room, but it suddenly occurred to him that Ferrer might be crouching at the very far end of the cupboard under the stairs, hidden
behind the junk that was in it.

Fetching the lamp from the end of the hall he opened the door
again and set it down on the floor just inside the cupboard. Now,
he was faced with a very dangerous situation. If he put his head
in and Ferrer was lurking there, and had a pistol, he might be shot
himself before he could shoot Ferrer.

The cupboard was only about three feet deep but about eight
feet long, its roof sloping downwards from inside the doorway
to within a foot or so of the floor. With a sudden movement he
thrust his pistol round the doorjamb and fired two shots blind
in the direction of its far end. If Ferrer had been there he must
either have been hit or made some spontaneous movement as
the bullets thudded into the underside of the stairs within inches of
him. But the crash of the shots was followed by complete silence.

Disappointed again, and more worried than ever that by now
Ferrer might be escaping from the house, de Richleau bent down
and picked up the lamp. As he did so it lit the whole cupboard.
He caught his breath and his eyes widened with excitement. They
had fallen upon part of a line on the floor that ran at right angles
to the floorboards.

The line emerged from under a big cardboard carton. Quickly
he set the lamp down again, pocketed his pistol, and hauled the
carton out of the cupboard. It was heavy and full of books. Beyond
it there were two others, but the removal of the first was enough
to show him that the line he had spotted was one edge of a

trap-door. It must lead to a cellar and all the odds were that Ferrer was down in it.

He would have gone to his bolt-hole at the first ring of the front door bell. In her hurry and in the semi-darkness of the cup-board Dolores had failed to pull the cartons into place after he had descended, so that they would completely cover the top. But for that, de Richleau realized, he might have searched the house with a toothcomb, then left it in the belief that either Ferrer had not been there or had escaped before he had had a chance to catch him.

The problem now was how to get at him. To go down the steps into the cellar would be to walk into a death trap. The man at the bottom would have an overwhelming advantage. He had only to stand round the corner to the stairway with his pistol levelled and, as the intruder emerged from it, shoot him. But de Richleau had behind him ample experience of house to house fighting, during which pockets of resistance had to be mopped up. It took him only a minute to decide what to do.

Having thrust the heavy carton of books back, so that with the others on the hinge side of the trap-door their weight would prevent Ferrer coming up and making a desperate bid to get away, the Duke hurried back to the kitchen. There, he collected some bundles of faggots, a tin of oil, some wax tapers and a rolling pin. With these items he returned to the narrow hall and set about preparing to smoke Ferrer out.

First he hauled all the cartons of books out of the cupboard so as to leave the trap-door free. He then poured oil all over the faggots and pushed a wax taper into each. Lastly he tied two of the oil-soaked faggots to raincoats that were hanging in the cup-board. The combination of oil and rubber when on fire would, he knew, produce the most suffocating smoke.

When he opened the trap-door no glimmer of light filtered up from below. That shook him a little, as he felt that Ferrer should have considered himself safe enough down there to light a candle. He became worried then that a man so experienced in being hunted as Ferrer would, quite probably, have made himself an escape exit, and by now might have crawled through a tunnel to emerge in the garden. But the thought did not deter him from putting the matter to the test.

He lit one of the tapers, waited until the oil-soaked wood of the faggot had caught, then pitched it down into the cellar. As quickly as he possibly could he got the others well alight and heaved them, with the raincoats, after them. Flames leapt up at

the bottom of the stairs. Above the crackling of the wood the
sound of hurried movement came up to him. His handsome, slightly
saturnine features broke into a grin. Ferrer was down there all
right, and now desperately engaged in trying to put the fire balls
out; but the odds against his succeeding were very heavy.

De Richleau quietly lowered the trap-door into place, so that
none of the smoke that was now billowing up should escape.
Picking up the rolling pin that he had brought from the kitchen,
he went up the stairs until he was standing above the door to the
cupboard. Leaning over the banister he waited.

The wait seemed interminable. Yet it was no more than three
or four minutes. Suddenly there came a loud bang, as the trap-
door was thrust up and thrown back. After that there came the
sound of someone gasping for breath, and eddies of smoke began
to seep out into the hall. For a full minute nothing further happened. Then a head, that peered swiftly right and left, emerged
cautiously from the open doorway of the cupboard.

But, to the Duke's amazement it was not Ferrer's head. Ferrer
had had brown hair. This man's was red – startlingly red – the
red that is known as 'carrots'. Nevertheless, with the head had
appeared a hand that held a revolver. Whoever he was, as an
occupant of this villa he must be an enemy. De Richleau leaned
forward over the banister and brought his rolling pin down hard
on the man's head. Without even a murmur his knees buckled
and he fell in a heap on the floor of the narrow hall.

For two minutes de Richleau remained where he was, waiting
for Ferrer to follow this other man out of the cupboard beneath
him. But no second head appeared, neither was there any sound
of footsteps on the cellar stairs. All he could hear were Veragua's
groans and a continuation of the muffled noises from the lavatory.
Putting down the rolling pin, he took out his pistol and came
downstairs. Having shut the cupboard door as a precaution against
Ferrer surprising him by suddenly emerging from that quarter, he
turned the body of the red-headed man over and stared down at him.

His features were clean-shaven except for a carroty toothbrush
moustache. For a moment de Richleau did not recognize him,
then he realized that, after all, the man was Ferrer. He looked
many years older than when the Duke had last seen him, perhaps
on account of his year in prison; and the violently red hair, coupled
with the fact that he no longer wore a beard, had entirely altered
his appearance. Picking up the lamp de Richleau moved it nearer
to him so that he could examine at close quarters the hair, now
worn *en brosse*, on the skull. By the brighter light he could see

that the violent dye used to change his hair to carrots had also stained the skin of his scalp. That dissolved the Duke's last doubts. The man was Francisco Ferrer.

De Richleau's next problem was to get his prisoner in to Barcelona. To take him as an apparently lifeless body in the open automobile or, worse still, when he came round as a captive shouting for help when they passed through the working class outskirts of the city, could have led to all sorts of trouble. For a moment he remained deep in thought, then he smiled to himself, for it had occurred to him to take a leaf out of the Ferrer family book.

Now he did open the door opposite to the one beside which Veragua lay moaning and retching. It led, as he had expected, into a sitting-room. At one end stood a table which, from the fruit and other things on it, was evidently used for meals; but in its centre the stained floorboards were covered with a coarsely woven Indian rug, measuring about six feet by eight.

Returning to the hall, de Richleau stuffed his handkerchief into the still unconscious Ferrer's mouth, picked him up, carried him into the sitting-room, laid him down at one end of the rug and then proceeded to roll him up in it. Having done that, he secured the tube from unrolling by pulling tight and knotting two curtain ties round it. Heaving the bundle up on to his shoulder he carried it out into the hall, put it down for a minute while he unlocked the front door then rolled it out on to the doorstep.

Leaving it there, he walked back up the hall and unlocked the door of the lavatory. The strange sounds that had come from it were then explained. Dolores had attempted to escape through the narrow window, but got stuck in it. Something about her fat posterior, from which depended skinny legs and feet shod in heavy brogues, the toes of which were beating a violent tattoo against the wall, struck him as incredibly funny. He roared with laughter, then with his open hand dealt her a mighty slap on the bottom. Her squawk of indignation came faintly back to him. Controlling his mirth, he took her by the ankles, stood back, and pulled hard upon them. She gave an agonized groan as the sharp tug freed her. Stepping forward he caught her as she fell.

Her eyes blazing hatred, she swivelled in his embrace, raised both her hands and clawed at his face. Instead of throwing his head back in an attempt to avoid her vicious attack, he brought it forward and downward in a swift, strong jerk. His forehead came into hard collision with her fleshy Semitic nose. She let out a scream, her hands flailed helplessly and, as he let go of her, she flopped down on to the lavatory seat.

Indifferent to the suffering of this woman who had helped to cause so much more suffering to others, he gave only a moment to looking down at her now hideous face: the nose flattened and streaming blood, the eyes blinded by tears. Then he said:

'I came to release you only because there is one of your murderous fraternity in the study who is on the point of dying in considerable pain. I have to get back to Barcelona quickly. Otherwise I may find myself with a corpse rolled up in a carpet on my hands; and I prefer that your friend Ferrer should be legally tried and executed. But if you have any morphia, laudanum or even aspirin in the house, give the lot to that misguided young fool who is dying.'

Turning on his heel he left her and hurried back to Ferrer. Heaving the roll of carpet up on to his shoulder, he plodded with it down the garden path and along the road to the triangle of grass on which Veragua had parked the automobile. Panting, he laid the roll in the back, cranked up the engine, then climbed up on to the high driver's seat and set off towards the city.

Twenty-five minutes later he pulled up in front of the Police Headquarters. Two uniformed men carried the roll of carpet in for him and upstairs to Urgoiti's office. As they set it down on the floor, the fat, bald Chief of the Security Bureau gave de Richleau a puzzled look, and said:

'I thought you meant to make an arrest. What's the idea of turning up with that old carpet?'

The Duke waited until the uniformed men had left the room, then knelt down, undid the ties, rolled the carpet back and removed the gag from Ferrer's mouth. Ferrer had recovered consciousness during the journey. He looked grey in the face, and woebegone. Struggling up into a sitting position he gave a violent sneeze. Kneeling behind him de Richleau smiled at Urgoiti, and said:

'I brought him wrapped up like this because I didn't want any trouble with him on the way. But here he is. The celebrated Señor Francisco Ferrer.'

The Police Chief had risen behind his desk. For a moment he stared at the captive, then he said, 'You've got the wrong man. That's not Ferrer.'

'Oh yes it is,' replied the Duke.

'It's not. I often used to see Ferrer taking his aperitif outside the Café Ronda. He was one of the best-known figures in Barcelona. He is a much younger man; he has brown hair and a beard.'

'Don't let his appearance deceive you. It's easy to shave off a beard, and his hair is dyed. As for his age, his year in prison wouldn't have made him look any younger.'

The red-headed man had come to his feet. Suddenly he burst into a violent spate of words. 'I don't know what you are both talking about, but I'll have the law on you for this. My name is Hernando Olozaga and I can bring a hundred people to prove it. This man,' he jabbed a finger towards de Richleau, 'broke into my house with another villain. I live out in the country. No amount of shouting would have brought help, and I was scared; so I hid in a cupboard. While I was there they must have quarrelled. There was a lot of shooting. When I thought they'd gone I peeped out of the cupboard. I saw the other fellow, a young chap with a beard, lying wounded on the floor of my workroom. He was clutching his stomach, and looked to me about all in. Next thing I knew, this man had coshed me and knocked me out.'

Urgoiti frowned at de Richleau. 'Explain, please. Where is Veragua?'

The Duke frowned. 'What our prisoner says about him is correct. He is probably dead by now.'

'Dead!' repeated the Police Chief, his eyes widening. 'Is it really true, then, that you shot him?'

'Yes. I had to; otherwise he would have shot me. It was only a minute before he held me up that I recognized him. By taking him on as a detective you have been nurturing a viper in your bosom. His name was not Veragua but Pineda. I knew him as a young anarchist and a student of Ferrer's when I was in Barcelona three years ago.'

'I cannot believe it.' Urgoiti shook his head. 'It is impossible that the police should have had such a deception practised upon them. And what, may I ask, were you doing in the city at that time?'

'Surely General Quiroga told you about me,' de Richleau said quickly. 'I was hunting anarchists, just as I have been doing these past two days; but then I was working on my own and posing as a Russian refugee.'

'Ha!' exclaimed the red-headed man. 'I recognize him now. He was pointed out to me by a friend of mine as a Russian nihilist, and his name . . . his name . . . yes, it is Nicolai Chirikov.'

De Richleau laughed. 'Of course he remembers me. It would be extraordinary if he did not. I got a temporary job in his school for assassins and succeeded in breaking it up.'

Urgoiti gave him a queer look. 'But you are a foreigner, aren't you? Your name is not really Carlos Gomá. The other evening, when we first met, Veragua also said he believed you to be a Russian refugee.'

'I am half Russian by birth. But what the devil has that to do with it? General Quiroga personally vouched for me to you, did he not?'

'Yes, yes; but he may have been deceived.'

'Deceived! What nonsense!'

'It is not nonsense. It is much more likely that he should have been deceived about you, who arrived here only forty-eight hours ago, than that I should have been deceived about Veragua, who has worked for me for months.'

'You are quite wrong about that. General Quiroga has had incontestable proof of my true identity. What is more, I first met him three years ago, soon after this man Ferrer had failed in an attempt to have me murdered.'

'I tell you the man is not Ferrer.'

'I tell you he is,' de Richleau retorted stubbornly. 'I agree that his appearance is greatly changed, but that is mainly because he has dyed his hair. You have only to look at his scalp to see that it is dyed.'

'It is not a criminal offence to dye one's hair, and he says he can bring plenty of people to swear to it that he is a Señor Olozaga.'

'Plenty of anarchists who are prepared to perjure themselves, no doubt; but there are many ways in which his real identity can be proved.'

'It seems to me that it is your identity that stands in greater need of proving.'

'God give me patience!' exclaimed the Duke angrily. 'I thought you an intelligent man, but tonight you are acting as though your head were made of wood.'

Urgoiti's plump figure stiffened with resentment. 'You will kindly refrain from insulting me.'

'And you will kindly refrain from questioning my integrity,' snapped back the Duke. 'Believe it or not, the man I have brought in is Ferrer. In General Quiroga's name I charge you to hold him for questioning. Should you fail to do so, I promise you it will cost you your job.'

'I'll hold him,' grunted the Police Chief, 'just to be on the safe side. But it looks to me as if he's someone you've got your knife into privately and are trying to frame.'

'Damn your impudence!' roared de Richleau. 'It now exceeds even your stupidity. I've had enough of this. I am going straight back to the Fortress to lodge a complaint about you with the Captain-General.'

'Oh no you're not.' Urgoiti pressed a bell-push on his desk. 'I'm holding you too. This man says you are a Russian nihilist named Chirikov. It wouldn't surprise me if you are, after what's happened to poor young Veragua. It looks to me as if he stumbled on the truth about you, and you shot him to keep him quiet. Anyhow, you admit yourself that you left him dying of wounds that you inflicted on him; so even if you turned out to be a Grandee of Spain, General Quiroga couldn't blame me for detaining you until we find out a bit more about what did happen. You're going to pass the night in a cell.'

That the Police Chief should have hit a bull's eye when making what he obviously thought to be the wildly improbable suggestion that Señor 'Carlos Gomá' might turn out to be a Grandee of Spain, almost made the Duke laugh. But to have declared at this stage that he was one would only have made Urgoiti still more sceptical about his *bona fides*, and the situation that had developed was now no laughing matter. To have triumphed in his mission only to be told that he had arrested the wrong man was bad enough; to have to spend a night in prison because he had succeeded in saving his own life, at the expense of that of a youth who had been on the point of murdering him, seemed positively intolerable. Yet the last word, in this place, definitely lay with Urgoiti.

In vain de Richleau asked to be allowed to speak to General Quiroga on the telephone. Urgoiti, evidently still smarting under his insults, flatly refused. A uniformed man appeared in answer to the Chief's summons, others were sent for and the Duke and the red-headed man were both marched away, the latter loudly protesting that it was an outrage and that his name was Olozaga.

Locked in a solitary cell, the Duke took stock of the situation. When he had calmed down a little he had to admit to himself that he was in part to blame for what had happened. He had made a particular point with Quiroga about not wanting it to become generally known among the police that he was that Count de Quesnoy who had three years before worked against the anarchists and brought about the closing of the *Escuela Moderna*; but he had assumed that, before his arrival in Barcelona, the General had confided his true identity to the Police Chief. Evidently that was not so and the General could only have told Urgoiti that he was expecting a special investigator that evening to whom he wished him to give his full co-operation.

That being the case, when Urgoiti learned that Señor 'Gomá' had just shot one of his most promising detectives, and a man whom Urgoiti did not believe to be Ferrer declared that he knew 'Gomá' to be a Russian nihilist named Chirikov, the Police Chief had certainly had grounds for holding 'Gomá' until a full investigation into the question of his identity could be made.

About that the Duke felt no concern. for it could be only a matter of waiting until the morning: General Quiroga would be informed about what had happened, he would be released, and Urgoiti made to look a complete fool. But he was worried about Ferrer.

For a few minutes he wondered if he could possibly have been mistaken. The red-headed man certainly had only a vague resemblance to the Ferrer he had known in the past, and Urgoiti had been so positive that he was not. Yet as the Duke went back in his mind over the events of the evening his vague doubts were swiftly dissipated. Teresa had told him that Ferrer was living out at San Cugat under the name of Olozaga with Dolores Mendoza. For Dolores to have been there with a man who resembled Ferrer but was not him was beyond any possible coincidence. Then Ferrer's account of what had occurred had diverged considerably from the truth. He had said that two men had broken in; but that was not so. He said that he had hidden in a cupboard; but in fact he had been down in the cellar and had had to be smoked out. And he had made no mention at all of Dolores – obviously because if Urgoiti had sent out to have her picked up she would at once have been identified as one of Ferrer's closest associates and so put the noose round his own neck.

No, there could be no doubt about the red-headed man being Ferrer, but the thing that worried de Richleau was that, before he could get into touch with General Quiroga in the morning, Urgoiti might question Ferrer further, become strengthened in his opinion that the self-styled Olozaga really was an innocent person, and have him released. To have Urgoiti sacked later for his blunder would be little consolation for having lost the chance to bring Ferrer to justice.

The Duke was still speculating with considerable anxiety on such a possibility when, after about an hour, two warders entered his cell and one of them said to him, 'Señor Chirikov, we have orders to search you.'

'Chirikov is not my name,' he replied with a frown. 'Here I am known as Carlos Gomá.'

The warder shrugged. 'Chirikov is the name you're under on the charge sheet and that's good enough for us.'

'Charge,' repeated de Richleau. 'What am I charged with?'

'With the wilful murder of Detective Veragua. His body has just been brought in. Come on, now. No nonsense. Get your clothes off and quick about it.'

For a moment de Richleau thought of protesting; but he quickly realized that it would be useless. The two men, evidently under the impression that he was a thug who had killed a member of the police force, were scowling at him and would clearly have jumped at the least excuse to give him a beating-up.

As he took off his clothes, garment by garment, they went through them. He had already been relieved of his own automatic, and the one that had belonged to Veragua, before being put into the cell. Now they took his police card, his wallet and his loose change, then returned his clothes and left him.

He re-dressed with a set face, now gravely alarmed by a new thought that had suddenly come to him. Could it be that Urgoiti had known all the time that the red-headed man was Ferrer, and be one of the police against whom Don Alfonso had warned him – a fanatical Catalan who was secretly doing his utmost to protect the anarchists? Could it possibly be that Urgoiti had twisted the situation to suit his own ends – that he meant to let Ferrer go, and to frame the man who had caught him for the murder of Veragua?

22

The Surprise of His Life

FOR a few moments de Richleau stood staring at the steel door of his cell. The thought that Urgoiti might be hand in glove with his enemies and that, if so, he had fallen into a trap, was an appalling one.

Then, with a shrug, he relaxed, convinced that he was letting his imagination run away with him. Urgoiti might be a self-opinionated and somewhat thick-headed official, but a man so high up in the service could hardly be a traitor. After all, he, de Richleau, had admitted to shooting Veragua, and now that the detective's death had been confirmed it was no more than normal procedure that he should be charged with it.

But why should he be charged as 'Chirikov' instead of as 'Gomá'? That could only mean that Urgoiti was accepting Ferrer's word rather than his. And it was Urgoiti who had selected Veragua to act as his constant companion during his investigation.

De Richleau sat down on the iron bed with which the cell was furnished. His thoughts were racing. He tried to persuade himself that everything would be all right in the morning. As he had said that he might not be back until very late Quiroga would not be waiting up for his return, but when he did not appear next day it was certain that the General would inquire of Urgoiti what had become of him. At the worst Urgoiti could only be keeping him out of the way until he had made a pretence of questioning Ferrer, then released him and given him a good start to get well clear of the city to a new hiding place. That was it. Then explanations would ensue. Urgoiti would make the most abject apologies; but Ferrer would already be beyond danger of recapture.

But Urgoiti was not going to get away with it. The Duke meant to see to that. Good tough old Quiroga, the scourge of the Barcelona anarchists, would support him. If need be he would go to the King. By the time de Richleau had done with him Urgoiti would have lost his job and his pension, and be extremely lucky if he did not have to serve a prison sentence into the bargain.

All the same, when the Duke lay down on the truckle bed and tried to get to sleep his mind continued to be harassed by so many unnerving possibilities that it refused to rest. Several times he tried to concentrate his thoughts on Gulia in her big warm bed and the joys they had experienced there, but, try as he would, he could not keep them on her; so during the long hours he did little more than doze, then start awake again with renewed anxiety at the extraordinary situation in which he found himself.

Morning brought nothing to allay his fears. On the contrary. At seven o'clock he was marched out to give himself a wash, and on returning to his cell a breakfast was dished out to him that looked so revolting that he decided not to eat it. For over an hour afterwards he sat gloomily on the edge of his bed, then a young Artillery Lieutenant was shown in to him.

Removing his kepi the young man introduced himself by the name of Navarez and announced that he had been nominated to act as 'Prisoner's Friend'.

De Richleau gave a start. As a soldier he knew well what the term implied. 'What!' he exclaimed. 'Does this mean that I am to be court-martialled?'

The young man nodded. 'Yes, of course. But we are lucky in that we shall not have long to wait this morning.'

'This morning!'

'Since the revolt a court-martial has been convened to sit at ten o'clock every morning. It administers summary justice to all political prisoners that have been brought in during the preceding twenty-four hours. But such cases have been much fewer during the past week, and we are the only one on today's list; so our case should be heard right away.'

De Richleau knew then, beyond all doubt, that Urgoiti did intend to frame him as Veragua's murderer. It was a terrifying thought. He stared aghast at the young officer who evidently disliked the job he had been given but had been made callous to it from having had to perform a similar function several times in the past month. He was going on with hurried unconcern:

'I understand that you are a Russian nihilist and that last night you killed a detective. If those are the facts I don't think there is much that I can do for you; but if you have any line of defence let me hear it and I'll put it to the Court.'

'Thank you,' said the Duke. 'There is only one thing you can do for me. That is to go up to the Fortress at once and tell General Quiroga that . . .'

He got no further. 'Take a message from a prisoner to that old tiger,' interrupted the Lieutenant derisively. 'Is it likely? He'd have my head off.'

'Very well then, let it be a written message that you can deliver without seeing him.'

'Prisoners awaiting trial are not allowed to send letters to anyone outside the jail.'

De Richleau drew in a sharp breath. 'Then I fear there is nothing that you can do for me. I prefer to defend myself.'

'That is not permitted. If all the rebels who have been before the Court during the past month had been allowed to talk their heads off the Court would never have got through. It would still be sitting next Christmas.'

'Do you mean,' asked the Duke with rising alarm, 'that I shall not be allowed to say a word in my own defence? That I must leave it to you to put the bare bones of anything I tell you before the Court, and that on that alone my life will hang?'

Navarez nodded. 'That's the usual procedure in these routine cases. And the Court doesn't take long to reach a verdict. If it does turn out that you didn't kill this 'tec you'll be a free man by about half past ten. If not . . . well.'

'Well what?'

For the first time the young man looked slightly uncomfortable. Fingering his small moustache, he muttered, 'You may as well know what to expect. These Courts are convened to administer summary justice. Establishing them was the only way to stop bombs being thrown into the better-class restaurants and officers walking in the streets being shot from windows. They have succeeded in that; but only because it is now known by everybody that any prisoner found guilty is given no second chance. In the yard behind the building in which the Court sits a firing squad is always kept in a state of readiness. If it's thumbs down you'll be taken out to it straight away.'

De Richleau had paled under his tan. He realized now that he was in desperate danger. Urgoiti had known the procedure and counted with well-founded confidence on events taking the course usual in such cases. It might be all over before Quiroga heard a word about it. Afterwards Urgoiti, with his tongue in his cheek, would bow to the storm and accept a reprimand. But he need not fear anything worse as he could plead a belief that it was Quiroga who had been deceived, and all he had done was to send up for trial a Russian nihilist who, to prevent himself being exposed in his true colours, had shot a detective.

'Well?' said Navarez. 'Time's getting on. If you have got a plea to make you'd better let me hear it.'

'If I told you the truth you would never believe me,' replied de Richleau bitterly.

'No harm in trying me,' remarked the Lieutenant with calm indifference.

'Very well then. My proper style and title is His Excellency Major-General the Duke de Richleau, Count de Quesnoy, Count Königstein, Knight of the Most Exalted Order of the Golden Fleece. I am a British subject and a personal friend of your King, with whom I have sat at table three times during the past month. I arrived in Barcelona . . .'

'That's enough!' snapped Navarez. 'What sort of a fool do you take me for? But perhaps you're trying to be funny. If so, let me tell you this is no time for joking.'

'As it is I who look like shortly facing a firing squad, and not you, it is unnecessary to remind me of that.'

'Let's have the truth then.'

'Apart from sparing you some of my lesser titles and honours I have told it; but I also told you first that you would not believe me. I don't suppose you will believe either that for the two nights preceding this last one, I was staying up at Montjuich as General Quiroga's guest.'

'Of course I don't,' the young officer's voice had become impatient. 'Is it likely that the Captain-General would entertain a nihilist?'

'You have no shadow of proof that I am a nihilist,' retorted de Richleau angrily. 'Do I look or speak like one?'

The Lieutenant shrugged. 'I am told that some of them are

educated men who have become mentally deranged. One of the most famous is a Russian Prince. I forget his name but it begins with K.'

'Kropotkin,' supplied the Duke. 'All right. You have me there. But at least I ask you to believe that for most of my life I have been a soldier. You are a soldier, too, so we both know that the quickest way to earn promotion is to display courage.'

'What has this to do with your case?'

'That it gives you a chance to display your courage. Go and see General Quiroga for me, or even telephone to him. He cannot eat you. On the contrary he will think the better of you for having bearded him rather than see a man condemned who may be innocent. I swear to you by all I hold sacred . . .'

'What? That you did not kill this detective?'

'No. I do not deny that I shot him, but . . .'

'Since you admit your guilt I'll be damned if I'll beard the Captain-General on your account.'

De Richleau sat down on the truckle bed and put his head between his hands. He had been in many a tight corner before but in nearly all of them he had at least had the chance to fight his way out. This time there was no such chance. He had been trapped under a false identity and caught up in a swift-moving judicial process designed only as an emergency measure to crush a serious revolt. It really began to look as though, should he fail to get word of his plight to Quiroga, he would find himself facing a firing squad before the morning was out. For a minute or more he racked his brains for a way to persuade or bully Navarez into acting as his messenger. Then a new idea occurred to him. Springing to his feet, he cried:

'I am a British subject. I demand to see the British Consul.'

'You told me you were when you made all those other damn fool claims about yourself,' the Lieutenant replied coldly. 'Have you any papers to prove it?'

'No. But as a British national I demand to see my Consul.'

'You are in no position to demand anything.'

'All right then. I request, beg if you will, that he should be brought here.'

Navarez shook his head. 'We've had dozens of foreign nationals through our hands: Frenchmen, Italians, Greeks; mostly seamen from ships in the docks who joined the revolutionaries. With the city under Martial Law they were treated like the rest. In an emergency formalities such as notifying Consuls have to be waived, and the emergency is still on.'

10*

Again they remained silent for a minute while the Duke strove desperately to think of a way out. Then the Lieutenant said, 'Your best plan is to cut out the fireworks about your being the King of Siam and plead that you shot this fellow in self-defence.'

'I did. If I hadn't shot him he would have shot me. But do you think the Court will believe that?'

'I doubt it,' again the young man fingered his moustache, 'still, it's about your only chance.'

As he was speaking a key grated in the lock, and the door was thrown open. Navarez stepped out into the corridor and two warders entered the cell. One of them snapped a handcuff on to the Duke's right wrist and snapped the other on to his own left wrist. Then they filed out and up to the ground floor of the building.

In front of it a prison van was waiting. As the Duke stepped out into the bright morning sunshine, he cast a swift look up and down the street. There were plenty of people in it going about their morning's business. If he could have cut and run for it he might have got away in the crowd. But as he was handcuffed to the warder such an attempt was out of the question. Filled now with such apprehension that he had broken out into a slight sweat, he allowed himself to be hustled into the van.

It set off at a trot, then as its pace slowed he knew that the horses were drawing it up the long hill of Montjuich. All the time his brain was working furiously, but it had now become sterile of ideas by which he might attempt to save himself. His one hope lay in the chance that when it reached the fortress some member of the General's staff who knew him by sight might be about, so that he could shout to them for help. But when the van pulled up and he was pushed out of it he saw that it had halted on the far side of the fortress from the General's quarters. Two minutes later his warders had marched him through a door and down a passage into a small bleak waiting-room.

Navarez left them, and for ten minutes de Richleau remained there, still cudgelling his wits without avail. Now that he was alone with the two warders he contemplated the desperate step of attempting to overcome them. Had he been free he might have succeeded, but he was still handcuffed to one of them. He knew that even if he had knocked the man unconscious, he would never be able to get the key and unlock the steel bracelet while the other attacked him, before shouts brought some of the soldiers he had seen at the entrance to the fortress.

An N.C.O. appeared at the door of the room and beckoned to them. Turning, he led the way down the passage, the Duke and the warders following closely on his heels. They went out through a door and crossed a small courtyard.

Twelve soldiers and a sergeant were lounging near their stacked rifles. De Richleau needed no telling that they were the firing squad that Navarez had mentioned as always being kept in a state of readiness.

The north wall of the courtyard was blank, without doors or windows. Half-way along it and about four feet from the ground there showed a long, irregular patch where the stone-work had been pitted by innumerable bullets. Obviously it was there, with their backs to that stretch of wall, that during the past six weeks hundreds of mob-leaders, anarchists, syndicalists, Communists, and probably quite a number of honest but unlucky workers, had met their death. The Duke lowered his eyes and could not prevent a shudder running through him.

They passed through another door, turned right and entered a largish room furnished only with a number of deal tables, chairs and benches. In the middle of a long table at the far end of the room three officers were seated close together: a Major, a Captain and a Lieutenant. Anxiously the Duke scrutinized their faces in an endeavour to assess the characters of the three men who were about to try him. The Major was elderly, square-headed and somewhat morose-looking. De Richleau judged him to be past further promotion at his age, so probably disappointed in his career and a harsh disciplinarian. The Captain was about twenty-six, a dark, handsome fellow with a fine upturned moustache. The Lieutenant was a vapid-looking youth wearing a monocle.

At smaller tables to either side and a little in front of the long one two other officers were sitting; one was Lieutenant Navarez, the other – a dark round-faced man of about thirty – de Richleau knew would act as Prosecutor. To the latter's right and a little behind him Comandante Urgoiti was sitting. At a fourth table, forming a T with the long one at the top, there was another officer with a number of papers and books in front of him. He belonged to the Legal branch and was there to play the part of Clerk of the Court. At the same table there were two N.C.O.s with pens behind their ears. Except for a uniformed policeman and two men who looked like detectives, the benches were empty.

In the doorway the warder to whom the Duke was handcuffed quickly unlocked the bracelet round his wrist. Both warders stepped aside then went to sit on the bench next to the policeman. Two soldiers with rifles and fixed bayonets took their place one on either side of de Richleau and marched him up to the end of the middle table.

The Legal Officer asked his name, and he replied in a firm voice, 'Jean Armand Duplessis, tenth Duke de Richleau. I have been brought here owing to a most iniquitous . . .'

He got no further. The officer cut in. 'Your name is given on the charge sheet as Nicolai Chirikov.'

'That was a *nom de guerre* used by me only for a few weeks when I was here in 1906, seeking evidence to bring to justice certain anarchists believed to have been concerned in the wedding-day attempt on His Majesty King Alfonso. I arrived here three days ago for a similar purpose. I was received by General Quiroga and spent two nights as his guest. I . . .'

The Major, who was acting as the President of the Court, rapped sharply on the table with his gavel and said, 'The Prisoner seeks to waste the time of the Court. Expunge his remarks from the record and proceed.'

The few preliminaries were soon over and the charge read out: 'That the said Nicolai Chirikov, being temporarily employed as a member of the special police, did on the evening of September 10th wilfully kill by shooting Detective-Officer Rodrigo Veragua, who had gone out to the village of San Cugat in his company.'

To that de Richleau replied, 'Not Guilty. The man I shot was an anarchist named Rubén Pineda.'

Urgoiti whispered to the Prosecuting Officer, who rose and said, 'We shall bring evidence before the Court to show that the murdered man was in fact Rodrigo Veragua.'

The first witness was called: a frightened-looking old woman who, after a moment, the Duke recognized as the landlady of the *pensión* at which he had stayed during his first visit to Barcelona. After peering at him she identified him as Nicolai Chirikov; upon which he said:

'I have already admitted to having carried out investigations to the advantage of the State under that name.'

'Silence!' said the President loudly. 'The Prisoner will speak only when he is addressed.'

The second witness was a foxy-looking little man who deposed that during August, 1906, he had been a frequenter of the branch of the Somaten that had premises down by the docks; that he had on several occasions seen the prisoner there and heard him talk with enthusiastic approval of the outrages committed by militant anarchists, and say that he had himself been exiled from Russia for nihilist activities.

De Richleau let that pass, only thinking grimly that Urgoiti must have spent a very busy night raking up these witnesses against him.

The third and fourth witnesses were the two detectives. They deposed to having been sent out to San Cugat the previous night at about half past ten. They then described the circumstances in which they had found Veragua's dead body and the injuries he had sustained. They also stated that they had known the dead man for a number of years as Rodrigo Veragua.

As Urgoiti would have been certain to choose men of his own kidney to go out to Ferrer's recent hiding-place, de Richleau felt sure that the two detectives had perjured themselves; but there was nothing he could do about it.

The next witness to be called was a sandy-haired little man with pince-nez. He proved to be a ballistics expert. The Duke's automatic was produced and three bullets that had been extracted from Veragua's body, which he testified had been fired from the weapon.

The Duke held up his hand. The President nodded. 'You may speak.'

'Sir,' said de Richleau firmly, 'I do not deny that I shot this man, but when I first met him he was an anarchist using the name of Pineda. And my name is not Chirikov. You have only to confront me with General Quiroga and he will order this wicked charge to be withdrawn immediately. He is aware of my true identity and I swear to you that he will vouch for it.'

The Major looked a little uncertain and whispered to his two colleagues. Hope rose in de Richleau's breast, but Urgoiti had been murmuring to the Prosecutor. The latter rose to his feet and said:

'May it please the Court, evidence has already been given that the Prisoner is in fact Nicolai Chirikov. I submit that to request His Excellency the Captain-General to leave his urgent duties in order to attend this Court, only to tell it that he has known the Prisoner under another name, would be a most unjustified waste of His Excellency's time.'

The three officers who formed the Court again whispered together. Pale with anxiety the Duke watched them, waiting for their all-important decision. At length it came. The President said:

'The Court is satisfied that the Prisoner is the nihilist Chirikov. In the circumstances it would be pointless to request His Excellency the Captain-General to attend and give evidence. Let the case proceed.'

The Prosecutor was still on his feet. He bowed and again addressed the Court. 'The Prosecution has shown that Veragua was slain by bullets from the Prisoner's pistol. It remains only to show that he was on the premises where the murder was committed at the time it took place. Next witness.'

De Richleau glanced round to the door by which the witnesses entered. To his utter amazement he saw Ferrer walk in. That Urgoiti should have had the audacity to produce him seemed positively staggering. Yet there he was, looking more than his age despite his head of carrot-coloured hair, but his bright, intelligent eyes proclaimed that his mind was as active as ever.

When questioned by the Prosecutor, he told the same story as he had at Police Headquarters the previous night, with only a few embellishments. He lived alone out at San Cugat with only a daily woman who came in to do for him. He had been working in his study when he had heard a window smash at the back of the premises. Fearing robbers who would do him violence he had hidden in a cupboard under the stairs, and so on.

As de Richleau listened he could hardly believe that he was not dreaming. That Ferrer of all people should be standing there swearing his life away seemed so fantastic that it could not possibly be true. Yet he was horribly aware that he was not suffering from a nightmare; this macabre travesty of justice was actually taking place.

The moment Ferrer stopped speaking the Duke burst into speech. Pointing an accusing finger at Ferrer he declared with passionate sincerity:

'The witness has told a tissue of lies. He is not the peaceful citizen, Olozaga, that he claims to be. He is Francisco Ferrer, the notorious anarchist. It was he who ran the *Escuela Moderna*, the school for assassins. He has been responsible for more murders than any man in Barcelona. I demand . . .'

'Silence!' roared the President, banging on the table with his gavel. 'Silence!'

The Duke ignored him and cried above the din, 'I demand that General Quiroga be fetched so that I can prove my true identity. I demand that Ferrer, this man who has instigated outrages that have led to the death of hundreds of innocent people, be brought to trial. This Court dare not condemn me. I am here as a result of a conspiracy. Comandante Urgoiti is at the bottom of it. He has hatched this plot to have me shot so that Ferrer may go free.'

'Silence! Silence! Silence!' shouted the President; and then, 'If you do not stop this minute, I'll have you gagged.'

Breathless and sweating, de Richleau subsided. Ferrer was glancing nervously from side to side; but the Prosecutor nodded to him and he scurried swiftly back into the room from which he had come.

After a moment's hush the President said, 'Proceed,' and, standing up, the Prosecutor again addressed the Court.

'I am confident,' he said, 'that the Court will disregard these wild accusations. It is obvious that they are no more than a bluff by which the Prisoner hopes to gain a few hours of life by beguiling the Court into an adjournment. But that he is guilty the Court can hardly doubt.' He then gave a very brief summing-up, ended by demanding the death penalty, and sat down.

The President made a sign to the Prisoner's Friend. Navarez stood up, bowed, fingered his little moustache, and said:

'May it please the Court, although I have been nominated as the Prisoner's Friend, I fear I can make only a poor showing in that rôle. When I interviewed the prisoner earlier this morning he would say little about himself except to make assertions impossible of belief, such as that he was a foreign Duke, a personal friend of His Majesty the King, had been staying in Barcelona as the guest of His Excellency the Captain-General, and so on. It is obvious that he suffers from delusions of grandeur. That would indicate that his mind is unbalanced, and the Court may wish to take his mental state into consideration. Apart from that I can only submit to you the statement he made to me, that he killed Veragua in self-defence; but, unfortunately, of that I can give the Court no proof.'

Had de Richleau not been so frantically anxious about the fate that might overtake him in the next quarter of an hour, he would have felt outraged by this travesty of a defence; but he had been prepared for something like it and his whole mind was concentrated on wondering if there was even a chance that the Court would agree on a verdict of 'Guilty, but with extenuating circumstances'. That would have meant imprisonment in the fortress and, given even a few hours, he might yet save his life.

In accordance with practice at courts-martial, the President put the question to the junior member of the Court first. 'Lieutenant Herrera, do you find the Prisoner guilty or not guilty?'

'Guilty,' replied the youth with the monocle.

The Duke's pulses raced. In his mind he saw again the courtyard outside and the lounging soldiers in it. On many occasions in Central America he had seen firing squads execute rebels, saboteurs and spies, and he knew that such executions could vary greatly. If the men ordered to do the job had never carried out an execution before, most of them hated it. They were either filled with pity for the condemned man, or reluctant to accept the guilt of having been a party to killing a fellow-human in cold blood; so they either fired over his head, or shut their eyes before pulling the trigger. That meant that the poor wretch up against the wall was rarely killed by the volley. Instead he dropped wounded and screaming, and the officer supervising the execution had to finish him off by putting his pistol to his jerking head and blowing out his brains. But if the men in the squad had had previous experience the majority of them aimed to kill. De Richleau thanked his gods that the men outside must have had ample practice at such work, so at least he could hope for a quick, clean death.

The President turned to the second senior member of the Court and said, 'Captain Escalante. Do you find the Prisoner guilty or not guilty?'

'Guilty,' replied the handsome Captain without a shadow of hesitation.

The word was hardly out of his mouth before de Richleau exclaimed, 'Captain Escalante! Is your name Juan?'

The astonished Captain looked at him and nodded.

'You are, then, making your addresses to the Señorita Mercedes, General Quiroga's daughter.'

The Captain frowned, but again he nodded.

'Then,' gasped the Duke, 'I will tell you something about her that you do not know.'

In an instant the Captain was on his feet. 'If you dare . . .' he began angrily; but de Richleau cut him short.

'It is nothing to the young lady's discredit. She is embroidering a pair of velvet bedroom slippers with your initials as a New Year present for you.'

Urgoiti jumped to his feet and shouted, 'I protest! This is irrelevant! Yet another pack of lies by the Prisoner in the hope of gaining a respite.'

The President banged the table with his gavel. 'Silence! You have no right to address the Court unless asked for your opinion.'

The Captain, still staring at de Richleau with a puzzled look, muttered, 'If this is true, how could you possibly know of it?'

'That is my point,' the Duke was trembling with excitement and new hope. 'How could I know it? Only because I have told the Court the truth. For the nights of the 8th and 9th I was a guest in General Quiroga's home and lived as one of his family. You have only to ask the General and he will tell you that I was that Count de Quesnoy whose wife was killed by the bomb thrown at His Majesty's wedding procession, and that I have been seeking revenge against the anarchists ever since. You need not even bother the General. Send for the Señora Quiroga, for the Señorita Mercedes, for their butler, for the soldier servant who valeted me while I was a guest in their house. Any or all of them will tell you that I speak the truth.'

As he paused, breathless, the three officers constituting the Court exchanged a few quick words. Then the President announced:

'I suspend the Court until further investigations have been made.'

At that moment there came a loud report. The windows of the room rattled. A spiral of smoke eddied up from just behind the table at which the Prosecutor was sitting. Comandante Urgoiti, realizing that it must now emerge that he had known the facts from the beginning, and that ruin, disgrace and death awaited him, had pulled his pistol from its holster and blown out his brains.

His act gave immediate confirmation of de Richleau's innocence. The officers present escorted him in a body through the long corridors of the fortress to the General's office. Quiroga berated them for a set of fools; but the Duke could now afford to be generous. He spoke up for them, saying that they had only been carrying out their duty and had been entirely misled by Urgoiti's skilful plot. The General then assumed his jovial aspect and invited them all over to his residence, where he ordered up champagne for them to drink a toast to his guest's eleventh-hour escape.

Señora Quiroga and Mercedes had joined them, and de Richleau asked his host and hostess to do him a great favour. He said that since the bedroom slippers Mercedes was making for Captain Escalante had been the means of saving his life, he begged that they would there and then give their consent to the young couple becoming engaged. Mercedes's mother hesitated for a moment, but the old General declared heartily that it would make a happy ending to what might so easily have been a terrible tragedy; so consent was given.

Yet it was not quite the end. After the little celebration was over and the officers had returned to their duties, de Richleau, not having eaten since the previous evening, asked for a light meal. When he had finished it he felt so utterly exhausted from his ghastly ordeal that he went upstairs and threw himself upon his bed. Ten minutes later he was sound asleep.

At five o'clock the General went up and roused him, to tell him that at midday he had given fresh instructions to the police, who had been busy collecting witnesses all the afternoon, and that he had convened a court-martial to try Ferrer that evening. Together they walked over to the Courtroom. Evidence was given that Ferrer had played a leading part in fomenting the July revolt, and de Richleau gave evidence about the anarchist's past activities.

He was condemned to death and an order given that the sentence was to be carried out at dawn the following morning.

As the Duke and Quiroga walked away from the Courtroom, the General said, 'You know, that Engineer Officer who acted as Prisoner's Friend did a better job for him than, from all accounts, young Navarez did for you this morning. Even now we haven't succeeded in fastening on him any act of violence carried out by himself. And those woolly-minded Liberals love him. They maintain that he stands for free speech and a broader form of education. There is going to be hell to pay when they hear that we've shot him. Radical bodies all over Europe are going to raise a tremendous outcry. I wouldn't be in the Prime Minister's shoes after Ferrer's execution has been announced for any decoration His Majesty could give me.'[1]

De Richleau shrugged. 'I don't give a damn what they say about my part in the matter. I know him for the cold-blooded viper that he is. By having him shot we are preventing him from plotting further outrages that would mean the death of hundreds more innocent people. That has been the real issue, and it is the duty of men like us to protect people who cannot protect themselves.'

That night the Señora Quiroga gave a small dinner party for relations and a few intimate friends, at which the engagement of Mercedes to Captain Juan Escalante was unofficially announced. Afterwards the handsome Captain and Mercedes overwhelmed the Duke with their thanks at having played the part of Fairy Godmother to them, and asked him to be Godfather to their first child. To which Mercedes added that she meant to make him, too, a pair of embroidered bedroom slippers for the New Year.

Delighted at having brought happiness to the young couple and with blissful thoughts of the happiness he would himself soon find again in Gulia's arms, he went up to bed.

He had arranged to be called early in the morning and a little before six o'clock he walked through the fortress to the small courtyard where executions were carried out. Soon afterwards, in the grey light of dawn, Ferrer was brought up from the dungeons, blindfolded, and put against the wall. An officer gave the order,

[1] *Historical Note.* Ferrer was shot on September 12th, 1909. Vigorous protests at his execution appeared in Liberal newspapers all over the world. So great were the demonstrations in Madrid against the Government that Señor Maura, the Conservative Prime Minister, was forced to resign. The Liberal leader Señor Moret stepped into his shoes on October 22nd. Nevertheless there can be no doubt whatever that Francisco Ferrer was morally responsible for the deaths and wounding of many hundreds of people. D.W.

a volley shattered the silence, and the anarchist fell riddled with bullets.

Having personally satisfied himself that no fresh piece of treachery by fanatical Catalans or anarchist sympathizers had enabled his enemy to escape, and that his poor Angela's untimely death had been avenged, de Richleau walked back to the General's house and made a hearty early breakfast. A few hours later he took leave of the Quirogas and left Barcelona on a morning train.

On the evening of the 14th he arrived back in San Sebastian. It was too late to send a message to Gulia letting her know of his return; but soon after midnight he went to the livery stable and collected the horse, which he had left instructions should be kept at his disposal. In the orchard behind the villa he hobbled it as in the past, then he got out the ladder from the gardener's shed and climbed up to Gulia's window.

Her relief and delight at his safe return were unbounded. They had been separated for a week so in the hours that followed the ardour of their passion for one another reached new heights and, since between their embraces de Richleau had to tell her the long story of his doings in Barcelona, they did not sleep a wink.

Next morning the Duke waited on Don Alfonso and was received most kindly by him. After the King had listened to his report, he said that all the parties of the Left would make so much capital out of Ferrer's execution that a very difficult time lay ahead. But he fully agreed that they had done the right thing; adding that if the people desired reforms they must bring them about in a constitutional manner, and that in the meantime it was the duty of the Government to protect the innocent from violence by criminal fanatics such as Ferrer.

That night de Richleau rode out to the villa again. Once more the two lovers took their joy of one another, but their transports of the preceding night had taken toll even of their seemingly insatiable desire, and during it they had hardly closed their eyes. In consequence, as they had often done before, at about three o'clock in the morning, clasped in each other's arms, they first fell into a blissful doze, then slept.

With a soldier's trained ability to wake at any hour, a little before dawn the Duke opened his eyes, freed himself from Gulia's embrace and sat up. He had just lit the bedside lamp so that he could see to dress, when he heard the sound of someone coming up the ladder. Next moment a cloaked figure scrambled in through the window.

As de Richleau stared in that direction it flashed into his mind that, naked as he was, he was at a considerable disadvantage in tackling a burglar. But at that moment the intruder turned towards the bed and the light from the lamp shone full on his face.

The Duke drew a sharp breath. For a few seconds he thought he must be seeing a ghost. But it was no wraith from the dead that stood scowling at him. It was a man of flesh and blood; and he was Gulia's husband, José de Cordoba.

23

Sunrise in the Bay

DURING the course of his thirty-odd years de Richleau had found himself in many dangerous situations and a certain number of embarrassing ones, but none more embarrassing than the present. Occasional contretemps with the husbands of lovely ladies were the hazards which had to be accepted by a virile man who had spent nearly all his life as a bachelor and was so fastidious in his choice of mistresses that he had never kept a *demi-mondaine*. But never before had he been caught naked in bed with a woman; much less the wife of a friend whom he had believed to be dead.

Temporarily bereft of speech, he stared at the stalwart, bearded figure. Then, finding his tongue, he exclaimed, 'I thought . . .'

'I can very well guess what you thought,' de Cordoba burst out, his face convulsed with rage. 'You thought that I was not returning from South America until the end of October. You would have been right, and free to continue to practise your vile treachery, but for the threat to the peseta brought about by the war in Morocco. Ruiz cabled me three weeks ago asking me to return and resume control here. I was three hundred miles up the Amazon when his cable reached me, but I started for home at once.'

As the Conde paused for breath de Richleau began again. 'But I thought . . .' then he checked himself. It had suddenly dawned upon him that if Ruiz had sent that cable towards the *end* of August he could not possibly have received news at the *beginning* of the month that his brother was dead. Therefore Gulia had lied. She must have invented the whole story about her husband's death.

Turning his head he shot a swift glance at her. She was sitting up in bed beside him, with the top of the sheet held up in front of her to hide her superb breasts. Her long Titian gold hair hung about her in disorder, her big eyes were wide and shining, her breath was coming fast; but on her beautiful face there was an expression of defiance as she looked straight before her at her husband.

Swiftly the Duke grasped the fact that he was in a cleft stick. Either he must reveal the deception she had practised on him, or allow de Cordoba to believe that he had deliberately seduced his wife during his absence. De Richleau had never been a man to kiss and tell. Within seconds he decided that, wicked as Gulia's trickery had been, he could not give her away. Feeling that his only course now was to carry the war into the enemy's camp, he began again, more firmly than before.

'Very well. I understand. But you might have spared yourself this unpleasant discovery if you had not returned like a thief in the night. It seems you must have been spying on us to arrive here at this hour and by way of the ladder.'

'I've done nothing of the kind,' de Cordoba retorted harshly. 'And it is you who are the thief. My ship docked at Bilboa yesterday evening. I thought that by hiring an automobile I could easily get home by midnight. But the cursed thing broke down and it was six hours before I reached a town where I could hire another. When I did get here, not wishing to wake the whole household I went round to the back of the villa to see if I could find a way to get in. I found one. Yes, I found a ladder leading up to my wife's bedroom. And what then? What a welcome home! I found a man whom I regarded with affection and respect in my wife's bed.'

'I sympathize with you in the shock you sustained,' replied the Duke calmly. 'What more can I say? That which is done is done. In such a situation an apology would only sound insincere.'

'Apology be damned!' the Conde exploded. 'By God, you're going to give me satisfaction, and that before you are much older.'

De Richleau sighed. 'Since you demand it, I am entirely at your service.'

'Demand it! Of course. What else would you expect? Now collect your clothes and get out of here. You can dress in the bathroom.'

'No,' the Duke shook his head, and his jaw became aggressive. 'That I will not do. I refuse to be humiliated by getting naked out of bed in front of you. And unless you wish to lower yourself by entering on an unseemly brawl you cannot make me. It is you who will leave this room while I dress at my leisure.'

For a moment de Cordoba glowered at him, then he sneered, 'One would hardly expect to find such delicacy in a man base enough to seduce the wife of a friend. But let it be as you say,

You'll find me down in the hall. Be quick about it. I'll stand for
no delay in making our arrangements.' Turning, he marched from
the room, slamming the door behind him.

As his footsteps faded away down the corridor, Gulia and de
Richleau took their eyes from the door and looked at one another.
'Well,' he asked coldly. 'What have you to say?'

Two great tears had welled up into her eyes and were running
down her magnolia-petal cheeks. Sadly she shook her head. 'Oh
Armand, my dear love, I never dreamed that things would end for
us like this.'

'Nor I; which is less surprising since I believed him dead,'
de Richleau replied bitterly. 'But you; you lied to me. You made
up that story about his having been mauled by a puma, and that
Ruiz had asked you to keep his death secret because if it became
known there would be a run on the bank. It's obvious now that
you knew him to be alive all the time, but did not expect him
back until the end of October.'

'Yes,' she murmured. 'It's true. But I beg you not to think too
badly of me because of that. We have had such a wonderful time
together. Think of the happiness I have given you. And your conscience, at least, is clear.'

'My conscience!' he burst out. 'Yes, but not my reputation in
your husband's eyes. Do you not realize that whatever may happen
now he will regard me with contempt – as a man who has sullied
his honour?'

'Honour! Oh Armand, why must you men make so much of
that? Surely love counts for more. You love me. I know you do.'
Suddenly raising her arms she threw them round his neck.

'Love you!' Breaking her hold he thrust her from him. 'After
what you have done, how can I do anything else than despise you.'

As she collapsed sobbing on her pillow, he angrily kicked the
bedclothes aside, jumped out of bed and started to dress.

By the time he was in his shirt and trousers she was sitting
up again, watching him with tear-dimmed eyes. In a hoarse voice
she spoke. 'Armand. This duel that he insists on fighting. It is
I who have brought it on you. Oh, I pray to God that you will
not be hurt. If you were killed I . . . I'd never get over it. I . . .
I . . .'

He felt calmer now, and quickly reassured her. 'You've little
need to let that worry you. I am used to arms, whereas he, poor
devil, is only used to handling butterfly nets. There's one chance
in a hundred that he might pip me at the regulation twenty paces,
but no more.'

Getting out of bed she stood in front of him, naked and as beautiful as Venus arisen from the foam. But her arms hung slack by her sides and her head was bowed. Choking back a sob she said:

'I don't think I am a wanton. I have refused the pleading of scores of handsome men. That I am a wicked woman to have behaved so despicably towards you I confess. But love drove me to it, Armand. From the very first moment I saw you I knew you were the only man that I could ever love profoundly. I wanted you desperately – desperately. I did everything I could to get you. I even lied about José. He was very far from being a satisfactory husband, but I've no reason at all to believe that he really kept a mistress in Madrid. Yet you were too honourable to give way to my tempting. It was then the idea came to me that if I could only free you from your scruples I'd get my heart's desire. My plan succeeded. But it was born neither out of greed nor ordinary wantonness. If I died tonight I'd die happy in the knowledge that for just a few weeks in my life I had had you for my lover. And you returned my love, Armand. You know you did. Can you not possibly forgive me?'

His heart melted within him. He suddenly felt that during the past quarter of an hour he had behaved towards her like a prig and a brute. Softly he said:

'I understand. Yes, I understand. And someone once said, "to understand all is to forgive all", didn't they. Anyway, I take back everything I said just now, and ask your forgiveness for it. Oh, my darling, what can I say to comfort you? It was I who, by putting honour before love, drove you to do as you did. That you should have had the strength and courage to carry through your purpose shows the depth of your feeling for me, and I humbly thank the gods that I should have been blessed with a love so great as yours.'

She lifted her face to his and once more her eyes were shining. Gently, he took her in his arms. They kissed, but with all passion drained from them, as two beings who for a little time had dwelt in heaven together, and, whether or not they met again in this life, would forever remain long-time friends.

Two minutes later he had put on his coat and left her. Down in the hall he found de Cordoba agitatedly pacing up and down. Without a word the Conde led the way into the small library. De Richleau followed him in. From the drawer of a bureau the Conde took an oblong mahogany box. Placing it on the centre table, he opened it, disclosing a pair of silver-mounted duelling pistols and compartments that contained cleaning materials and shot.

'These will serve our purpose,' he said tonelessly. 'Be good enough to take your choice, and put a few bullets in your pocket.'

'Surely,' protested the Duke in astonishment, 'you cannot be suggesting that we should fight here and now.'

'No, down in the private bay. One could hardly find a better place to fight a duel than on its flat, firm sands, and it will take us only a few minutes to walk down there.'

'But . . . But one cannot fight a duel without seconds, and a doctor within call.'

'I see nothing against doing so.'

'There is a great deal,' replied de Richleau promptly. 'However intense your resentment against me, Conde, I beg you to exercise a little patience. Put away these weapons for the time being. Although as the challenged party I have the right of choice I am willing to accept them. But allow me to return to my hotel. Send two of your friends to me there and I will ask two friends of mine to make proper arrangements with them. Then I will meet you at any time or place they may decide.'

De Cordoba shook his head. 'No. We will go down to the shore and settle this matter without delay.'

'But why this unseemly haste, Conde? Why?'

'Because I have no mind to allow witnesses at this affair. You have sullied your honour, but mine remains unbesmirched. How could we fight in the presence of others yet prevent them from talking afterwards? Whatever pretext we might give them for our meeting they would suspect the truth. For you to have reached such a degree of intimacy with Gulia, you must first have been a great deal in her company. It will be said that she betrayed me with you and I found her out. I have the honour of my family to consider, and I refuse to submit to the humiliation of having my Condesa's name bandied about as that of a whore.'

'That is the very last thing I would wish, either for her or for yourself,' the Duke agreed. 'But there are other considerations; and most serious ones. A duel is a duel and, although illegal, if carried out according to accepted traditions no serious notice is taken of it by the authorities. For two men to discharge pistols at one another when alone and, as might emerge later, with a cause for anger, is a very different matter. Should one of them have the misfortune to be killed the other would be accounted guilty of murder.'

'That risk can be overcome,' replied the Conde stubbornly. 'I will leave a note on the hall table for my butler, asking him to have an early breakfast ready for us at seven o'clock, and saying that you and I have gone down to the shore to practise pistol shooting at the seagulls. Then, when it transpires that one of us has been wounded or killed it will be taken as an accident.'

De Richleau shook his head. 'Such an explanation would not bear investigation. Is it likely that on returning from a long absence overseas, and before your household even knows that you are back, you would stroll down to the beach to practise with a pistol? And what am I supposed to have been doing here at this hour?'

'I thought that at least you were a man of courage,' sneered the Conde. 'But your cowardice is in keeping with the character of a wife-stealer.'

The Duke's face suddenly went white and he said softly, 'You shall pay for that. To insist on this is the act of a fool. You are a fool, too, to have challenged me. I doubt if you could hit a hay-stack, whereas I could put a bullet through your brain at fifty yards. But you shall have your way. Your blood be on your own head.'

Taking the nearest pistol from the case, he broke it, squinted down its barrel, slipped a few bullets into his pocket, and walked out of the room.

De Cordoba followed him and caught him up. Side by side, maintaining a frigid silence, they walked along the path fringed with pines, tamarisks and myrtle that led down to the beach. The tide was going out and had left a quarter-mile-long stretch of smooth, clean sand. As they reached it and halted, the Conde said:

'I have never before fought a duel, so I must request you to state in detail how we should proceed.'

During their walk down to the shore de Richleau's anger had cooled, and he said quickly, 'Then why fight this one? I know that I have done you a great wrong, but for one of us to wound or kill the other cannot undo that which has been done. Will you not . . .'

'No!' the Conde cut him short. 'One expects a certain frailty in women, and in view of the relations between Gulia and myself I do not blame her overmuch. But men are made of sterner stuff. For you there can be no excuse, and with God's help I hope to punish you for your despicable behaviour.'

'Very well, then. We load our pistols and stand back to back. I will ask you if you are ready. When you reply "Yes", I shall then say the one word, "March". On that we shall both walk ten paces away from one another then turn about face to face. Either of us may fire instantly upon turning, or hold his fire to take more careful aim. Ten paces, you understand. And may I

suggest that when you take your stance to fire you should stand
sideways, so that your body presents a minimum width of target
to me.'

'Thank you. I appreciate the chivalry you display in making that
suggestion.'

Having loaded his pistol with the single bullet that the duelling
weapon held, de Richleau looked out over the bay. A sick nostalgia
seized him as he thought of the many happy hours he had spent
there with Gulia. Whatever might be the outcome of the duel
he knew that never again would they swim there together or sit
side by side talking and laughing on these golden sands. It had
been for them an earthly paradise, and now her husband had
come back, like an avenging angel with a flaming sword, to drive
him out of it for ever.

With a sharp word de Cordoba recalled him to the present.
They took up their positions back to back. 'Are you ready?' asked
the Duke. 'Yes,' replied the Conde. 'March,' cried de Richleau,
and in swift strides each covered his ten paces.

The Duke knew that if de Cordoba took a snap shot at him
immediately upon turning, only by an extraordinary fluke could
the bullet fail to go wide. Therefore, to have any hope of hitting
him at all, the Conde must give at least ten seconds to taking
aim. He, on the other hand, was a crack shot. Two seconds would
be ample for him to draw a bead on his opponent and fire. In
consequence, when walking down to the beach, he had decided
to put a quick end to the matter by winging the Conde in his
pistol arm before he had a chance to discharge his weapon.

Yet now, at the last moment, he changed his mind. It was he
who had wronged the Conde, unwittingly it was true, but that
did not alter the fact. And there was always the chance that if
he took a snap shot the bullet, instead of lodging in the Conde's
arm or shoulder, might ride a trifle high, hit him in the neck,
and kill him. When de Richleau recalled how de Cordoba had
cared for him like a brother after Angela's death, and the way
in which, after he had nearly died in Barcelona, he had been nursed
back to health and strength in the villa, he felt that he could
not bring himself to injure him, let alone take a chance that might
rob him of his life.

Five seconds after the two men turned the Duke fired, but
he had deliberately aimed high. The bullet passed a good foot
above de Cordoba's head. No longer having anything to fear
the Conde took careful aim before pressing the trigger of his
pistol, but the bullet whistled harmlessly past his adversary.

The two men walked towards one another and de Richleau said, 'I have given you the opportunity you desired. I trust you are now satisfied.'

'Certainly not!' the Conde replied in a still bitter tone. 'And I shall not be until one of us is too seriously wounded to continue. Let us reload.'

With a resigned shrug the Duke again loaded his pistol. They followed the same procedure as before. Again de Richleau fired high, but this time de Cordoba's bullet tore a little strip of cloth from his coat low down near the thigh.

Grimly he walked back to prepare for the third round. Brave as he was, it required no little courage to stand still and be shot at, and small beads of sweat had broken out on his forehead. Yet he felt that there was nothing he could do except pray that he would soon receive an injury which, without being too serious, would be sufficient to satisfy the Conde.

Again they loaded, stood back to back, then marched to their stations. But now, instead of making any pretence of aiming, the Duke turned the point of his pistol straight up and fired into the air.

As the bullet sailed heavenwards de Cordoba lowered his weapon and came striding towards him.

'How dare you?' he cried. 'How dare you? I see now the reason why you have twice missed me. It is because you are not trying. Is not the injury you have done me enough without adding this insult to it? The fact that you happen to be a soldier well practised in arms gives you no right to treat me with contempt as an antagonist.'

De Richleau sadly shook his head. 'Believe me, Conde, nothing was further from my thoughts. But after all the kindness you showed me in the past, should I happen to kill you I would never forgive myself. Even to injure you would be a shameful return for the support and comfort you gave me after my poor wife's death.'

It was no use. A temporary madness seemed to afflict the Conde, making him deaf to all reason.

'Shameful return,' he echoed furiously. 'Have you not made it already? You are one of the few men in whom I would have placed unlimited trust. It is not the seduction of Gulia that I desire to avenge, but your betrayal of my belief in you. I am determined that you shall either be carried from this bay with a wound that will long remain a reminder of your treachery, or that having put a bullet into a man who once had complete faith in you will permanently plague your conscience. Come! Reload; and take your punishment one way or the other.'

They were just about to place themselves back to back for the fourth time when a shout of 'Stop! Stop that! Stop!' reached them.

Turning towards the slope that ran up to the villa they saw a female figure running down through the pine wood towards them. Both recognized it instantly as that of the Infanta. Instinctively they stepped apart and waited as she hurried towards them.

Although only in her late forties Maria Alfonsine was a bulky woman, and now she looked even more so than usual, for she had no corsets on under the thick dressing-gown that was swathed about her. When she reached them her face was scarlet from her exertions, and wisps of her hair, which she had hastily done up in a bun, were floating untidily about her ears. But her high-nosed features displayed the habit of authority and her dark eyes flashed angrily, as she panted.

'Holy Mary be praised that neither of you is yet injured. There is to be no more of this. I forbid it.'

Made more furious than ever by her arrival on the scene, de Cordoba barked at her, 'Go back! Go back to the villa! Leave us this instant. You have no right to interfere.'

'I have every right,' she retorted. 'It is obvious that you have forced this duel upon the Señor Duke; and I know you to have done so under a misapprehension.'

De Cordoba gave a bitter laugh. 'Since I have a pair of eyes in my head that is impossible. The cause of our quarrel does not concern you; but you may rest assured that no man ever had better reason to call another out.'

'In that you are wrong,' the Infanta insisted. 'I have just come from Gulia, and she has told me how you took her by surprise by coming through her window.'

'So she has admitted her shame. I had hoped that everyone other than myself might be spared the knowledge of it. Since she has confessed to you how can you possibly suggest that I had no grounds for challenging this viper whom I believed to be my friend?'

'Gulia has confessed to more than taking him as a lover.'

'To what more could she confess?'

The Infanta waved an impatient hand. 'Be quiet, José, and listen. An hour ago I was wakened by angry voices. There came the slamming of a door and footsteps past my room, then ten minutes later more footsteps. I felt that I must find out what was going on. I went to Gulia's room and found her sobbing her heart out. She told me of your unexpected return and that you had caught her *in flagrante delicto* with the Señor Duke. Then that twice, three years ago and again this summer, she had done her utmost to persuade him to become her lover. But he had proved adamant in rejecting her advances.'

'It's said the road to hell is paved with good intentions,' sneered the Conde, 'yet the fact remains that he thought too little of his honour to stay the course. Had he possessed the integrity with which I credited him, he would not only have repulsed but left her.

'Wait, José. Wait! Having failed to seduce him from his loyalty to you, she hatched a most subtle plan. She told him that your valet had returned from South America with the news that you had been attacked by a puma and died of your wounds. According to her story the man had brought a letter from you expressing your last wishes. They were that Ruiz should conceal your death for the next two months, and meanwhile call in all doubtful loans; so that the bank should be strong enough to withstand a run upon it when your death was publicly announced. Only then, believing her to have become a widow with the right to dispose of herself as she wished, did the Señor Duke agree to become her lover.'

The anger suddenly drained from de Cordoba's square-bearded face. Turning towards de Richleau, he asked, 'Is this the truth?'

The Duke nodded. 'Yes, that is what happened. But it was not for me to tell you so.'

Tears sprung to the Conde's eyes, and he exclaimed, 'Oh my poor friend, I see now that I have done you a terrible injustice. And you! With what chivalry you have behaved. For the insults I heaped upon you I could not have blamed you if you had killed me. Yet you stood there as a target for my bullets and would not even use your skill to render me *hors de combat*. Can you ever forgive me?'

'Willingly,' smiled de Richleau. 'Most willingly. I am overjoyed that out of this unhappy affair we should at least have salvaged our friendship. You cannot guess the distress that I have suffered in this past hour from knowing that you believed so ill of me.'

Overcome with emotion, the Conde opened his arms in the Spanish fashion and the two men embraced, kissing one another on both cheeks. But the Infanta's voice caused them to turn again to her.

'To see you reconciled is a great joy to me, but you do not yet know everything. Gulia tells me that in mid-August she believed herself to have become *encinta*, and a few days ago she became certain of it.'

'What!' exclaimed the Duke. 'She is going to have a child!' Swinging round he met the Conde's eyes, and faltered, 'I . . . I had no idea of this. How . . . what are we to do?'

Maria Alfonsine said quietly, 'I feel this is a matter which can only be settled between you. May the good God in His wisdom give you guidance.' Then she turned and left them.

When she had covered a little distance, de Richleau said, 'I imagine you could find some pretext to secure an annulment. If so, I should, of course, be willing to marry her.'

For a few moments de Cordoba remained deep in thought, then he shook his head. 'No. To secure an annulment would take at least two years. If I put her from me and long before she can be married to you she has a child, that is certain to become known. It would bring dishonour upon my family, and later reflect on her, on you, and above all on the child. It is better that she should remain with me.'

After a brief hesitation, de Richleau said, 'About the child you are unquestionably right. But we have also to think of her happiness.'

'True. And at the moment I have little doubt that she would prefer to leave me for you. Time, though, as we know, is the inevitable destroyer of passion. Hers for you would be bound to suffer an additional strain if until the annulment came through she had to live as your mistress in furtive secrecy. Afterwards there would be the constant strain upon you both of never knowing when some woman of position, such, for example, as Maria Alfonsine, having learned that Gulia had lived with you before your marriage, would refuse to receive her. Within a few years I fear you would have tired of one another, yet find no compensation in a happy social life together.'

'There is much in what you say,' the Duke admitted. 'But what if she remains with you? Are you . . . would you be willing . . .'

'To forgive and forget,' de Cordoba finished for him. 'Yes. Gulia is not alone to blame for this. When I persuaded her to marry me I was already too old to do her full justice. Experience tells one that few young and healthy women, unless they are deeply religious, do not on occasion succumb to nature's urges. Therefore I have no real right to complain if she takes a lover now and then; provided she is discreet about it.'

The Conde paused a moment, then he went on, 'There is another thing that I will tell to you, but would tell to no one else. I have known for some years that I am no longer capable of begetting a child. But to have one would be a great joy to me. And I know no man whom I would rather have had to sire an heir for me than yourself.'

De Richleau lowered his glance. 'You could not pay me a greater compliment, José. In fact you overwhelm me. May I . . . may I take it then . . . ?'

'That I will not act harshly towards Gulia? Yes, you may rest content about that. She has made a punishment for herself, in that she is certain to suffer for some time to come from having lost you. But now she carries the child that is to bear my name I shall lose no opportunity to cherish her.'

Side by side they left the golden sands and walked up the slope. At its top they shook hands and, having wished one another good fortune, parted, the Conde to go into the house, the Duke to collect his mount from the orchard.

As he rode away from the villa, now that all the tension and uncertainty were over, a terrible depression descended on him. The thought that never again would he hold Gulia in his arms distressed him beyond measure. Yet he knew that de Cordoba had been right, and that her prospects of future happiness were far brighter if she remained with her husband than if he had taken her away. In fact, with this new bond of the child to bring them together there was every hope that in due course they would achieve as great a state of contentment as fell to most married couples.

It was he who was left in the air. Angela and the prospect of having a child by her had been taken from him; now he had been thrown back into much the same state of loneliness and indecision as he had been shortly after her death. He had many friends and innumerable acquaintances, but no family. He owned a fine property and a great mansion, but they were situated in the most sparsely populated area of Central Europe, far from any city or cheerful community of neighbours. He was a highly trained officer, with experience of many forms of warfare, but no army worthy of the name was open to him. He was intelligent, wealthy and ambitious, but his life as a soldier had left him ill-equipped to enter on any other career. Yet he loathed the thought of idling away his life in one pleasure resort after another.

In this unhappy state of mind, he had ridden only about half a mile towards San Sebastian when he saw two other horsemen cantering towards him. As they came nearer he recognized Don

Alfonso, evidently out on an early morning ride attended only by a groom.

With a cheerful shout of recognition, the young King reined in his horse. De Richleau dutifully made his service. The King gave an amused glance first at his face, then towards the villa, and said with a smile:

'From your unshaven chin, Duke, it looks as though you have given up keeping butterflies for your friend, and been out all night giving your attention to a beautiful moth.'

There could be no mistaking the King's meaning, and it would have been churlish to pretend not to respond to his gay rallying; so with a wan smile in reply, the Duke said:

'Alas, Your Majesty, I have had to surrender my enchanting charge into the hands of the friend for whom I was looking after it.'

'What!' exclaimed the King. 'Is José de Cordoba back from South America, then?'

'Yes, Sir. He returned last night.'

'And you? I fear the cessation of your duties as custodian will leave a sad gap in the pleasant life you have been leading in San Sebastian.'

'It will indeed, Sir. In fact I fear to find this place so dull that I intend to leave it not later than tonight. Permit me, therefore, to take this opportunity of asking Your Majesty for my *congé*.'

'I am sorry that you are leaving us, Duke. Where do you intend to go?'

De Richleau shrugged. 'I hardly know. I am at a loose end. I may pay a visit to my late in-laws in England and shoot pheasants with them. Or perhaps I'll return to Central America and shoot some more unfortunate Indians. I expect that is where I shall end up.'

For a moment Don Alfonso remained thoughtful, then he said, 'The advice you gave us at that conference of Generals I asked you to attend was taken. I am forming another Cavalry Division. Although you are a British subject, as a Knight of the Fleece you also owe allegiance to the Crown of Spain. It has just occurred to me that I could find no man better fitted to command it.'

'A Cavalry Division!' gasped the Duke, his face suddenly lighting up. 'Can Your Majesty possibly mean it? To command a Cavalry Division has been the ambition of my life.'

A new and bright horizon had opened for him.